PRAISE FOR LISA DE NIK

Beautiful, sexy, exciting, mysterious, dangerous and twisted. Those words can be used to describe not only the alluring locations depicted in Lisa de Nikolits' thrilling novel *The Witchdoctor's Bones*, but also some of the eclectic characters fatefully traveling together on a tour bus through South Africa and Namibia. A suspenseful page-turner that will bewitch you until the end.
— ALEXANDER GALANT, author of *Depth of Deception* (A Titanic Murder Mystery)

Imagine you've signed up for a low-budget safari in South Africa and find yourself cheek-to-cheek on a battered van with the most bizarre travellers you've ever met — except in some ways they do remind you of characters you've encountered in a late-night screening of *Moulin Rouge*. You know, the kinds of people you don't naturally gravitate toward but whom you're unable to ignore. You're drawn in. Illicit love, rejected love, misfired love, machinations of all sorts, and all involving characters of dubious integrity and (in some cases) of questionable sanity. Such are the players in Lisa de Nikolits's, *The Witchdoctor's Bones*, who've embarked on a journey that soon seethes with peril (physical and psychological), and not solely because of the wild creatures roaming the bush veld.

By planting her characters in the untamed landscape of the South African wilderness, de Nikolits has stripped away the niceties and rigours of polite society. Nothing is familiar. Nor do people even speak the same language. Tour leader Jono whispers in his Khosa tongue, only to be drowned out by the harsh words of Stepfan, the German. One imagines sweet-talking Kate, the Canadian, is the closest thing you get to a heroine in *The Witchdoctor's Bones*, as proof that the best woman will be left standing. As safari guide Jono cautions his guests early in the novel, "This is a land of heat and dust and you will wonder how anybody survived?"
—DOUG O'NEILL, Executive Editor, *Canadian Living*

Fascinating South African lore comes to life in *The Witchdoctor's Bones*. De Nikolits gives us more than an intriguing mystery — a look at the dark side of the human soul and the healing power of love.
—D. J. MCINTOSH, author of *The Witch of Babylon* and *The Book of Stolen Tales*

Take sixteen travellers from around the world, gather them on a tour bus bumping its way along the rough roads of South Africa and Namibia, add jealousy, sexual obsession, secrets, violence, magic, poison, mental breakdown and the breathtaking arrogance of tourists treating Africa (and Africans) as their playthings, and you have Lisa de Nikolits' psychological thriller, *The Withdoctor's Bones*. As the travellers and their guides slowly reveal their true (and sometimes twisted) natures, the tension ratchets higher and higher in a narrative that draws deeply on African lore and history, with echoes of Christie's classic *Ten Little Indians*, Katherine Anne Porter's *Ship of Fools*, and Chaucer's *The Canterbury Tales*.
—TERRI FAVRO, author of *The Proxy Bride*

Lisa de Nikolits has done it again. This time she shines her characteristically unflinching but loving and humour-filled gaze on the land of her birth, deftly weaving Africa's ancient witchcraft practices, superstitions, breathtaking beauty and disturbing struggles into the journey of a group of modern-day tourists — whose motives for coming on the "trip of a lifetime" are in some cases highly suspect. The myriad conflicts between the characters are handled so subtly and the physical terrain of southern Africa painted so vividly, you won't be able to tear yourself away from your own seat on the bus, even as the body count begins to rise.
—BRENDA MISSEN, author of *Tell Anna She's Safe*

Put together an international group of travelers, each with their own secrets, in a bus touring Africa and you have the makings of a very suspenseful tale! Lisa de Nikolits does a masterful job of drawing the reader in and not letting go until the last delicious word! Set against an exotic backdrop of Africa and Namibia, this story is a great read!
—JOAN O'CALLAGHAN, editor and contributing author of *Thirteen*

What I really enjoy about Lisa de Nikolits is her refusal to be pinned down to a particular genre. Besides the fact that *The Witchdoctor's*

Bones is so different from all her other novels, it's also incredibly difficult to classify it in its own right. Part travelogue, part psychological thriller, part sociological and anthropological study, *The Witchdoctor's Bones* entertains, educates and fascinates all at the same time. It's a gripping read that draws you into the heart of darkness, both in the literal and figurative sense; the action takes place in untamed Africa, but it's the darkness in the human heart that de Nikolits portrays with such chilling precision. It's a page-turner that will keep you biting your nails right up to the bitter end.
—BIANCA MARAIS, http://biancamarais.com/ Musings of a Wannabe Writer

A cast of intriguing characters is thrust together for an African adventure. What results is far more perilous than anyone could have imagined. Against the beautiful backdrop of South Africa and Namibia, danger and death lurk around every bend in the road, as the trip of a lifetime becomes the holiday from hell. Within the pages of *The Witchdoctor's Bones* multiple mysteries emerge, as Lisa de Nikolits takes the reader on a suspense-filled journey that won't soon be forgotten.
—LIZ BUGG, author of the *Calli Barnow Series*

In *The Witchdoctor's Bones*, Lisa de Nikolits drives a busload of seemingly normal souls into the heart of Africa, revealing the baggage they've dragged along, piece by sweaty piece. Against a backdrop of Bushmen tales and geography she clearly loves, de Nikolits creates by turns a lusty dusty romp and excursions to the nastier regions of human desire. Passions both wandering and misplaced pull the story ever deeper down a bumpy road. Well worth the trip!
—ROB BRUNET, author of *Stinking Rich*

If romance, suspense and serial killers under the African sun are your cup of tea, this book is for you.
—DUNCAN ARMSTRONG, writer, poet, spoken-word performer, TOpoet.ca

Copyright © 2014 Lisa de Nikolits

Except for the use of short passages for review purposes, no part of this book may be reproduced, in part or in whole, or transmitted in any form or by any means, electronically or mechanically, including photocopying, recording, or any information or storage retrieval system, without prior permission in writing from the publisher.

  Canada Council   Conseil des Arts
for the Arts   du Canada

We gratefully acknowledge the support of the Canada Council for the Arts and the Ontario Arts Council for our publishing program, and the financial assistance of the Government of Canada through the Canada Book Fund.

We are also grateful for the support received from an Anonymous Fund at The Calgary Foundation.

Cover design: Lisa de Nikolits.
Cover artwork: Wopko Jensma.

Library and Archives Canada Cataloguing in Publication

De Nikolits, Lisa, 1966–, author
    The witchdoctor's bones : a novel / by Lisa de Nikolits.

(Inanna poetry & fiction series)
ISBN 978-1-77133-126-5 (pbk.)

    I. Title. II. Series: Inanna poetry and fiction series

PS8607.E63W57 2014   C813'.6   C2014-902297-2

Printed and bound in Canada

Inanna Publications and Education Inc.
210 Founders College, York University
4700 Keele Street, Toronto, Ontario, Canada M3J 1P3
Telephone: (416) 736-5356 Fax: (416) 736-5765
Email: inanna.publications@inanna.ca   Website: www.inanna.ca

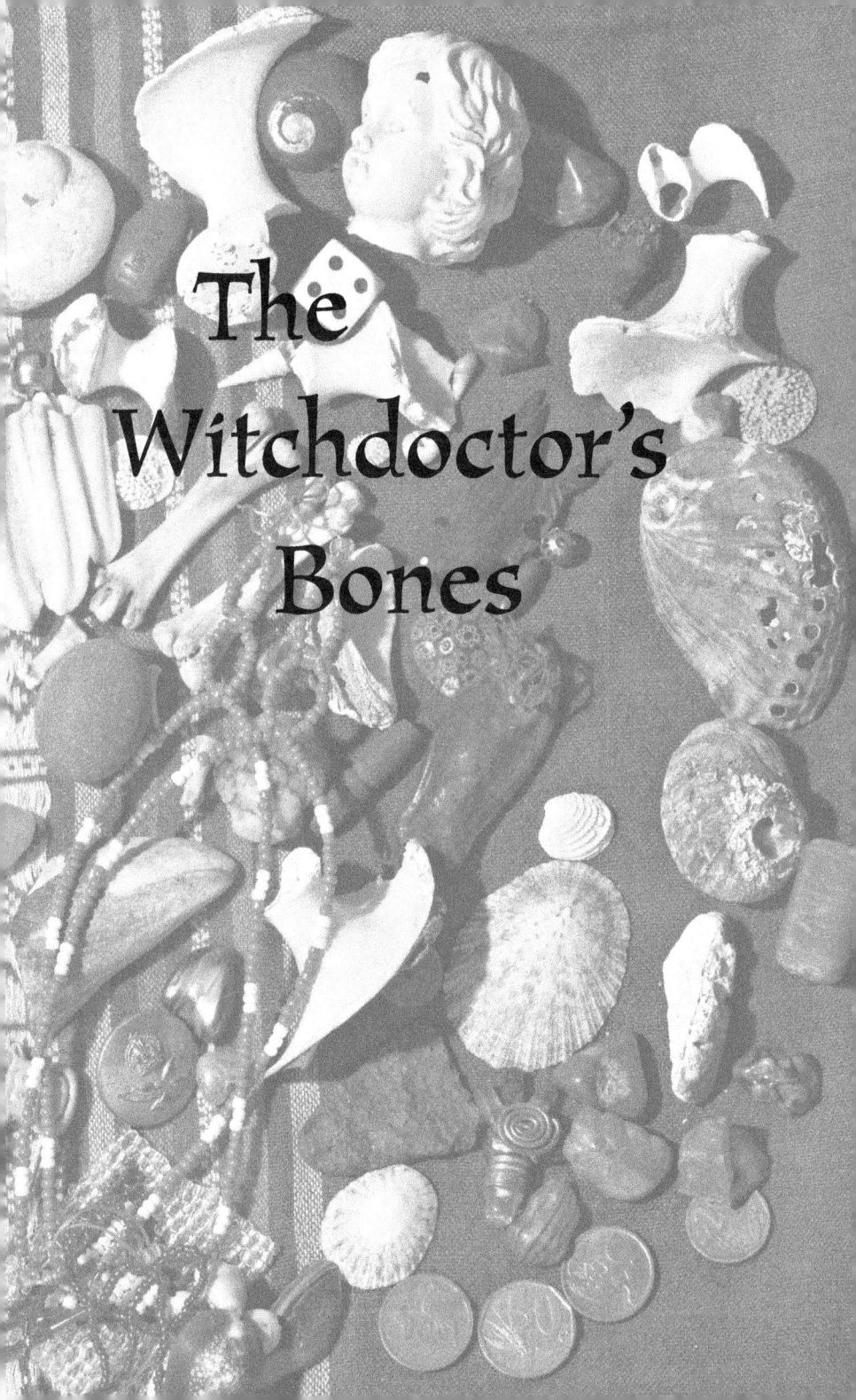

The Witchdoctor's Bones

ALSO BY LISA DE NIKOLITS

A Glittering Chaos
West of Wawa
The Hungry Mirror

The Witchdoctor's Bones

a novel by

Lisa de Nikolits

inanna poetry & fiction series

INANNA PUBLICATIONS AND EDUCATION INC.
TORONTO, CANADA

*This one's for Dad.
And as always, Bradford Dunlop.*

The Bushmen Tell a Story of Porcupine, Tiger and Xau

"Xau was a man who liked to throw thorns..." the storyteller began.

"Throw thorns?" asked a man.

"Yes. Throw thorns between a man and his best friends. It is an ugly thing to do, something we forbid our children to do. Then one day Xau sat high in a tree trying to see where the gemsbok cows were grazing. He looked for the gemsbok but his heart longed to visit his beloved who lived in the grass. Suddenly he heard something approaching. He looked, turned his head, and saw Porcupine and Tiger.

"Porcupine was playing on his harp, singing "Jicky-jick ... and one day when I am king of all the animals, Lion will have to carry the ashes away from my camp and Elephant will have to bring me tambootie grass. Jicky-jick ... Jicky ... jick... One day when I am king of all the animals, Warthog will have to dig roots for me, and Antbear will have to kill the ticks with his thick tail."

Tiger was delighted to hear that Lion, who always robbed him of his food, would have to carry ashes. And he said to Porcupine: "My Brother, you and I have black and white spots. We must always walk together. We must always be friends. I shall be your watchdog, and will see that Lion does not leave ashes in your fire-place."

When Xau heard them talk of a watchdog, an idea occurred to him. And he hurried to Tiger with his idea. He gladdened

Tiger's heart with these lying words: "Man-of-whose-teeth-Lion-is-afraid, you are king of all the animals. I am king of all the people. Let us walk the same road. Then our wives will not be angry when we visit our beloved friends. When I go to see my beloved in the grass seeds, you must keep watch."

But Rain, the woman of heaven, who can see into everyone's heart, saw how Xau wanted to cheat on his wife. She was very angry that the daughters of the earth should be treated this way and so she sent a Winterwind to kill all the grass so that Xau could not see his beloved in the grass seeds.

So then, Xau said to Tiger: "Man-of-whose-teeth-Lion-is-afraid, you are king of all animals, I am king of all people. Let us walk the same road. Let us find gemsbok together."

But wherever Xau and Tiger went they found only the tracks of gemsbok in search of new pastures. They searched and searched but found only the tracks. Then Tiger's feet started to hurt him and he said to Xau: "The places you visit are too far away. My feet hurt. Look, they are bleeding. Porcupine never asked me to walk as far as you do. I want to go back to the black and white king who sings to me."

But Xau entreated: "Just over this one sand dune and another one and then one more after that."

Then Rain, the woman of heaven, commanded Winterwind, saying "Throw frost into the hollows, so that Tiger's feet will crack."

And Winterwind, who had no sympathy with the menfolk, pulled a heavy white blanket over the hollows through which Xau and Tiger had to walk. But Xau was a man of many plans. And he carried Tiger across the first hollow. Then Rain said to the Winterwind: "Push them from the front."

Winterwind did so and she threw them over backwards. Tiger, who cushioned Xau's back and head, struck the ground first. His back was broken.

Xau gazed at him and then looked again and said: "You good-for-nothing, you with your back made of grass, why didn't you stay with your harp-playing king?"

Tiger's throat constricted when he saw Xau was walking away from him through the white hollows.

Alone in the veldt, with a broken back, he knew he would soon be a meal for Wolf. Then Tiger wept bitterly. And Winterwind took up his cry and carried it to the listening ears of many wolves.

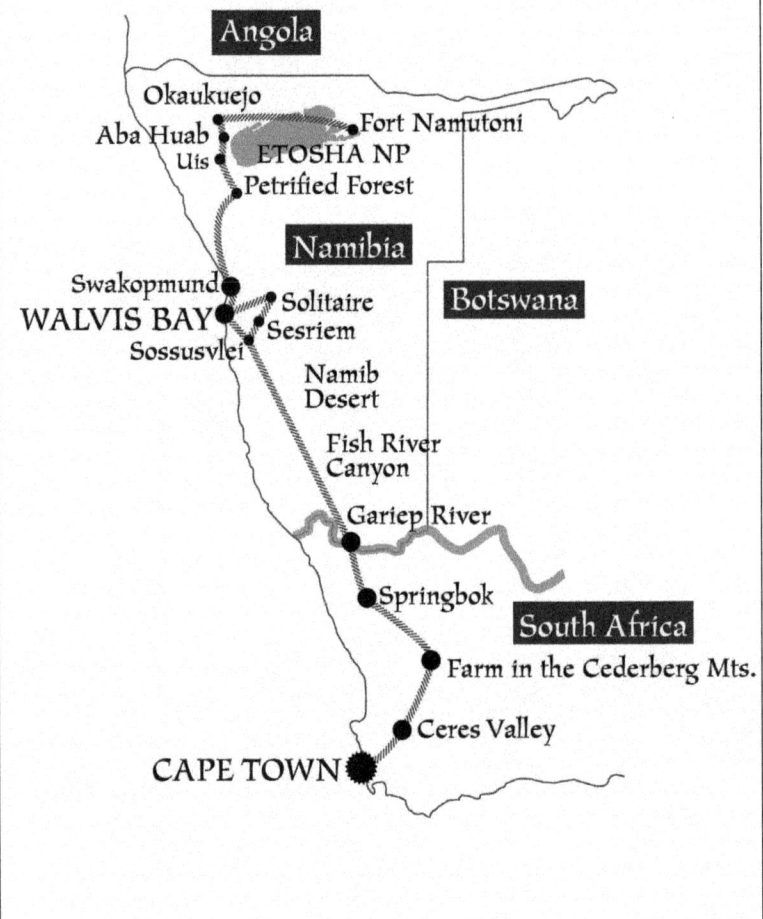

The First Night

SIXTEEN STRANGERS WAITED IN A HOTEL ROOM in Cape Town. Some had come to holiday, others to murder.

Kate chose the tour on a whim and now wondered what on earth she'd let herself in for. The itinerary said: *Briefing at 8:00 p.m. All information will be supplied at this time.* It was already well past the appointed hour and the guide had yet to show up.

"This is ridiculous." A man shared his discontent loudly, his German accent pronounced. "If this is how the trip's going to be run, I'm not going to be happy, I can tell you that right now." The man was catalogue-dressed for a safari; his khaki shorts boasted ironed pleats and his leather hiking boots shouted newness, cracking as he rocked back and forth on the balls of his feet. His wife patted his arm but she too looked anxious and unsure. "This is Africa," another man offered. "Things run differently here."

Kate guessed the new speaker was Eastern European. He was in his forties, with a broad forehead and a sharp, pointed chin and when his efforts to lift the mood failed, he frowned and started flicking through the pages of a spiral-bound notebook.

A heavy silence filled the room and Kate turned to the gothic girl standing next to her. The girl's eyebrows, nose, and dimples were pierced; the latter giving her the appearance of smiling slightly even when she was not. Kate forced her attention away from the girl's facial decorations and stuck out her hand, quickly withdrawing it and feeling stupid, this was not a business meeting. "I'm Kate."

"Eva," the girl said, grinning. "What do you think of the décor? Floral rules, man! And what's with the shipwreck painting? Maybe it's an omen."

Kate was about to reply when another man stood up, yawned widely and stretched. "I simply must go and brush my teeth," he announced with polished British vowels. "And splash my face with cold water or I'm in dreadful danger of nodding off rather rudely. We've been on a plane all day, we dropped our bags off and came straight to the briefing."

He was tall, in his thirties, and had strong features: a bold, hooked nose and close-cropped, reddish-ginger hair. Kate found his accent to be at odds with his appearance although she couldn't say why. "I'm Richard Conlon," he added. "Perhaps one of you would be so kind as to come and give us a shout if the guide ever arrives, which I'm quite sure he will do, eventually. We're in Room 10."

"No problem, I'll come and get you," the Eastern European man offered, looking up from his notebook.

"Fantastic, thanks. Come on, Mia, my love."

He reached for his partner who scrambled to her feet, tugging her sweater down over her generous chest. She giggled, embarrassed. "I think I nodded off for a bit," she yawned, rubbing her face. "Hope I weren't drooling or nuffink." Her voice was breathy and girlish and she was as round as her partner was hawk-like.

"This is completely unacceptable." The German man spoke up again, hands on his hips. "Here we are, heading off into the middle of Africa with this kind of non-leadership. All of you are very calm about it, if you ask me." He crossed his arms and shook his head.

"Thinks he's Ernest Hemingway, spoiling for a fight while waiting for his buffalo-kill photo op," Eva whispered to Kate who smiled and nodded in quick agreement.

At that moment, a stocky African man rushed into the room, his dark skin glistening with sweat. He had an untidy sheaf of papers under one arm and was struggling to catch his breath. The British couple sank back into the sofa.

"Good evening, everybody!" The man smiled as he mopped his forehead on the sleeve of his T-shirt, "I am very sorry to be late! I hope you will forgive me. But I am here now, so let us get started. I am Jono Odili, your tour guide and I would like to welcome you all to Africa." Jono's English was thick with melodic Xhosa.

"I am late because the photocopier in the hotel is not working and so I had to run around to try to find one but that is another story. More importantly, I welcome you to this very interesting twelve-day journey from Cape Town to Windhoek and on our tour, we will travel through some of the most historic parts of Africa, not to mention the most beautiful. This is a spiritual land, the land of our forefathers, a land that has seen war and bloodshed, a land that literally shone with diamonds and gems, as if a hand from heaven decided to bless this part of the world, so that the sparkle could be seen from the sky. This is a land of heat and dust and you will wonder how anybody survived? But they did and we will learn how. You will also ride bikes across the sand dunes, canoe down rivers, hike into valleys, go sky diving, ride a camel, anything you like."

His listeners leaned forward, enraptured.

"If you don't mind," a sharp tone broke the spell, "can we cut to the chase? I have to be somewhere else right now." The woman was tall and lean and her cropped T-shirt revealed a blue jewelled navel ring that flashed and glittered on her smooth belly.

"Of course," Jono replied, "and once again, I apologize for the late start. As you know, this is a camping tour and you will be responsible for putting up and taking down your tents, which are provided. Breakfasts and suppers are prepared for you but you will take turns washing dishes and making lunches. We leave tomorrow morning at 8:30 a.m. The bus will be parked right outside the hotel. Does anybody have questions?"

"I do," the Eastern European man piped up, his notepad at the ready. "I'm Harrison Petrenko."

"Harrison?" Eva whispered. "What's with *Harrison*? Boris or Viktor yes, but Harrison?"

Kate shrugged.

Harrison continued. "All camping equipment is in good working order and all non-camping accommodation has been secured? The bus has been serviced and the tires are in good condition?"

There were a few snickers and Harrison glared as he tried to find the culprits.

"Please sir, do not worry," Jono reassured him. "The tents are fine, the lodges have been booked, and the bus is in good working order. Anything else?"

"Yes," Harrison nodded. "What about water? We are going into the desert after all."

"We will stop regularly for supplies," Jono said. "But, each person is responsible for their own drinking water."

A new voice joined the conversation, high-pitched and uneven. The man twitched at his clothing as he spoke, a crooked smile on his face, his eyes looking down at the floor. "Rydell Adam Jackson here. Must we use bottled water for brushing our teeth?"

"Tap water is fine for brushing your teeth," Jono said, "just do not drink it. And now, if there are no more questions, here is a list for each of you, with the names of everyone who is on this trip. I am going to read off the names and you can say if you are here or not."

"How can you say you're not here, if you're not here to say it?" the hawklike British man enquired.

"If you are not here," Jono replied, "we will determine that you are not here by a process of elimination. Let us get started. Charisse Masellis?"

"Here," a husky voice called out. Charisse was long-limbed in tiny denim shorts.

"What's the bet she's a soap-star actress from L.A.," Eva whispered to Kate. "Or a lingerie model."

"Cheerleader," Kate said.

"Brianna Hau?"

"Here," a petite Asian woman replied from her spot next to Charisse.

"Jasmine Moir?"

"Here, and happy for it," a heavily overweight blonde cried out, her words tangy with an Australian accent.

"Enrique Franco?" Jono moved through the list in no apparent order.

"I'm Enrique," a young man with bad acne raised his hand.

"Sofie Sveinson?"

"Here, I am here," a young woman jumped up and waved, causing her long blonde braids to bounce. She was wearing baggy jodhpuri salwar pants that curtained down in pleated folds of gold and aqua daisies and narrowed sharply at her ankles. The apparel seemed incongruous; she looked more suited to beer steins than vibrant Indian pantaloons.

"Helen Harding?"

"That's me," the tall brusque woman spoke up. "I'm the one who has to leave soon. I thought we'd be done by now." She forced a smile.

"Do not worry, we will see you tomorrow," Jono said. "But first, do you and Sofie know that you are sharing?"

"We met hours ago." Helen waved at Sofie and rushed out without a backward glance.

"I'm glad I don't have to share with Helen," Kate whispered. "She's scary."

She was about to ask Eva who she was sharing with when Jono called out another name. "Ellie Lawrence?"

"Yes, I'm sharing with Jasmine, we're traveling together." This from a bony girl who was folded into the sofa next to Jasmine.

"Mia Teller?"

"That's me, yeah," the British girl said, looking mildly confused for no reason Kate could fathom.

"And I'm Richard Conlon," her partner announced. "I'm with Mia."

"Good to meet you, sir," Jono said. "Marika van Breytenbach?"

There was no answer, only a couple of bewildered stares.

"Marika?" Jono asked again. "Marika, are you here?"

"I guess we can answer that one for her," Richard said, "Hi, I'm Marika and I'm not here."

"Does anybody know where she is?" Jono ignored him. "Is anybody here traveling with her?"

"Shouldn't you know that, not us?" the German man burst out. "Are you not the tour leader for God's sake? How on earth are we supposed to know such things?"

Jono took the aggression in stride.

"Let us conclude that Marika is not here," he said, "I will follow up on that. Kate Fraser?"

"That's me," Kate stuck her hand in the air and just as quickly pulled it down again. "I'm Kate Fraser."

Jono made a note on his pad. "I see here that you're sharing with Marika, the one who is missing." He looked at Kate again and she thought he blushed.

"Ha! You've got a fan," Eva whispered, laughing. "Jono likes you, did you see that?"

Kate was about to reply when the German man spoke loudly. "My wife and I are exhausted. We've also just arrived, we'd like to give you our names, take our papers and go to our room. Does the hotel offer room service?"

"Unfortunately not, but the front desk can recommend a number of good restaurants close to this area although I suggest you do not wander too far or stay out too late. Or, you could eat downstairs in the bar where they serve supper until 10:00p.m. What is your name, sir?"

"I'm Stepfan Brummer and this is my wife, Lena, and thank you, we'll have a meal at the bar. We've no desire to be killed in Africa on our first night after waiting a lifetime to come here. We'll see you all in the morning. Unless," he said, swinging around to direct his attention to the long-legged Charisse, "you wish to join us at the bar?"

"A drink would be good," she agreed, her voice languid. "And we haven't eaten supper either."

A masculine woman in her early forties piped up. "I'm Gisela and I'd love a nice big drink."

"We're ready for a few cold ones too," Jasmine and Ellie chimed in.

"And we never say no to a drinkie-poo," Mia declared, shrugging off her former tiredness. "Bring it on!"

Stepfan appeared disconcerted by the sudden additions to the party but he smiled and nodded. "Lena and I are going to freshen up. We'll see you there shortly." He strode out, a bow-legged bantam, with Lena gliding effortlessly behind.

Jono marked off Gisela's name. "Who do we have next? Harrison Petrenko, that is you, yes?" He turned to the man with the notepad.

"Yes, I'm Harrison," the man replied. He examined the papers that Jono had given him. "I don't see the exact times of departures and arrivals marked here. And where are the daily kilometers we will travel? And where will the list be posted of who's responsible for what duties?"

"I can give the kilometres to you each day," Jono assured him. "Treasure, our cook, makes the lists of duties and sticks them on the inside of the bus door. The exact times of departure and arrivals are hard to say until we actually get on the road, and even then…"

"I can see that I will have to be in charge of my own documentation," Harrison commented. He sounded grim although he smiled as he spoke, his blue eyes bright. "We must be precise. Well, Mr. Jono, good night and thank you." With that, he picked up a thin leather briefcase, bowed slightly and left.

"Did I leave anybody out?" Jono asked, looking at his list. The room was emptying.

"Yes, me," Eva said. "I'm Eva Leifsdottír and I am in Room 12. Is anybody else here who is also in Room 12? Room 12 that does not have a Gideon bible but does have a blue plaid carpet."

"I'm in Room 12." Gisela called out.

"*Haw*, but those are interesting clothes you are wearing for our journey," Jono said, then paused, his eyes resting on Eva's amused face. "Surely you will be very hot?"

Eva was wearing a long black sweatshirt with black leather knee-high platform boots, ripped black stockings and a short black skirt. She laughed. "I'll be fine, don't worry."

"Do you just dress the part or do you live it?" a sly tone interjected with a slight stutter. "I bet you only dress it, you don't mean it."

It was Rydell, the man who had asked Jono about the bottled water. Rydell had thinning light brown hair, a long aristocratic nose, and full lips which he licked nervously. His small dark eyes were deep-set and he blinked rapidly, his gaze darting from Eva's face to the floor.

Eva looked down at him and frowned. "You couldn't handle me, little man," she said, and Rydell turned beet-red and scuttled out the room, leaving only Kate, Jono and Eva, who was also ready to leave. "I'm going to my room to freshen up, meet you down in the bar in half an hour?"

"Sounds good," Kate said. "I just want to ask Jono something."

"With pleasure, my dear," Jono said, his smile wide. "But please excuse me, Kate, I must sit down for a minute. *Haw*, but I am very tired tonight. I have recurrent bouts of malaria and this time, it was very bad."

He eased himself onto the floral sofa next to Kate. "Even if I was not sick," he continued, "the briefing is always a very hard thing for me. I feel like I must be a salesman to everyone." He rubbed his face and gave a small laugh. "*Eish*, I must be tired, to be telling you these things."

Kate was used to strangers pouring out their hearts to her; even her friends and family found it natural for her to be waylaid by people wanting to share the intimate details of their lives.

"Everybody's nervous and tired," she said. "And that makes them seem wound up. This does seem to be quite the collection of characters though. Is it usually such a mixed bag?"

"Um, we do seem to have a few more unusual ones this time. I have never had anybody ask me for such particular details as Harrison, and Rydell, with his funny body twitches and dressed in so many layers of clothing, and Stepfan seems like such an angry little man ... and then there is Eva! I have never had a punk girl on my bus before! *Eish*, I should not judge. Treasure is not going to have much patience with them, I can tell you now," he laughed.

"Treasure's our cook, right?"

"Yes, but she organizes a lot of things too. Everybody loves Treasure. But I am worried about her." He burst out the last bit and then clamped his mouth shut.

"Why? You can trust me." Kate was happy to be discussing someone else's life, her own woes a distant memory for the moment.

Jono hesitated. "She is seeing a married man. A white, rich, married man. And she thinks he is going to leave his wife but he will not. They never do. And her heart will get broken, again. She is so beautiful but she picks the wrong men."

"I'm sorry," Kate said. "Heartbreak is horrible."

Jono looked at her. "Is your heart broken?"

She shook her head vehemently. "I've got a wonderful boyfriend back home." She was not sure why she lied. "He's great about my coming on holiday. But who of us hasn't known heartbreak and I hate people to be sad."

"Yes, she is very sad. I also think she may be pregnant. She already has a six-year-old son back in Zimbabwe. Her mother looks after him. She cannot afford another child. It is very stupid, really. I do not know why I am telling you all this, I must still have a bad fever."

"Don't worry, I won't say anything. Maybe this married man really loves her? If she's so beautiful, then most likely he does. Men will generally do anything for a beautiful woman." Kate realized she sounded bitter and changed the subject. "Jono, can't you take anything for malaria?"

"It is too late for medicines, the mosquito swims in my blood forever. I just need a good night's sleep and I'll be fine in the morning."

"I had better go and get ready to meet the others," Kate said and stood up. "Would you like to join us downstairs?"

"No, but thank you. Did you not want to ask me something?"

"It was about the tents. I've never camped before and I am a bit worried about it, but I didn't want to say so in front of everybody."

"*Ai*, Katie, it is very easy and I will show you how to do everything, please do not worry."

"Okay! See you tomorrow then," Kate bade Jono goodnight and went down to the bar leaving a cheerful Jono.

Jono could not recall the last time he had really spoken to a woman and he could not help but appreciate that Kate was remarkably lovely although it seemed she was quite clueless to the fact. He thought about his own life and how loveless it had become, not by intention but by time, distance and the ever-constant companion of exhaustion. And while his head cautioned him there was no way that a white woman would fall in love with him, his heart could not deny the flicker of excitement he felt at the thought of seeing Kate the next morning.

Kate, flanked by Gisela and Eva, was soon enjoying a large glass of white wine in the pub.

"From the smell of it, more beer was spilled in here than drunk," Eva wrinkled her nose. "But I love the décor, it's very colonial."

"I hadn't really noticed," Kate said, and looked around. The pub had a gold and red paisley carpet and striped burgundy and yellow wallpaper with framed prints of British fox hunts. An elderly black man in a white jacket and red fez was standing behind the bar, polishing wine glasses and keeping the drinks flowing.

"You're right," Kate said. "I need to be more observant, like you, Eva. Gisela, where are you from?"

"Sweden. How about you?"

Kate was impressed by how well almost everyone on the tour spoke English. Europeans, she thought, were always so far ahead in this regard than North Americans. "Canada," she replied, wishing she could speak another language as effortlessly. "And you, Eva?"

"Iceland. I was studying psychology but I failed my exams, so I came to Cape Town as a volunteer and now I'm having a holiday before I go back home."

"Volunteering is very noble of you," Gisela said. "I just got tired of the darkness and the cold of December and I decided to give myself a hot summer vacation."

"I'm not noble," Eva downed half her beer. "I'm a poet with writer's block and I thought coming here would help, but nothing has happened. My head and heart are still empty."

"I wish my heart was empty," Kate blurted out. "My heart's full of hurt and questions."

"He, or she, will come crawling back." Eva spoke with conviction. "You're much too gorgeous for them not to."

Kate blushed. She had not meant to bare her soul to people she had just met. "You think so?" she added, somewhat cheered by Eva's prognosis. "He doesn't even care enough to know that I've come on this trip. He's too busy enjoying the benefits of an open relationship with a socialite who wears a lot of Tiffany bracelets. But I'm sorry I mentioned it, let's talk about something else."

"What do you do for a job?" Gisela picked a safer topic.

"I very recently, and without any kind of regret, mind you, left my job as a publishing assistant, where I worked for eight very long years. I left, just like that. My entire life is stored in two big boxes in my best friend's apartment and here I am."

"In that case you need another drink," Eva said.

"True, I do," Kate agreed. "Although I've never drunk this much in my life."

"You've only had two glasses of wine," Gisela was amused. "How old are you?"

"Thirty-one," Kate said, "I know, I'm so boring. All I wanted to do was marry Cam, that's my boyfriend, and do whatever came after that. But now that's all gone."

"If you ask me, my dear," Gisela said, "coming on this trip is the best thing you could have done. It'll clear your head and give you new perspective." She laughed. "That's what I'm hoping for anyway. And now, if you'll both excuse me for a moment, I'm going outside to have a cigarette and I never apologise for my habit. I love smoking."

Behind them, Stepfan was complaining theatrically about the food. "One would not think it possible to ruin such a simple thing as a hamburger but they've succeeded. The meat's been deep-fried in what tastes like old fish oil. The bun is stale and these slices of raw onion are big enough to give me halitosis for the entire trip. But," he paused for comedic effect, "what truly fascinates me, is this piece of orange. Let me present to you Exhibit A. I've never seen an orange garnish a hamburger before, particularly not speared onto a toothpick and accompanied by two red cocktail onions." He thoroughly enjoyed his joke.

"Horrible old wolf," Eva shivered. "No, wolf's too good for him. He thinks he's so charming."

"I feel sorry for his wife," Kate said, watching Lena pick

quietly at her dinner without comment while Stepfan directed his observations at Charisse who laughed her deep slow laugh and agreed with his assessments. Charisse's friend Brianna drank steadily, lost in her own world while Jasmine and Mia leaned across the bar counter and giggled while they threw back shots.

"Oops-a-daisy," Mia exclaimed. "Nearly missed with that one! Got most of it on me bleedin' face. What a waste. Here, luv," she turned to Richard and offered him her sticky face. "Sambuca. Do us a favour and lick it off, won't you?"

Richard wiped her face clean with a napkin and gave her a kiss.

"Don't get too hammered," he cautioned her.

"Right, look who's talking," Mia laughed. "Come on, luv," she said to Richard, "let's have a nuvver round of shots, not just me and Jasmine, all of us. You both, too," she called out to Eva and Kate. "And you," she pointed at Rydell who was sitting off to the side in a red velvet chair.

He shook his head, licked his lips and fussed with his sleeves. "No shots for me," he stammered. He examined the glass of beer in front of him, holding it up to the light before venturing a cautious sip. Then he crossed his legs tightly, shoved one hand into his pocket and fingered something nervously.

"No alcohol for us and anyway, it's time we went to bed," Stepfan announced. He threw the cloth napkin onto his ketchup-covered plate and got to his feet. "Come, Lena. I want us to go through our backpacks one more time. We will see you all in the morning, good night." He bowed in Charisse's direction and walked out with Lena trotting behind him, her food largely untouched.

Gisela returned to the bar to find them all another round down.

"You've got to catch up with shots," Mia said bossily but Gisela shook her head.

"Another nice big vodka will do me fine. Neat, and make it a double."

"Hardcore," Richard said admiringly. "Oh, bollocks, in for a penny, in for a pound." He threw back his drink and ordered another round.

An hour later, the party was in full swing and Kate could not remember ever being so drunk. She stood up and spotted Rydell who was still sitting alone, watching everyone. He stared at Kate and gave her a strange, lopsided grimace and shook with silent laughter. Kate tried to make sense of the unspoken exchange but the room was blurring and she left the bar unsteadily, gripping chairs for support on her way out.

Rydell watched her leave and fingered the small knife in his pocket, experimenting by pricking the pad of his thumb. No, he was fine, he did not need the release of pain. It was true that he had been alarmed when he first saw Kate; she reminded him strongly of the early Vegas showgirl pictures of his mother, having the same leggy full-bodied appeal, but it was more than that. Her features were similar; her full lips, her high oval cheekbones and the fall of her long dark hair that refused to stay tucked behind her ear.

"Nothing will stop me this time," he hissed under his breath. "Not even you, Mother. Not this time. I'm not going to let anything stop me, do you hear me? Not you or anyone else."

From Cape Town to the Cedarberg Mountains

KATE WOKE EARLY THE NEXT MORNING with a blinding hangover. She was afraid to move but lying down felt worse and she eased herself up with deliberate slowness, opening her eyes to see the room spinning at her like a bowling ball thrown through a fish-eye lens.

She lay there cursing herself. The first real day of her holiday and she was sick as a dog. Half an hour later, she decided a walk would help and she dressed gingerly, putting on her sunglasses and pulling on her jeans and a T-shirt.

She stopped in the lobby to lean her forehead against the cool wall and overheard a woman talking.

"Hello? Jono? This is Marika van Breytenbach; I'm with your tour. I was supposed to be here for the briefing last night but my flight got rerouted because of a snowstorm and I was lucky to get here at all. The bad news is that South African Airways lost my luggage. Could you phone them? You'll have more authority than me. I've got a contact name and number for you; I'm hoping they can find my luggage before we leave Cape Town."

Ah, her roomate, the missing Marika.

"O...kay..." Kate heard Marika say hesitantly and then she listened for another moment, quickly responding with a heartfelt yowl. "I can't have a shower, Jono, because I haven't got any luggage. No soap, no towel, no clothes. I don't even have a hairbrush."

She sounded despondent and Kate felt bad for her. "You're right, we'll sort this out later. Thank you, Jono." With an audible sigh, the woman hung up the phone.

Kate went up to her and held out her hand. "I'm Kate, your roommate, I'm sorry to hear about your luggage. What can I do to help?"

Marika was older than Kate had first thought, in her mid-forties at least. Kate was glad she was wearing sunglasses because Marika was dressed in a startling explosion of colour.

"Wow, are you an artist?"

Marika laughed. "Shows does it? Yes, I'm an illustrator." She grinned and spoke with a thick South African accent. "I missed the briefing, what's the plan?"

Kate checked her watch. "Jono said the bus leaves at 8:30, so we've still got lots of time." She let out a groan. "This really isn't like me, Marika but I've got a shocking hangover and I feel really sick."

"You're going to find me very boring to room with, I'm not much of a drinker," Marika smiled.

"Neither am I, believe me, and after last night, I plan to drink even less, although we did have fun. Let's go up to our room, you can wash your face at least and I'll give you a clean T-shirt although I haven't got anything as bright as yours."

Marika grinned. "Sounds good to me. What a nightmare journey. First I got rerouted and then..."

Kate suddenly rushed past her on the stairs, pushed her key card into the lock and made for the bathroom where she threw up until there was nothing left but painful dry heaves.

"You poor thing." Marika followed Kate into the bathroom and pulled Kate's hair back from her face. "You'll feel better now."

"So embarrassed," Kate muttered, flushing the toilet with one hand while resting her head on the side of the bathtub.

Marika patted her shoulder. "We've all been there. Listen, I'm going to have a shower, okay? Can I borrow your towel?"

Kate made agreeing noises and crawled to her bed, covering her eyes with a sweatshirt.

By the time Marika emerged, her short blonde hair dark with water and her face stripped of makeup, Kate was feeling better. Slightly.

"Time to go down to the bus," she said and Marika obligingly grabbed her camera bag. "This is heavy," she commented. "Are you a professional photographer?"

"I wish," Kate said. "My dad said it was no way to earn a living."

"One could say the same about illustrating, but I manage."

"I lack the courage of my convictions," Kate admitted. "This trip is the first thing I've ever chosen for myself."

They went outside and found Gisela leaning against a large white overland tour bus, smoking a cigarette.

"This is Marika, my lost roommate," Kate made the introductions. "Gisela, how come you're not hung-over like me?"

"Maybe because I only ever drink vodka," Gisela shrugged.

Kate went green. "Please don't mention alcohol." She looked up at the bus. "Can we go inside and explore?"

Gisela laughed. "It's like a big shoebox on wheels. The door's open. I've already put my luggage inside."

They climbed in and found the bus utilitarian in the extreme, with a narrow white-painted metal frame and low-ceilinged grey metal racks above the seats. The riveted-steel floor had two bucket seats on either side of the aisle and the seats had thinly cushioned backs covered in a worn gray fabric. Kate searched in vain for cup holders and pouches on the seat backs and tried a window, which opened with some persuasion. "It's quite rustic," was all she could manage.

"Definitely seen some serious mileage," Marika agreed as she turned to Kate who had slumped down into a seat, looking green again.

"Listen to that lovely noise out there," Marika said to distract Kate from her hangover. "Taxi horns, African music, people shouting. I love Canada, don't get me wrong, but I miss this a lot."

"I'm from Canada too," Kate said, her eyes closed. "How long have you lived there?"

"Nearly twenty years. A long time, not that you can tell from my accent."

The flow of minibus taxis increased, with the noise level rising and Marika studied the resigned faces of the taxi passengers staring at nothing in particular on their way to work. A black woman walked by in threadbare clothing, a large bag balanced on her head, a baby swaddled against her back, and a toddler clinging to her hand.

"I'm quite sure I wouldn't be able to live these people's lives, not even for a day," Marika said. "And I wonder if anything has become any easier for them since apartheid ended? From what I've heard, they work as hard as before and so many of the promises turned out to be lies."

"No matter what, it must be better now," Kate said from her slumped-down seat. "Their lives were violated before in the most evil and unspeakable of ways."

"Ja, I know of course you're right, my friend. I just wish for happier endings, that's all."

Marika watched a tall lean woman throw her arms around a poster-perfect surfer boy who recoiled slightly from the embrace. "People are joining us," she said.

Kate carefully sat up and peered out the window. "That's Helen. She seems very uptight. I wonder who the pretty boy is with her."

"Whoever he is, he's not keen on her," Marika commented.

"You're right. There'll be no happy ending there, there never is."

"Speaking from experience?"

Kate's eyes filled with tears. "I'm so stupid. But this is between you and me, because I told Jono I've got a boyfriend. I don't know why I lied, maybe I don't want to admit it's over. I also got the feeling Jono might be interested in me, and there's no interest from my side, but I wouldn't want to hurt his feelings."

"Got it," Marika said. "We can talk more later, I think the rest of the gang is here."

One by one, the group clambered onboard, with Jono bringing up the rear. He searched the bus for Kate, and he smiled and waved at her. She summoned a grin and waved listlessly back.

"Good morning, everybody!" Jono was much more energetic than the night before.

"Good morning, Jono," they chorused.

"How did everybody sleep?" he asked.

A volley of replies gave assorted answers.

"That is very good to hear," Jono said, when the din subsided. "Now let me introduce you to our cook, or should I say, our chef." He put his arm around a beautiful woman in her mid-thirties, with full lips, high cheekbones and sleepy almond eyes. The thin, worn fabric of her navy pants and faded T-shirt did nothing to diminish her grace.

"Treasure has been on many tours such as these and fed many more than you and has received the highest praise for her cooking."

The group clapped and shouted greetings and Jono smiled.

"And now, to the second thing," he said. "Has all the luggage fitted?"

"We had to use the entire back seat but yes, it fit," Harrison jumped up. "But I don't think the things are well-secured in the luggage racks." He strained to look up, "Please, Mr. Jono, check, I'm worried."

Jono walked down the aisle, prodding and readjusting. "It is fine," he said.

"Isn't there any space on the roof we could use to store a few things?" Richard asked.

"No, my friend, that is full. One piece of advice, try not to acquire too many souvenirs along the way and if you must buy things, try to keep them small," Jono grinned.

"Does that mean I can't have one of those giant six-foot

carved wooden giraffes I've heard about?" Jasmine joked. "But Jono, getting one of those was the main reason for my trip."

"Then I suggest you wait until Swakopmund," Jono advised her, "where you can buy a lot of brown paper and post one home to yourself. Even better, give him your address and let him swim home to you."

Jasmine sighed with a crestfallen expression on her face and Jono laughed. Kate could not understand why no one seemed as hung-over as she felt.

"I am being a very bad host," Jono said. "Everybody, we must welcome Marika who happily has arrived, although her luggage was not so fortunate. But it will get here in the end. Marika, where in South Africa are you originally from?"

"A farm in Underberg, Natal," Marika said. "Jono, did South African Airways...,"

"Underberg? Near Himeville?" Helen interrupted.

"Yes, exactly," Marika was surprised that Helen knew such a remote town. "How do you know it?"

"I've been volunteering there for the past year. That's incredible, what are the odds? And why are you *here*," Helen persisted, "on *this* tour, when you come from the most spectacular place in the world? If I had a farm in Underberg, I'd never leave it."

Marika was uncomfortable at being put on the spot. "I guess I want to see the Africa that lies beyond my father's farm and I've always been fascinated by the Bushmen. They were so advanced and such amazing, peace-loving people."

Rydell, across the aisle, gave a loud derisive snort. Marika turned to Kate for an explanation but Kate shrugged.

Helen thought how small the world was and while it was true that she had loved Underberg, she had been excited to leave with the promise of a wonderful new life beckoning. However, as she had rudely realised the previous night, that shiny promise had been no more than the false hope of fool's gold. She swallowed hard, not yet ready to acknowledge the truth.

"Let us be on our way," Jono said, "Our bus is named

Mandoza, after a popular South African musician. One day I will play some of his music for you. Everybody, let us go!"

In the privacy of the cab, Jono and Treasure exchanged glances as they settled into their seats. "Here we go," Jono referred to the riotous chatter behind. "It begins again."

"Hmmm, yes." Treasure suppressed a smile. "But there's something different this time, Jono, *yebo*? I saw that girl, how she caught your eye. I have never seen you like that before. *Haw wena*. Since when do you like tall American girls?"

"She is from Canada but I am quite certain I do not know what you are talking about," Jono said, grinding a gear.

Treasure laughed and smoothed her hair with long, capable fingers. "*Yebo*, I was right on the money. But you've always told me you could never trust a white girl, when it comes to matters of the heart?"

"You are right. Do I think a white girl could ever really fall in love with a black man like me? No. That aspect of apartheid is still strong for me. How are you, this morning anyway? I thought you would have a sore head from coming home so late."

"No sore head for me, my friend, I'm fine thank you, you worry about yourself."

Jono concentrated on the road, thinking that while Kate had a boyfriend back home, she was travelling by herself and that had to say something about the relationship. He acknowledged the flicker of hope in his heart and thought that stranger things had happened than a tourist coming on holiday and falling in love with the guide. The legacy he had grown up with, the forbidden relationships between black and white, that bitter old voice whispered that Kate would reject him out of hand because of his black skin, while his rational mind argued that she was not like that, that things had been different for a long time, and that anything was possible.

Treasure put her bare feet up on the dashboard and picked up a magazine, happy to be distracted from her own worries by teasing Jono, oblivious to the fact that she was being stared at by Rydell, stared at with singular and uncompromising focus.

From the moment he laid eyes on Treasure, Rydell realized she was The One. Overwhelmed by his good fortune, he tried to remain calm but he felt as if ants were crawling under his skin. He was simultaneously ecstatic and panic-stricken. He had not expected to find her so soon. And now that he had her in his sights, quite literally, he had no idea what to do.

Yes.

He twitched with delight and twisted the fabric of his trousers with plump, pale fingers.

Yes, Treasure will know how to make a man feel like a man, not like the painted whores in Kansas City.

He thought back to the red-clawed women who had tried to trap him in cheaply-perfumed cages of sagging tired beauty and broke out in a cold sweat, wiping his forehead and upper lip with the sleeve of his shirt. *They wrapped their arms and legs around me and tried to suffocate me with their flea-infested feathers.* Not that Rydell was opposed to restraints and vices, that binding punishment provided necessary release. Being chastised by a dominatrix was the only way he had found to momentarily quieten the anxious fevers that jostled for real estate in his tormented mind. He deserved to be tied up and whipped, he needed it, and besides, that brutality was honest. What he could not bear was the mockery of social pretense.

He snuck a quick glance at Treasure and greedily drank in the sight of her. Treasure, unaware of him, licked the tip of her finger and turned the page of a magazine.

Rydell felt his erection straining against his trousers and he shifted in his seat. He thought back to his book and how it had shown him his destiny. He had nearly gone mad from being so alone but the book had changed his life. He tugged the floppy brim of his hat, filled with fury at the thought of how hard his life had been, how he had been called an *odd little boy*, and then, *an odd little man*, despite his remarkable intelligence.

I'm not odd. They're the ones who are odd; the ones who think I'm not right in the head for wanting the things I do — as if I can help it. They're the ones who make me sick, they want to eat me, they want to stick their feelers inside me and suck out my juices.

Filled with panic, he found it hard to breathe, and he reached into his pocket and clutched the small serrated knife he carried with him. He dug the sharp edge into the palm of his hand, cutting into his flesh and the pain helped to clear his head. He glanced back at Treasure, willing her to lick her finger again with the tip of her dark pink tongue.

He knew that she was not a Bushman woman like the ones in the book, but Africa was Africa and a woman was a woman. He just hoped she was not too emancipated. The book had said the Bushman women were the least emancipated, which was what he wanted, but now he had fallen for Treasure and he had make it work with her, no matter what. He wet his lips. He imagined the pungent smell of her sweat and he wanted to bury his face in her hot, wet armpit and drink her salt. His face turned purple with desire.

He sensed someone looking at him and he turned to find that girl, the one who reminded him of his mother, staring at him. Rydell paled and felt as if he had been doused in icy water.

Why was she watching him again? He hated the way she looked at him, as if she could read his thoughts. But what could she know of his thoughts? Nothing, nothing at all. He returned her look evenly, his face quickly blameless and composed but when she smiled at him, he was disconcerted. He managed an uncomfortable half-smile in return, his lips twisted to one side and then he looked away. He eased his grip on the knife, telling himself that everything was fine, that he was in control even although he knew it was not true. He had never been in control and he jiggled his knee in anxious irritation, shrinking from the inescapable memory of his countless shames. He had been laughed at all his life because he did not see the world as others did. He tried so hard for normalcy, but the fingers of his mind would scrabble and lose purchase and he would fall back to lonely ground where the only balm to his vicious anger was pain — someone, or something, always had to pay.

He glanced up at his luggage, reassuring himself with the thought of his medications. Yes, he had done the right thing, seen his family doctor. He had tried to pass his concerns off as mere travel stresses but the doctor knew him too well.

"I'm glad you came to see me. That shows an impressive maturity, Rydell. I wish you would stay on meds all the time. There's no shame in it you know, it's not your fault, it's a disease, an illness like any other."

"I didn't come here for a lecture," Rydell said softly in his light, pale voice. "I came for a prescription and I'll need enough for three months."

"Three months? Why such a long time?" the doctor had asked as he scribbled on his pad.

"Not that it's any of your business but I might have to stay in Africa that long. I'm going to find something special and I don't know how long it will take."

"Here you go. Come and see me when you get back," the doctor handed over the prescription and wrote in a file.

"Why? So you can interrogate me?" Rydell got to his feet and brushed imaginary dirt from his trousers. "Don't worry, Doctor, I plan to be a very good boy. If Mother were still alive, she'd be proud of what a good boy I'm going to be."

"But Rydell," the doctor said, disturbed, his notes forgotten, "your mother is still alive and you know it."

Rydell had turned white. "My mother is *dead*. Now I remember why I try not to see you, Doctor. You always *upset* me." And with that he had left.

Rydell shuddered.

"Are you cold?" tall, boyish Enrique enquired. He was sitting next to Rydell and Rydell nearly fell off his seat in fright.

"What are you talking about?" he asked nervously.

"You gave a great big shake, you know, like when you're cold. But you shouldn't be cold, you have the most clothes on, out of all of us," Enrique smiled at him.

Rydell wanted to hiss at him but he could not, so he tugged at his sleeves and pretended to be laughing. "I'm not hot, and I'm not cold either. Tell me about the first time you kissed a girl and I'll tell you about mine."

Enrique was taken aback. "No way," he said and Rydell turned his back to him and stared out the window.

The bus reached the beach stop and Jono assembled the group. "Everybody! You have ten minutes to walk on the sand, take your photographs of Table Mountain and maybe dip your feet in the ocean. But remember, the water is very cold."

Kate knelt in the soft white sand and smiled up at the young woman with the long, blond braids who had walked up to join her. Even this morning, she was clothed in flowing Indian trousers; today's pair were bright yellow cotton, patterned with enormous red and lilac flowers. "In case you do not remember from last night, I am Sofie," the girl introduced herself again. "I just arrived from travelling through India, which I loved. I do not know if I will love Africa as much, though. India is such a spiritual land."

"This beach certainly is wonderful," Kate said, running the fine sand through her fingers.

"True." Sofie sat down next to her and played with the tiny shells and bits of seaweed casually strewn around her. "The mountain looks incredible from here — a pefect summer day." Sofie spoke with an odd lisp and Kate found it hard to understand what she was saying.

"Time to go, everybody," Jono called. "Richard and Mia, come on."

Mia, standing on the edge of the shoreline, let the icy waves tease her toes as she glanced up at Richard. "Nice, innit," she whispered, "'aving our own dark little secret?"

Richard laughed. "Not so little really. Yes, it does feel quite thrilling. But you do realize that we have to be patient? That we might only get to have the chance to do it near the middle or end of the trip?"

Mia looked grumpy. "Yeah, I know, you don't need to keep yammerin' on."

"Mia," he said, "patience isn't one of your virtues, my love, and I worry about you."

"Well, bleedin' don't," she said, linking her arm through his as they walked back to the bus. "I know what we've got to do, pretend to be 'appy little holidaymakers, blah blah – don't worry, it's all under control."

"Come on," Jono called again, "it is time to go."

An hour later, Jono brought the bus to a stop outside a suburban shopping mall on the outskirts of Cape Town. "Everybody! We are going grocery shopping now," he called out. "You have one hour."

"Thank goodness," Marika said. "I'm going to buy a towel and a few things."

"I forgot, Marika, I have good news," Jono announced. "Your luggage has been found and it will be with us tomorrow."

"Excellent! I've been in these clothes for what feels like forever." She brushed at her T-shirt and jeans while the rest of the group tumbled off the bus.

Kate and Marika headed for the T-shirt section inside the main store. "Here's a nice one," Kate said, holding up a lime green T-shirt with a blue sequined butterfly on the front.

"Perfect! Well done," Marika exclaimed.

Stepfan startled them by popping out from between the racks. He flashed a wolfish grin and held up a sheer pink wrap. "This would suit you, Kate."

"I'm not a stripper," Kate retorted and Marika pulled her away. "Ignore him," she said as they weaved through another aisle of casual clothing and made their way toward the front of the shop.

They bumped into Jono and Treasure who were loading up the cart with canned goods and offered to help but Treasure waved them on.

"I'm going to check out the other shops in the mall and see if there's anything worth photographing," Kate said to Marika. "You okay?"

"I'm fine, dear, see you out there."

Watching Kate leave, Treasure nudged Jono.

"I'm sure," she said in Xhosa, "that you would have been nice and happy to have your princess at your side, so you can begin to charm her."

Jono gave her a sharp nudge. "*Haw!* What nonsense you talk. Anyway, you have an admirer already, Did you not notice?"

"What are you talking about?"

"Don't look now, but over there, by the tomatoes, no Treasure, I said *do not* look now. You see that man?"

"How can I, if I don't look?"

"Look out of the corner of your eye, like a spy would. That man over there has a thing for you, I can tell. He is one of the unfortunates whose heart you are going to break. But, usually there is more than one," he teased. "So, who is your other victim?"

"*Haw!* You!" She shoved him, "I don't do anything. *Ei,* but why does *that* man like me? He's very strange with all the clothes he wears and look at how he is sniffing that tomato. What is he is going to do next, lick it?" She laughed. "He looks like he's never been with a woman in his life! He must not think he is going to start with me." She nudged Jono with her shoulder and they walked off, bantering playfully in Xhosa.

Standing next to the tomatoes, Rydell felt the blood red

haze of anger fill his vision. He was certain Jono and Treasure been laughing at him. He had seen Jono nod in his direction followed by Treasure's quick and dismissive glance and her careless, amused shrug.

Filled with savage hurt, he squeezed the tomato in his hand so hard it exploded. Disgusted by the mess he had made and fearful he had been seen, he quickly wiped his hand on the stack of displayed fruit, reached for his handkerchief and delicately cleaned between his fingers. He inspected his clothes for stains, but they were clean. Momentarily appeased, he told himself that Treasure had no idea what he had to offer, and that he must not feel discouraged but his efforts to reassure himself failed and a voice crawled out of his past and into his lonely place, echoing like a vinyl record in a forgotten and empty room.

Georgie Porgie, Puddin' and Pie,
Kissed the girls and made them cry,
When the boys came out to play,
Georgie Porgie ran away.

The voice stopped, silent for a moment, then it began again, reedy and thin, mocking and unmistakable. Alone among the fresh produce, with the oft-told nursery rhyme ringing in his head, Rydell listened to his mother's cruel voice and came to a decision. "No," he said out loud and this time his fury was white. "No, not this time." No matter what it took, this time, he was not going to be Georgie Porgie.

He closed his eyes and began to chant and hiss at the grinning crone-ghost of his mother, at the too-close image of her wrinkled red lips, her lipstick spreading into the fine cracks of her skin like blood.

Sticks and stones, I'll break your bones, but words will never hurt me. When you're dead and in your grave, you'll be sorry for what you called me.

He opened his eyes and gave his hands one last careful wipe, his mother silenced.

The mall was decorated for Christmas. Mary and Jesus loomed behind two children with hymn books, their mouths stretched open in frozen song. Kate knelt down next to the life-size tableau. There was something oddly obscene about the children's faces; they had rudely-painted features, a parody of childhood beauty with yellowed teeth, cornflower blue eyes and bloodied nostrils.

Kate, an avid reader of horror novels, thought the children looked like they had been chewing on raw flesh. She imagined they were Steven King characters that came alive at night and ran amok. She was peering into the boy's nostrils, enjoying her macabre fantasies when she was startled by the brush of fetid, hot breath on her neck and she nearly crashed into the tableau.

It was Stepfan, leaning over her. "Are you alright?" he asked. "Let me help you up. I was looking over your shoulder to see what you were photographing. I didn't mean to frighten you."

Kate gathered herself, pointedly ignored his outstretched hand and tried to forget his stale breath.

"What's going on here?" Marika arrived, a plastic bag in hand.

"Nothing, nothing," Stepfan held up his hands. "Don't twist your little panties into a knot." He wandered off.

"I really wish he'd stop popping up," Kate said. "What an awful man and I get the distinct impression he thinks he's God's gift to women. His poor wife."

"His wife's Katharine Hepburn á la *African Queen*?"

"Yep, that's the one."

Marika looked at her watch. "Enough time left to quickly pop into the pharmacy."

They bumped into Charisse at the entrance to May's Chemist. She was pale and had a hand on her belly. "My stomach's killing me," she said by way of a greeting. "I'm hoping the drugstore will have something that will help."

Richard and Mia were also inside, in the middle of a heated argument with the pharmacist.

"Now see here, old chap," Richard insisted loudly. "My girlfriend here needs her prescription filled, and no, for the fifth time, you can't phone the doctor who wrote it. He's in London, for God's sake."

Richard was trying to appear amicable, but his jaw was clenched and his hands were balled into fists at his sides.

"Come now," he tried again, forcing a smile, "I don't understand what you're making such a fuss about. We're here for a long holiday and we're going to be on the road, travelling all the way through Africa and who knows when we'll get to a pharmacy again? Come on, old chap, be an obliging fellow and give us a hand."

"But it is a most strong tranquillizer," the Indian pharmacist objected with a strong Delhi accent. "And not one I am used to having to give out. Plus, you wish to acquire a hefty amount. It would be irresponsible of me to fill this out without enquiring further. I am only wanting to know that this is all above board." He studied the prescription with a frown.

Kate, Marika and Charisse watched Mia gaze at the pharmacist with a pleading expression. It might have been the conviction of Richard's speech, or Mia's desperate look, but the pharmacist suddenly gave in.

"All right," he said with obvious reluctance. "Come back in fifteen minutes. Next?"

Richard and Mia exchanged a glance. "Excellent, old chap, thanks," Richard said and he and Mia left, acknowledging the waiting girls with a grin.

Charisse began explaining her stomach woes to the pharmacist while Kate and Marika turned their attention to the candy display.

"Sweetie Pies," Marika exclaimed with delight. Turning to Kate, she explained, "they are thin chocolate shells filled with the most delicious, soft fluffy vanilla marshmallow stuff. I'm buying the lot!"

Kate laughed. "Okay, Ms. Sweetie Pie, you get those and then I want to pick up a sandwich. My stomach feels better and I'm starving!"

"Stupid bleedin' wanker," Mia muttered to Richard as soon as they left the pharmacy. "And I mean you, ducky, not him. I told you we should have got more when we were in London, but no, you 'ad to do it your way as per bleedin' usual." Her face settled into petulant lines, her thin lips pressed tight.

Richard ran his fingers through his short ginger hair. "Whatever, Mia, whatever. I'm not going to argue with you. Remember, we're here to have *fun* okay? We're here to make all our fantasies come true, okay?" He put his arm around her and jiggled her. He was so tall that she fitted neatly under his arm. "Come on," he said kissing the top of her fine blonde hair, "put on your party face, we've worked so hard to get here, right?"

She grunted in reply, not ready to forgive him. "Would of been fucked without it, yeah? Could of ruined everyfing."

"We would have made a plan," Richard said with confidence, "you know that. When have we ever not? Come on Mia, have I ever let you down?"

She sighed and relaxed into him. "Yeah, okay. Anyway," she poked him in the ribs, "you don't need to tell me why we're 'ere, whose idea was all of this anyway, sweet cheeks? Mine. Oy, you don't think Charisse and them heard us do you?"

"Sod it if they did." Richard was cheerful, encouraged by her improved mood. "I can't help it if my girlfriend's a neurotic wreck who needs her happy pills, can I now?"

They both laughed. "We may as well stock up on a couple of other things we might need," Richard said. "We've got most of what we need but it doesn't hurt to have extra. There's the other party equipment we'll need, but we'll pick that up later, we've got time."

"I love it when you talk dirty," Mia linked her arm through his. "Lead the way, Macduff."

Kate and Marika went outside and Marika showed Eva and Lena her purchases while Kate joined Gisela who was standing alone, smoking a cigarette under a palm tree and watching Mia laughing with Jasmine.

"Hello," Kate said. "I'm glad to say I'm finally feeling a bit better. I'm never drinking like that again, I felt poisoned all morning. I've got no idea how Jasmine and Mia do it."

"I'd say they do it often," Gisela said. She sighed.

"What's wrong?" Kate asked.

"I guess I'm lonely." Gisela admitted and she pushed her sunglasses up her freckled nose. "It's been so long since I've been with anybody in any kind of real way. I thought I was used to being by myself but right now I wish I had somebody to share this with. Why can't I find someone? It took me years to get over my last relationship catastrophe but I did and I thought I was ready to move on, ready for the next love but there was nothing waiting. I failed at online dating too, though I tried so hard, with men and women and no one, not one person was right for me."

"My heart's still too broken for me to feel lonely," Kate said. "I can't imagine being with anyone except Cam. I say be happy you're not currently in a state of actual heartbreak. I'd trade with you," she joked and Gisela laughed and ground out her cigarette.

"Putting it like that, I do feel better. And I mean really, this is a dream come true, being in Africa and here I am, feeling sorry for myself! Thanks, Kate. Let's join the others. What is Richard doing, climbing up onto the roof of the bus?"

Treasure and Jono arrived with armfuls of groceries. Both turned to look at Richard who was inspecting the roof.

"When we're in the desert," Richard enquired, suspended on the ladder, "can we travel on the top of Mandoza the bus?"

Jono shook his head. "Out of the question, my friend. That would be too dangerous indeed. Anyway, you will see the whole world through your window and that way I can send you back to your family in one recognizable piece."

"Where's the fun in that?" Richard climbed down. "Let me help you with those groceries, my good man. I must say, how much do you chaps think we eat? There's enough for an army here."

Settling into his seat, Rydell thought back to what had happened at the mall. He realized that Treasure had not laughed at him in a dismissive way; she simply had not wanted to let Jono know that she was interested. Which also explained her casual shrug. Rydell acknowledged how badly it had hurt when he had thought she scorned his affections but he now understood, and he also told himself that he had not been mistaken when he saw her glance coyly back at him over her shoulder as she and Jono walked away. He told himself it was her modesty that caused her to laugh, like a geisha girl giggling behind her hands to hide her hot desire.

Rydell cast a quick glance through the connecting window at Treasure who was dozing and felt a powerful connection to her.

The bus traveled steadily through the winelands and mountains of the western Cape, past lush green farmlands with old-fashioned windmills standing sentry to horses that grazed idly. Past flowing rivers that sparkled in the sunlight and bubbled over rocky beds.

"This feels so good," Sofie shouted above the noise of the bus, her scarf held out to catch the hot breeze that blew through the open windows.

"Yeah, really," Jasmine cried, "we are on holiday. Yeehaw!"

"I feel like I'm going to throw up," Helen announced loudly. "Can I please exchange my aisle seat with someone who's got a window? I hate to ask but I feel really carsick."

"Sure," Marika offered. "Take my seat."

Kate sat up. "Uh, no, don't go..."

But it was too late, Marika had gathered her plastic bag and her purse and Helen was ready, waiting.

Kate sighed. She could not help it, she did not like Helen with her brusque and self-centred manner.

"That's much better," Helen leaned out the window and took great gulps of fresh air.

Kate quickly reached for her iPod, hoping to get the earbuds in place before Helen could start chatting but she it was too late.

"You're from Canada too?" Helen asked.

Kate sighed. "Yep, I am."

"I love Africa much more than Canada and I was having the best time ever but then I made the stupid mistake of falling for the wrong guy. He turned out be *so* different to what I thought."

Like it or not, I'm going to get Helen's Heartbreak: The Unabridged Version. Kate tried to feel more charitable towards Helen but could not.

"I was volunteering at this mission, right?" Helen continued. "Getting them organized. You'd be amazed by how haphazard these places are; I've worked at so many and they're well-meaning but chaotic. And there was this girl there, a total airhead, a do-gooder with not a hope in hell of organizing a box of matches at a campfire. And she thought I was a bitch, I could tell. But then her brother, Robbie, came to visit her and I fell for him, just like that. I didn't mean to but I did."

Her eyes filled with tears and she fumbled in her bag for a Kleenex, also digging out a photograph that she thrust at Kate. It pictured Helen, lovely and smiling, being hugged by a cherubic looking fellow with a wealth of blonde curls and big blue eyes, the same person who had bade Helen farewell at the bus.

"Nice," Kate handed the picture back to Helen who put it carefully into her bag. "Don't tell me, he had a girlfriend that he forgot to tell you about?" She couldn't help asking.

Helen shook her head. "No, he fell for me too. At least he

said he did. He even stayed for two weeks when he'd only planned on coming for a couple of days. We were together for every single minute from the time he arrived, and it was the best time of my life. He emailed me every single day when he went back to Cape Town; twice, three times a day. He talked about our future together, we discussed having kids and doing volunteer work around the world. He said I must come and see him before I went on this trip — I'd already booked this when I met him. *Come and see me before you do your big trip,* he says, *I'll show you my world, our new world."*

Helen blew her nose loudly. "I went to see him last night and there was nothing.... It was like we'd never met before. A complete and utter rejection. He even made me sleep in the living room. I wondered if his sister said something to turn him against me but he already knew she didn't like me. I don't know why he did this but I hate him, I hate him."

Kate had no idea what to say. Despite her recent similar heartbreak, all she could think was that it must have been because Helen was such a hard-assed bossy know-it-all but she knew that wasn't fair.

Helen blew her nose again. Kate looked around, wondering if anyone realized Helen was crying, but the bus was loud and they were all engrossed in their own chatter.

"I'm going to get over him, I will," Helen said. "First thing I'll do is go for a long run as soon as we get to wherever we're going. A long, long run. Then I'm going to dig out all his emails, I printed them all, and I'm going to mark them with a highlighter and post them to him, so he knows he lied. I'll send them back to him saying *liar, liar."*

"I don't think that will do you any good," Kate said. "He'll think you're a psycho that he's lucky to be rid of."

Helen thought about that. "You're right. Hmmm. But I want revenge. I do. Any advice?"

"Enjoy your holiday. I know, it's easy for me to say, but you're here now, try to let it go."

"I can't." Helen's eyes filled again. "He was my *future*. I have *nothing* without him. I'd been alone for so many years, and it was tough but I was okay, and then he came along and he was my everything. I don't know how to be alone again. And I don't even want to try."

Kate knew that feeling. And she had no desire to imagine the reality of her life after the trip. Talking to Helen was making her horribly uneasy; it was triggering all the pain that had for the moment subsided. She had forgotten what her real life felt like and now Helen was bringing it all back to her.

"I still feel very hungover," she lied. "I must have a nap. I'm sorry, I don't mean to be rude."

Helen seemed not to have heard her. She was staring out the window, clutching her wad of sodden tissue, deep in thought.

Kate closed her eyes and, without intending to, fell fast asleep.

When she woke, Jono was shouting. "Everybody! Off the bus! We have ten minutes here! Off the bus!"

Kate looked around confused, then stepped off the bus, still half asleep. They were at the top of a mountain with a valley far below.

"This is the top of the Cedarberg mountains," Jono explained to the gathered group, "and from here we begin our descent into the Ceres Valley named after the goddess of fertility. Our lodge for the night is on another mountain very close to here."

Helen sat down on the top of the pebbled stone wall at the edge of the lookout and peered at the valley below.

"Lots of thorn trees and brush scrub," she commented. "I wouldn't like to fall down there. It'd be quite the punishing tumble for sure."

Gisela looked at her. "Are you okay?" she asked. "You're very pale, you know."

"I've got a huge headache," Helen lied. "Must be the relief of being on holiday, you know what that's like, you suddenly let go and then it hits you."

"I think it's the party you had last night, that's hitting you,"

Sofie said. "I couldn't help but notice your handsome boyfriend this morning. I am sure you didn't do a lot of snoozing last night."

"You are so right," Helen said, "I hardly slept a wink. But Robbie's not my boyfriend, not anymore, it's time to find some new blood. Turned out he was quite weak and not the kind of man I want in my life. Pretty yes, but not much substance or brain power."

"I would have kept him around as eye candy," Ellie said, flicking at a large ant.

"Too much candy causes cavities," Gisela commented. "To sustain you in life, you need real food."

"You got it," Helen agreed. "I need a good thick steak to sink my teeth into."

"Sounds rather painful for the steak," Richard commented idly. He was chewing on a piece of veldt grass, one leg casually up on the stone wall.

Kate watched Helen turn towards him, her eyes widening and she smiled. "All depends on the technique," she drawled.

"And practice makes perfect, I'm sure," Richard said.

"Do I sense a *vakansie romansie* between those two?" Marika appeared next to Kate.

"A what?"

"A holiday romance."

Kate shook her head. "He's with Mia, over there. They were in the pharmacy together, remember?"

"Right. But Helen's very predatory, if you ask me."

"Yep. When we get back on the bus, I want to sit next to you again," Kate said. "I don't like her. She's so … I don't know … tough as nails. Some guy broke her heart and she's out for revenge, and now it looks like she's after a rebound man too."

Kate, walking back to the bus next to Charisse, asked her she was feeling any better and Charisse shrugged. "Much the same really."

Brianna was concerned and placed her hand on Charisse's

arm. "You didn't tell me you weren't feeling well," she said and Charisse shot Kate a look.

"Because it's nothing." She smiled, put her arm around Brianna and planted a kiss on the top of Brianna's head. "I'm fine."

"Enough of this lesbian activity," Stepfan grumbled, herding them in front of him. "Let a real man pleasure you, Charisse, and you'll never look at a woman again."

"And you're the man for the job, eh?" Kate asked, unable to stop herself.

"No," Stepfan said, weakly. "I'm a happily married man with a beautiful wife. I am just saying *if* Charisse found a real man to pleasure her, *then* she would never have a lesbian idea again."

"Timeout, people," Charisse said. "Let's hit the road and discuss something a little more interesting than my love life."

The bus drove through rich orchards and farmlands, finally turning into a steep gravel driveway lined with heavy fruit-laden lemon trees. Abundant purple and orange bougainvillea twisted around the branches of lilac jacarandas, while the scent of coffee jasmine filled the air with a soft vanilla fragrance.

"Oh my," Kate climbed off the bus, closed her eyes and inhaled the air. "Yes, it's official, I'm in heaven."

She opened her eyes to see Rydell watching her with a very strange expression on his face. She opened her mouth to speak to him but before she could say anything, he twitched and moved off.

The Cedarberg Mountains

THE LODGE AND CAMPSITE WERE SET HIGH on the mountainside with a circular garden and a fire pit in the centre and an open, thatched rondavel to the side. The garden was filled with tall trees and abundant flowerbeds that offered a profusion of spectacular colour. To the rear, the towering mountain was piled with great rocks splattered with bold dashes of red as if an artist had thrown ochre paint or blood.

Kate was open-mouthed with wonder. She turned to Marika who was standing next to a heap of folded and canvas and steel supports and ran over to help her, examining the array of tent poles that Marika had emptied onto the ground. Following the others, they assembled their tent, stood back and surveyed their abode.

"Our tent looks like its trying to lift off and fly," Marika said, "but the others are the same. Once we have our stuff in them, they'll be weighed down better."

"The campsite's like a botanical garden," Kate commented. "I imagined something a lot more Saharan." She shaded her eyes. "Even though it's summer here, it's quite cold. I'll need a sweater later."

"It's because we're in the shadow of the mountain," Marika said. "If we were in the sun, we'd feel the heat for sure. I'm going to get some floor mats for us."

She returned with the mats and crawled into the tent, with Kate following.

Marika lay down on her bare mat. "*Ag ja*, it feels so good to lie down."

"I'd forgotten," Kate remarked, "you don't have a sleeping bag or anything."

"It's not good," Marika agreed. "Foolish of me, but I had hoped my luggage would be here when we arrived. Hey, is that Jono calling?"

She and Marika climbed out, zipped up the tent and walked over to the group.

"Everybody, there is a walk; it is only ten rand and the guide, Kleine Skok, is very knowledgeable. How many of you are interested?"

The gathered lot held their hands in the air and a commotion erupted near the fire pit as the guide arrived, accompanied by a pack of barking dogs leaping around with excitement. The guide was slender and short, wearing a large knitted reggae cap and holding a beautifully carved walking stick. He beamed at the group and revealed four missing front teeth.

"Hello *mense*. I am very glad to see all of youse here. Thank youse for joining me on my tour of this, my home country. Now, do not go off the path, there are lots of very poisonous snakes."

He smiled happily and led the group around the side of the rondavel, holding the low thorny branches aside to let them pass through. The path was narrow and steep, ascending the mountainside sharply and passing between precariously balanced rocks of staggering heights. Kleine Skok led them at a brisk pace, chattering and pointing out this and that. The path itself was dusty, with patches of slippery broken stones that had to be navigated carefully and the group climbed upwards for a while until they burst out into the shoulder-high grasses at the very top. There was blue sky for miles around and an endless and lush valley below and everyone exclaimed in delight at the breath-taking scenery.

"Now *mense*, and that means 'people' in my language, the

Afrikaans language, you must wait for me here. I am going to look for a tortoise for youse because they are special creatures of this earth and you must see one. But if I take too long, youse must please shout for me."

"Okay," they chorused and sat down on the lichen-covered rocks, enjoying the cool breeze. Kate and Enrique whipped out their cameras.

Enrique was in his element, with his nose up close to tiny grasses and flowers. "I studied all the plants of the places I planned to visit," he told Eva, "and it's wonderful to see them all in real life."

"So what are all these ones called?" Eva teased him and he blushed.

"The grasses and plants are called fynbos, which is a collective term for all the shrubland that you see. It's not good grazing but it's lovely for us plant lovers. See those yellow flowers there? That bush is part of the proteoid family, which includes the famous protea."

"Impressive," the group gave him a round of applause.

Except for Mia. "Good Lord," she commented. She had a smudge of dirt on her upper lip and forehead and she looked like a disheveled Kewpie doll. "Get a freakin' life, son. While you're pouring over the botany books and all that crap, there are randy girls out there waiting to be shagged, pubs to be visited, drinks to be drunk."

"Thank God, Mia," Sofie commented, "that we're not all like you."

"And what exactly is that supposed to mean?" Mia demanded. She thrust out her belly, her hands on her hips.

"Actually, Mia," Enrique interrupted any retort Sofie might have made, "you may think what you do is fun but I wouldn't exchange my interests for yours or anybody else's. I'm going to give you one more fact; Britain, in an area three and a half times larger than this, has only 1,500 plants, meanwhile there are 8,500 species right here."

"I'm glad if that gets your rocks off, Professor Flowerpot," Mia countered, unapologetic, "you can do my learning for me, I can't be bothered, mate." She sat down and glared at Sofie who was meditating with her eyes closed while she clutched a dancing Ganesh necklace.

Enrique shrugged and turned away while Stepfan and Harrison broke into a noisy argument about a bush; whether it was the one that Kleine Skok had said would cure liver ailments or if that had been another. Kate was snapping photographs, while Marika was enjoying the view. Lena sat quietly to the side looking like a *Vogue* model. Her long tanned legs were stretched out in front her of her, and she trailed her hand over the tiny stones on the surface of the soft, cool soil. She was wearing white tailored shorts and an orange sleeveless tank top covered with a long-sleeved sheer white shirt and a large, broad-rimmed linen hat hid her face.

Mia was talking about how she was longing for a pint or three, with Jasmine and Ellie concuring with vocal enthusiasm. Sofie was talking at high speed and loud volume to Helen about yoga and Pilates and they announced they would hold a class each evening.

Stepfan interrupted his argument with Harrison to say he would love to join the yoga class, in fact, he would lead it and advise. Yoga was then met with less enthusiasm.

"We will do it and not tell him," Sofie whispered to Helen. Kate saw Lena wince and she wished Sofie did not talk so loudly; even her whisper was clearly audible.

At that moment Kleine Skok reappeared, disconsolate. "I cannot find me a tortoise. There was one there this morning but he left and now I can't find him."

The group tried to reassure him they were fine without a tortoise but he remained unconvinced.

"Now, I could not find me a tortoise but I did find me these." He dug into his pockets and brought out two large scorpions that scuttled up his bare arms.

As one, the group recoiled.

Kleine Skok laughed. "This one is the male," he pointed to his right arm, "and the other is the female. Now me, I was once bitten by a scorpion. If you is bitten by a scorpion, you must get the nicotine from an old man's pipe and rub it immediately into the area of the bite. But the day I was bitten, it was a Saturday night and you know, *mense*, my people, they likes to drink, most particularly on a Saturday night.

"I could not find me an old man with a pipe with good nicotine because all the old men was drunk and their pipes was dead. I did find me one old man and my knees were already shaking and he said to me *ei nee* man, you is dronk Kleine Skok, no scorpion did bite you, go to bed, man, and take some disprins."

Marika explained that disprins were aspirin that could be dissolved in water.

"*Ja mense*, that is correct. I drank me lots of disprins and I went to sleep. In the morning I could not move my legs and they had to take me to the hospital for a month with wires in my body with liquids and then they did give me crutches and it was four months before I could walk properly again. So people, they are very dangerous, these animals."

He put them down carefully on the dry, dusty ground, watched them disappear and searched among the bushes for his next treasure.

"*Ja*, I found it!" He held up a coal size lump of black tar. "Tell me, people," he grinned toothlessly and the late afternoon sun cast long shadows on his face, "what do you think this is?" He glanced around but no one had any idea.

"Licorice?" Jasmine guessed and Kleine Skok laughed.

"*Nee mense*, it's the monthly blood from the women dassies; the little rabbits. All the women dassies in the area come to the same place and eventually it becomes like this. Smell it," he offered it on an outstretched hand.

The group recoiled in a wave again. Kate recovered first and took the black lump from him, not really wanting to touch it but not wanting to hurt the little man's feelings. "It does smell bloodlike," she sniffed it, "and it feels like thick plastic that melted in the sun."

"We'll take your word for that," Sofie laughed. "Sorry, Kleine Skok but I am not touching it."

Kleine Skok took back the congealed dassie blood and put it in his pocket. "My people use this to cure kidney problems. When it gets hard and black like this, they boil it up with some of those green leaves I showed you earlier for the liver and then they drink the tea and their backs and kidneys is much better. I have a friend, his back was so bad he could not play soccer and he was very heartsore by this. He just lay on the ground groaning something terrible. My people boiled him up some of this, with that leaves, and next thing he was fine."

"Is that something a witch or a *sangoma* would use?" Richard asked.

Kleine Skok looked anxious.

"*Ei, nee man,* you must be very careful with that," he whispered, and he peered around furtively and shook his head. "Witches is stoned to death or they is buried alive. My people are healers, *mense*, not witches, *nee man*, there is no witches here." He walked off, glancing around nervously, his expression worried.

"You frightened him, you silly tosser," Mia scolded Richard as she poked him with her forefinger.

"I simply asked him a question," Richard swatted her hand away.

"Witchcraft is big here in Africa," Helen climbed over the rocks and came up behind them. "I can tell you what I know, if you like. I learned a lot about it, working here for a year."

"Ta, I'd appreciate that," Richard replied. "It's an area that really intrigues me."

Harrison rushed up to Kate, whispering urgently. "Wash your hands clean of that terrible rabbit's blood. Here's some water, hold out your hands, I will pour it for you."

Kate obediently held out her hands, washed them and dried them on the back of her jeans.

"And here's hand sanitizer," Harrison handed her a small bottle.

Kate squeezed a dollop onto her hands and rubbed vigorously.

"Happy?" she asked Harrison who nodded, relieved.

Kleine Skok stopped, waiting for Kate to catch up. He watched Harrison, his expression inscrutable.

"Now, people," he said, "I wants to show you something very precious, something me did only find very recently."

He led them across the mountain, through the tall grasses and gnarled wild protea trees to a shaded and quiet area and walked up to a wall of ancient rocks, pointing proudly at the Bushmen art.

"Me did find some printings only two weeks ago. Oh, Kleine Skok was so excited, he ran down the mountain shouting. Meneer Hennie, my boss, said he thought I was bitten by a snake, me was so excited."

He showed the group the paintings, explaining how they depicted a kill at which all the food had been eaten, not a scrap was left; all the bellies were full, swollen and sore.

Stepfan was convinced one of the images was a pregnant woman but Kleine Skok insisted it was a man replete from the feast. Stepfan was finally persuaded by the others to stop arguing, even if he did not agree.

"Let him tell his story," Sofie declared. "Why do you think that you know better than him, Stepfan? This is his home, his heritage."

"Our Stepfan is the resident expert of everything," Harrison commented. "He is Mister Encyclopaedia of the Universe."

"And you are the documenter of a thousand irrelevant facts, you and your little notebook. How many steps did you take up and down this hill? I'm sure you've got it all written down already." Stepfan retorted.

"Boys, boys," Helen admonished, "come on now, play nice."

"He started it," Stepfan declared.

"I can't believe you actually said that," Gisela was incredulous. "Would you like to compare dick sizes too?"

"Kleine Skok is waiting to tell us something," Kate said. "We're being very discourteous."

They turned back to Kleine Skok who was waiting patiently. "*Mense*, I know youse don't believe me but we can eat a lot when we eat. People is shocked by how much we can eat. And then our stomachs is like this," Kleine Skok rounded his hands far away his belly. "So truly *mense*, that is a man there, with his stomach sore and swollen from the feastings."

"Don't worry, Kleine Skok, we believe you," Sofie gave Stepfan a dark look. "Ignore that man there, you are the expert here."

"I read a most interesting thing about the Bushmen," Marika said, pointing back at the paintings and ignoring Stepfan who was about to say something. "You see these angles of the animals in movement? How they seem almost contorted? Later when photography was invented, it was discovered that the Bushmen's eye was so accurate that they could see things that we couldn't; things we could only see when captured on film."

"Yeah, brilliant," Richard commented. "I also think they imbibed some magic medicines, shall we say, to help them see more clearly. Tell me my friend," he said to Kleine Skok, "I see you are wearing Rasta colours. I take it you are a man of herbal means?"

Kleine Skok was confused.

Richard made a specific smoking motion.

"*Ei mense*, youse is too naughty," Kleine Skok blushed. "Nee, mense, no *dagga* for me. I am good."

"Dagga?" Jasmine asked.

"Marijuana," Helen explained, and Mia gave a broad smile and a thumbs up.

"And tell me my friend, have you heard of tik tik?" Richard pursued his topic.

Kleine Skok turned pale.

"*Nee man, tik is baie gevaarlik mense, praat nie van tik nie, ai.*"

"What did he say?" Jasmine asked, "I didn't understand a word of that. He's terrified. Richard, you're doing a good job of scaring him."

"He said don't talk about *tik*, it's very dangerous," Marika translated. "Richard, what is *tik*, anyway? I've never heard of it."

"It's the South African word for chrystal meth," Helen said. "It's called *tik tik* because of the noise it makes when it heats up. They smoke it out of old light bulbs and it makes a ticking noise. But surely Richard, you wouldn't be interested in that?"

"Of course not," Richard was jovial. "It's simply that I read online you could buy it just about anywhere and I thought I'd ask, to see his reaction."

"I'd say you scared the crap out of him," Mia said. "Jasmine's right, Richard, he's beginning to look at you like you're the bleedin' devil or something."

"Stupid people take stupid drugs," Rydell declared loudly in his high-pitched, nasal way. The group stared at him in surprise, he'd hardly uttered a word on the walk.

"When I grow up, I want to be frightfully stupid," Richard commented and Mia chortled.

Kate noticed that Kleine Skok was looking quite tired out. "That's the end of our walk," she said, "let Kleine Skok take us back. We've exhausted him, poor man."

Kleine Skok led them back through the orange orchards behind the lodge and was quick to wave goodbye. "Goodbye *mense*," he shouted before vanished, his dreadlocks bouncing, "and remember, be careful, Africa can be a very dangerous place."

"As long we follow my systems of washing," Harrison remarked wryly, "and don't drink the dried menstrual blood of rabbits, I'm sure we'll all be just fine."

"That was a cure, not a poison," Kate corrected him.

"You know what the man means," Stepfan said, retying his

camouflage bandanna around his head. "You were stupid to even touch it."

Kate stared at him. "I'll touch whatever I like," she said, through gritted teeth, "but go ahead, have the last word, Stepfan, if it makes you happy."

He started to say something but she stalked off before he could finish.

Stepfan shrugged. "I'm only trying to help," he said to Lena who nodded vaguely, holding an orange blossom to her nose.

The Second Night

LATER THAT NIGHT, SUPPER WAS OVER and the group was waiting for Jono on the grass around the fire pit, with the small fire offering little more than sparks and smoke.

"I'm shattered, yeah," Mia said, "it's all this fresh air, I'm not used to it." She had plopped herself down and was leaning back on her hands with her face turned up to the sky.

"She's like a child," Helen muttered under her breath to Kate, "a somewhat retarded child." Kate ignored her and wished Helen would leave her alone.

"What are we waiting for anyway?" Jasmine put another log on the fire. "I wish we had some marshmallows. We should have thought of it when we were at that big store."

"We're doing introductions of the self," Richard said. "Getting to know each other and all that jolly bonding stuff."

"I feel like we already know too much about each other," Eva commented quietly to Kate who grinned in agreement.

"I want to get down to some serious drinking," Mia joked and banged her feet together.

"And some serious sleeping," Marika yawned.

"You party animal, you," Mia said.

"I only arrived this morning," Marika said, defensively.

"I want to write in my journal," Sofie unbraided her hair and gave a jaw-splitting yawn.

Jono arrived at the campfire, holding a mug of coffee. "Good evening, everybody!" he said. "And how is everybody?"

A chorus of responses rose from the sprawled lot.

"Sweet Mary and Jesus," Mia sat up, "it's bleedin' freezing up here. This is Africa, for pete's sake, and the bleedin' desert too, it's supposed to be hot, yeah."

"It does get cold at night," Jono agreed. "You should be prepared for all temperatures, it goes from very hot to very cold. Are we ready to begin our introductions?" he asked.

"I'd like a pint in hand," Mia said, "and a nice warm cardy. Richard, would you be a luv?"

"Of course," he said, getting up. "Anybody else for a beer?"

"Yes please," Ellie, Jasmine, Charisse and Brianna called out and Richard looked slightly dismayed.

"And some socks, luv," Mia yelled after him. "My nice thick ones, not the bleedin' thin ones."

Finally, they were all settled, ready to start.

"Who will go first?" Jono asked.

"I'll go," Charisse said in her deep, husky voice.

Stepfan immediately leaned forward, his elbows on his knees and Kate glanced up in time to see Lena wince.

Kate's throat filled with bile and she had no doubt that Stepfan, like Cam, was a believer in *an open relationship*. Stepfan reminded her of a young Charlton Heston, good-looking in a classical, sensual-lipped, strong-jawed, chiselled nose, high-cheekboned kind of way, but despite his movie star appeal, she found him obnoxious. She glared at him while he, unaware, was openly admiring Charisse who was still wearing her tiny gold shorts but had added added a fluffy pink angora sweater.

"Bree and I've been in Cape Town for six months," she said, wriggling her painted toenails at the fire. "We plan conferences and events and we've been working eighty hours a week so we haven't seen much of anything at all. We're both from Chicago and that's our story. My story, anyway. Bree can tell hers."

"You've got such an incredible voice, you should be on the radio," Stepfan said. "Then again perhaps not, you'd have all the men crashing off the road." He was the only one to laugh at his joke and Jono nodded at Brianna to go next.

Brianna yawned. "Hello, I'm Bree and my story's like Charisse's so I don't have anything to add, except that I hope we see lots of lions and elephants." Brianna was clearly not enjoying the cold; she was sitting cross-legged, bundled up in her sleeping bag, with only her small freckled face peeking out.

Enrique was next. "Hi, I'm Enrique Franco. I've just come from Thailand, Vietnam, China and Japan and it was totally amazing. Now I'm traveling around Africa and after that I'm going back to South America to my home in Peru where I'm going to study to be a doctor." Enrique was long-limbed and gangly, with thick unruly sandy hair and pleasant features which were mostly hidden by a bad crop of acne.

Stepfan, next in line, cleared his throat loudly. "I'm Stepfan Brummer and this is my beautiful wife, Lena. We've dreamed of coming to Africa all of our lives and we decided now is the time; we must do it now or never. We are both much older than all of you, how much older we will not say, but we take good care to eat well and exercise a lot and so our bodies are in excellent shape. I'm trained in several martial arts and I also do yoga regularly. Anyone who would like to join me in a daily routine of yoga is most welcome. After sitting on the bus all day, I would highly recommend we stretch our bodies and keep them in good working order."

Kate thought it was a pity that Stepfan was on the tour; the man found it impossible to shut up about himself.

"We're originally from Germany," he continued, "although we've lived in New York City for many years, and that is where we're now retired. I was in human resources and Lena was an accountant."

"I was a financial director," Lena burst out, her hands tightly clenched in her lap.

"And that's our story." Stepfan beamed, ignoring his wife.

"And would the lovely Lena, financial director, like to add anything?" Gisela asked dryly. She was huddled inside a pale-blue fleece jacket with the collar turned up, blowing cigarette smoke into the wind.

Lena laughed and the tension drained from her body. "No, that covered everything, but thank you, Gisela." She blushed slightly.

Stepfan scowled at Gisela who met his glance with amusement.

"I've got a question for you, Stepfan," Harrison pulled out his notebook and licked the tip of his pencil, "and this one's for the record, as they say."

"Anything." Stepfan said, generously.

"Where on earth did you get that tracksuit, my friend? The abandoned wardrobe of *Saturday Night Fever?*"

Stepfan was wearing a tight white sweatsuit with silver stripes down the side and the group broke out into raucous laughter. The only one not amused was Stepfan. "What's wrong with this?" Stepfan was genuinely puzzled. "It's Versace."

This had the group rolling around again. Even Lena was laughing, her hand to her mouth.

"I'm going to get a cup of coffee," Stepfan said sourly and he got to his feet, "and when I get back, perhaps you will have composed yourselves. Or am I the only adult here?"

For some reason this set the group off again.

Jono held up his hand. "Everybody!" he called, "come on now, everybody, please, settle down, give the man some peace and quiet. Who is next to go?"

"That would be me," Jasmine said. Kate noticed that Jasmine had unusually distinctive and beautiful eyes; they were enormous and slightly cat-shaped, the iris was a clear grey green, and she had long thick eyelashes. "I'm Jasmine Moir and I'm from Sydney, Australia. I work as a medical assistant where I process zillions of samples in a lab. Kind of like CSI but it's not like anything on TV. I also want to say that I have a severe vitamin B deficiency and a thyroid problem which is why I'm bigger than some people." She cast a look at Charisse who was adding wood to the fire and did not notice. "But I'm very fit and active. I do a lot of hiking as well as yoga. I'm a certified yoga teacher and I also love to knit when I'm not travelling. I even spin my own yarn. I love all things organic and I've also wanted to come to Africa my whole life."

Her attentive audience erupted into a another loud round of applause but it could have been that they needed an outlet to make a noise after their amusement at Stepfan's expense.

Jasmine smiled and nudged Ellie who seemed to have forgotten it was her turn to go.

Ellie sighed and stretched her long bony limbs out in front her. She was a plain girl, with a sallow complexion, a sharp nose and thin lips. Her sparse hair was an untidy cap, a feather pixie cut in need of a trim. "Righto, it's my turn. I'm Ellie Lawrence. I work with Jasmine. She mentioned this trip to me and I thought it sounded interesting. I needed to shake my life up a bit ... and so, here I am."

Kate thought Ellie looked as though life had served her up one disappointment after another and it had sounded as if she had wanted to add more but she stopped, twisting her large, pale chapped hands and signalling Richard who was next.

"Righty ho, me next," Richard was jovial. "Hi, my name is Richard Conlon. Gosh, this way of introducing ourselves sounds like an A.A. meeting or something. Only joking, not that I'd know. Anyway, we've not been to Africa before but it's fantastic to be here." He smiled and chugged a long swallow of beer and signaled for Mia to speak.

"Hi, yeah, I'm Mia Teller, Richard's partner, and it's like what he said."

Eva, next in line, pulled her sleeves down past her fingers. She was still dressed in black but her attire was casual and ordinary, black sneakers, thick sweatpants and a long-sleeved hoodie with Celtic insignia in white on the front. Her long purple and black hair spilled out from under her hood. "I'm Eva Leifsdottír from Iceland. I'm a psychology student but I'm actually a poet. The end."

Rydell was next and he peered around uneasily without saying a word. Then he sat up, tapped his tin cup a few times with his teaspoon and recited: *"Yankee Doodle came to town, ridin' on a pony. Stuck a feather in his hat and called it macaroni."* The group stared at him, silenced. Rydell smiled his crooked, wet smile and looked down at his cup.

"I'm Rydell from Kansas." His voice was so quiet that the others had to lean forward to hear him. "I do a lot of different things for important people. I have many talents that most people don't even know exist. I'm here to find a special *treasure* in the desert and that's all I have to say." He gave a strangled chortle, flushed beet red and studied his hands.

No one seemed to know how to respond.

"Me next," Marika said into the waiting silence. She was still wearing the same clothes she had arrived in and she was glad that at least her jeans were her favourites, soft and comfortable. She wore a brightly-coloured, Picasso-styled T-shirt with geometric puzzle-piece faces, topped with a bright pink polar fleece jacket and a lime-green pashmina that was edged with fluffy balls. Given that the night was cool, she was grateful that she had travelled in such warm gear. "I'm Marika van Breytenbach and I'm originally from South Africa but now I live in Toronto with my husband. I didn't leave South Africa because of the crime or anything but for an interesting life in a different country. I'm an illustrator, mainly of children's books and I love colour, as you can no doubt see from my clothing! I'm on my way to see my parents for Christmas. They still live on the farm as I mentioned this morning. I love Canada very much but I miss the smell of the African dust, I miss the heat, the dryness."

Kate was next. "I'm Kate Fraser and my job's very boring, and my boyfriend's in sales, and I came here on a whim and I really don't have much of a story." Kate hated to tell a lie and she shot Gisela a knowing look, with a small shrug.

"What about your boyfriend? Doesn't he mind that you're

here all alone with strange men?" Rydell piped up unexpectedly.

"Cam doesn't mind what I do," Kate said, wishing it was not the truth.

"Little Jack Horner's been left all alone in his corner," Rydell was dismissive. "And he won't be so happy when you find a new boyfriend." He giggled as if he had discovered a dirty secret.

"Not going to happen," Kate was firm. "Sofie, you're next."

"Hello," Sofie said, with her strange accent and twisted lisp. "I finished travelling through India, which I loved very much, as you can see from all my jewelry and clothing. Now I am travelling through Africa and then I go back home. I am originally from a small town in Denmark, but now my family lives in New Mexico. I do not really have a lisp; my accent is a bit convoluted, that's all, so please do not ask me about it. People always ask me and it is very irritating. I teach mathematics and biology and that is my story." She smiled.

Harrison was next. "As you all know, I'm Harrison Petrenko." He turned to Kate then added firmly, "I should have gone next in the line of telling my story, not Sofie," though smiling to lessen the rebuke. "We must keep the accurate order of things, Kate. I am an architect and I am originally from the Czech Republic but now I live in Seattle. I'm here to travel through Africa and I have also wanted to do this all my life." He paused to look pointedly at everyone in the group and continued, "I am older than many of you, but not as old as Stepfan nor am I as fashionable." Grinning at Stepfan to take the sting out of his words, he added emphatically, "I would also like to say that we must be vigilant in washing our hands before preparing food or eating. I have a system I will show you tomorrow that will save us from e-coli and other such diseases. Thank you." He tucked his notepad and pencil into an inner pocket of his khaki jacket.

"I think we should drink a lot of neat scotch, Harrison, that'll kill any germs," Jasmine broke the silence.

"In absolute agreement." Richard applauded and Mia nodded with enthusiasm.

"Who is next? Has everybody gone?" Jono asked.

"No, they have not, I haven't gone." Helen admonished him. "Neither has Gisela. I'm Helen Harding. I'm a Phys. Ed. teacher…"

Her introduction was interrupted by Mia who let out a high-pitched squeal. "You missed it," she cried, hitting Richard on the back. Richard spluttered, having swallowed his beer the wrong way.

"A shooting star," Mia pointed at the sky, "it was brill and you totally missed it."

"Probably because they know how to listen politely," Helen muttered. She had moved away from Kate and was sitting closer to Richard.

"Along the path of our travels together," Jono said, "I am going to introduce you to folklore and legends of the African people and this is a perfect example of one of them. A shooting star is not, as you might think, a piece of the solar system rushing headlong towards earth, but rather the spirit of a sorcerer, travelling with its eyes wide open."

He immediately had the group's attention and he continued. "It is said that there are two types of people in this world; there is the good, normal, friendly peace-loving African and there are the *ndkoki*, the wicked destroyers of life, health and happiness. A sorcerer, or *ndoki*, is a man or woman who wishes to harm other people.

"With sweet words and a double tongue, the *ndoki* will invite you to his or her house and offer you delicious-looking food but it is served with dirty hands and under the *ndoki's* nails there are tiny grains of a magic powder, so the victim very quickly becomes sick with indigestion and a headache and a fever and he goes home and dies. Then, when he is dead, the *ndoki* turns himself into an insect, an ant maybe, or a mosquito, and he goes into the bedroom of the dead person and he drinks all the blood of his victim. Then the *ndoki* steals the body and he makes a very magic poison with the body. *Ndokis* love to eat young girls the best of all, because he finds their blood very tasty. And when the *ndoki* himself finally dies, his eyes stare wide open, and you cannot close them and their spirits wander about and are seen by us as shooting stars. There is your first African story."

"Excellent, old chap," Richard commented, applauding loudly with the others.

Kate had noticed that Richard was very fond of peppering his speech with quaint British bonhomie that sounded forced to her, particularly when compared to Mia's east end slang patois.

"You see," Harrison was jubilant, "that is yet another reason why we must abide by my hand-washing system. So none of us can be killed by the poisonous dirt under the fingernails."

The group howled at him.

"Kate," Richard called to her, "swat him on the head for us, won't you?"

"I'm not the *ndoki* mosquito," Harrison protested. "There will be no swatting of me."

"Everybody!" Jono said, "please let us continue, we must be attentive to the others who have not yet spoken. Where were we?" he asked. "Ah yes, Helen was telling us she is a school teacher. Go on, Helen, I am sorry for the interruption."

She smiled tightly. "I was saying before we got distracted," she shot a glance at Mia who was blowing her nose loudly and missed the look, "that I teach physical education. I love to run; I must run every day, so Jono, please fit that into our schedule. I've been living and working in Underberg for the past year and this trip is my treat before I go home to Canada to resume my normal life. I've come to love my African life a lot, so I'm not sure if I'll be able to give it up. I like to do good in the world but in an organized way."

Gisela was next. She lit another cigarette and pushed a lock of dark hair back from her forehead. "I'm Gisela Klasson from Sweden. I'm a sports therapist there and I treat a lot of celebrities. Importantly, I am also here to see the Big Five. Most important are the zebra and the giraffe."

"Zebra and giraffe are not part of the Big Five," Stepfan and Enrique corrected her at the same time. "The Big Five are the lion, elephant, buffalo, rhinoceros and leopard."

"What about the hippopotamus?" Jasmine asked. "I thought that was a Big Five one also?"

"The Big Five are based on how hard they are to hunt," Jono explained, "not on how big they are."

"What about cheetah?" Brianna enquired from the folds of her sleeping bag.

"I don't think there are cheetah here?" Ellie chewed on a nail.

"You do get them but they are quite rare and you would be very fortunate to see one," Jono said.

"It's your job to make sure we are fortunate," said Stepfan. "Is that not so, my friend?"

"It is my job to try and put you in places where they might be," Jono agreed, "but I cannot make them come out and perform tricks for you. Has everybody had a turn to introduce themselves?"

"What about Treasure?" Rydell clutched his tin mug tightly. "We haven't heard from her."

The group looked over at Treasure who was equally startled by the attention. She was sitting to the right of Jono, on the stone steps of the rondavel.

"*Eish!* I don't have much to say," Treasure wiped her hands on her blue pants and pulled her T-shirt down. "I'm just the cook. And people have never gotten sick from my food, so you don't need to worry," she laughed and looked over at Harrison who did not seem at all reassured.

"But where are you from? Do you have family?" Rydell was purple with the effort of asking.

"I'm from Zimbabwe, like Jono," Treasure said, "and my

family are still there. Now, you must please excuse me to wash the dishes."

"Do you need me to boil some water for you?" Harrison jumped up.

"No, really, there's a lot of hot water here," Treasure told him, "stay and listen to Jono." She nodded in his direction.

Jono looked around. "It was very good to hear about all of you," he said. "I am a Xhosa, originally from Zimbabwe and I have been a tour guide for eighteen years. It is an interesting job because I meet a lot of fascinating people." He seemed to be directing his comments to Kate.

"Tomorrow," he continued, "we go to the Gariep River and set up camp there. It is a first-rate place for canoeing since there are no crocodiles because the water is too cold for them and if you search carefully and are very lucky, you may find a diamond on the banks of the river, but the chances for that are not good. We leave tomorrow at 8:00 a.m. Breakfast is at 7:00 a.m. Any questions?"

There were none and Lena, Sofie, Ellie and Gisela got up and bade the others goodnight.

Stepfan immediately sidled up to Charisse whereupon Brianna wordlessly gathered her sleeping bag and disappeared.

"I'm going to grab another coffee," Kate said, "I love it. Especially with condensed milk."

Marika laughed. "Aha, the Ricoffy addiction claims one more! I'll join you."

Lena made straight for her tent and sat down on her sleeping bag, seething with rage. *He promised me he wouldn't do this. He promised. He swore he was done with all that. And I believed him. I thought that I, that we, would be safe from that stupid madness, safe in Africa on a tour group adventure. I thought that I'd be able to relax for once in our thirty-seven years of being married. Thirty-seven years of putting up with this. And only once did I ever make a fuss.*

She recalled the incident clearly. She had greeted Stepfan with a sharp letter opener in the early hours of the morning when he had returned from being overly attentive to the new concierge, a busty brunette with a creamy cleavage and an inappropriate sense of what "taking care" of the condo owners meant.

After Lena had rushed at Stepfan, shrieking and flailing, and after he called their family doctor to issue a sedative, and after the girl was urged to seek alternative employment and Stepfan and Lena enjoyed a second honeymoon in the Seychelles, only then did things return to normal and Stepfan was careful to keep his cuckoldry far from home. Which meant that while Lena had her suspicions, she was without proof and Stepfan could not be held to account. But now, here, he was accountable and this public display of faithlessness was simply unacceptable.

Lena chewed on her lip in a fury and scowled at the tightly zippered tent door. Something would have to be done about this.

Kate and Marika made coffee and rejoined the others who were huddled around the fire pit while Stepfan and Charisse had moved off to one side and were deep in a private conversation.

"What's the big discussion about?" Kate asked, sitting down.

"I'm trying to explain what *sangomas* are," Helen said, sitting back on her heels. "I thought I knew but, I realize I'm confused. Jono, maybe you can help us out?"

"I can," Jono said, accepting a beer from Richard. "Thank you. First, some facts. Eighty-four percent of all South Africans consult a *sangoma* more than three times a year and there are more than 200,000 *sangomas* in South Africa alone. A witch and a *sangoma* are not the same thing whereas a witch*doctor*," he emphasized the last word, "is the same thing as a *sangoma* but the term witchdoctor is considered to be a perjorative one that came from the European settlers. *Sangomas* are practitioners of complementary medicine and they serve a long apprenticeship learning to become intermediaries between the world of spirits and the world of the living. Witches are a whole other thing;

they are evil and dangerous and if they cannot be cured, they are stoned to death or buried alive."

"They certainly gave Kleine Skok the heebie jeebies," Richard stretched his feet towards the fire. "Poor fellow, he had this godawful lump of dried up rabbit's blood and I asked him if that was something a witchdoctor would use and he nearly shot right off the mountain. I felt quite dreadful for asking."

Jono laughed and took a drink of his beer. "I can imagine that frightened him in a big way. More than six hundred people have been killed in the last ten years in Gauteng alone, because they were accused of being witches, so even the mention of such a thing is frightening for many people."

"Can you cure someone of being a witch?" Eva asked.

"You can but it is not easy," Jono said. "There are many kinds of witches, one of which is the night-witch who is invisible during the daytime but then at night, changes into an animal; a crocodile, a hyena, a lion, a wolf maybe. Night-witches devour human bodies, dead or alive during the night, and they can been seen flying at night, with fire coming out of their bottoms."

"They fart fire?" Mia found this hysterically funny and the rest of the group joined in, laughing. "Oh lord, fire-farting witches, knock my bleedin' socks off."

"Isn't it true," Helen queried when the laughter died down, "that Western doctors found a high correlation between schizophrenia and epilepsy in individuals who have been accused of being witches?"

Jono nodded. "Which would explain the hallucinations they have," he said. "And some of them have also been found to be manic-depressives and schizophrenics. But if you ask me, this does not mean that Western medicine has any kind of increased knowledge in this area, it is just that you call your witches by a lot of medical-sounding names and find different ways to treat them."

"Touché," Richard exclaimed while Helen nodded enthusiastically.

"The *sangoma*," Jono said, "or the witch-finder, is the one who sniffs out the witches. *Sangoma* is a Zulu word for the traditional healer and he or she will be invited to cleanse an entire village of witchcraft by giving them emetics, or sneezing powder, or making incisions into which medicine is rubbed, or by many other methods."

"How does the *sangoma* know what to do?" Kate asked.

"They receive their knowledge from the spirits and there are more than sixty documented methods to ask the spirits — reading the stars, throwing sticks, studying lines in the sand, observing the blood trickling from a victim, even by looking at how birds are flying or how they are sitting on a tree. A lot of people think that diviners are not good because they are trying to know God's secrets before God wants us to know them, and we should not be attempting to steal divine secrets."

"I'm divining that it's high time for schnapps." Mia got to her feet, and brushed embedded grass from her legs. "I'm getting the Archers. Go on, you lot." She waved and walked across the grass. "Don't wait for me."

"Yes, carry on, Jono," Richard said, "Mia won't mind, she's not into this sort of thing."

"I find it incredibly amazing," Helen spoke up quickly, "I wish I'd had time to learn more. Well, better late than never." She smiled at Richard who cracked open another beer and missed her meaningful glance.

"The *sangoma* tries to cure the witch…" Kate reminded Jono where he had left off.

"Yes," Jono said, "but curing witches is a very small part of what the *sangoma* does as his life's work. The main function of the *sangoma* is to heal and protect people in the community. *Sangomas* are generally very respected members of the community. Even Nelson Mandela was circumcised by a *sangoma* when he was sixteen by a famous *ingcibi*, a circumcision expert. *Sangomas* conjure up potions, known as *muti*, to make you better, and *muti* is made from all sorts of herbs and things. Then the *sangoma* dances herself, or himself, into a trance, usually with his drum which also has a spirit, and this is how they contact the spirit. Then they will alter their voice and begin to talk, using two voices, relying on their powers of ventriloquism."

"I was told you can recognize a *sangoma* by their dress which is covered in beads, and is very ornamental, in red which is *bomvu*, black which is *mnyama* and white, *mhlophe*," Helen said, hoping to impress Richard with her knowledge.

Jono nodded. "The medicine the *sangoma* mixes can be based on colours also. The *sangoma* mixes opposite colours together, uniting them symbolically and then real life harmony follows. Light colours represent life and masculinity, dark colours are death and femininity."

"I knew it." Richard poked Mia who had returned with the bottle of schnapps and a sleeping bag, "you women are the death of men."

Mia tittered, slapped him on the shoulder and wrapped herself in the sleeping bag. She opened the bottle, took a long swig and passed it to Jasmine.

"Is it true," Marika asked, "that *sangoma*s study for as long as doctors?"

"Yes. It takes seven years for the *sangoma* to study, and he, or she, studies a lot of things; techniques of divination, treatment of psychological, mental, physical conditions, animal and plant medicine use, the anatomy of the soul, ritual mastery, prayer and invocation, throwing the bones, chant and song, channeling souls, soul ascension, case study, tradition and culture, and finally, techniques of investigation. *Sangomas* are also very good detectives and great historians and guardians of local culture and learning."

"Impressive," Kate said. "But the witches sound horrible."

"They are. Witches operate on fear, superstition and rumour," Jono said. "The evils of gossip. Nowadays even some of the churches use witchcraft to bring new worshippers, convincing them their problems are due to supernatural witch curses that only the church can cure. Some churches even preach that diseases like AIDS and leprosy, blindness, deafness, impotence, and infertility are *muti* curses by witches."

"Before we left," Richard said, "I read an article about how Tanzanian witchdoctors have been killing albinos and harvesting their body parts because they think it will bring them good luck. What's with that? Why albinos, why body parts for good luck?"

"What have you been reading, my friend, to hear that?" Jono asked and Richard's expression became guarded.

"General research and whatnot. One's interested in studying up before a trip, and what with the Internet, it's astounding what one comes across. Some scary stuff actually. But why albinos, Jono?"

"Because they are considered to be very sacred. They are treated with deep respect because they are believed to be spirits born as human beings. And the whole *muti* body parts thing, well, that's a whole other area, my friend, that is a dark thing for sure."

"I'd be super keen to hear the whole bangshoot," Richard said.

"Maybe you are, my friend but it is not a discussion for the faint-hearted," Jono warned. "And yes, Richard, I know the events of which you speak. But one last word on witches: they are also accused of inciting adultery, alcohol abuse, and theft. Witches also have immense power to turn innocent people into witches and therefore it is possible to become a witch without even being aware of it, simply by eating contaminated food or picking up an 'impure' object."

"Do not, for the love of God, tell Harrison any of this," Richard said. "We're all sworn to secrecy. Can you image what he'd be like if he heard these sorts of things? He'll be rubbing everything, including us, in antiseptic."

"All for one and one for all, we say nothing," Helen assured him. "Jono, what about *tokoloshes*? I've tried to find out about them but no one would really tell me anything."

"Ah," Jono said, "the infamous *tokoloshe*. Helen, here is the secret to creating one: you remove the eyes and tongue from a full size corpse, then you blow a secret powder into its mouth and it comes to life and will obey your every wish. But there is a high price for creating a *tokoloshe*, including the death of a relative within a year, because the spirits do not give life freely. If you are prepared to create an unnatural life, then you must be prepared to destroy a natural one."

"An unnatural life," Kate echoed and even the fire seemed to flicker and dim. Mia offered her the bottle of schnapps but she shook her head. Mia shrugged and passed the bottle to Jasmine.

"The *tokoloshe*," Jono continued, "is a spirit in the households of witches and warlocks and they speak with a lisp…"

"Sofie speaks with a lisp." Mia sat up, giggling "She must be a *tokoloshe*. I suspected it all along."

"But she is not small and brown, nor does she have a penis so long it has to be slung over her shoulder," Jono said. "Sorry, Mia, but she falls short of many of the physical characteristics needed."

Mia found this so hilarious she nearly fell into the fire.

"Easy there, cupcake," Richard said, kicking a burning log further away from her.

"I'm fine." Mia protested, "perfectly composed, fank you very much. It's the thought of Sofie with a giant penis slung over her shoulder, lisping…" She and Jasmine hung onto each other, hooting with laughter.

"The *tokoloshe*," Jono said, "is very unusual in that he has a single buttock. Apparently Satan was unable to replicate this uniquely human feature, of our lovely, well-rounded bottoms. Therefore, if you wish to scare away the devil, you must bare your buttocks at him and he will be frightened by that which he cannot have."

"That's why mooning is such a handy tool," Mia yelled. "Never mind crosses for vampires, just pull down your trousers and scare the bejesus out of the devil. Richard luv, show us your moon."

"Yes," Helen chimed in, "show us."

"I respectfully decline the invitation," Richard said. "Go on, Jono."

"I am too worried to continue," Jono said. "I am afraid this discussion is being a health hazard to Mia."

"I'm fine," Mia gasped, "but my stomach hurts from laughing. Bleedin' hell, this is too hilarious."

"Part of the *tokoloshe's* duties," Jono said, "is to make love to its witch mistress, which is why he was created so well-endowed. As a reward for fulfilling these sexual duties, the tokoloshie is rewarded with milk and food."

"Milk?" Kate was perplexed. "Why milk?"

"Milk is considered a sacred drink in many parts of Africa," Jono explained. "It has many healing powers. If you do see a *tokoloshe*, do not annoy it by talking to it and most certainly do not point at it because it will vanish immediately."

"How on earth can I not look," Mia shook with laughter, "when it's hung like a bleedin' donkey?"

Despite having downed half the bottle of schnapps, Mia was surprisingly coherent, unlike Jasmine, who had abruptly fallen fast asleep and was snoring slightly.

Jono finished the last of his beer and looked regretful. "Well, everyone, that is all for tonight. I must go to sleep or I will be a bad driver in the morning. Thank you very much for listening."

He looked at Kate who grinned at him.

"Thank *you*," Richard said. "You're incredibly knowledgeable, Jono, and I look forward to more stories about *muti* and witchdoctors and the like. Anyone else like one for the ditch? Last call, people, last call."

"I'm going to bed," Eva said. "Thanks Jono, thanks everyone."

"Yeah, we're calling it a night too," Kate and Marika said, getting up.

"Me too," Helen said. "That was fascinating."
"I'll have one more," Mia said, "lay it on, baby."
Jasmine was still fast asleep and Mia patted her head.

"I'm going to brush my teeth," Kate said to Marika who was tucked up in borrowed sheets and blankets and already half asleep.

Kate unzipped the tent and walked across the grass. She swung the washroom doors open and saw Helen sitting on one of the slatted wooden benches, crying. Kate's heart sank. The last thing she wanted was another heart-to-heart and she walked over the basin without saying a word.

"That was a fun night." Helen said, drying her eyes and blowing her nose loudly. "I even forgot about Robbie for a bit, but now I feel sick again. It'll be good for me to have some fun, let my hair down for a change. I'm always so serious even when I try not to be. That Richard, he's so hot, don't you think?"

Kate, her mouth full of foam, made gargling noises. Helen continued.

"Even just sitting next to him had me all worked up; I could have pounced on him right there. I need him to help me get over Robbie. Mia's so stupid. I don't understand what he sees in her. Hopefully, as time passes, he'll see he has other options, options that he's got more in common with."

"She's his *girlfriend*," Kate said, having rinsed vigorously. "It's not good karma to steal another man's girlfriend."

Helen shrugged. "It's not a nice world, what can I say?"

Kate, filled with fury, walked out without saying another word.

To Springbok and into Namibia (the Gariep River)

THE NEXT MORNING, KATE WOKE BEFORE DAWN. She unzipped the tent as quietly as she could and climbed up the mountainside using the path Kleine Skok had shown them the day before. The dark blue sky was freckled with stars and a pale yellow ridge in the east lit the mountain top. The air was cool, carrying myriad African fragrances of woodsmoke, dew-wet grass and aromatic flora, and Kate, listening to the cry of the ring-necked dove, closed her eyes and felt happy. She lost track of time; heartbreak and her real life seemed a million miles away and then, worried she should be helping Marika with the tent, she hurried down, threading her way through the mountain grasses, thorny trees and castle-turret rocks.

She passed Helen running laps up and down the gravel mountain driveway, her hair pulled back in a tight ponytail and her face hard and focused, and she bumped into Treasure coming out of the washroom, with Harrison close behind her.

"I'll help you with breakfast," he said, and Treasure grunted a reply.

Kate laughed and told Marika while they dismantled the tent.

"*Ja*, that Harrison, he's something," Marika said. "We're done, let's grab some breakfast, I'm starving."

They found most of the group gathered at the rondavel, with Harrison hovering over Treasure and examining cutlery while Treasure ignored him and arranged slices of bread and poured milk into plastic jugs.

"Plastic holds a lot of germs if it's old." Harrison held a jug up to the light. "The germs get in the little cuts from the wear and tear."

Treasure ignored him.

Richard groaned. "I couldn't eat a thing. My head's killing me, my eyeballs are soft-boiled eggs set to detonate. I don't know why I'm so hungover when I drank scads more the night before and I was fine."

Mia laughed and dunked her tea bag in her mug. "Maybe a witch poisoned you. How do you feel, Jazzer?" she asked Jasmine. "How's your head?"

"Fine," Jasmine said, "Did you guys put me in my tent? I don't remember."

"Yeah, you were dead gone. That was a good laugh, last night."

While the others hung around the breakfast table, Marika went to find Jono. "Did my luggage come during the night?" she asked, her expression expectant.

"It is not here yet," Jono said, carefully balancing a bowl of cereal, a plate of toast and a cup of coffee, and still managing to eat and drink. "But please, do not worry my dear. It will come, it always does."

"There's no hot food except for toast," Jasmine commented, "if you can count that as a hot food. I could have done with some fried eggs and sausage."

Two cups of coffee later, Kate popped off to the washroom. She was drying her hands on some paper towel when Charisse emerged from a stall, her hand pressed to her stomach.

"My stomach's still killing me," she said.

"The meds you picked up still aren't helping?" Kate asked.

"It would appear not." Charisse straightened up and took a deep breath. "Don't tell the others though."

Kate said she wouldn't and they walked out to help load the bus, while Marika hurriedly finished washing dishes with Helen drying and Harrison offering a running commentary. "Germs,

germs. Everywhere I look, germs. We are in dire need of new buckets to put the dishes in, look at these, scratched and old."

"Harrison, if you're going to try to replace all the things in Africa that are scratched and old, you'll have a big task on your hands," Kate heard Helen say, with Marika agreeing.

"Not all of Africa is my worry," Harrison remarked, "but our health and safety is."

"These are fine, Harrison," Helen was curt. "Trust me, I know. What? Do you think I'd put my own health at risk?"

The argument died down and they got all the bits and pieces on the bus and were just about ready to leave when Treasure climbed up into the passenger area of the bus. "Good morning everybody. There's a rule Jono forgot to tell you. Everybody must change seats every day, so you get to know each other and make new friends."

"What about the couples?" Richard, Mia and Lena enquired, wanting to stay in their pairs while Stepfan was noticeably quiet.

"Couples may stay together."

Rydell, close to Treasure, bent down, as if to pick something up off the floor while he admired her feet. He stretched out his hand to touch her but forced himself to straighten up. "I wasn't sitting here yesterday, so I can stay here?" he asked her.

"Yes, you can stay there. Who's sitting next to you?"

"No one. You should come and sit here with me," he added boldly, flushing with pride at the retort. He had woken to find the ghostly voices silent and was feeling clear-headed and whole.

"Thank you but I must stay up with Jono. It's my job to keep him awake when he's driving."

The group laughed.

"Everybody except the couples, switch around," Treasure insisted. "Come now."

Grumbling, people switched seats.

"Right, now we are ready to go," Treasure climbed down the steep narrow stairs, closed the door of the bus and took her place beside Jono in the sectioned-off front cab.

Kate settled into her seat next to Rydell, determined to put him at ease. "What made you choose Namibia? I came here out of the blue."

Rydell chortled. "Not me. I planned this down the last detail and there were lots of reasons but the most important one is the Bushmen."

"The Bushmen? I don't know much about them except that they're a peace-loving people and very clever. That's what Marika said, remember? She also loves them."

Rydell gave her a look. "Clever? Peace-loving?" He snorted again, a high-pitched laugh and Kate wished he would stop.

"What do you mean?" she asked, more to stop his mirth than to get an answer.

Rydell rubbed the palms of his hands on his trousers. "I found a book that was published in 1899 and it changed my life. Do you want to hear about it? It might upset you."

"I'd love to hear about it," Kate said, having no idea what she was letting herself in for. "I'm always interested in learning things."

Rydell cocked his head to one side. "The writer begins by asking what is the lowest of human races? And the answer, according to the book, is the Bushmen — because of their filth, how they never wash and he also quotes one missionary who reports they have 'few ideas but those of vengeance and eating.'"

Kate was startled and Rydell continued.

"The writer quotes an explorer who says that 'no meat, in whatever state of decomposition, is ever discarded by the Bushmen.' Another quote says that 'while necessity has given them acute sight and hearing, they might almost be supposed to have neither taste, smell or feeling; no disgust is ever evinced by them at even the most nauseating kind of food, nor do they appear to have any feeling of even the most striking changes in the temperature of the atmosphere.'"

"Do you have a photographic memory?" Kate asked, trying to distract him from his disturbing topic. "That sounds word-for-word." She glanced over at Marika and saw that she was looking miserable too. She was staring down at her hands, while Harrison was shouting in her ear.

Rydell was oblivious to Kate's discomfort.

"I'm highly intelligent and yes, I've got a photographic memory." He gave her a sideways glance and a half-smile.

"First off, that book of yours sounds totally archaic with the funny old language and how it's written, and secondly, if we lived in the desert, we might also eat anything too, in any kind of state. And just because the Bushmen didn't run around with a bar of soap in hand, or dressed in Western clothes, doesn't mean they are filthy. If we had to hunt to survive, there'd be some degree of violence in our society too." She was sure she had convinced him but Rydell made his snorting noise again.

"How's this for violence," he hissed in a quiet whisper. "One explorer said, 'No other savages betray so high a degree of brutal ferocity as the Bushmen. They kill their own children without remorse.' A missionary reported that 'when a mother dies whose infant is not able to shift for itself, it is, without any ceremony, buried alive with the corpse of its mother.' Another missionary tells of 'instances of parents throwing their tender offspring to the hungry lion, who stands roaring before their cavern, refusing to depart till some peace-offering is made to him.' "

Kate stared at Rydell. "My word." She was sorry she had opened this particular can of worms and was desperate to stop the flow of conversation.

"There's more," he said. "After a fight between husband and wife, the one who is beaten is likely to take revenge by killing their child. And, on various occasions, parents smother their children and cast them away in the desert, or bury them alive without remorse. Murder is an amusement and is considered a praiseworthy act. When fathers and mothers become too old to be of any use, or can no longer take care of themselves, they are abandoned in the desert to be devoured alive by wild beasts."

Kate was not sure if she were more disturbed by what Rydell was saying or by the manner in which he was speaking, and she wondered if he was harmlessly strange or really dangerous. He refused to look at her while he spoke and he leaned forward in his seat, his face bright red, with beads of sweat forming on his forehead.

"Good heavens," she said, slumped down, resigned to her fate of having to listen to detailed of acts of torture.

"Yes. And there is no good reason except for fun. They do it for fun, your peace-lovers."

"Timeout, Rydell. I must ask you this," Kate was curious despite her intention to end the conversation. "You said you came because of the Bushmen. Why, then? You like their brutality?"

"No." Rydell spat on her with his vehemence. "Sorry," he wiped her arm with a cold, damp touch. "I'm here because the book said 'there is love in all their marriages.' In *all* their marriages. The explorer, James Chapman, said that 'although they have a plurality of wives, which they also obtain by purchase, there is still love in all their marriages, and courtship among them is a very formal affair.'" He came to a standstill at last and fell silent. "If I'm to understand you correctly, you're here to find a Bushman wife?" Kate joked.

"Yes," Rydell whispered, "but you can't tell anyone. I'm swearing you to secrecy. Promise me you won't tell anybody. I don't know why I told you. I shouldn't have told you." He folded his arms tightly, visibly distressed.

"Of course I won't tell anybody," Kate said.

Rydell was reassured and Kate's seeming empathy encouraged him to confide further.

"I've got money, you see. I'll be able to pay for a good wife. But now I've changed my mind anyway, because I've already found what I'm looking for and she will be The One. It's all changed now. But I'm not going to say anything else to you, I've said too much already. I don't know why I talked to you so much." He said the last with resentment as if it was Kate's fault, and that she had tricked him into revealing his secret.

He shook his head violently, turned his back to her, and stared out of the window. Kate, disconcerted by his sudden anger, tried to make some sense of what he had said, but at that moment, Jono pulled over at a gas station for a washroom stop and to fill up with petrol.

Inside the Opei Take-Away Café adjoining the gas station, the group studied the hand-written menu behind the counter. "Toasted mince, pork trotters, vetkoek, meatball, chakalaka wors, quart chicken, pork ears, pap and vleis, Vienna sausage, hot dog," Eva read out loud. "Boewewors roll, russian roll. Look, it says 'egg', just like that, 'egg' one rand fifty. And don't forget the chicken burger, toasted burger, and chicken macaroni."

"Stuck a feather in his cap and called it macaroni," Richard said absently.

Helen glanced at him. "What are you talking about?"

"Rydell. Remember he said that last night. The macaroni reminded me."

"Hmmm, yeah, I'd forgotten." Jasmine said. "Definitely not playing with a full deck of cards, that one."

She waved to Kate and Marika, "We're over here."

Kate pointed Marika in the direction of the gathered group.

"Simba chips," Marika said dreamily, "roar with flavour. And Willards Big Corn Bites, Eet-Sum-Mores, Marie biscuits, Sparletta Sparkling Grenadilla."

"Is she delirious?" Richard asked Kate.

"I'm fine," Marika objected, "just stressed about my lost luggage which I really was stupid enough to think would be here this morning. I mean if they found it yesterday, why isn't it here? How'm I supposed to manage without any of my things? The sun's like a blowtorch on me in the bus, and I don't have a hat or any cool clothes, my jeans are suffocatingly hot and I wish I had sandals and I'm so uncomfortable on a hundred levels. And Harrison ... let me tell you, that man can *talk*."

"So can Rydell," Kate said. "Marika, you are pale you know."

"*Ag*, really, I'm fine. Good lord, man," she said peering into the glass counter, "look at that food. Please, let me assure you that most South African food does not look like this. These could be movie props for a bad axe-murderer story."

They resisted the local delicacies offered by the café but raided the ice-cream freezer. Marika bought a Marlboro cowboy hat for thirty rand and headed outside to find Jono, with Kate jogging at her side.

"You have a hat, I see," Jono said. "Good idea. I just got off the phone with South African Airways and they want you to tell them any identifying marks or labels on your luggage."

Marika stopped deadstill in the hot sun and looked over at the aloes with their fire-red flowers and at the small African children playing on the swings, screaming with laughter. She was trying her best not to get upset.

"But Jono," she said, scuffing the dusty ground with her foot, "you said yesterday that the luggage had been found and that it was on its way? Now they want to know what it looks like? That means they haven't found it."

"Yes, that is what they told me yesterday and this is what they are telling me today. Take Treasure's cell phone and try to text message the woman at SAA; she said you have her number."

"Why must she use my cell phone?" Treasure argued, "I've hardly got any money left on it and I'm waiting for an important call."

"Because I do not have any money left on my phone either," Jono was insistent, "and I cannot buy a card here. I thought I could. I used up my time by calling SAA."

"Great," Marika said. She wanted to sit down in the thick red dirt and weep. "My luggage is lost, I'm in the middle of nowhere, and between the two of you, I can't even phone anyone."

"Do not worry," Jono said, "we will get a phone card at the

next stop. It is a bigger town there and I am sure it will be fine."

"Jono, we go into the desert tonight and I don't have a sleeping bag or any clothes, or any toiletries or a torch or anything at all. How will they get it to us if they haven't even found it yet? We're two days away from the airport now. There's no way it'll get here in time."

"Do not worry," Jono repeated. "It will be fine. Now we need to get back on the bus so that we can continue our journey. Everybody! Back on the bus!"

"What are you going to do?" Kate asked Marika sympathetically.

"I've got no idea. I feel sick about it. I wish I could sit next to you," she whispered to Kate. "Harrison's killing me! He won't shut up for a second."

"I bet Rydell's way weirder than Harrison, I'll tell you about him later. Listen, try not to worry about your luggage, we'll make a plan, okay? You're not alone in this."

The bus jolted off the sand back onto the tar road. Jono and Treasure were arguing. "You should have given Marika your phone," Jono said, hanging onto the steering wheel while he spoke.

Treasure was obstinate. "I am waiting for a call."

"A call that will never come. Do you think I am stupid? *Aikona*. Do you think I do not know that he left you and you cried all night? You pick bad men, Treasure."

"At least I have a love life. And now you have fallen in love with your American princess, what foolish dreams do you have in your head? She's got a boyfriend, she told you."

"Treasure, she is Canadian and I know she has a boyfriend at home. You are just angry because she has got a man and you do not. But that is not the point. You should have given Marika your phone. She is very worried about her luggage." He looked at her. "You are pregnant, is that not so?"

She stared at him, picked up a copy of *Cosmopolitan* and

put her feet up on the dashboard.

"Maybe," she said quietly. "Okay, so yes." She sighed. "I'm not in the mood for all these people. And that Harrison, I tell you Jono, he makes me so angry. 'Wash this like this, wash this like that.' He's obsessed."

"Yes," Jono agreed. "He is like that with me too, always asking me how many kilometers we are going and exactly when we will arrive and depart. But we must be patient. It is our job to put up with these people. I know it is not easy."

Treasure sighed again and opened her magazine. "I keep waiting for my Prince Charming to come on one of these holidays," she said. "Waiting for him to tell me that I'm his bride and that he's come to take me home to his mansion with as much hot running water as I like and many rooms for my child. Children. But it is like dreaming of winning the lottery. *Haw!* Jono, the next stop, I am buying a lottery ticket. I have more chance with that."

In the back of the bus, a fierce argument had broken out between Sofie and Stepfan. It started out with Stepfan playing devils' advocate to Sofie's left-wing politics but it soon became nasty and eventually Kate had enough and she stood up. "Come on, people," she called out. "What is with all this racket?"

"We are having a discussion," Sofie paused for breath.

"No, you're not, you're arguing and very loudly too. Why don't you both wait until you can walk somewhere far away from the rest of us and you can shout to your heart's content? In the meanwhile, it's very unpleasant."

The rest of the group cheered.

"Political discussion frees the mind," Sofie objected.

"Not when it's a shouting match between two people with opposite opinions," Kate said. "Now, you two talk about something else or change places, I mean it."

"I do like a strong woman," Stepfan smiled wolfishly. "You

look like Sandra Bullock. Has anyone ever told you that? When she was younger, I mean."

Kate ignored him and sat down next to Rydell who had not said one word to her since they had returned to the bus.

They arrived in Springbok in the early afternoon.

"An announcement, everybody!" Jono addressed the group who were eager to get off the bus. "This is the last big town before we cross the border from South Africa and go into Namibia and the desert. You should buy enough water to last for at least a day and a night. We are going to need a lot of supplies."

"I'll have to buy things to sustain me for the rest of the trip," Marika said to Kate. "My luggage is dead."

Kate nodded. "I'll help you," she said.

Eva leaned across the aisle. "Me too," she offered.

The three of them went shopping while Harrison insisted on helping Treasure and Jono with the groceries. Rydell vanished down a side alley while the rest of the group set off to explore the town.

Marika grabbed a sleeping bag, a spare blanket and a hasty selection of clothes. "I came on this holiday in search of adventure," she said wryly to Kate and Eva as they entered a pharmacy, "and I'm certainly getting that in spades. Although I've got to admit, lost luggage wasn't quite what I had in mind."

"You're doing wonderfully," Kate picked up a can of Black Mamba deodorant. "What a great name for a deodorant!" She gestured around the pharmacy. "I love how this store is called a chemist. When I first arrived, I thought chemists were traditional African shops."

Marika laughed. "Understandable." She gave a small shudder. "All that stuff Jono was telling us last night made me remember something. When I was young, I was always off exploring places other white people wouldn't be seen dead in, and I came across a bag of witchdoctor's bones. It was a little black bag and it came with a guide on how to throw the bones – that's what they call it, throwing the bones, to tell the future. I was so excited, I rushed home and showed our housekeeper, Anna, who was horrified. She told me that I was inviting great evil into our lives and that she didn't want to be in the house as long as I had that bag of bones."

"What happened?" Eva and Kate were keen to hear.

"Strange things started to happen almost immediately. Pictures fell off my bedroom walls in the middle of the night, or I'd wake to find that ornaments and books had moved. And then when my two goldfish died, I panicked and I asked Anna what to do and she and I buried the bones out in the veldt."

"And the trouble stopped?" Eva asked and Marika nodded.

"It stopped. So, my dears, we must be respectful of the African ways. Those who use them in ignorance will be brought to task and those who use magic for ill will pay the price."

"Maybe I can find some magic to help me get my poems back," Eva looked hopeful.

Marika laughed. "Eva, the magic lives inside you. I've got everything, let's pay."

They went to the cashier and Kate got into a conversation with the tiny woman behind the counter, explaining Marika's lost luggage woes.

"*Ag nee Mevrou*, I'm sorry for you," the tiny, prune-wrinkled woman commiserated and she grinned toothlessly at Marika, her eyes bulbous behind her coke-bottle glasses. "*Eina*, that would hurt, having to spend this money again."

"*Ja*, it hurts a lot," Marika agreed. "How much time's left before we have to get back on the bus?" she asked Kate who was trying on sunglasses.

"We've still got twenty minutes," Kate said.

"Those look great on you." Marika said. "You're very Audrey Hepburn you know."

"Oh, I'm so *not*." Kate went bright red. "Audrey Hepburn was a tiny toothpick of a woman compared to me. Did you hear Stepfan call me Sandra Bullock? Right, with this big gap between my teeth."

"A gap is sexy," Eva said. "But I agree with Marika, you're more Audrey than Sandra. Audrey with long hair."

"I'll buy these sunglasses and the deodorant," Kate handed the money to the tiny woman and they all left.

"Look there," Kate bobbed her head vigorously towards a small street in between an abandoned construction site and some old buildings. "It's Rydell, but what is he doing?"

"Looks like he's stalking something," Marika said, peering down the street.

They watched him disappear out of sight.

"He's the weirdest person ever." Kate shook her head.

They tried to see if they could spot him again but he was gone. "I must tell you all the crap he told me, about how the Bushmen are the lowest form of human filth but he's here to find one for a wife."

"I beg your pardon?"

"Yes. I'm telling you, he's very odd. He's got this terrible ancient book that he's learned off by heart and he keeps quoting from it. He's totally freaky. "

"Maybe he's socially inept and very shy?" Marika offered but both Kate and Eva snorted.

They went inside a liquor store where Marika bought a bottle of Old Brown Sherry and they wandered back out into the sunshine. "We've still got enough time to check out that Rasta market stall over there," Marika said, "I admit it freely, I'm a souvenir-addict."

"I'm not as interested in souvenirs as photographs," Kate said, "Cam used to complain that I took too many pictures but now I'm free to take as many photographs I like."

"That's the spirit," Marika said, grinning, and they lugged their bags towards the Rasta stall.

In the shady quiet of a garbage-strewn street, Rydell washed the blood off his hands under a tap and felt better. The cold water turned the red dust, mixing with the blood, into brown mud.

Rydell had wanted to go shopping with Treasure and Jono but Harrison beat him to it. Rydell was beginning to think he would have to do something about Harrison. He watched the three of them disappear into the grocery store and a blinding rage overcame him. He dug his nails into the palms of his hands as hard as he could and pierced the pad of his thumb but he quickly realized he was going to need more than that.

He set off at a jerky pace to seek privacy and an innocent victim, sensing it would not be difficult to find either. He was right and, his heart pounding at the thrill of the chase, he quickly got his hands on what he had been looking for: a small runty dog who was happy to receive attention and never realized the warm caressing hands would end his life.

"Good puppy, good puppy," Rydell rubbed the little stray's back, amused by the wagging tail and innocent naïveté. He ran his hands over the thin body, digging deeper and deeper until the dog let out a sharp yelp and tried to scramble away.

"No escape stupid dog, no escape."

He took his time venting his frustrations and once he had cleaned up, he was a poster child for sunny self-control. Back on the bus, he still could not look at Harrison without wanting to spit and he was reassured to see that Treasure seemed to find Harrison's attentions as irritating as he did.

He closed his eyes and thought there had to be a way for him to get close to Treasure. He would find a way.

The group crossed the border into Namibia in the late afternoon and cleared customs without mishap although Kate made some of the others nervous by boldly photographing everything.

"I don't fink it's a good idea for her to have her camera up the nose of every bleedin' official," Mia whispered to Richard in the lineup, "what with us and the contra on board. She's getting on my nerves."

"I'm not worried," Richard said, although he looked ill at ease. "They don't have any reason to search the bus or go through all our belongings but you never know."

"You know, luv," Mia said, "I reckon this trip's got more than its fair share of nutters."

"All the better for us. If we can get through this and into Namibia, no one will notice anything we do. We'll be home free."

Mia giggled and nodded.

"Look," Richard said and his expression cleared, "we're done, everyone's getting back on the bus, we're in the clear, my sweet girl. I'm not sure how I would have explained an entire set of monogrammed surgical tools with me."

Mia looked petulant. "Still don't know why you had to bring those ones, yeah? They were a present from me and what if they get lost?"

"I brought them for good luck and I'd never lose them. I must say, I do feel relieved that this hurdle of the journey has been surmounted."

"You must say, must you?" Mia teased him. "I must say I prefer it when you aren't talking like such a toffee-nosed geezer but yeah I know, everyone trusts a toff. Come on, luv, time to get back on the old scrap heap of metal."

While Kate scrolled through her photographs, Rydell hummed and smiled to himself and plucked at his clothing. Kate, unnerved, decided that she preferred the previously morose, depressed version of his persona.

In the back of the bus, another socio-political argument had broken out but this time more opinions entered the fray. "The end justifies the means," Stepfan insisted.

"I still vote for the greatest good for the greatest number," Sofie argued.

"You both have it backwards," Richard asserted, "because we don't do any of the things we do, for the good of mankind. We do what we do because we crave war. Man's natural state is that of war and we will find any reason we can to wage warfare. And if we can't find a reason to be at war, we'll make one up."

"Yes," Ellie, usually dour and quiet, was eager to agree, "I agree with you, peace is so boring."

"You cannot really mean that…" Sofie protested but she fell silent as the bus came to a stop next to a spectacularly unusual tree.

"Incredible," Enrique exclaimed.

"We must get off and take pics," Kate jumped to her feet and nearly fell off the bus when Treasure opened the door from the other side.

"Before you get off, I must make an announcement." Treasure climbed up into the passenger area of the bus, with Jono craning his head through the joining cab window. "You see that tree out there? That tree is the kokerboom or quiver tree and it is called that because the Bushmen made their quivers out of its branches since they are hollow and very light. And do you see that big bush to the left of the tree?" She made sure that the group knew which one she was talking about. "That is the Melkbos bush and it is very, very poisonous. Do not touch it. The Bushmen used to dip their arrows in the juice from it and the poison is so powerful it can kill a very big buck or deer as you would say. Now you have ten minutes to take pictures."

Kate bounded off the bus and ran up to the poisonous bush which looked like a large, spongy green sea coral with fleshy, podlike dusky pink seeds.

"Forbidden fruit," Stepfan grumbled. "That girl's going to get herself into trouble one day."

"Don't be so grumpy," Lena told him, "she's just having fun. Look, those poisonous bushes are everywhere."

Stepfan didn't answer. He followed Charisse and Bree, leaving his wife behind and alone. Only Gisela saw the quick flash of hurt cross Lena's face and she moved toward her, but Lena walked away briskly with her head down.

Ten minutes later, Kate followed Charisse and Stepfan into the bus. They were laughing and Kate saw Stepfan put his hand on Charisse's back to "help" her climb the stairs, and she watched him cup the girl's buttock with just the flash of a touch.

Kate bit her tongue and wondered what Charisse was thinking. Did Charisse not care that she was behaving badly for all the world to see? Apparently not.

A few seats behind, Stepfan admired the slender curve of Charisse's neck, the clean line of her jaw. He glanced down at Lena dozing beside him, her neck pillow in place and earphones on — classical music no doubt. If he had an inkling of the rage building inside his seemingly serene wife, he would have been speechless with shock and more than just a little concerned.

The next camping ground was a strange new world. "It is like we're on the moon or something," Sofie commented.

"It's all white and brown," Marika marveled, "as far as the eye can see. It's bleached and otherworldly."

"Rocks and stones," Enrique added, "no sand, no vegetation."

"Very harsh," Richard agreed. "And it's jolly hot too. You could fry an egg on my forehead. I'm going to put some ice in my bandana and wrap it around my neck."

"Good thinking," Helen said.

"Don't be using the ice for such cavalier things," Harrison admonished. "Jono just refilled the cooler and it's got to last until tomorrow."

"What's a few ice cubes between friends?" Richard said, twisting ice into his bandanna.

"And if we all did that?" Harrison asked. "Then what?"

"Then we'd all have nice cold necks," Richard shrugged.

"And not-nice hot water to drink," Harrison said. "You think very short-term. And selfishly too."

"Give it a break," Richard returned to his seat. "What I do with my share of the ice cubes is up to me."

Harrison clamped his jaw tight and an uneasy silence filled the bus just as they pulled into a manicured campsite, leaving the barren road behind. The prospect of setting up for the night offered a welcome respite from the noisy jolting and their spirits immediately improved.

"An oasis in the desert," Lena fanned her face and surveyed the campsite. "All we need are camels and palm trees."

"Camels are dirty animals with fleas," Stepfan grumbled. "Come on, Lena, carry the mats."

"Carry them yourself," Gisela called out as she walked past.

"Thank you, Gisela," Lena said, gracefully picking up her backpack.

Rydell waited until Jono pitched Treasure's tent and then he moved in close. The peace from his earlier release in Springbok had long since left and he burned with fever, his skin crawling. He was determined to talk to Treasure but she left quickly to prepare supper.

Meanwhile Kate and Marika set up for the night. "I'm like a homeless person," Marika laughed, "with all my little bags! Would you like to come for a walk?"

"Nope, I'm on kitchen duty tonight, I'm going to help Treasure."

Kate walked over to the thatched rondavel and found Treasure in a flurry, chopping vegetables. The table was piled high with half-prepared food and it seemed like every pot, pan, plate, cutting board, knife and bowl was in use. "Can I help you?" Kate offered.

"Yes, my baby, please." Treasure wiped her forehead. "Jono is cross with me because supper is late but we just arrived. And now I am trying to cut this butternut but it's not working, *Aikona*."

"Here, give me that." Kate took the butternut found a better knife.

Jono walked in and hovered at the edge of the table close to Kate, absentmindedly prodding the grated cheese with a fork. "Tell me, Kate, do you like Africa so far?"

Kate grinned. "I love it."

"And you live in Canada?" Jono asked, feeling foolish for asking such inane questions. "You must like the heat here because it's very cold there?"

"Actually," Helen interjected, returning red-faced and breathless from a punishing run. "Africa feels much colder than the States or Canada. I nearly froze to death my entire year in Underberg. There's no insulation and people put a space heater in the middle of a room and think that counts as central heating. Then you've got the wind that blows right through the windows. Can I help with anything here? I'm also on kitchen duty."

"No thanks, we're good," Kate said.

"Then I'm going to shower," Helen said, "I'll do double washing up later."

Talk of the cold weather in Underberg reminded Helen of Robbie and how they had laughed together while huddling in front of a tiny heater, and she was abruptly broken-hearted all over again, having forgotten for a fleeting moment that he was extinguished from her previously hopeful future.

"I've come to inspect the hygiene of the cooking situation." Harrison appeared without warning at Kate's side.

"I realize you're not joking," she said. "Search away, Inspector. I'm sure you'll find we're following health regulations precisely."

"Do you have enough hot water to wash the dishes?" he asked, lifting the lid off a steaming pot.

"*Aikona wena*. Harrison!" Treasure had enough. "Get away from my cooking, *eish!* You can clean after I am done if you like but right now, I'm cooking." She shooed him away and he left looking miserable.

"There," Kate washed her hands, "the butternut's all chopped. Is there anything else I can help you with?"

"I'm fine, thank you," Treasure said.

"Then I'm going for a walk along the river and try to find a diamond."

"Good luck," Jono called after her.

"You like her," Treasure teased Jono. "You know you do."

Jono groaned and rubbed his head. "Yes, fine, I admit it. But I say such stupid things to her, that is when I can even say anything. I am making a fool of myself."

"A very sweet fool," Treasure patted his shoulder. "Don't worry about it, you're giving your famous Bushman lecture tonight, she'll be impressed. But just don't look at Kate because then you will start saying the same sentence again, and again … the Bushman, the Bushman…"

"Enough *eish*, I get the picture," Jono got up, "thank you for making me feel much better and yes, I am being sarcastic. I am going to have a shower."

"See you later. Hey, Jono," she shouted after him in Xhosa, "and don't worry. I'll always love you!"

The Third Night

LATER THAT NIGHT THEY FEASTED at Treasure's table. "I am so full," Sofie sighed and patted her stomach, her plate balanced on her lap. "I ate too much but it was so delicious. That fish was wonderful and the sauce was incredible. What was in it?"

"The fish was snoek," Treasure said, "and the sauce was a mix of apricot jam, olive oil, soy sauce, a little bit of white wine, some chili sauce and lots of spices. I am very glad you liked it."

"It was superb," Helen agreed. "Treasure, you are going to make us all fat."

"I liked the mashed potatoes the best," Enrique leaned back, stretched his arms out and yawned. "I think I ate most of them myself."

"I loved the butternut," Gisela said. "What was the secret ingredient in that, Treasure?"

"Three secrets," Treasure said. "Syrup, butter, and cinnamon."

"Delicious," Stepfan commented. "Your husband is most fortunate to have you as his wife — not only are you beautiful but you are an excellent cook. The perfect woman."

"I want to kill you, Stepfan," Sofie said, pleasantly. "There is more to the perfect woman than cooking and good looks."

"Actually, there isn't. I just tell it like it is," Stepfan beamed proudly.

Rydell was tormented because Treasure had not answered Stepfan. He had wanted to ask Treasure if she was married but he could not find the words, and he twisted his hands, turning purple with frustration.

Treasure smiled at the group and ignored Stepfan. "I hope you have room for my world-famous dessert — ice cream with hot chocolate sauce made from Bar Ones, which are like Mars Bars but much better."

The group groaned. They were sitting on camp stools around a roughly-hewn wooden table that was piled high with the aftermath of a much-enjoyed safari dinner party; every tin plate, bowl, dish, cup and knife and fork had been used.

Kate surveyed the mess glumly, thinking it would take half the night to clean up.

Treasure jumped to her feet and blushed slightly at being the centre of attention. "I would like to introduce Professor Jono who will honour us with his world famous talk on the Bushmen. Get comfortable, sit back and enjoy the entertainment."

She curtsied to a boisterous clamour of appreciation.

Jono laughed. "It is true that I would like to tell you some things about the Bushmen and I hope that I will not disappoint you."

"Excellent, old man," Richard said, "Hang on a minute though, anyone for more beer? I'm going to fetch a few cold ones."

"While you do that, I'll move these dishes to the sink," Kate said, getting up.

"Good idea, Kate," Harrison jumped up. "Let me help you. Let's soak the dishes. That way the food will not sit here rotting and making germs."

Kate left him to it and returned to her seat.

"Do we need to take notes?" Jasmine asked. "Is there a test at the end of it and what happens if we fail?"

"If you fail, you have to clean the whole bus with a toothbrush and with Harrison in charge of you," Jono joked.

"A toothbrush," Harrison said brightly, dropping a spoon into boiling water. "An excellent idea, it would get right into the cracks. Jono, my friend, you're a genius."

"Here we are," Richard returned and passed around beers, "Castle Lagers all round."

The group fell silent and Jono got started. "Good evening, everybody! To begin with, a question. What is the link between pianos of the 1850s and the Bushmen?"

"That's easy," Rydell spoke up quickly, "elephants and their tusks." He blushed scarlet and examined his nails.

"The man is a winner." Jono declared. "Treasure, he gets a double serving of dessert."

Rydell looked at Treasure and blushed even harder.

"Seven million elephants were butchered, all for pianos and while a lot of ivory came from East Africa, Namibia supplied a large proportion before the depletion of herds in this country. The Bushman were great shots and many white hunters armed them with rifles and then traded them tobacco for ivory. The Bushmen loved tobacco very much and they would trade just about anything for it, even their wives."

"I can understand that," Gisela commented as she lit another cigarette and waved the smoke away. "I might trade one of you if I run out of tobacco."

"Us motley crew," Sofie joked. "You'd be lucky to get one cigarette per person. I cannot believe how many elephants were shot, and just for piano keys."

"Simple commerce, my dear," Stepfan folded his hands behind his head, "market need. A matter of supply and demand...."

"Anyway," Jono interrupted Stepfan, "the Bushmen played a big part in this ecological devastation and were not always the guardians of wildlife as some might imagine. But although they were profitable traders, they were not considered to be men, but rather the missing link in the evolutionary chain; that which came between the ape and man."

Rydell snickered quietly and snuck a glance at Treasure,

wondering if anyone would notice if he moved his chair next to hers.

The Queen of Hearts, she made some tarts, on a summer's day. The Queen of Tarts, she stole my heart on this summer's day.

He snickered again, oblivious to what was going on around him, adrift in a sea of thoughts.

"But whether or not," Jono said, "they were considered the missing link or first man himself, they had a bad reputation, because my friends, they were considered to be cruel and 'untameable.' One anthropologist said the cruelty with which the Bushman would carry out his raids put him 'outside the pale of humanity.' It was said he can never be trusted, that he is the true anarchist of Africa."

"Jolly good," Richard said, "the outlaw wild man."

"Except that no one thought it was good and by 1905, the life of a Bushman was worth nothing. You see," Jono explained to his attentive audience, "the Bushman had no respect for money or for the white man values of daily hard work, of always preparing for the future. He lived for his freedom and his tobacco, not for a house and a farm and a routine, and he suffered greatly for it. He was hunted, chained, punished and killed for any number of offences: laziness, stock theft, disobedience, vagrancy, desertion, insult, drink, escape, robbery and murder. He was punished for disobeying the white man's rules, most of which he had no idea even existed; he just lived as he always had."

"We did the same to the Native Indians and Inuit in Canada," Kate said.

"And the U.S. did it to the American Indians and the black slaves, and Australia to the Aborigines," Lena chimed in.

"South America and the Incas," Enrique offered.

"Yes, we get the picture," Stepfan was sour. "It's a world-trend through the ages."

"Which does not make it right." Sofie cried out. "It's no less shocking because it's historically prevalent."

Stepfan shrugged. "Man is man. We like to pretend we're civilized but when it comes down to it, we're not."

"By this time," Jono said, ignoring Stepfan, "the Bushmen had been divided into three groups: the 'wild', the 'semi-tame' and the 'tame' and all Bushman behaviour was categorized according to this. White settlers believed that a 'tame' Bushman was the ideal one because he would stay and work on the farms as cheap labour. But 'tame' Bushmen were rare because staying in one place was contrary to their ways; Bushmen were nomadic by nature and tradition. Being nomadic did not mean that he wandered aimlessly; he knew exactly where he needed to be at different times of the year according to nature and the seasons, but this did not accommodate the white man's needs for cheap labour and his lifestyle was declared illegal. And then things got worse. It was posited that the semi-erect penis of the Bushmen was a distinctive racial characteristic which was then used to identify him."

Stepfan jumped to his feet. "What does it mean when you have a huge penis that is constantly erect? I must be a Bushman of the first order."

"Stop it." Lena pulled him down.

Jono sighed out loud. "The point is, it was a very shocking thing to do, to stop a man and take a measurement of the angle of his private parts." He exchanged a glance with Treasure. "Are you ready for some dessert?"

"We're ready." Ellie and Jasmine leapt to their feet.

"The chocolate sauce is ready too." Treasure announced. "Jono, would you please fetch the ice-cream from the ice box in the bus?"

"I will." Harrison said quickly. "The ice box is most efficiently organized and Richard, I hope you did not disrupt my system when you got your beers."

"God forbid," Richard muttered, cleaning dirt out from under his fingernails.

Harrison returned. "It was not too badly upset," he said

sternly to Richard who tried not to laugh.

"I'm so relieved," he said dryly.

"Treasure, this is truly heaven," Sofie dug into her dessert. "Oh, oh, oh."

"Tonight's ice-cream soft-porn melting moment is brought to you by Sofie," Stepfan said. "Listen to Sofie as she takes it in her mouth and wait, will she, won't she, yes, she swallows."

"You're so disgusting, Stepfan," Kate said, with Sofie and Gisela agreeing loudly. Lena seemed lost in her own world and was gazing out into the darkness.

"Come now ladies, have a sense of humour. I'm only joking around a bit. Lighten up."

"Charisse," Treasure asked, "won't you have any dessert?"

Charisse blushed, wishing Treasure had not said anything. "Keeping an eye on my figure," she joked.

"And a very fine figure it is too," Stepfan piped up and Lena clenched her jaw.

Jasmine's enjoyment for her dessert vanished; she had watched Charisse and noticed that she hardly ate a thing and Jasmine took this as a personal slight, as if every mouthful Charisse did not eat was a reproach for every one that Jasmine swallowed. Jasmine had no way of knowing that far from subsiding, Charisse's stomach pains were getting worse.

Jasmine pushed her bowl away and turned to listen to what Jono was saying.

"Treasure's dessert has made me forget where I was with my story..." Jono said. "To continue, the Bushman calls himself Ju, which means 'people', in the same way one might say lion, or elephant. They see people as only one of the numerous species of Creation permitted to walk on the face of the earth. We humans are not superior to other creatures but are simply fellow eaters of food, fellow dwellers on this planet. Life in the wilderness is a struggle between equals who have equal rights to live, eat, die, and be eaten. The Ju say they have words in their bodies and by this they mean that they have dreams that are premonitions and that is why they are powerful and highly respected diviners."

"Words in their bodies." Lena leaned forward. "How lovely."

"Not as lovely as you," Jono blurted out, surprising himself and the others. "You are the supermodel on this trip, Lena. How is it you are never dirty, or wrinkled or tired?"

"I trained her well," Stepfan stated proudly and Lena slapped him lightly on the arm.

"You trained nothing."

Jasmine, uncomfortable on her tiny stool, felt even more bitter. Another example of the importance of looks. Lovely Lena and cheerleader Charisse, getting all the applause and attention. Jono would never compliment her, not in a million years, and she wished everyone had to live in her body just for one day, because then they would change their way of thinking, yes, they would. It made her sick that even Jono thought like that and she was disappointed in him. She looked at Lena and felt a wave of dislike.

Jono gave a small bow in Lena's direction.

"There is one final fact I would very much wish to share with you. Will you indulge me?"

The group nodded encouragingly.

"You all know of the Nazis, yes?"

"Of course," the group was disoriented by this turn.

"Hitler was not the first to use concentration camps. The British implemented secured 'camps' for civilian enemies during the Second Boer War in South Africa. Boer women and children and black civilians were put in these concentration camps and a lot of them died. But that is not all; the connections between Nazi totalitarianism and South African apartheid can be traced to right here in Namibia."

"What do you mean?" Marika spoke up. "I've never heard that."

Jono nodded. "Back when Namibia was a German colony called German South West Africa, war was being waged between the Herero and the German settlers and General Lothar von Trotha put the Herero into concentration camps and killed close to 70,000. This General also invited a certain Dr. Eugene Fischer, an anthropologist, to come and study the captured Herero.

"Based on his visit, Dr. Fischer wrote *Principles of Human Heredity and Racial Hygiene,* in which he claimed that the Herero were animals and that the German race was superior and he applauded von Trotha's concentration camps. Adolf Hitler read Dr. Fischer's book in jail and it contributed to his writing of *Mein Kampf.* This same Dr. Fischer was put in charge of training the SS doctors who later performed experiments in the concentration camps."

"Oh my God," Sofie said, "it's all entwined."

Jono nodded. "And it gets even more so. Marika, do you know who Dr. Hendrik Verwoerd is?"

"Of course. He was a prime minister of South Africa and the so-called architect of apartheid."

"Quite correct. And Dr. Verwoerd also studied under Dr. Fischer in Berlin which gives evidence of a very strong link between the origins of Nazism and apartheid."

Marika was horrified. "Jono, how come I didn't know?"

"History is written by those in power." Jono shrugged. "We are told what they want us to know."

"But what about now? Why hasn't this been brought to anyone's attention now?"

"Because," Stepfan flicked at the ground with a twig, "no one cares. People like you think you're supposed to care but in reality, no one does. Life's about power and money, and there's no profit to be made by talking about ancient history."

Kate looked over at Lena and wondered how she could be married to such a man. Lena was staring down at her clasped hands, her face closed.

"Stepfan, there is no point in even trying to talk to you," Sofie said.

"I outwit you my dear, it's as simple as that."

"You see," Enrique burst out, "that's why I like flowers better. They don't torture or kill each other like men do." He'd been quiet throughout the evening, listening intently.

Eva, sitting next to him, nodded.

"What a nice fireside chat this is," Stepfan frowned and leaned forward. "Do you have much more you'd like to share with us, Jono?"

"Does it make you uncomfortable to hear some hard truths?" Harrison asked. "Too close to home for you perhaps?"

"We Germans are always blamed for everything." Stepfan retorted. "I can't even go on holiday without finding myself accused of some genocide or other. It gets very boring."

"Stepfan!" Sofie cried out.

"What? You armchair moralists, what do you want *me* to do about it? Say that I'm sorry? It's all the fashion these days, to apologize, as if that fixes anything. I'm so bored of it — the guilt, the shame. We need to move on. That's all in the past. We need to get on with our lives and I, for one, want to get on with my holiday."

"Leave if you're not enjoying yourself," Harrison gave a dismissive wave of his hand. "Unlike you, Stepfan, I like to know about the people in whose land I am a guest."

Kate shot a glance at Rydell, wondering if he would pop up and recite something from his book on filth and protuberances but he was lost in his own world. She watched his lips moving silently, as if he was reciting a prayer or a poem. He was dressed as always from head to toe in pale, wrinkle-free attire and he must have sensed her gaze because he looked up at her. She smiled at him and he offered his wet twisted grimace in return, immediately looking away and flicking at his trousers.

"Does anybody have any questions?" Jono asked.

"I do have a question," Richard said. "It's about the Bushmen and trance dances. I'm dying to hear more. Mia and I are hoping to attend one ... or have one or some such..."

"Enough talking, it's nearly 9:30 and we must do the dishes..." Harrison said.

"Dishes ... forget the stupid dishes..." a chorus rose.

"I don't think the dishes will suffer, waiting for another half an hour," Helen's tone was cutting and she leaned back on her stool with her hands in her pockets.

"I've been thinking about paper plates..." Harrison began but he was shouted down.

"The trance dance," Jono said, "has the women sitting in a circle around the fire, clapping and singing. The men dance around them, trying to enter a trance. They believe that when they are in this state, they gain supernatural powers from some of the animals they respect, and from their ancestors. Then they lay their hands on the sick people and the sickness comes from them and goes into the medicine man, who is also known as a shaman, and it comes out through a hole in his neck, called the '*n//au*' spot."

"Is this the same as the *sangoma* dance we talked about last night?" Richard frowned in concentration.

"There are similarities but it is different. The end result is also to heal but the way of doing it varies, although both tap into ancestral spirits and ask them for help. The shaman is the one who enters the trance in order to heal, to protect from evil spirits, to foretell the future, bring good weather, and generally look after the well-being of his people."

"These fellows aren't crazy like the *sangomas*?" Jasmine asked.

"They are not filled with the *sangoma* madness we were discussing, nor are they trained in the same way as the *sangoma*, who spends years learning his craft. These are ordinary people who use dance to channel energies to receive visions and help to heal. Dancing has always been an integral part of African society; we dance to celebrate, to heal, to offer prayers; all sorts of things. Every African was born to dance."

Mia put her fingers to her mouth and gave a loud whistle of appreciation. "How, exactly do you make a trance dance happen?" She pulled her cardigan tightly around her, unscrewed a bottle of vanilla vodka and signalled to Jasmine who dragged her chair to sit beside her.

"The first few hours are relaxed and sociable and the women sit and clap and sing while the men dance around them. The men have rattles on their legs made from dried seed pods," Jono explained.

"Bleedin' sexist," Mia objected, "I want to dance, not sit and clap and I also want to wear seed pods on me legs."

"I suppose you can do whatever you like," Jono said, "but it is generally a man thing. Anyway, the dancers go faster and faster until they start to hyperventilate and that, with their intense concentration and the rhythm of the dancing, makes the potency of the moment come to a 'boil' as they call it, and they alter their state of consciousness. If a shaman is inexperienced and cannot control his concentration, he falls unconscious to the ground. The shaman also sweats a lot and breathes heavily and he has a glassy stare, like he is 'seeing beyond', which is how they describe it."

"Sounds like a sort of self-hypnosis," Eva commented.

"Or like an intense meditation," Sofie said, "where you kind of leave your body and enter a spiritual world."

Jono agreed. "Shamans often have nose bleeds and experience terrible physical pain because trying to access this other world hurts a lot. When they are in the trance, they lay their hands on people and perform the most important of all their tasks, that of curing people. They draw the sickness into their own bodies and with a high-pitched scream, they expel it through the hole that I told you about."

"Where does the sickness go, once it comes out of the neck?" Eva enquired.

"It is thought that it goes back to its source and the source is wicked, unidentified shamans," Jono explained.

"Have you ever seen a trance dance or been in one?" Gisela asked.

"No, but I have spoken to a lot of people who have attended them and you will meet one such person when we get to Sossuvlei. His name is Thaalu and he is a wonderful Bushman, who will take you on a walking tour and you can ask him all your questions."

"A trance dance is really like a rave, isn't it?" Mia said. "Who knew a rave was a spiritual ceremony. I think we should have one with just us."

"Having a hole cut in my throat and a nosebleed isn't my idea of fun," Helen was scathing. "But each to his own."

"I don't think we should fool around with things like that," Marika hugged her arms to her chest. "You never know what kinds of evil you might stir up."

"Afraid of a little black magic are you?" Richard joked, "I'm not afraid."

"Then you are foolish," Jono looked at him steadily. "There are always consequences and you should have respect for that which you do not understand."

"He understands," Mia asserted. "Take drugs, dance around a fire, wave your arms and see visions. Our kind of party."

"Jono, last night you mentioned that you knew about *muti* killings and such, can you tell us about them?" Richard asked.

"That is a whole different kettle of fish," Jono replied, "and I'm very tired now, so *muti*, which is traditional African medicine for those of you who do not know, is a topic for another time. And now I must change the subject entirely and ask who wants to go canoeing tomorrow morning? I must let them know at the lodge office."

Richard, Mia, Ellie, Jasmine, Brianna and Enrique put up their hands.

"A big round of applause for Professor Jono." Richard said and the group clapped enthusiastically.

Jono smiled and set off across the lawn. He had found the

group to be very tiring but he hoped that Kate had been impressed by his knowledge — that at least would have made the evening worthwhile.

Kate and Harrison were left to clean up the mess, while the others settled down at the pub where multi-coloured lights hung from the trees and there was the faint smell of citronella on the breeze.

Mia drew patterns on the wooden table top with a melting ice cube while she and Jasmine made inroads into the beer, shooting back vodka on the side.

"Look Richard, *MheartR*."

"Very nice," Richard patted her back.

"Sounds like a riot," Mia said, "the old trance dance. We should 'ave one."

Richard agreed. "We'll need to get masks and drums for a start."

"We should have one every night," Ellie piped up. "It'd be better than history lessons on the Bushmen."

"I bleedin' second that." Mia high-fived her across the table.

"We should do one around Rydell's tent to cure him of snoring," Richard commented. "Have you heard him? Snores like a hyena on steroids."

"I heard him alright," Stepfan was bitter. "I didn't sleep one single wink last night because of him and then I slept all day on the bus and missed everything — great."

"I've never heard anything like it," Richard said, swigging beer.

"Be careful, here he comes," Sofie warned.

"Who cares?" Stepfan said. "With that sort of medical condition, he shouldn't inflict himself on us normal people trying to have a holiday."

Rydell sat down and ordered a beer.

"As well as the trance dance, I really want to learn how to do the Marula," Mia said. "I saw a fing about it on YouTube, it's a famous African dance."

"Yeah, right, elephants get drunk on the fruit from the Marula tree," Jasmine said. "And there's that liqueur made from it too. Let's get some in the next town."

"Jasmine," Stepfan said suddenly and Gisela saw Lena stiffen. "May I please ask you a question?"

"Sure you can," Jasmine was affable. "Ask away."

"How is it, and why – and mind you I'm only concerned for your well-being – are you the big size woman that you are? Because you are, or could be fairly attractive. Why you don't try to lose some weight?"

The others, horrified by the turn of conversation, did not know what to say.

"My goodness," Jasmine was shocked, tears welling in her eyes, "No one's ever asked me anything like that. I've told you before, I've got a lot of medical issues and I do exercise a lot so this is just me."

"A calorie's a calorie, you either burn it off or it gets stored as fat. You must eat more than you burn off. Why don't you stop yourself from doing this? It's not healthy, never mind the damage it does to your attractiveness level."

Jasmine was searching for a reply when Rydell piped up.

"If you were a Hottentot, you'd be considered very beautiful. The Hottentots love a fat girl so much that young girls preparing for marriage drink liquid fat. The fatter they are, the more value they have and a big bottom is especially good."

"They drink fat?" Gisela said. "That's revolting."

"It is, but that's because they're dirty," Rydell was emphatic. "They find peculiar pleasure in dirt and stench and are among the filthiest people in the world, although they're not considered *the* filthiest. The women eat the vermin that swarm in their clothing and the details of their marriage ceremonies are too monstrous to talk about." He giggled.

"Crikey Moses, where on earth do you get these dodgy facts?" Mia enquired. "You sound like *National Geographic* gone haywire."

"From a book called *Primitive Love and Lovestories*. So," he turned toward Jasmine but she had vanished and he looked disappointed.

"*How to Win Friends and Influence People*," Richard said dryly. "Well done, Rydell."

"I'm going to take a shower," Lena stood up, "See you in the morning."

She walked off and Gisela jumped up to follow her.

"I'm going to find Jasmine," Ellie untangled her gangly limbs from the bench.

"Tell her chin up," Richard said, "some opinions just aren't worth getting upset about."

Charisse arrived, freshly showered and sat down next to Stepfan. "What did I miss?"

"Not a thing," Stepfan said, rubbing her leg under the table.

"We're calling it a night too," Richard got to his feet. "We've got to be up bright and early for canoeing."

"I was thinking of taking a walk down by the river," Charisse said, "any takers?"

"I'll come," Stepfan got up and they disappeared into the darkness leaving Rydell alone at the table.

Eva arrived, looking for Kate.

"She must still be doing dishes. I didn't realize it was only you here, Rydell."

"I heard you're a poet," Rydell's eyes glistened. "Do you want to hear a real African poem?"

"Some other time," Eva was firm but he grabbed her and recited:

"*My lioness.*
Are you afraid that I may bewitch you?
You milk the cow with fleshy hand.
Bite me."

He stared at Eva and she tugged her hand free and ran back up to the tents.

Left alone at the table, Rydell smiled to himself but then all at once he frowned and slammed his hand hard on the table. "It's not going very well at all," he said out loud. "Not well at all."

A couple of hours later, Rydell lay snuggled against the side of Treasure's tent, hoping for sounds of her readying for bed. She muttered a few times, slipped into her sleeping bag and gave a few deep sighs which gave way to small keening noises. Rydell smiled. That she was troubled boded well for him; her life stresses would no doubt increase the appeal of his offer.

The temperature dropped sharply but Rydell, lying on the damp chilly grass, did not feel the cold. Undetectable in black clothing and settling in for the night, he was startled when Treasure unzipped her tent and he crept around to see her padding across the grass to the washroom.

Rydell dove into her tent and searched for a memento but Treasure's possessions were meager. He opened her toiletry bag and grabbed a small white soapbox. He rushed out and hid behind the tent, worried that Treasure would notice something when she came back but she climbed back into her sleeping bag muttering under her breath and soon fell asleep.

Lost in a fantasy in which he lay close to her naked warmth, Rydell popped open the soapbox and undid his trousers. He inhaled the rose-scented fragrance like an addict, and tried not to groan as he pumped with increasing urgency, soon ejaculating in a hot rush. Filled with glory, he went to the washroom to clean up. For once, he liked what he saw in the mirror. He washed his hands sparingly with Treasure's precious soap and then he went to bed, soon shattering the peaceful reprieve of the noiseless night.

To the Fish River Canyon

KATE WOKE EARLY AND LISTENED to Rydell's noisy exhalations, thinking about the strange poem he had recited to Eva.

Eva had bumped into a weeping Jasmine, followed by Ellie who told her what had happened at the pub. "Stepfan pretends to love women but deep down he hates us," Eva said. "He makes me sick. And if you ask me, Harrison's obsessive compulsive but not dangerous, while Rydell is weird with the definite capacity for violence."

"But would they let a seriously deranged person on a trip?"

"How would they know the difference? They wouldn't. It's not like we've got to give them a Hello-I'm-Sane certificate. Pay and you're in. But in my feedback to them, I'm going to suggest they do some sort of psych evaluation before letting people sign up."

Tucked into the cosy warmth of her sleeping bag and thinking about what Eva had said, Kate was tempted to snooze but she did not want to miss the beautiful African sunrise and she got up, careful not to disturb Marika. It was still dark out, with birds singing a multitude of songs and flitting from tree to tree. The broad river was black in the predawn light, with the far-off mountains ghostly gray shapes against the sky and the bulrushes' tall silhouettes standing silent sentry.

Once the sun came up, Kate went in search of fossils and later, in excellent spirits, having filled her camera bag with rocks, she joined the others for breakfast and found them sitting morosely in a circle in silence. "Holy Mackinaw," she said, thinking she sounded like her father, "what happened? Did someone die?" She helped herself to breakfast cereal.

"They did not," Stepfan said. "Not yet, anyway. I couldn't sleep all night because of the *noise*," He glared at Rydell who was spooning cereal into his mouth, lost in his own world.

"Treasure is upset with me because I want to help her with the food preparation," Harrison said, looking up from his notebook.

"I'm not surprised she wasn't happy," Kate looked over at a clearly disgruntled Treasure. "Treasure's got her way of doing things and we shouldn't interfere."

Treasure shot her a grateful look.

Just then the canoeists arrived, sunburned and smiling.

"It was excellent." Mia was wide-eyed and breathless. "Never had so much fun in me whole bleedin' life."

"A ringing indictment of our relationship," Richard commented dryly, "But I concur, it was fantastic and Jasmine was positively masterful."

Jasmine beamed in appreciation and glowered at Stepfan, still smarting from his comments from the previous night.

Stepfan, massaging his muscled arms appreciatively, did not notice her venom.

Jono arrived and poured a cup of coffee. "Good morning, everybody! We will be leaving for the Fish River Canyon in an hour. I am glad to see that everybody is having a good time!"

Kate found an empty seat next to Harrison and the bus was soon rumbling up the steep rocky slope and out onto the long, pale dusty road. While Kate was lost in a daydream of fossils and rocks as big and perfectly round as soup bowls, Harrison fussed with his notebook and rearranged his bag. When it was organized to his satisfaction, he launched a missile of chatter at Kate about his travels, his hobbies, the tenants who shared his house and his work history. Half an hour later, she was ready to scream and it was clear that he had only just begun. Harrison did not converse; he discoursed, amphetamine-style, and Kate thought that while Rydell's repartee had been bizarre, at least he had been somewhat interesting.

Rydell had an empty seat next to him and Kate eyed it longingly. Also, Harrison's 'optimal ventilation system' was searing her eyeballs with a blistering wind. She looked around in desperation and caught Marika's eye. Marika laughed and nodded, making a spiraling motion next to her temple with her forefinger. "Cuckoo," she mouthed and Kate nodded in fervent agreement and after a while, she decided she had to move.

"Harrison," she interrupted him, "I'm going to sit next to Rydell," and she rushed over to Rydell before Harrison could say anything further.

Rydell was pleased to see her and he was in the mood to chat. "You remember our conversation?" he immediately asked her.

"Yes..." Kate said cautiously, thinking that he smelled slightly perfumed and oddly feminine.

"Remember I told you my plan had changed and that I had found The One?"

"Yes, I remember. Who is she?"

"I'll give you a clue," Rydell wet his lips. "She's something you hunt for and she's a gift when you find her," he clasped his hands together in glee.

Kate was bewildered. "Easter eggs?"

"Easter eggs? You're no good at this. Here's another one. She's what you find at the end of the rainbow."

"A pot of gold?" Kate was baffled than ever.

"Are you being stupid on purpose? Come on, *think*. Try this one; what do pirates find?"

"Hidden treasure," Kate gave the quick reply and then stopped. "Treasure? Do you mean *our* Treasure?" Her gaze shot to Treasure who was paging through a magazine with her blue baseball cap low on her forehead and her bare feet up on the dashboard. Treasure felt Kate's gaze and she turned and smiled and Kate smiled back.

She turned to Rydell. "You want to marry Treasure? But she's a tall Xhosa from Zimbabwe, which is a far cry from a small Bushwoman from Namibia."

"Africa is Africa," Rydell was dismissive. "It's all the same. Lobola and a wife for life who does whatever you want."

"It doesn't works like that, Rydell. It's not like buying a slave from hundreds of years ago. Nor do I think Treasure's the sort of woman who'll do whatever you want her to. She strikes me as very intelligent and independent. Does she know how you feel?"

"No, and you can't tell her. Promise me. I must court her properly."

"Are going to hunt an eland and present her with the tail or some other Bushman tactic?" Kate joked.

"No," Rydell was serious, "I'm going to hunt *her*."

Kate's amusement vanished. "What do you mean?"

"You'll see," Rydell was coy.

"I'm sure she mentioned something about a husband in Zimbabwe," Kate lied.

Rydell tittered. "I know you don't know that, you just don't want me to have her. But she will be mine. Remember you promised not to tell anyone what I said."

"I promise. Rydell, do you have any medication?"

Rydell was terrified. "What do you mean?" he demanded and there was a fleck of spittle on his lips.

"Headache meds. Harrison's darn 'open ventilation system' blew a furnace on my face and I've got a killer headache."

Rydell was relieved her request was so harmless.

"No, I don't. I don't believe in taking pills of any kind. My mother died from an overdose."

"Oh, I'm so sorry Rydell, I really am. How thoughtless of me." Kate did not want to sound unsympathetic but she felt that something about what he said did not ring true.

"It wasn't thoughtless, you didn't know," Rydell cocked his head sideways. "She was a beautiful singer and an exotic dancer in Las Vegas. A very good one. She had all kind of connections. She liked dangerous men and a glamorous life. And once she was sucked into that world, she couldn't get out except by killing herself." He spoke with an odd self-importance, once again sounding false and rehearsed to Kate.

"And what about your father?" she asked.

"My father's an extremely important man but he had his other family, his socially acceptable, legitimate family so he didn't have much time for me."

"How old were you when your mother died?" Kate had the distinct feeling that none of this was true.

"Sixteen. I've been on my own ever since. I'm fifty-one."

Kate was surprised. "I would have sworn you were about forty. How do you keep your skin so nice and smooth?"

Rydell grew uncomfortable under Kate's scrutiny. "Good genes, I guess," he squirmed.

Kate rubbed her temples and Rydell stopped fidgeting around. "What a tough life you've had," she said. "You never married?"

"Not yet. But soon." He wet his lips in his nervous way. "Until now I haven't found the right woman. Women want to eat you up; they're big fat hairy spiders in tight satin dresses with fake fat breasts and fat mouths filled with plastic. Makeup put on with a trowel, shiny wet red lips. No thank you."

"My head's killing me," Kate said, thinking she had to deflect the conversation or least be drugged to listen. "I've got to find some meds. Who'll have, do you think?"

"I've got no idea," Rydell pursed his lips. "If you ask me, this is a very strange bunch of people."

Kate suppressed a smile and decided to start with Jasmine. She had heard Jasmine offer all kinds of antihistamines to Brianna and her instinct proved correct.

"Acetaminophen, aspirin or ibuprofen? Or Robaxicet?" Jasmine was sitting next to Ellie who was fast asleep.

"I don't know. Ibuprofen, I guess. Thanks, Jasmine."

She took the pills and clambered back to her seat, relieved to find that Rydell had withdrawn into himself and had his back to her. She swallowed the pills, plugged in her earphones and waited for the pain in her head to ease.

Next to her, lips moving silently, Rydell rehearsed what he would say to Treasure later that night. He was once again furious with himself for confiding in Kate. It was as if he both wanted and loathed her approval, which was exactly as it had been with his mother. He had thought he was beyond such concerns but clearly not. He pushed those thoughts away and imagined taking Treasure aside and letting her know his intentions. He told himself he could do it, that it was his destiny, and when his courage faltered, he sniffed the tiny piece of soap he had wrapped in his handkerchief.

Several seats behind, Lena looked at her sleeping husband and came to a conclusion. She had to get rid of that little tramp Charisse. Make her sick enough to leave the trip. Because Lena could not go on this way. She looked over at Charisse who was innocently reading a book and felt a surge of hatred. *Go and find your own man. Stop chasing my man. He's mine, mine.*

She stroked Stepfan's head and he grunted slightly. She admired his classical features, his strong jaw, his dimples, the cleft in his chin. He was her husband and she had to fight for him, just like she always had. She tried to forget how he had hurt her over and over again with his shameless affairs, and she told herself the same thing she always had: *I'm his wife. No one can ever take that away from me. I'm his wife.*

She had to poison Charisse. Just enough to give her a stomachache and get her off the bus. She had not been planning anything when she broke off a piece of that lethal bush. Yes, Stepfan had cut her to the quick when he left her to follow Charisse but she had had no particular thought in mind when she had found herself alone and before she could consider her actions, she folded her bandanna, wrapped it around a branch of the poisonous bush and twisted hard. Something about the action made her feel powerful, invincible.

Stepfan grunted in his sleep and shifted on her shoulder.

I can't be alone. I've always had Stepfan to take care of me. I don't care if it's weak, it's who I am. I can't live this life alone. Yes, I had a good job but the backbone of my life has always been Stepfan.

She just had to find a way to put a tiny piece of the plant in Charisse's water and then everything would be fine.

"Tell me, my friend," Treasure said to Jono, her feet up on the dashboard and a magazine balancing on her legs, "are you enjoying this group of crazies or what?"

"*Ei*, Treasure, funny you should ask that…"

Treasure put down her magazine. "What's on your mind, Jono?"

He rubbed his arms as if he had a chill. "I get a bad feeling from this group."

"Why?"

"Really, I do not know." He was reluctant but needed to say what he was thinking. "I thought maybe, that first night, that they would be a good lot but now I have changed my mind. They are too restless and so many of them are unhappy, there is an undercurrent and I do not know why I feel it this strongly but I do. *Ei*. And we are only starting really, there is so much road ahead of us and already I feel like there is trouble brewing."

Treasure nodded, sighed and patted his arm. "We'll do our best along the way. We've always been fine, you and me, we're a team of survivors, isn't that right? Try not to worry about it."

Jono was not reassured.

Treasure pondered for a moment and reached for her cell phone. No messages. No missed calls. She sighed again and picked up her magazine.

By the time they reached the next campsite, Kate's headache was gone. She grabbed a tent bag and joined Marika who had secured them a spot under a tree.

"We're definitely in the bush now, just a lot of sand, rocks, dust, thorn trees and aloes. No more manicured green lawns or flower beds."

"I like this one better," Kate said and Marika agreed.

While Marika crawled into the tent and changed into her bathing suit, Kate picked up her camera and ambled down the dusty road.

The first thing Helen did, once her tent was pitched, was grab her running shoes. Her craving to enter the numb zone was so strong she could think of little else. *Like mother like daughter. I'm an addict too.* She half-listened to Sofie chatting nineteen to the dozen about her spring wedding, her dog, and her happy life back home while scrambling through her mess of things to find her bathing suit. "Excuse me," she smiled grimly at Sofie, "I simply *must* run."

Rydell emerged from his tent and watched her as she did a few stretches and eased rhythmically into her stride. *One, two, buckle my shoe, see how she runs, see how she runs. They all ran after the farmer's wife, did you ever see such a thing in your life? She's a blind mouse, she's a blind mouse.*

Then he watched Jasmine, Ellie, Richard and Mia head off to the swimming pool, all of them doubled over at a joke Richard had made. *Birds of a feather flock together, and so will pigs and swine; rats and mice will have their choice and so will I have mine.*

He looked thoughtfully over at Treasure's tent. *Rydell, Rydell people-eater, had a wife and couldn't keep her. Put her in a pumpkin shell and there he kept her very well. Yes, put her in a pumpkin shell and there he kept her, very well.*

When Kate got to the swimming pool she saw Stepfan splashing

Charisse, with an unhappy Lena watching. Richard was lying on a towel on the parched grass, next to Mia who was also baking in the hot sun. "Hi, Kate," he said, looking up at her as she leaned over the waist-high white fence.

Kate laughed. "Talk about mad dogs and Englishmen. It's over 40 degrees. Are you both crazy?"

"Surfing the high wave of Vitamin D," Richard shaded his face with his hand to look up at her.

"Must soak it up while we can," Mia said in a muffled voice. She was lying on her stomach with her forehead on her crossed arms and her pale skin was turning a painful scarlet.

"What a Casanova not, eh?" Richard said to Kate, nodding over at Stepfan. "Really thinks he's Mr. Charming but what I find unfathomable is why a girl like Charisse laps it up like she does."

"Low self-esteem and daddy issues," Mia said, raising her head off her arms, with deep towel creases on her forehead. "She tarts her body around, finking she doesn't deserve love so she takes it wherever it's offered. Odds are she was abused when she was little, and she probably hates herself for the fings she does but she's addicted to getting attention and she's got no bleedin' idea of what love really is."

"Thank you, Nurse Teller," Richard said. "I can always rely on you."

"You're a nurse?" Kate could not have been more surprised. She was surprised by the focus with which Mia had offered up the diagnosis. Kate was used to tipsy Mia, out-of-control, party girl; this somewhat-articulate persona was new and unexpected.

"Yeah, but a psychiatric nurse, not a blood and guts one," Mia rolled over and lay on her back. "For pete's sake, don't tell anyone. Once people hear you're a nurse, they're full of a thousand bleedin' aches and pains they want you to fix and truth is I don't give a flying sparrow's fart about their crap, I'm on holiday."

"I understand," Kate leaned on the white wrought-iron fence. "Gisela told us she's a sports therapist and next thing, Helen asked her to look at her knee. But enough sun for me, my poor little Canadian brain's boiling. See you later."

She walked back to the cool quiet of the old Colonial-style washrooms. She loved the chunky round-handled faucets, the silvered mirrors speckled with age spots and the uneven mosaic countertops. She was trying to find the best angle for a shot of the curtains fluttering above the old-fashioned cisterns when she heard a familiar laugh.

"Why am I not surprised," Eva said, resting against the toilet door, her red and black Mickey Mouse towel wrapped around her waist. "Everyone's at the swimming pool, eating ice cream and sun tanning and where are you? In the toilet, taking photographs."

"It's a dirty job but someone's gotta do it." Kate grinned.

Eva ducked into the washroom stall emerging a few minutes later to wash her hands. "You'll have to excuse me my friend, I actually have to use one of these. What on earth are you photographing anyway?"

"The plug hole," Kate was bent over the basin, "Look at the shape of it, Eva, it's a work of art I tell you."

"A masterpiece. But I must drag you away from your Picasso plug hole or you'll be late for the Fish River Canyon walk."

"It's more like a Salvador Dali plug hole..." Kate started to say and they both laughed.

"This is me in front of the Fish River Canyon, the second biggest canyon in the world," Sofie announced.

Rydell hovered at the edge of the canyon. "If you fuh-fell down there, you would die." he stuttered. He seemed upset, more distracted than usual and kept tugging and adjusting his clothing.

"Try not to put it to the test old chap," Richard said, peering down into the canyon. "The view's certainly incredible but not nearly as incredible as how fantastic that swim felt. This is magnificent and all that and I hope none of you think I'm a stick in the mud, but I'm getting a bit tired of this dust. I wouldn't have minded hanging about the pool for the whole afternoon, wallowing in the glorious hydration aspects of it all."

"Oy, me too," Mia groaned. "I'm tired of this walking, I want to lie next to the pool and get quietly pissed."

"Not your style my love," commented Richard, "the quiet bit I mean."

She punched his shoulder playfully.

"Ouch," he objected, "my sunburn."

"I also wish we were swimming instead," Jasmine said and Ellie, Charisse, and Bree quickly agreed.

Gisela and Lena had strolled up ahead, with Stepfan and Harrison setting off at a run, racing to see who could make it back to the bus in the fastest time.

"Let's hotfoot it back to the bus," Richard said, "and suggest to the others that we don't hang about for the sunset but go back and swim instead?"

"Yes," Rydell shouted, "let's get back to the camp as soon as we can." He set off at a run, his jerky style causing a contradiction of movements, his arms and legs wind-milling at odds with each other.

"Mad as a hatter, poor chap," Richard said, watching him and he turned back to his little party. "All in favour of getting this over with say 'aye'."

"Aye," they all hooted loudly and they set off at a fast pace.

Kate, Eva and Marika looked at one other.

"Do you think they'll leave without us?" Eva asked, "because I for one am not rushing this."

"Me neither," Enrique appeared from behind a large pile of rocks, where he had been photographing a tiny cluster of desert flowers.

"I'm with you," Sofie said, climbing up from a ledge.

"Me too," Helen said, back from a short run to explore the opposite trail.

"Then," Enrique said, "let's do this our way and enjoy every moment."

They took their time and watched the darkening light wash the canyon valleys with dark paint, and as the world turned away from the sun, the earth glowed a fiery, brilliant red.

The Fourth Night

"Did you have a good time?" Treasure asked when they returned. "I made a South African favourite for supper: Curried Pilchard Macaroni Bake, to give you lots of energy after that exercise."

Charisse groaned loudly.

"I don't think my stomach could handle anything as heavy as pasta with fish. Treasure, I'll just have a piece of toast if you don't mind."

Jasmine rounded on her. "Pasta's one of the best foods for you. You've got it wrong."

"I don't comment on what you eat, so back off." Charisse did not want to admit that her stomach was hurting more than ever and that she was hardly able to eat a thing. She hated being sick, hated being the centre of attention that illness brought, and she hated appearing to be vulnerable in any way. She was determined not to let the pain interfere with the hot romance between her and Stepfan, and she hoped the annoying virus, or whatever it was, would work its way out of her system soon.

"It's none of your business, what she eats." The generally quiet Brianna spoke up in Charisse's defence. "Just leave her alone."

"I'm entitled to my opinion," Jasmine countered but Treasure intervened.

"Stop fighting, all of you,," Treasure said. "Charisse, I will make you some toast."

Charisse thanked her and glared at Jasmine who returned the look.

"Wash your hands, remember to wash your hands." Harrison called out. He had stayed behind at the camp to prepare supper with Treasure, much to Rydell's anguish and Treasure's dismay. Rydell had only noticed that Harrison was missing when they were on the bus heading for the canyon and it was too late for him to change his mind and stay too.

"There are two bowls here," Harrison said, "one is for washing your hands with soap and the other is for rinsing your hands, and there is a hand towel that must be used for nothing except the handwashing. There is also hand sanitizer next to the hand towel but that is optional. People, please get into a line to wash your hands."

"Harrison's a bleedin' freak show," Mia whispered to Richard who nodded. "I'm going to get my cardy," she said and she headed off to their tent with Richard in tow.

"I'm so pissed off," she hissed at him, digging through her bag for her sweater. "They ruined it, those bleedin' nature freaks. We had to wait there for bleedin' hours and we lost out on our swim. I'm so angry I could spit." She was shaking with anger and close to tears.

"Sssh," Richard pulled her close, hugged her and patted her back.

"I know you're upset, love, but you have got to remember the real reason we are here. It's not to swim or look at animals or say the desert's so lovely or get a tan or any of those things. Don't lose focus, this is all part and parcel of what we have to do to get what we want right? This is our dream, remember?"

He put his arm around her, and stroked her tangled hair. "Come now, my little chickadee, I know you're tired of this fucked-up flock of tossers, of the dust, the heat, the crappy food, the endless hours on the bus, oh, that nightmare of a bus, God, could they have got anything cheaper, hotter or more noisy? I don't think so. I'm so over it too — taking those ancient bloody tents up and down, having inane conversations and giving shit-eating grins all the time. At least Jono's got some interesting stuff to say, he's an unexpected treat."

"Argggh. I'm sick of him too." Mia wailed. "Those bleedin' lessons, it's like I'm back at school or something. I hate it."

"Ssssh. I know you're tired but keep fantasizing because it will all be worth it, I promise you. Now, we should get back to the others."

"Richard luv, hang on a mo', don't go yet," Mia's voice was suddenly small. "I've got to tell you somefing." She hesitated briefly and gave a shuddering breath. "I'm preggers."

Richard stopped dead, then he swung around quickly and came up close to her. "What the fuck?" he whispered, his breath hot on her face. "How the fuck did that happen, you stupid tart? That's your area to take care of, and you fuck it up. And *now*? Like *now's* the time? Oh fuck. Oh you stupid, stupid cow."

He ran his fingers through his hair and rubbed his face. "Are you sure?" he asked her through gritted teeth.

She nodded. "I got some test thingies in Springbok. I'm sorry, I really am, I don't know how it 'appened. I can't have it taken care of when we get home, it'll be too late. I even thought maybe we could get it seen to here but we don't stop in any of the towns for long enough."

"We can't do anything here, too dangerous by far," Richard said, shortly. "We can't have you out of action if anything goes wrong." He thought for a moment while his mind raced to compute the unexpected problem.

"Fucking preggers. And you think your mum's going to raise this one too, do you? I don't think so. We were lucky she took Moira off our hands, not that she had much choice, you being fourteen would have made a great mum, yeah?"

"I said I was sorry, didn't I? And you can't blame me for Mo." She looked away. "Richard," she said, her voice still small. "You could do it. You know you could. You could take care of getting rid of it."

He went white and shuddered. "Not a chance in hell, Mia. Are you crazy?"

"I trust you. I'd trust you with my life. I know you could do it."

"Well, stop thinking about it because I can't and I won't." He fell silent, thinking.

"We'll stick to the game plan," he said, staring into the dark bush and scratching his chin. A few minutes later, he added, "Ignore the little fucker, pretend like it doesn't exist, right?"

Then he turned back to Mia. "Here's the torch," he said, holding it out to her. "Go to the little girl's room, fix your hair and wash your face. You look a right tart. Go, get cleaned up, come and get some supper. And when you get back, remember, proper jolly, right? No sniveling or nothing, you're Mia party animal, keep it up, keep smiling, remember what you came here to do, yeah?"

"You'd better watch yourself there, laddie." Mia's voice was cold. "Your accent's slipping." She snatched the torch from him. "I'll go and fix me face while you stand here and try to find your hoity-toity self, that sound good to you, Dickyboy?"

She marched off into the darkness and he heard her crash and curse her way through the trees, her light fading as she walked away.

The rest of the group dutifully washed their hands according to Harrison's instructions and piled their plates high.

"The pasta is delicious," Jasmine called out to Treasure, shooting a look at Charisse who ignored her.

Rydell kept staring at Treasure, his lips moving as if he was talking to himself.

Lena watched Charisse, eyeing her water bottle, her eyes narrowed and her senses sharp. Much to her frustration, and not for lack of trying, she had not found an opportunity to slip a piece of the poisonous bush into the girl's water.

Treasure, meanwhile, dished up the food, thinking about the phone message she had finally received. She was on her own with her growing baby. There would be no help coming from her married white man.

"Good evening, everybody!" Jono said, the whites of his eyes bright in the light of the campfire. "And how is everybody tonight?"

"Good, thank you," the chorus came back.

The fire pit was a small area ringed with curved wooden benches and the group squeezed together, balancing tin plates on their laps, with smoke from the fire whipping and blowing around their heads. The logs crackled and popped with sparks and the low hanging acacia branches kept the circle enclosed.

"Excellent. Now I must warn you that we have a very long, very tough drive ahead tomorrow. I want you to be prepared for it and we must leave early. We are going to Siesriem which is near to Sossuvlei, the heart of the Namib Desert and is a most special place. The day after tomorrow there is a guided walk there, with Thaalu, who is a very knowledgeable Bushman and I hope that you will all join him."

"How much is the walk?" Stepfan asked, attacking his food with noisy enjoyment.

"It is more expensive than the one with Kleine Skok because it also pays the entrance fee for Sossusvlei and a portion of the money goes towards the Bushmen such as Thaalu who look after it there. It is 180 rand per person," Jono said.

"That's ridiculous." Stepfan scraped his plate with his fork.

"For heaven's sake, Stepfan," Kate objected, "that's not even $25 and this is one of the highlights of the trip. I'm in for sure."

"Neither Lena or I are going." Stepfan said, picking his teeth. "It should be free, part of the trip."

"I'll do it," Harrison decided.

"And me," Rydell echoed. Treasure had disappeared and he was not sure if she was gone for the night. His need to talk to her was becoming unbearable and he scratched hard at his arms knowing he was drawing blood but that the darkness would hide his secret.

"I've got dessert for everyone," Jasmine said eagerly. "I got ingredients for smores for us at that little store we stopped at."

"Smores?" Gisela asked. "What are smores?"

"It's a campfire tradition," Ellie explained. "You toast a marshmallow, put it between two crackers and add chocolate. It's sort of like a dessert sandwich."

"I thought smores were Canadian, not Australian?" Kate asked.

"Nah, we've got them too. Maybe we borrowed them from you lot. I'll go and get the stuff, you guys get the sticks ready," Jasmine rushed off to her tent.

"Rydell," Ellie asked suddenly, "have you ever tried a smore?"

Rydell looked up, not pleased to have been drawn into the conversation. "No," he said shortly, swatting wildly at a small mosquito. "I haven't."

"Then I will have to come and sit next to you and show you how to do it," Ellie was being unmistakably flirtatious.

The others looked at her in surprise. Quiet, little Ellie had woken up but those familiar with Rydell's eccentricities could not understand her sudden interest and neither could Rydell who could not even remember her name and thought she was like a bony, graceless moth. He was focused on Treasure, trying to will her to return to the group and now he had big moth-girl in his face. He scowled.

Jasmine returned. "I'll go first and show you how it's done, then help yourselves."

"When will we be getting a full moon, Jono?" Richard asked. "I hear there's all kind of magic and power associated with an African moon."

"Full moon in two days. And yes, the moon is very important to African people. It is said that the King of the Universe gave the earth, and all the people in it, to the moon and when the

Sun arrived, he was so furious that he burnt the moon's face, which is why she still looks ashen to this day. But some say the moon and the sun are lovers and that when the moon vanishes for three days, she is with the sun, making love."

"Whimsical," Helen said, casting a glance at Richard and wondering where Mia was. She had noticed that Mia had been uncharacteristically quiet during supper and seemed to be in a bit of a disheveled state but then again, Mia was always a mess; she had to be the sloppiest, most untidy person Helen had ever known. Which was not true, and Helen's heart sank at the unwelcome reminder of her mother but rather than think about that, she looked over at Richard who also seemed distracted, as if he was making an effort to be jolly when it was not how he really felt.

Helen hoped there was trouble in paradise. She would love nothing more than to return to Cape Town with Richard on her arm, and find a way to bump into Robbie. She had reread Robbie's emails dozens of times and the bitterness she felt towards him was so strong it was like bile in her mouth. And while she had tried to insinuate herself into Richard's awareness at every possible instance, he hardly seemed to notice her.

"It's very lovely to think of the moon and the sun as lovers," Gisela said and Lena, sitting next to her, agreed. Stepfan looked up and glared at both of them.

"I find the reference to three days very interesting," Lena said, "It's like Easter, with Jesus rising from the dead after three days."

Jono agreed. "*Yebo*. In African stories of creation, and there are many different versions of this, the three day resurrection is often found also."

"Tell me," Sofie asked, "where do the Bushmen stand on reincarnation?" She played absent-mindedly with her Ganesh necklace as she spoke.

"*Ei* little Sofie, *haw!* but you like the complicated questions." Jono laughed. "All I can tell you is that African people believe very strongly in life before birth and in the existence of spirits, but the opinions on life after death are more varied. That is one you will have to research yourself and now, I must go to bed and prepare for tomorrow." He took another smore offered by Ellie and tried to meet Kate's eye but she was yawning and standing up to leave with Marika.

"We're going to bed too," Lena and Gisela said. "See you all tomorrow."

Rydell accepted that Treasure would not be coming back and he got up to go to his tent, much to Ellie's obvious disappointment. A lively life-after-death discussion erupted as he walked away, with opinions shouted from all sides, Stepfan and Sofie among the loudest.

Rydell was depressed by Treasure's disappearance. He had been preparing to talk to her the whole day. It was not fair, he never seemed to have any luck, as if his life was cursed from the moment he was born.

Kate and Marika were startled to be woken at midnight by Jasmine. "Come quickly, there's an elephant, I saw it, come with me." They quickly followed her and joined the rest of the pajama-clad lot.

"Where is Stepfan?" Lena asked. "Has anyone seen him?"

Brianna could not find Charisse either but she kept quiet. "I'm sure he's fine," she said to Lena, "probably in the washroom. Let's go and see this elephant, I was fast asleep and I want to get back to bed."

Jasmine led them through the camp.

"Is someone in the swimming pool?" Sofie asked. "I can hear splashing."

"The swimming pool's on the way," Jasmine herded them. "Let's go past and see." She led them to the pool and shone her flashlight on the swimmers. Fully illuminated and buck-naked, both Charisse and Stepfan screamed in horrified surprise while the group stood in shocked silence.

"We didn't need to see this," Brianna said, when the real purpose for Jasmine's urgent call became clear. "You've had it in for Charisse all along. This was none of your business, Jasmine."

Jasmine set her mouth in a stubborn pout. "They deserved it."

"Maybe they did, but did Lena?" Gisela was angry. She turned to see Lena disappearing into the darkness and Gisela rushed after her.

Stepfan and Charisse climbed out the pool shivering, and Brianna rushed over with their towels.

"We weren't doing anything wrong," Stepfan was defensive. "It's a hot night, we were taking a swim, that's all."

"Pull the other one, why don't you?" Richard said, "but who am I to judge? Come on, Mia, let's go back to bed."

The group walked off, followed by Brianna, Charisse and Stepfan. Jasmine was left alone. Despite her righteous anger, she felt ashamed and sad, and she sat down and wept in the darkness, her body shuddering.

To Siesriem

THE FOLLOWING MORNING, breakfast was a quiet affair. The group avoided eye contact and the only sounds were chattering birds and clinking tin plates.

Jono and Treasure exchanged glances and Jono's look asked Treasure a hundred questions but she shrugged and shook her head. She had no idea what had happened and she had even less interest in finding out. Her world felt weighed down and she was trapped and afraid. There was no rescue in sight and now she had another mouth to feed, another child to school, clothe, and look after. Who would help her now? Nobody.

She packed the pantry in silence, wordlessly stacking things passed to her by an equally subdued Harrison who had been dismayed by the incident at the pool; the entire situation had depressed him by its sad and sordid nature.

Everyone was relieved to get back on the bus, looking forward to being buffered in their own worlds by the noise of the engine and the jolting of punished steel on the rough road.

But when Kate climbed up, she spotted Ellie waving her over to an empty seat beside her. "I saved this one for you," she beckoned loudly and Kate sighed inwardly; something was going on with Ellie and she was about to find out, like it or not.

Kate glanced over at Charisse whose eyes were hidden by dark glasses, her skin blotchy and swollen. Brianna, next to Charisse, was clearly ready to challenge anyone who confronted her friend, glaring up as people made their way to their seats.

Jasmine's eyes were as equally as swollen and she looked the most miserable of the lot. Lena, sitting next to Harrison, was inscrutable apart from a certain set to her jaw.

Stepfan glared at Harrison, hoping to get him to move but Harrison ignored him. Out of deference to Lena, Harrison did not launch into his usual barrage of chatter.

Kate reluctantly sat down next to Ellie. "We've got a long way to go today and I feel very tired," she said, hoping that Ellie would get the hint, but Ellie needed to talk.

"Have you ever fallen in love with someone you shouldn't have?"

"Can't say I have," Kate sighed audibly this time. "I've been with my boyfriend forever."

"I'm here on this trip because I met this guy about a year ago and I fell for him just like that." Ellie snapped her fingers. "He came to install some glass at the lab and our eyes met and it was one of those electric things." Her face, suddenly lit with happiness at the memory, and just as quickly clouded over.

"My friends never liked him and they weren't wrong. He's a loser for sure, I know that. But he did something to me I can't explain. It's like I was addicted to him even though he treated me so badly; like he'd come and see me for sex at two or three in the morning and I'd let him, no matter what time it was. I was just so happy to see him and I gave him money for drugs. He deals drugs, nothing serious, just some cocaine and pot and ecstasy, but sometimes he'd run out of money and I'd help him. I could never say no even though he never paid me back."

"Are you still seeing him?" Kate asked politely. She wasn't overly surprised by what she was hearing; Ellie was a vacuum waiting to be filled.

"No. But," Ellie admitted with reluctance, "it's more like he's not seeing me. He dumped me for a high school cheerleader, can you believe that? When he left he told me I was never his type anyway — too tall, dark, and plain."

"You're better off without him." Kate was blunt. "He sounds like a real jerk." She realized she was feeling the same way about Cam, and that she was increasingly relieved to be free from the relationship she had once thought she would die without. She was also discovering that she enjoyed her own company; it felt good to be doing things for and by herself.

But Ellie didn't hear a word. "I did things for him, with him, that I never dreamt I'd do, that I'd never had occasion to do. He was the most exciting person I've ever been with. It's like I was free for the first time in my life and now everything's so *boring*. The sex was off the planet, wild. We had sex anywhere, anytime, in public places, you name it."

More information than Kate needed.

"And then, when you've had a taste of heaven, how do you adjust to normal life? It's all such a yawn. My stupid job, my stupid life, everything's boring. That's why my parents paid for this holiday, to try to get me excited about life, and I work with Jasmine who made it sound fantastic so I figured why not?"

Her face soured. "I thought it would be wild and dangerous and so far it's just history lessons, stupid fights and being on this bus like *forever*. It's as boring as the rest of my life."

"It depends on what you were expecting. I'm loving every second. How flexible you are makes a difference too. You need to see the best in a situation and take it from there."

"Yeah, really! That's *exactly* it. Make the best of things. I knew you'd understand. That's why I wanted to sit next to you because I want to ask you something. Rydell's a very interesting man and you've been sitting next to him a lot so you must know him best of all of us. Do you think he'd be interested in me? He's very sexy."

"I beg your pardon? Rydell? You find him sexy?"

"Yeah. He's got this like, mysteriousness to him. He's hot."

Kate could not have been more astonished if Ellie had told her a local ostrich was the new Brad Pitt. Rydell hot? She tried to see him from Ellie's perspective. She supposed he was not a bad-looking man when he stopped jerking and twitching.

"How old are you, Ellie?"

"Twenty-three."

"Here's what I think," Kate said, knew that whatever she said would not be be well-received. "Sometimes it's hard to see things for what they are. I understand, here you are, recovering from a broken heart and looking for adventure and a good time..."

"Totally." Ellie interrupted her. "Exactly. You totally get it."

"But Ellie," Kate tried to explain, "there are some men one should stay away from and truly, Rydell's one of them. He's different to us, to the rest of the world..."

"Who says different is bad? Different is good. Different is exciting."

"I can't tell you what to do but all I'm going to say is, be careful. It's up to you, I'm not going to advise you one way or the other."

"You want him for yourself!" Ellie hissed and she took off her baseball cap, thin hair plastered to her skull. "You take up all his time and attention. I've watched you. You always sit next to him, you're always talking to him. You should give other people a chance to get to know him. You're unfair about him in the things you say and I'm not going to listen to a word of it. You're just jealous that he might be interested in somebody else. You can't fool me."

Kate was taken aback. "Do whatever you want, Ellie. I won't get in your way but don't tell me about it or ask any more questions because I'm not interested. As far as I'm concerned, he's all yours." She put on her earphones and reached for her water bottle, hoping the next stop would come soon.

A couple of hours later, Jono pulled into a gas station. "Everybody! Time to get petrol. You have got fifteen minutes."

Kate shot off to the washroom, then ran into the local store to buy a supply of local newspapers and chocolate. She made good use of the photo opportunity, in no hurry to rejoin Ellie.

"Who are you sitting next to?" Marika joined her on the dusty red road. "I'm next to Jasmine who's depressed and keeps crying although she pretends not to. I know I should be more sympathetic but they created that whole mess."

"I couldn't agree with you more. I got stuck with Ellie who told me to stop monopolizing Rydell because he's such a sexy, *hot* and interesting man and she wants to get to know him better."

"Are you serious?" Marika stopped, amazed. "Hot? I can't believe she said that. What level of crazy is she? Even a blind man could see from a mile off what a weirdo he is. He's the closest thing to normal when he's around you which is probably why he likes hanging around you. Well, let her have him and vice versa. I wish we could seat Ellie and Jasmine back together and you and me could sit next to each other again but I guess that wouldn't be very nice of us?"

They discussed various ways of orchestrating the move but short of being rude, they realized they would have to continue with their depressed and angry seatmates. Except that when they got back on the bus, Jasmine and Ellie were sitting side-by-side, dark glasses on, no explanations offered.

Kate laughed. "And to think we worried about our manners," she whispered to Marika. "Look, Enrique's gone to sleep up on the luggage rack. I'm surprised Harrison let him. It must be bumpy up there. This is one of the worst roads so far and Jono said it's one of the longest ones too."

"I'm pretending it's Namibian massage therapy," Marika said, folding a blanket to sit on. "If you relax and don't fight it, it jolts the bones and muscles in a way that loosens them all up."

"You always see the positive," Kate laughed at her. "I'll give your way of thinking a try."

The bus stopped at a crossroad that boasted nothing but miles of thick ginger sand and a single acacia tree. "Everybody! We will have lunch here," Jono called out as he climbed down from the bus.

"Now," he said to the assembled gang who were stretching and yawning, "here we are, at a crossroad. In some African myths and legends, a crossroad is no ordinary road but an intersection of dimensions; a place where the world of the dead and the world of the living connect, a place where you can make choices. So here, now, you can change your life forever."

They pulled out the camp chairs and sat under the tree waiting for Treasure and Harrison who had waved off offers of help. Stepfan was quiet, and avoiding Charisse who was silent and withdrawn, attended to by a hovering Brianna. Richard had succeeded in joking Jasmine into a better mood and Kate made sure to steer clear of Rydell and Ellie. Ellie had made a beeline for Rydell and was sitting next to him but Rydell was lost in his own world. He was desperate to talk to Treasure and had reached the point where he could hardly sit still.

"Jono," Richard said, "while we're out here, out in the middle of nowhere, waiting for lunch, how about you explain *muti* to us? Seems like as good a time as any, what do you say?"

Jono opened his mouth to reply when a loud crash sounded from the back of the bus and Treasure jumped down, seething.

"I've had *enough!* You're making me crazy. No one gets sick on my trips, ever. I want you to leave me alone to do my work. Why can't you do that? Why can't you leave me alone? You and your stupid rules for everything. I'm sick and tired of you, Harrison." She turned and stormed down the sandy road.

Harrison emerged from the back of the bus, his expression miserable. He looked over at the group who stared wordlessly back at him. He glanced questioningly at Jono, holding his hands out to the side, as if asking Jono what he should do but Jono just shrugged. Harrison sat down for a moment, watching Treasure's furious stride. Then he got up and went after her.

Rydell smiled.

"I guess we can safely assume that lunch is delayed," Richard commented. "Which means we've got the time to chat, Jono."

"Or maybe we should get our own lunch," Sofie stated. "Poor Treasure's at the end of her tether."

"Good idea," Kate agreed

"I'm in," Marika got to her feet.

"Us too," Lena and Gisela said.

Jono looked at Richard. "Perhaps tonight my friend," he said and Richard was clearly disappointed.

"Treasure! Stop!" Harrison yelled as he ran after her. "Treasure, I'm sorry, believe me. I never meant to make you crazy. I know I can be strong-minded sometimes but I never wanted to upset you or insult you. Please stop and talk to me."

Treasure came to a sudden stop. She stood still for a moment, her shoulders heaving, then she dropped down in the middle of the thick sandy road and cried even harder. She pulled her knees up to her chest, put her head down and sobbed, her whole body shaking.

Harrison sat down next to her, not sure what to do. "Treasure," he said cautiously, "are you alright? I know I upset you by what I said about the food storage system, and I know I make you crazy but you do seem more upset than one would think. I mean, shout at me yes, but crying like this, I don't understand. Please Treasure, please, tell me what's going on."

"Fine. I will tell you," Treasure shouted and she looked away from him. "But you cannot tell anybody. Do you promise? Jono knows but you cannot talk to him about it. Tell me you promise?" She wiped her face with the back of her hand.

"I promise absolutely." Harrison glanced around anxiously. They were sitting in the middle of the road but he thought it wasn't the right time to mention it. He tried to focus on her as well as keep an eye on the traffic, of which, thankfully, there was none.

"Tell me," he said and his voice was kind.

"I'm going to have a baby," she wailed. "I thought I would

happy and I thought I would be a strong and brave woman but now I'm only frightened. I'm very scared and I'm not happy at all. How can I afford a baby when I can barely afford the son I've already got? Tell me? I work twenty ones days on, four days off then twenty days on again. How can I keep working and have this baby? And I could never kill my baby; there are women who could do that but I could not."

She started to sob again. "But how will I live? And how will my baby live? My mother, she is old, she is the one who already looks after my son. I cannot give her a new baby too and now things are so bad in Zimbabwe, everything is very bad. I don't know what to do, *haw*. And this man, the father of the baby, he told he loved me and now he won't even pick up the phone to answer my calls. He has walked away from everything."

With that, she put her head in her hands and wailed again.

"Treasure, come here." Harrison moved closer to her and wrapped his arm around her. "Let me tell you this," he said, while a part of him registered that her bare, sun-warmed skin was soft and smooth to the touch. "Come now, stop crying for a moment and listen to me, because I want to tell you something."

Treasure drew deep gulping breaths, calmed down and hiccupped slightly. She stared at the ground, despondent. There was nothing he could say that would make her feel better; he knew nothing of the hardships of her life.

"After I left the Czech Republic, I worked in the Middle East, trying to help with rebuilding and I've seen men and women and babies survive in conditions that no one would believe possible. Which doesn't mean it's easy, it's not, but what I do know is this: we survive. We survive because we have to, and because we must, because it is our human instinct to try to stay alive for as long as we can. The fight for life is like a flame that cannot be extinguished except by the most terrible of tragedies."

He rubbed her back and he felt her anguish ease a fraction. He had the vague thought that she smelled wonderful, of washing detergent and clean soap, and she reminded him of his wife, back when she loved him and he had no reason to doubt her.

"You are a beautiful, strong woman," he said, "and I know this baby is very lucky. There is a belief that each baby chooses its mother carefully, so this baby chose you. He or she knows all about you, you have no secrets from it; it knows all your pains, your dreams, your weaknesses and your joys and it chose you, above all other women."

Treasure let out a deep, shuddering sigh and wiped her face on her T-shirt sleeve. Harrison dug into his pocket and brought out a large wad of toilet paper and Treasure laughed.

"*Ei*, Harrison," she said, "you are always so prepared." She blew her nose vigorously.

"Of course. Listen Treasure, try not to be afraid, let yourself be loved by this baby and let yourself love it. Enjoy the miracle of having a baby, having it grow inside you, it's a wonderful thing. And now I give you my word, my promise that I will help you. I will send you money every month, no matter where I am, or what I'm doing. You'll never have to afford this baby alone. I will help you."

Treasure froze, mid-nose blow. "Do you mean that?" she whispered, half of her face covered by crumpled white toilet paper. "Why would you do such a thing? I am a stranger to you."

"Because…" Harrison started and then he stopped.

"Tell me," she said.

"I was married," he began, and the words did not come easily. "To what Americans would call my high-school sweetheart. We were married for twelve years. And then my wife got pregnant. The only trouble is, I could not have been the man to make it happen because I cannot make babies although I wanted to, more than anything. When I asked her how it happened, she told me that she and my best friend had fallen in love and that was how it happened. I didn't want to get in their way, so I left them to their happiness and I went to the Middle East but I couldn't stay there long and after that I went to America because I wanted a new beginning, I wanted to build my own life from the ground up, just like the buildings I am so good at making happen. I changed my name too, I wanted to take the name of a man who had been told he'd never succeed but then he succeeded more than most people ever do."

"Harrison is not your real name? What do I know of white men's names anyway?"

He laughed. "No, Harrison's not my real name. It's the name I chose for my new life, and I picked it because everybody told Harrison Ford that he'd never make it in the movies, and look, he did!"

"Harrison Ford! Tell me then, what's your real name?"

He shook his head. "Maybe one day. But back to the baby. Now you see, why I mean what I say. In this way, I too can help a child, I can make a difference too. "

He rubbed her back again and looked up at the rich blue sky. "Treasure, can I say something?"

"Anything." She wiped away the last of her tears.

"We're in the middle of the road. Not that sthere's a lot of traffic which is a very good thing but please can we continue this discussion on the side where it is safer?"

Treasure laughed, a happy, joyous sound. She climbed to her feet and dusted the sand off her shorts.

"Yes, Harrison, we can move off the road. We had better get back anyway, the others will be wondering what happened to their lunch."

"Who cares about their lunches?" Harrison stood and beamed at her, his teeth flashing white in his sunburnt face. "They are adults, and they can get their own lunch."

Treasure laughed even harder at this and he joined in. They walked back to the bus and the sounds of their mirth reached the others before they did.

"Look who's coming back," Richard announced. "Good

God. And they're even laughing. Jono, is there such a thing as desert fever? Because when they left, she was in tears and now they're the best of friends."

"The desert does strange things to people," Jono agreed. "But for now let us be grateful that things are better again and that we will get our lunch."

"Richard," Jono asked, "now that things are back to normal and Treasure and Harrison have resumed the sandwich-making, what do you want to know about *muti*, about which you are so insistent? And why, if you do not mind my asking, are you so curious about it?"

"There's nothing macabre or evil in my interest," Richard said. "I'm just curious to know which African myths are true and which are urban legends. For example, I came across an article that said a human head could fetch more than a thousand British pounds and I thought surely that couldn't be true?"

Jono was thoughtful. "I can tell you exactly because I make it my business to know. But Richard, while you may wish to know, do the others? This is very disturbing. The discussions we have had about *sangomas,* witches and *tokoloshes* are nothing compared to this. Perhaps you and I should chat in private later."

"I don't care," Stepfan rocked on his campstool. "It would take a lot to shock me."

Kate had been watching Rydell's reaction to Treasure and Harrison's return and had not been paying much attention to the discussion, but she turned to Jono and said, "I'd rather know than not."

"Me too," Ellie said, her gaze focused on Rydell, sure that he too would be interested.

But Rydell, offering no explanation, got up and walked away, his head down, shuffling his jerky little steps.

Ellie disgruntled, crossed her arms and scowled.

"I'm sure I heard much worse at the mission," Helen said, "and besides, we should know the truth."

"Should we?" Jono asked. "Sometimes I am not sure that all truths need to be known. In answer to your question, Richard, that is not an urban legend but a true fact; a human head can sell for more than a thousand pounds. The price depends on whether the victim was alive when their head was cut off. If they were alive and screaming, then their head will be worth more because their screams would have woken up the spirits. The louder and longer the screams, the more the supernatural pays attention and the stronger the *muti*."

He took a long drink of Coke, leaned back in his chair and continued. "The majority of traditional healers will have no part in this kind of thing but if you find an unscrupulous *sangoma*, he may decide that traditional ingredients such as herbs, roots, and animal parts are not powerful enough to achieve the desired results and he will insist that he needs body parts to make the magic happen. He does not commit the murder himself; he tells the client what is needed and the client hires a hit man.

"Generally speaking, the word *muti* means medicine in the way you would normally understand it, but when it is called 'strong *muti*', it refers to magic which uses body parts and people usually want this kind of magic for protection or good luck. Does it work? People believe it does. But the most terrible thing in all of this is how many little children are killed for their body parts."

Helen leaned forward. "Yes, I knew that an incomprehensible number of children vanish. But I had no idea they were taken for *muti*. Do you know how many children are taken?"

"*Yebo*. More than 1,500 children disappear without a trace every year."

The group was quiet, shocked. From the kitchen area of the bus, they could hear Treasure and Harrison joking and the sound of their carefree calls seemed a million miles away.

Jono continued. "There is a big trade in Africa in human body parts and each body part is used to create a particular potion. For example, a brain gives knowledge, while breasts and genitals bring virility; a nose or eyelids can poison an enemy, a tongue can smooth a path to a girl's heart, fat from breasts and the abdomen bring good fortune and wealth, and a penis brings good luck in horse racing."

"Is that all?" Stepfan asked, "I'd have thought my substantial member would be worth far more than a good win at the track."

Jono ignored him. "You might ask where the police are in all of this, particularly since the suspects are usually fairly easy to identify. The police fear they will be cursed if they investigate and so they say that the victims have been eaten by fish or crabs after drowning in the river, but what kind of fish only eats the private parts on a human body?

"Police also say it is quite easy to identify a *muti* murder as being such because body parts are removed in a straightforward surgical way with no trace of gratuitous violence or evidence of passion as there would be in a sadistic or serial killer murder."

Jono shifted on his stool and wiped his forehead. "A former member of the South Africa's occult-related crimes unit estimates that close to 900 of the missing children are killed for *muti*. There was a horrific case that came to light of an elderly couple who killed five children. The police found the little bodies in a rusty old car in the backyard of the couple's house. Can you believe that? Grandparents killing children and throwing their bodies away like rubbish. Three- and five-year-old children, just little babies." He took a deep breath.

Helen got up and walked off without a word, her jaw set, her fists clenched.

Jono watched her go and was silent for a moment. "Family members are often killed for *muti* but never enemies because the energy is not good. The victim is seen as a sacrifice to the gods. People wanting the *muti* are grateful to the victim because they see the killing as being for the good of themselves or society. They see it like an animal sacrifice but much more powerful. Some people even justify it by saying well, Jesus was sacrificed for the good of man, so how is this wrong?"

This caused an immediate uproar. "That's disgusting! How can they even compare?" Lena shouted. "Jesus died to save mankind, not to be a good-luck charm for some evil bank robbers."

Others voiced similar agreements.

Jono held up his hand. "*Aikona wena*, I am just the messenger, please, do not shoot me. I told you this is very upsetting. Do you want me to carry on?"

"We have listened to this much, we must hear the rest," Sofie said, pale.

"You must stop for lunch anyway," Treasure announced as she joined the group. She put a hand on Jono's shoulder. "There are meat and vegetarian hot dogs on the table. Why do you want to know these terrible things, *ei*? I'm not going to sit with you for lunch if this is what you're talking about. I'm going to sit on the other side of the bus and enjoy the sunshine."

"I'll join you," Lena said. "Sorry Jono, but I can't listen anymore."

"I'm going to join Lena and Treasure," Gisela said. "It's not that I don't care, I do. Too much." She got up, followed by Eva.

"We've had enough too," Jasmine and Ellie picked up their chairs. "Thanks Jono, but that's all we can take."

"I don't blame any of you," Jono said.

When the remaining group returned and were sitting with their lunch plates balanced on their knees, he continued. "The murders are not limited to children. Even old men have had their hearts cut out and one girl was found with half of her face cut off which was done while she was alive. At least one *muti* murder is reported a month, and many others go unreported.

"Do you all remember our first night together when I was

talking about witchcraft? We digressed into an amusing talk of *tokoloshes* but in case you think any of this is a light-hearted matter, it is not.

"Right now, in Angola, adults are turning against children as young as five years old and accusing them of witchcraft. Children have been hanged, stoned to death, raped, burned and downed in rivers after they were accused of sorcery."

"But what damage could a five-year-old child cause?" Sofie asked. "I don't understand."

"It is how people explain the endless misery of their lives. After nearly thirty years of brutal civil war, after rebel assaults, government counterattacks, violence, disease, mass starvation, scattered families, people have lost all sense of hope in justice and society, and in what has been labeled a post-traumatic stress reaction, adults have turned the blame to witchcraft because they have run out of reasonable explanations."

"When we can no longer explain the horrors that we inflict on each other," Sofie said, "we turn to the supernatural and the religious?" She stared down at her plate, her food untouched.

"*Yebo*, that is it, Sofie," Jono agreed. "Even AIDS has been explained as a curse that children put on their parents and and the grandparents punish them for it. If the children are lucky, they escape with their lives but have to live on the street. I have heard it said that even the most hardened of human-rights workers cannot believe what they are seeing; even babies are accused of being witches.

"And then there are those who claim to be able to 'cure' these children by making them jump and dance in the hot sun for hours in order to 'cleanse them' of their magical powers. They are beaten until the magic is broken down, chili powder is put into their eyes, boiling oil dripped into their ears. These things are done by religious communities and if children survive, they have to pay off their 'debt' for being healed by working for the people who 'cured' them. They are not safe anywhere.

"And that, my friends," Jono concluded, "is the reality of witchcraft. There is nothing charming or funny about it. It is terrible and evil and only getting worse as people's misery increases. Now," he said, into the silence, "I have told you all I know, please, do not ask me to talk about it again. It is one thing to read about it in a London newspaper or on the Internet," he looked reproachfully to Richard, "and quite another to live where it happens."

Richard looked somber and ran his hands through his hair, nodding apologetically.

Sofie scrambled to her feet and knocked her food over. "We should do something! We should do something *now*."

"Like what exactly?" Stepfan asked. "Go on, you tell us."

"Angola is not far from here. We should drive there and rescue the children and tell the adults that what they are doing is wrong, that it is a crime against God and nature. How can we be on holiday, relaxing in the sunshine and eating ice cream when there are children suffering like this? How? You tell me?"

"*Eish*, man has a great and terrible capacity to enjoy the frivolities of life while others have to endure the tortures of it, you know that, Sofie," Jono said. "And this very capacity also ensures our survival. I understand your desire to help but we cannot just go and save people although there is nothing I would rather do. What do you think? That we can drive across the border, load our bus with children and then what? Take them where? To America? To Canada? Where? It does not work like that, that is kidnapping, and illegal. I understand how you feel but there is nothing we can do. When you get home, you could start a foundation but I tell you now, the money you collect will be stolen; not one cent will reach the children. Or maybe," he said and his voice rose to a shout, "go and work there yourself and achieve what? You have nothing to offer, no power, no money. Maybe try to adopt one child; you think maybe you can make a difference that way? You would not be able to afford it, it would bankrupt you and the paperwork alone would take a hundred years. *Aikona*, you think you are the only one who cares?"

He stopped and looked down at the ground. "Sofie, I am very sorry. I am sorry I shouted at you. I too find this very upsetting. I am going to wash my hands and take a small walk to rid myself of this talk and then we will get back on the bus and continue with the holiday, can we be in agreement?"

Sofie ran up to him and threw her arms around him. "I am the one who is sorry. Please, forgive me."

"There is nothing to forgive." He patted her shoulder awkwardly.

"Everybody," he called, "we will get back on the bus in fifteen minutes. Please pack up lunch."

"Good lord," Richard said after Jono walked away, "listen people, heartfelt apologies, *mea culpa*. Seems I opened up a big old can of worms, I had no idea. You know how it is, darkest Africa and all that, I was curious what was true. I'm sorry I subjected you to hearing it."

"Don't worry," Enrique said. He had been silent throughout, listening quietly. "You didn't know. Anyway, it helped me. I really want to be a doctor now. Maybe I can do something helpful with my life, something that will make a difference."

"I need a stiff drink," Mia said, "I feel quite pale."

"Me too," Charisse agreed.

"Sofie, are you okay?" Brianna went over to her. "Come here, let me give you a hug."

"I feel sick about it," Kate said. "But I'm glad I know and one day I will do something to help, I just don't know what, yet." She looked over at the bus. "Who's on dish duty today?" she asked. "I'm going to see if I can help."

"We are good, we are good," Harrison said, when Kate arrived. "We've got a very fine system, Treasure and I. We don't need your help here but if you'd be so kind as to sweep the floor of the bus that would be excellent. The broom's over there."

"Harrison," Kate said, "we're in a *desert*, yes, spell the word with me now, and in a *desert* there's a lot of *dust* and *sand*. But if it makes you happy, I'll sweep the floor."

"It will make me very happy." Harrison said, "and when people climb up the ladder, I will sweep their feet with a small brush to lessen the dirt that infiltrates."

Amused, Kate walked off, thinking there were preferable levels of madness and that compared to *muti* murders, Harrison's obsessions were mild and harmless. She had just started to sweep inside the bus when a large shape crawled out from under one of the seats, startling her and she let out a cry.

"Fraidy cat," Rydell said, standing up. "That's what I'm going to call you from now. Fraidy Kate. I was picking up something I dropped. What are you doing?"

"Sweeping the bus," Kate's heart was still pounding. "Harrison wants me to sweep the bus."

"Of course he does," Rydell advanced. "And, like a good little girl you're doing it. Tell me something, are you always such a good little girl, Fraidy Kate? Even late at night, when you're by yourself alone with your secrets, are you such a good girl then?"

Kate was taken aback by his anger. His dark eyes glittered and his thick red lips were wet with spittle.

"Do you ever do the things you really want to do or do you just dream about them? Do you even know what you are capable of? I bet you don't. I bet you've never been challenged in your whole life to do something extraordinary, something powerful. All you've done is say yes to the men in your life. What have you ever done that's your own?"

"Why are you attacking me like this?" Kate edged towards the door, feeling trapped by the tight seats and the mountainous piles of backpacks, magazines, food and water bottles. "What have I ever done to you except be nice to you? I just came to clean the bus."

"I'll do it," Rydell snatched the broom out of her hand. "Go for a walk, Fraidy Kate, and think about your obedient little life, how you're a puppet, an ordinary, boring little puppet."

Kate did not need to be told twice. She shot out of the bus and ran up to Marika and Jono. "Rydell just attacked me for no reason, he really scared me. He's not normal, Jono, he's not, and you don't know the whole story."

She told Jono what Rydell had said to her about wanting Treasure to be his wife and how he was going to hunt her down.

"Kate, my dear," Jono said, "calm down. Rydell is angry right now because Harrison and Treasure are friends, and that is why he attacked you. I have been with Treasure on many trips and men always get crushes on her and then the fights start, although mostly it is the wives who get cross. Please, do not worry about Treasure, she can take care of herself. Rydell is a strange man, but he is not a dangerous one, I know the difference. Believe me, I will take very good care of you, nothing bad will ever happen to you." He blushed.

Kate looked doubtful in response to his rationale. "I don't know. I agree with you about why he vented on me but I don't think you are right, Jono, I think he *is* dangerous."

"I agree that he has the potential for violence but he wouldn't be so stupid as to attack you with all of us around," Marika said. "And why would he attack *you* anyway? I mean think about it, what would he gain from that? Out of all of us, he likes you the best, he was just upset, that's all."

"Hmmm," Kate considered what Marika had said. "Maybe you're right. I hope so." But she was still doubtful.

"I will sit next to my wife now, thank you very much," Stepfan said to Harrison when they got back on the bus. Harrison nodded but looked questioningly at Lena who gave a hint of a smile and nodded back.

"Fine, no problem. Sofie, I'll sit next to you."

"No, you won't," Sofie replied quickly with unmistakable firmness. "We've already been seatmates, so you sit next to

Charisse and I will go next to Brianna because we haven't had the chance to talk. Is that alright, Charisse and Bree?" She gave them a pleading look.

"Sure, why not?" Charisse agreed.

Sofie gave a sigh of relief. "He talks nonstop," she whispered to Brianna. "I couldn't do it again."

Brianna nodded and smiled. Despite her run-ins with Jasmine and the tensions about Charisse and Stepfan, she was looking more relaxed than she had at the start of the trip; she was tanned, her dark hair was shiny, and her worry lines had eased.

"This bus is full of all kinds of stuff," Sofie commented. "Not helped by the fact that Helen hangs her running gear everywhere. It's like we are inside a travelling laundry. And whose bananas are those, perched over the big water bottles at the front?"

Brianna looked up. "I hadn't noticed them. I know the avocados are Richard's, he's trying to ripen them. You're right, the bus is very lived-in; it's like we're the circus."

Eva, listening, leaned forward. "A travelling circus," she said, with delight. "Hah! I feel the start of a poem." She scrambled to find a piece of paper.

True to form, Harrison chatted to Charisse at high speed, covering a hundred different topics a minute. Charisse seemed interested and even laughed now and then.

Enrique climbed back up into the luggage rack nest he had made for himself, while Ellie threw a mat on the floor of the bus, near the water bottles, close to Rydell's feet and lay on her back, reading.

Kate glanced around and saw Rydell staring daggers at Harrison and she sighed. She turned to tell Marika but her seatmate had her eyes closed and was either napping or listening to music.

Several long hours later, the bus came to a shuddering halt

amid a cloud of red dust that whirled around the hot, ticking vehicle. They had arrived at Siesriem.

The road had been a true test of the adventurers' stamina. Even the most avid readers had given up on their books and had resigned themselves to being jolted instead. It was impossible to concentrate over the noise of grinding steel on the corrugated weather-beaten road. There was no point in trying to listen to music or talk. Harrison was the only one who continued to chat, forging a conversation with a flung-about Charisse who had long since stopped listening.

The bus had passed through terrain both remarkable and unworldly and the heat was devastating. Every window was open but this merely circulated a relentless gale of scorching dust-infused air that scalded eyeballs and leached already parched throats. The group held onto one another or clutched the seats in front of them and watched rocks become veldt scrub which in turn became black and orange canyons that eased out into flat, pale blonde dust as far as the eye could see. Then the landscape changed back to talon-gouged red canyons while skyscraper dust-devils wove across the land with chimeras dancing alongside in the searing heat.

They finally came to a stop and no one moved until Treasure forced the door open. She took one look at the wild-eyed, wind-burnt travellers and burst out laughing. "Yes," she said. "That is the road here. Overlanders must be tough. There is ice-cream in that shop there. You should all go and get one. I promise it will make you feel better."

But not even the lure of an ice-cream oasis could get the group moving at more than a snail's pace. They unfolded their shocked bodies, and got slowly to their feet, grunting.

"Good Lord," Richard groaned. "Feels like I've been locked in a barrel and sent over a cliff or two. I wouldn't be surprised if I'm suffering from internal bruising."

"Arrrggh…" Enrique let out a wail. "Sorry," he apologized, "I had to do that."

"We must do a stretch class tonight," Helen said to Sofie who nodded in agreement.

One by one they staggered off the bus.

Kate noticed Charisse leaning against the side of the bus, her complexion an unhealthy green. "Are you okay?" Kate went over to her. "You don't look so good."

Charisse groaned. "I'll be fine. That road was worse than I expected. I thought I was getting dehydrated so I drank water the whole way but it didn't help, my stomach is worse than ever."

"Can I get you an ice-cream?" Kate enquired.

"God no, but thank you anyway. Brianna's getting me more water and I'll lie down for a bit once we get our tents up. Don't worry, I'll be fine. I gotta tell you, that Harrison can talk. Even when it got so noisy, he carried on. No wonder Sofie palmed him off on me. Maybe that's why I feel sick, it's the aftermath of being held captive by a talk-aholic," Charisse hugged her stomach.

"Yep, he's special. We're really in the desert now," Kate said, taking in the scenery. "It's sort of like a prairie except that the sand's a foot or two deep." She held her arms out to the sky and took a deep breath, enjoying the smell of veldt grass baking under the hot sun and mixing with the spicy dust. The sky stretched a vast deep cerulean above the golden grassy plains and the air was so hot it seemed solid, with the horizon a distant shimmer.

Marika returned from the store and handed Kate a raspberry-flavoured jelly-filled water-ice. "I got you a Frogz Eggz ice cream." They got back on the bus, eating quickly, with the ice cream melting down their hands.

The wheels of the bus spun and the big old white truck fishtailed as they slowly ground through the soft deep sand to their campsite, a small circle under the umbrellaed shade of a giant Camel Thorn tree thick with large, grey, boomerang-shaped seedpods, a majestic green canopy in the middle of the vast veldt.

"Everybody!" Jono shouted as soon as they arrived. "Please, pay attention for a moment! You have got two hours to put up your tents and do whatever you like, but please be back at the bus at 5:30 p.m. for the Siesriem canyon walk. Treasure will stay here to make supper. I would like to suggest an early night because our wake-up call tomorrow morning is 4:00 a.m."

Shrieks of horror greeted his announcement and Jono laughed. "There is a very good reason for it. You will watch the sunrise from a place of great beauty."

Jono had decided he needed to be more proactive when it came to Kate because time was passing and, with it, opportunity. He made his way over to Kate and Marika and said, "I've come to help you two."

"That's fantastic of you, Jono. My eyeballs feel like someone's held a hairdryer on them for the past three hours, so all in all, I'm not feeling too strong," Marika said.

"Don't put us anywhere near Rydell," Kate said. "Jono, did you ever get a calling card for your cellphone? Although you probably wouldn't get a signal out here anyway. What if something bad happens? We are so far from everywhere."

"You worry too much, Katie," Jono said. "Nothing bad will happen."

"You might want to check on Charisse," Kate said. "She looked quite nauseous."

"A guilty conscience will do that to you," Marika muttered in an undertone. "I must go and do some laundry. I should have bought more clothes in Springbok."

Later they were all gathered under the huge tree. Sofie was doing yoga, her concentration fierce. Helen was frowning and clipping her toenails. Brianna was standing outside her tent, focusing on the dunes in the distance and shading her eyes with one hand.

Harrison and Treasure's happy chatter and the clanging of their pots and pans were the only sounds floating over the campsite.

Richard and Mia were reclining on camp stools, drinking beer and Gisela and Lena had just returned from a stroll.

"I'm too knackered to go on a walk later," Mia announced. She was stretched out, with her toe ring sparkling in the sunshine and her toenails sporting the remains of chipped purple polish.

"It'll be good for us," Helen filed her nails vigorously.

"Bollocks to things that are good for me." Mia matched Helen's firm tone of voice. "And I wish this place had a bleedin' swimming pool. It's the hottest place ever, why doesn't it have a pool? And it's bleedin' miles to the ice cream shop. I'm not walking through all that sand, though I'd kill for a Toffee Magnum. Just getting to the toilet's a bleedin' trek through the Sahara."

"I'd get you a Magnum," Richard offered idly, "but it'd melt before I got back." Richard had foregone shaving and he had a sunglasses tan. He was the Lone Ranger around the camp fire at night, only his was a sickly pale mask.

"I'm going to stay here this afternoon," Enrique announced, appearing with Eva at his side. "It's absolutely incredible. I could shoot for days." They were odd companions. He was tanned and boyish in his shorts and a faded T-shirt while Eva was gothic glam in designer sunglasses, a black midriff tee and black shorts.

"Can one stay?" Kate asked. "Is that an option? I thought we had to go on the walk?"

The others were amused by her earnestness.

"This isn't school, Kate," Richard said, his face to the sun. "You can do whatever you like."

"Then I'd like to walk around all by myself with my camera," Kate declared.

The moment was shattered by an angry shout.

"Where's Charisse?" Harrison ran up to them. "Where is she? She drank all my water. That is not right."

"How do you know it was Charisse who drank it?" Sofie asked from the Lotus pose, her hands in a prayer pose.

"Because she was sitting next to me and she said she'd drunk all of hers and she asked if she could have *some* of mine. Of course I said yes but I never said she could have all of it. Where is she?"

"Sssh, Harrison, she's feeling really sick," Brianna walked up to him quickly. "She probably drank it because she wasn't feeling well and wasn't thinking straight. She said was feeling dehydrated and now she's very nauseous. Please don't shout at her. We can buy you more at the store in the morning and in the meantime, you can share ours, I got some when we stopped for ice cream."

"Come on, Harrison," Sofie got up and shook her mat. "Mistakes happen. Don't make a big thing of it, let it go."

"All right," Harrison grumbled. "For the sake of international goodwill, I will let it go."

"Is everybody ready for the walk?" Jono called from the bus.

"I'm staying here," Kate said. "This area is absolutely magical."

"The canyon is magical too," Jono said. He had been hoping to take Kate aside and finally have a real conversation with her.

"I am sure it is, but I'm going to explore by myself."

"I'm going to stay here to help Treasure," Harrison said.

"I'm going to stay here and do bugger all," Mia said. "Oh hang on ... I'm going to drink beer and work on my a suntan, that counts as something."

"You do that, my love, have fun and enjoy," Richard pulled on his T-shirt.

"Let us be off then," Jono said, "we will see everybody for dinner in two hours."

Out in the middle of the field of blonde grass, Kate dusted the sand from her shorts. She walked towards a small red sand dune and lay down on her stomach, studying the tiny remains of a bleached white beetle. Then she sat up and looked around, digging her bottom deep in the soft, almost oily, cinnamon-coloured sand.

"Hey Cam," she said out loud to her ex-boyfriend. "If you hadn't been such a jerk, I'd never have seen this. Thank you for being such a jerk."

The Fifth Night

THAT NIGHT THE SKY WAS THICK with stars and the hazy band of the Milky Way spread a broad crystal swathe across the darkness while Mars glowed like a pinprick ruby among the diamond delights.

"Supper's ready," Treasure sang out.

"This is the plan, everybody," Jono said. "We get up at 4:00 a.m. tomorrow morning and then we drive like the wind to sand Dune 45, the second highest dune in the world. From there you will watch a spectacular sunrise. Then you will come down off the dune and enjoy a hot breakfast which Treasure, and most probably Harrison, will be preparing for us."

"No, I'm going up the dune." Harrison said. "I'm very excited. I will be the first at the top."

"No, that will be me," Sofie said.

"No, me," Helen insisted.

"I'll give gold stars to the winners," Mia said.

"I'm more excited about getting a hot breakfast," Stepfan said. "The morning offerings have hardly been adequate. It should be more like a traditional Continental breakfast with slices of assorted cold meats, different kinds of cheese with different breads and pastries and pots of freshly brewed coffee…"

The others stared at him.

"Stepfan," Sofie said, "let me ask you a question. Where are we? As in where in the world are we? We are in the middle of nowhere in Africa. And you want assorted cheeses and pastries. Sometimes the things you say blow my mind."

"If certain things have not been as I thought they would be, so what?" Stepfan retorted. "I'm allowed my dreams. I imagined a desert safari, with buffet tables covered in white cloths. I thought there would be lions strolling in front of us. I thought we would be riding through large herds of big game, and at night sleeping in big tents with draped mosquito netting. I thought our bus would be air-conditioned and comfortable, so you would be able to hear yourself think. I thought 'participatory tent assembly' meant that somebody would put up my tent for me and I would participate by sleeping in it."

"*Haw!* Sleeping in a tent does not count as participatory assembly," Jono finished his hamburger and wiped his fingers on a napkin. "With regards to your other comments, there is a questionnaire you can fill out at the end of the trip and you are most welcome to write all of that down. We would not wish to believe we have misled you."

"Ignore him," Lena put her empty plate down on the sand. "He's just being difficult. He knew exactly what it would be like. There was nothing misleading in the brochure. Despite all of this being new to me, I'm having a wonderful time."

The group was surprised. It was true, she looked good. Relaxed, tanned and happy.

Treasure walked up with her hands on her hips, concerned. "Where's Charisse? She didn't come and get any supper."

"She's still feeling very sick," Brianna replied, "she's sleeping. She didn't even come on the walk to the canyon."

"She drank all my water as well as hers," Harrison said.

"I thought you were going to let that go, Harrison," Helen said.

"I'm trying to show Treasure how thirsty she was," Harrison objected. "Although she was most talkative. I would not have said she was not feeling well."

"Let us know how she is," Jono said to Treasure and he

returned to his introduction of the area but he was clearly distracted, reciting facts in a monotone.

"We are in the Namib Desert and the word Namib comes from the Nama word which means desert or large plain. Siesriem, which is where we are now, is the gateway to Sossuvlei, one of the prime tourist attractions in Namibia. The word 'Sossusvlei' means 'dead-end marsh' and the area is made up of giant red-coloured sand dunes as well as large salt and clay pans, which are dried-up shallow pools baked dry by the desert sun. The pan never sees water unless the Tsauchab river floods, which happens very seldom. The red colour of the dunes comes from the iron oxide in the sand and the colour of dunes changes, depending on the time of day and the light. Tomorrow you will climb a dune and take a walk with Thaalu. Are there any questions?"

"That's it?" Richard asked. "That was an awfully short story for an area this big."

"And it will have to suffice, my friend," Jono said. "I am going to check on Charisse."

"I'm going to bed to look through my images," Kate said. "See you all tomorrow."

"You never stay and sit around the fire after supper," Rydell said, appearing suddenly at her shoulder.

Kate was startled. "There's plenty of great company here already," she said shortly. "No need for me to stay."

She hurried off, suspicious of his creepy version of friendly after attacking her earlier on the bus. She stopped at Charisse's tent just as Jono and Treasure emerged. "How is she?"

"Not good," Jono's expression was worried. "This does not feel right. If she had a stomach flu, it would be one thing but this is another. We shall see tomorrow."

"What if she's not better?"

"I will get a car to drive her fast to the hospital in Walvis Bay. But I'm hoping she will be better."

"Is there anything I can do?" Kate asked.

"No, but thank you," Jono said. "She even tried to take her emergency antibiotics but couldn't keep them down."

"I tried to give her some Gravol but she could not keep that down either." Brianna was miserable.

"Sounds like she's a lot worse," Kate commented. "When we arrived she was just a bit green in the face. Call me any time, if I can help."

Kate crawled into her tent and lay staring at the small domed canvas roof with her hands behind her head. Marika returned, her hair wet from the shower and Kate updated her about Charisse.

"I'm beginning to wonder if this trip is cursed," Marika said. "If all that talk about African magic sparked off something bad, like that bag of bones I bought that time. I lost my luggage, it seems like there's so much arguing, that monkey business between Stepfan and Charisse, all the talk of little children being murdered, Rydell being so odd..."

Kate looked thoughtful. "But Charisse said her stomach was sore right when we started the trip, remember? I'm sure there's a logical explanation for everything."

They heard the campfire party breaking up for the night and they tried to fall sleep but Rydell, who fell asleep immediately, seemed to have added nightmares to his four-snore symphony and although their tent was furthest from him, they could still hear every nuance of his moans as he thrashed around.

They were not alone in their sleeplessness. No one, apart from Rydell, Mia and Jasmine, was getting any sleep. Helen lay awake, gritting her teeth and furious with Rydell for keeping her awake at a time when she had nothing to do but contemplate the cracked fragments of her hopes and dreams.

Stepfan, seething with rage at the snoring, tossed, grunting loudly, fuming at Lena's unexplained absence.

Brianna flicked on her flashlight and whispered words of encouragement to Charisse who groaned softly, her face slick with cold sweat. Brianna wondered if she should call Jono but figured there was not much he could do. She poured some water onto a cloth and and gently wiped Charisse's face.

Eva lay awake, alone in her tent, wondering if they should suggest to Rydell that he sleep on the bus at night, with all the windows tightly closed.

Enrique and Harrison, snug in their sleeping bags, struck up a conversation about the architecture and beauty of the natural wonders of the world, while in the tent next to them, Jono sat upright, his legs crossed. He was filled with a terrible sense of foreboding.

While the others called it a night, Gisela and Lena remained at the fire pit. "It's so nice," Lena whispered to Gisela, their camp chairs touching, "to be sitting here in the silence of bush with nothing but the desert around us and the amazing starry sky above."

Gisela laughed softly in agreement and lit a cigarette. "I'm glad to see you're happier."

Lena hesitated before replying. "Yes, I am but Gili, can I tell you something?"

"You know you can tell me anything," Gisela flicked ash into the dying fire.

"I nearly did a very bad thing." Lena stopped.

Gisela made no effort to interrupt her or encourage her; she simply waited.

"I wanted to save my marriage so badly that I nearly destroyed myself and everything I stand for. I contemplated the unthinkable — hurting another person."

"She would have deserved it," Gisela cried out quietly. "That tramp."

"That's what I thought too. But Stepfan's much more to blame than she is. I mean sure, she got involved with him but it's odd — when the worst thing in the world happened to me — when everyone saw them together that night, that was my worst fear ever. It's what I've dreaded my whole married life; public disgrace. But once the initial shock wore off, it was almost a relief, like the worst has happened and now I can get on with my life. Does that make any sense at all?"

"Yes, it does."

"And I realize that I have few feelings left for Stepfan. My love for him was almost an obsession, tempered by my constant fear of losing him. Now, stripped of that fear, I look at him and see an arrogant man who's really quite terrible. The things he says! And to think I once thought he was so funny, so intelligent and so incredibly charming."

She looked down. "But here's the thing," she said, her voice low. "What if last night at the swimming pool hadn't happened and I had gone through with it? Because I was going to, I kept looking for her water bottle and I was going to do it, Gili, I was going to poison her water. I'm a terrible person."

Gisela threw her cigarette in the fire and hugged her.

"You're not a terrible person at all, Leni, and it's going to be fine." She stroked Lena's hair.

Lena sighed and her breath was soft against Gisela's neck. "I won't contemplate doing something like that again, but now I know we all have a breaking point and I reached mine. Not because my husband was naked in a swimming pool with a girl young enough to be his daughter but because of me, because of what I was prepared to do. But you know the biggest gift at all? I don't care about Stepfan any more. I don't even like him. I'm free, for the first time in my life. Free."

Then, her heart pounding with her own daring, she cupped her hand behind Gisela's neck and pulled her in close.

Sossusvlei, Walvis Bay and Solitaire

FIVE A.M. THE BUS WAITED at the gateway to the park. Several cars were lined up in front of the bus and it was still dark outside.

"Why does the man not open the gate?" Stepfan called out loudly, and the rest of the group ignored him. Everyone was pensive and the mood was dislocated; concerned looks were cast at Charisse who was dozing, her skin grey and clay-like. Various degrees of loathing over the sleepless night were directed at an oblivious Rydell who was distracted and tormented for his own reasons. He twitched and rubbed his legs, unable to stop fidgeting.

"Where did those cars come from?" Richard said. "We were the only ones at the campsite last night." No one answered him and he shrugged.

"You could cut the tension with a knife in here," Enrique commented. "It feels we're waiting to go to war or something."

"Ah! I see the man, the gate opens," Stepfan craned his neck and reported. "Jono, the man is there."

"Yes, I see him, Stepfan," Jono replied from the front cab, "but there are cars in front of us. I have to wait until they move before I can."

"That's highly unreasonable of you, old chap," Richard said. "Stepfan's thinking along the lines of you barreling through, take no prisoners and all that."

"Very funny," Stepfan said sourly.

Because the gatekeeper had been late, Jono wanted to make up time. He pushed the bus at such a rate that Marika grew quite nervous.

"Speed is one thing," she said to Kate who grinned, "but this is a bit much. If we hit something, like a deer, or if we have to swerve, we're all dead."

Her concerns were not shared.

"Bleedin' great!" Mia shouted at the top of her lungs. "Full throttle, yeah, baby, yeah."

"Extra X-treme." Jasmine yelled.

They roared into a lay-by an hour later, coming to an abrupt stop. The old bus creaked and moaned and shuddered.

"Old Mandoza sounds like a horse that's been run too hard." Sofie patted the bus as she climbed down. "Good bus, good job."

"That is your dune there," Jono pointed, "up you go."

With a cry of delight, the group rushed at it.

Kate high-tailed it a quarter of the way up and stopped to take a breather, her thighs burning. Then she looked down and nearly screamed. It was if she was standing on a narrow ledge twenty-stories high. She quickly planted her bottom in the sand and decided to watch the sunrise from where she was.

"Kate? Are you alright?" Marika asked.

"Fine," Kate said, hating to acknowledge her fear of heights. "You go on, I'll wait here."

Sofie, Harrison and Helen ran upwards with the rest following. Stepfan, bringing up the rear, tried to persuade Kate to continue with him.

"I'll hold your hand the entire way," he offered, looking enthused at the prospect.

"No thank you, I'm happy right here."

She watched her fellow compatriots as they climbed the dune, with the hardiest becoming tiny specks on the high ridge above.

She looked at the tiny bus far below and thought about Charisse resting inside. Charisse had been able to talk in small bursts, insisting she was able to do the walk, that she would be fine, that she had to meet the real Bushman. But Kate had her doubts. Charisse's face was pale as a ghost's, her eyes circled with bruises.

Kate wondered why Jono had not her taken to the hospital in Walvis Bay as he had said he would. She wanted to ask him but had not managed to get him alone.

Her thoughts were interrupted by Rydell, Ellie and Jasmine coming back down.

"Too cold up there. We're going down to walk the perimeter instead," Rydell said. "Come with us," he offered but he sounded forced and Ellie glared at Kate.

"Thanks but I'm happy here."

"Do you need any help going down?" It was Brianna. "I'm going back. I don't want to leave Charisse alone for too long."

"Yes, thank you, I'm a bit nervous."

"Hold your arms out to the side, like this," Brianna showed her, "it feels safer this way."

Kate did as she suggested and found it worked.

"Kate, I'm sick with worry about Charisse. We've been best friends since we were kids and I've never seen her like this. I don't know what to do. I suddenly feel so far from anything civilized or safe. Of course Jono's civilized but the place, you know what I mean? We're so far from home. I don't know what to do here whereas at home I'd know exactly."

"I don't even know what to suggest, Bree. What about getting her to Walvis Bay like Jono suggested?"

"I asked him and she said she felt better and that the Bushman would know what to do. But I don't think she looked better."

They walked the rest of the way down in silence and back on the bus, the sight of Charisse was not reassuring although she tried to insist she was on the mend.

"I think I feel bit better," she said, though her voice was not its usual sexy contralto but a cracked, broken rasp. She tried to smile but the effort exhausted her. "Can't wait to do the walk." But she could not raise her head from the window ledge and Kate thought there was no way Charisse could even get off the bus, never mind do a walk. Her lips were dark, bruised and oddly dusky.

"Must see the dunes and do the walk, I'll be fine," Charisse said, and then fell back into a doze. The spittle around her mouth had formed a fine foam and Kate went to get hot water from the breakfast kettle.

"What shall we do, Jono?" she asked outside of Charisse's hearing. "She needs serious medical attention, which is more important than a walk."

Jono was deep in thought. "We will have a quick breakfast when the others get down and go onto Sossuvlei as fast as we can. Thaalu will know what to do."

The others began to tumble off the dune in high spirits.

"I was first to the top." Harrison declared.

"By three seconds." Sofie said. "What's three seconds?"

"It's a *win!* I am the dune climbing champion of the desert." Harrison held his arms aloft in triumph and strutted around in a circle. "A round of applause please."

"I was a close third," Helen said. "That was the best thing ever, I loved it. Can we climb another one this afternoon?"

"Yes, maybe." Jono was distracted.

Stepfan, the last to return, limped to the bus. Lena, chatting to Ellie and Jasmine did not seem to notice or care.

"Lena's definitely her own woman now," Richard said to Mia, mopping up his runny eggs with a piece of toast and enjoying every bite. "I wonder how Stepfan the wonder-man hurt his leg. He won't like that, the stupid wanker."

"Let's go, please," Brianna called out. "I know you haven't finished breakfast but I'm very worried about Charisse. Come on, please, let's go now."

Kate went in search of Mia and found her under an acacia tree where she and Richard were deciding what sort of animals the dead trees resembled.

"Definitely a dog," Mia said, "a dog shagging another dog."

"I don't see that. It's a deer with big antlers and things, a reindeer. Father Christmas was flying across Namibia and one of his reindeer fell out of the sky and became a tree."

"Mia," Kate said quietly, "can't you help Charisse? What with you being a nurse?"

"Nah, sorry luv, I can't," Mia said in an undertone, exchanging a quick glance with Richard. "I don't know nuffing about sick bodies. It's probably a stomach bug, or something she ate, who knows."

"And I'm afraid I can't be of much help either," Richard was apologetic. "I'm into sales insurance which is pretty hopeless in situations like this."

Kate went over to Jasmine and Ellie who were finishing their coffee.

"Disgusting stuff," Ellie declared and threw the dregs on the ground, "I can't wait to have a nice big strong flat white when I get back. I'm craving an iced coffee and a cappuccino."

"Yeah! I want a sausage roll or three and toasted Turkish bread with thick Vegemite."

"And a meat pie and a big vanilla slice...,"

Kate interrupted them. "You two work in labs, that's medicine and science, so can you help Charisse? She's so much worse."

Jasmine shrugged unhelpfully. "Negatory Scotty. All we do is process samples. It's not like on TV where lab people solve crimes and detect things. You've got as much chance of helping her as we do." She walked off to rinse their coffee cups.

"I'll look in on her," Enrique said, having overheard, "I wish we had cellphones that worked," he whispered to Kate, "but I've got no idea who we'd phone anyway. This area of things really should be better organized."

"Come on everybody, let us go," Jono called.

Jono drove as fast as he could but the thick sand only got deeper, causing the unwieldy bus to swerve from side to side and it was another hour before they arrived at Sossuvlei. Jono pulled the bus to a quick stop, jumped out and ran over to a tall man leaning against a small white utilitarian van with an open back.

The others climbed off the bus and Richard and Enrique carried Charisse out of the bus and laid her on a mat, thinking the fresh air might do her some good but she flopped down like a rag doll with her eyes closed.

"She's gone into a coma," Brianna shrieked.

"Jono! Come quickly!" Kate cried and Jono and the tall man ran over to them.

"*Praat hierdie mense Afrikaans?*" Thaalu asked Jono who shook head. *Do these people speak Afrikaans?*

"*Nee, hulle verstaan nie,*" Jono said in that language. *They don't understand.* He had forgotten that Marika understood every word.

"She's been poisoned," Thaalu said, in Afrikaans. "There is no cure; she will die very soon."

Charisse suddenly arched her back as if she had been hit by a bolt of lightning and retched a fountain of blood. Some of the circle took an involuntary a step back.

"Do something!" Sofie and Brianna screamed at Jono. "Why don't you do something?"

Thaalu knelt down and held Charisse's head. Her body writhed as if she was having a seizure which did not sit well with Gisela who doubled over and threw up her breakfast with Ellie following suit.

"Charisse! Stop it! Charisse! Somebody do something!" Brianna shouted and tried to grab hold of Charisse's hand and it seemed as if the thrashing continued for an endless time while Thaalu held Charisse's head. He was soon covered in blood, as was Brianna.

Sofie and Marika were crying loudly while the other women were horrified and quiet. The men were transfixed and motionless.

The bleeding finally stopped and Charisse hacked up thick green bile.

Thaalu looked at Brianna. "It will end soon," he said, and sure enough, Charisse stopped shaking and writhing and began to quieten. Then she opened her eyes wide, gave a gurgling gasp and flopped back, motionless.

"She is dead now," Thaalu announced bluntly.

"Do something!" Brianna screamed. "She can't be dead. We're on holiday. You don't die on holiday. She's my best friend." She began to cry hysterically, her breath coming in gulps.

Kate rushed over to her. "Don't look anymore," she said and hugged Brianna tight. "Come now, come now, come with me, over here." Brianna leaned into her and wailed.

"What on earth happened here?" Richard said. "What happened? She's dead for God's sake. How did this happen? Someone close her eyes, for God's sake."

The others began to slowly turn away in shock.

"Kate," Marika said, "I've got some medication I travel with, to help me with flying. It's a normal tranquilizer. I think we should give Brianna a couple, what do you think?"

"Good idea," Kate agreed and Marika trotted off, returning with the pills.

"Bree," Kate said softly, "these are tranquilizers. You're not allergic to them are you?"

Brianna shook her head, sobbing so intensely she was hardly able to breathe.

"We want you to take two," Marika told her and she tried to wipe the blood off Brianna with a cloth. "A terrible thing has happened, please my dear, you need to take them."

Brianna shivered and she continued to cry but she swallowed the pills.

"Good girl," Kate stroked her back. "Keep breathing slowly."

"Do not touch the body," Thaalu said sharply, in response to Richard's suggestion that they close Charisse's eyes. "They must do a proper autopsy in Walvis Bay. This girl did not die of natural causes." His statement was greeted with shouts of horror.

"What are you saying?" Helen demanded, "That one of us killed her? That's impossible. We're civilized people here."

Thaalu regarded her evenly. He was not, Kate reflected, how she'd imagined a Bushman to be. She had thought he would be ancient and tiny, toothless and wrinkled like a prune while Thaalu was lean, graceful and elegant.

"There is no such thing as a truly civilized man in the way you like to think there is. We all have the potential to kill each other and sometimes, for reasons known only to ourselves, we do. We need to cover the body." He conferred with Jono who opened the side door of the bus and pulled out a thick plastic ground sheet which Thaalu spread on the ground next to Charisse.

"Now," he instructed Jono, Richard and Harrison, "we'll each take a side of her mattress and put it with her on top of the sheet."

They lifted Charisse carefully and Thaalu folded the sheet over her and covered her up. "I need something to secure her. Do any of you have rope or tape?"

"I have rope," Jono said.

Thaalu secured Charisse's body in the back of the bakkie and the group were even more shaken by the sight of the body bag than they had been by Charisse's wide-eyed dead stare.

"Here's what I will do," Thaalu announced, "I'm going to drive her to Walvis Bay. Does her friend want to come with me or continue with you?"

"Of course I want to go with her!" Brianna shouted. "How can you even ask such a thing?" She was still crying but less hysterically.

"Then you need to get your things and the dead girl's too, all her papers and her passport."

Kate helped Brianna gather her and Charisse's belongings off the bus and put them in the back of the van with Charisse. At the sight of her friend's body, Brianna began to sob again and Kate led her to the front of the tiny truck and put her inside.

"Wait for me," she said to Brianna and went back to Thaalu and Jono.

"I'm coming with you to Walvis Bay," she said to Thaalu, who had taken off his bloodied T-shirt, and was pulling on a clean one that Jono had just handed him. "Jono, you're in Solitare overnight and you'll be in Walvis Bay tomorrow? You can pick me up there. Thaalu, may I come?"

"It will be a bit of a tight squeeze in the front of the cab but yes, that would be helpful."

"Let me get my camera bag," Kate told them. "I'm going to leave the rest of my stuff here."

"It's good of you to go," Helen said, and the others agreed when they heard the plan.

"It will take us some time to get out of this sand," Thaalu said to Kate when he got in and started up the van, "but hopefully, once we are on the good roads, it will not take us too long to get to Walvis Bay."

Horrific circumstances aside, Kate could not help but notice the beautiful and harmonious way that Thaalu spoke.

She stroked Brianna's hair and settled down for a long drive. She would use the time to try and figure out what had happened.

Back at the bus, a fierce argument had broken out. "But why do we need to go straight to Solitaire?" Jasmine protested. "There's nothing there except a camp ground and famous apple pie, you said so yourself, Jono. Meanwhile here we are, at one of the highlights of our trip and now we're going to leave without seeing a thing. All I am asking is that we stay here for an hour, see the sights and then go. I'm sorry about what happened to Charisse but it's unlikely I'll ever be here in my life again and I really want to see more of Sossusvlei, especially the salt pan and petrified trees. This is one of the main reasons I booked this trip."

"You are disgusting," Sofie was accusing, "a girl is dead and all you can think of is yourself. You never liked Charisse anyway, we all knew."

"Don't call Jasmine names," Mia said. "She can say whatever she finks. Oh God, I could use a drink."

"And all you want to do is get drunk and lie around doing nothing," Sofie bit back.

"Careful now," Richard warned. "We've had a horrid time of it but there's no need for us to start attacking one another."

"Start?" the usually calm Gisela shrieked. "What do you mean *start*? A girl's been murdered, and by one of us. It's gone way beyond 'start' if you ask me."

"Now, we do not know for sure that she was murdered," Jono said. "I would suggest we wait for the autopsy results before we jump to any conclusions."

"But Thaalu said…" Helen began.

"I know what Thaalu said," Jono said, "but he is not a doctor and he is not always right."

"How do you know?" Richard fired. "Why, has he been wrong about a murder before? Is this like a common thing, to be right or wrong about a dead body on a holiday trip?"

"*Eish,* everybody," Jono held up his hands, "please try to remain calm. I know this is a terrible thing. I really do. But we have to stay calm." His look pleaded with them.

At that point another small van drove up and a man got out wearing the same uniform as Thaalu. He walked up to Jono and shook his hand. They conversed in Xhosa and Jono turned back to the group.

"This is Charles. Thaalu radioed him to come here in case there was anybody who still wanted to do the walk."

"I do," Jasmine said immediately.

"And me," Helen echoed.

"Anybody else?" Jono asked. "It might be a good thing, help to calm us down."

"Yes, a walk after a murder is always calming," Richard

said, sarcastically. "Mia, what do you want to do?"

"Let's go for the bleedin' walk," Mia said with a shrug.

"We'll go too," Gisela said, pointing to Eva and Marika.

"Me too," Lena said.

"Lena, we are not going on the walk remember," Stepfan said.

Lena looked at him curiously. "Stay if you like. I'm going."

Stepfan glared at her with quiet fury, turned on his heel and limped off.

"Come with me, ladies and gentlemen," Charles said. "Climb onto the back of that little truck over there, which we call a 'bakkie.' There's room in the front for two of you."

"Hold on tight." He shouted out his window once they were settled and he pulled off at high speed.

"You'd never think we had just witnessed a murder," Eva whispered to Marika. "Here we are, taking a drive like nothing happened. I feel very odd. I don't know what to think."

Marika agreed. "Who poisoned Charisse? I agree with the Bushman, it must have been poison. It was like she was vomiting up her insides. It was the most terrible thing I've ever seen. I've never even seen a dead body before. I don't know if it's right for us to be going on this walk but what else could we do? Go to Solitaire and sit around, waiting for tomorrow? No, it's better we keep ourselves busy."

"There's something alien about the sand dunes," Eva said, looking around at the vast red dunes that lay like enormous ships of sand anchored in an isolated harbour, shadowed by the passing clouds. "They're how I'd imagine the pyramids to be. Huge. Inscrutable entities that hold timeless secrets we'll never know."

The early morning clouds thinned, making way for patches of powder blue sky. The air was quiet and cool and the dawn mist was backed away, like a curtain being pulled off-stage.

The bakkie came to a halt and Charles got out.

"This is where we start our walk," he announced and he led them across to the dunes. The landscape was spectacular:

thick, thorny bush-like acacias fought with tall veldt grasses among the twisted stone carcasses of dead black trees that had been sculpted by the weather and time.

The dense scrub opened to reveal flat white pans burnt and bleached by the kiln of the sun, and broken into puzzle pieces by the freezing nights.

"I'm sorry Kate's missing this," Eva said to Gisela. "She would have been photographing everything and beaming from ear to ear."

"Yes. I'm still so shocked by what happened. Do you really think Charisse was murdered? I can't believe anyone here would do such a thing, do you?"

"How about Lena?" Eva suggested, stepping carefully across white clay-like stones that crumbled beneath her feet. "Charisse was making a fool of her with Stepfan, maybe she'd had enough?"

"Not a chance in a million years." Gisela snapped, and looked around quickly to make sure Lena had not heard, but Lena was up ahead with Charles. "Get that thought out of your mind this second. Lena's a lady and the only fool was Stepfan. If you ask me, it was Jasmine. She hated Charisse, I'd bet it was her."

"Jasmine?" Eva was astonished. "Why?"

"Because for some reason, and I don't know why, she hated Charisse. You heard how she spoke to her and she was the one who shone the light on Stepfan and Charisse."

"Shining a torch on two naked people in a swimming pool is one thing, murder is quite another. Oh, let's admit it, we've got no idea who did it or why. Maybe Stepfan killed her because she ended it after they got caught in the pool and he was angry, although I don't know who ended it, do you? But I don't think he would be that violent, do you?"

"I have no answers except to say that he's a most unpleasant, horrible man," Gisela said.

Up ahead the group was paying careful attention to what

Charles was saying while Rydell, unnoticed, brought up the rear. His level of distress had plummeted to new depths, even for him, and he was muttering to himself.

"Stupid, stupid, stupid," he repeated, a mantra of self-hatred. "Why were you so stupid? You should have found another way. The room for error was too wide. But we never drink from each other's water, never. It's a rule. That stupid girl, it's her fault, she broke the rule, it's her fault, not mine. She wasn't meant to die, I don't understand why she died, there wasn't enough poison to kill a person, I just wanted to get him out of the picture, throw him off course, have him get off the bus so he'd have to recover somewhere for a while. Anything, as long as he was distracted from Treasure. Why did that stupid girl have to die? I never get things like that wrong. There's no way anyone can prove anything, I got rid of all the water bottles but how am I going to stop him now? I can't do the same thing again but I've got to get rid of him, he keeps getting closer to her, I can see that. I'll have to find another way."

Rydell's lightweight cotton trousers and long-sleeved shirt filled with the breeze while his large floppy khaki hat was firmly tied under his chin. He glared at Harrison, up ahead, running around shirtless.

He caught up to the group who was watching Charles unearth a baboon spider by lifting the door to its nest in the sand. The spider poked out cautious feelers, expecting prey but finding nothing.

Rydell waited until the others had walked ahead and when he was sure no one was watching, he kicked heavy sand onto the spider's trapdoor and brought his heel down hard on the mound, stamping a few times for good measure.

"Eensy weensy spider, down goes the spout. Die, die, die!"

Jono was frightened. While the others were with Charles, he and Treasure sat under a tree and discussed in whispers what had happened. "*Haw!* Treasure, I am sick with worry," Jono admitted, and he snapped a twig into tiny pieces.

"Was it my food?" Treasure was equally alarmed and her lovely face creased in a worried frown. "*Aikona wena*, do they think she died from my food?"

"No, Treasure, you must not worry. She was poisoned. I saw it in the army when I was in Zimbabwe. I thought that yesterday but it was already too late and there was nothing that could be done."

"*Eish*," Treasure exclaimed in alarm. "What poison? Who would even do such a thing?"

"Poison from that bush we told them not to touch. I think somebody put it in the water. Kate warned me about a certain person but I thought she was frightened and taking things the wrong way but now I do not know so much."

He told Treasure what Kate had told him, about how Rydell wanted Treasure to be his wife, and how angry Rydell was when Treasure and Harrison had returned as friends from their argument.

"No!" Treasure's eyes were wide, "Truly not. I can't believe that. That he would kill somebody. But Jono, he killed Charisse, that has nothing to do with Harrison and me."

"Charisse drank all of Harrison's water yesterday," Jono explained. "I believe that Rydell poisoned Harrison but the wrong person drank the water. I looked now on the bus, for the empty water bottles but he is clever, they are all gone. I want you to be very careful Treasure, he is a madman."

"But what about Harrison? I can take care of myself but what about Harrison? He has no idea. We must tell him."

"No, we cannot tell him." Jono immediately insisted. "We have no proof, this is supposition only. Promise me. Thaalu should not have said anything about poison until we have proof. He will stay with them at the hospital until they have proof and he will phone me. Thaalu is a good man, I thank God it was him who was with us."

"I still think we must warn Harrison," Treasure replied stubbornly. "If this is true, he is in danger."

Jono swung around, knelt in front of her and held her by the shoulders. "Treasure, please, please promise me you will not say one single thing to him. You have my word that I will watch Rydell very carefully from now on. You can rely on me and you know that, but please, promise me."

"I promise," Treasure said with reluctance and she looked away. "What a terrible man. You mentioned that he had a crush on me, in the Pick 'n Pay that time, but what gave him the idea I would even look at him? He is very strange, I could see that from the start. He never looks you in the eye and he wears all those clothes, with his shirts buttoned right up and his sleeves pulled right down. And he has that terrible smile, he puts his head to the side like this and he wets his lips and he looks like he knows a terrible secret and now we know this is true, he does. *Eish.*"

"You would not have thought any of that if I had not told you," Jono was cross, "so do not start to see problems now where there are none. I will have to reassure the group but I do not know how I will even begin to do that. Oh, this is such a big trouble. In all my years, I have never had such a tour as this! Why all this bad luck?"

He stood. "I told you Treasure, I had a bad feeling and now look, it is true. It is because they want to know about *muti* and terrible things. I should never have discussed any of that with them. But they should never have asked. *Eish!*"

He smacked his forehead with the flat of his hand, "I am going for a short walk, I need to think about what to do. I will see you later. I will get back before the others, they still have more than an hour to go."

In the small van that hurtled along the asphalt road, Kate was also thinking about the murder. She was convinced Rydell was responsible for what had happened. She had seen him on the bus, he had said he was getting something from under the seat but he must have been poisoning the water. He had meant to poison Harrison but Charisse drank it by mistake.

Kate found it hard to believe she was driving along a road in Africa with a dead girl lying in the cargo hold behind. She was not sure what she was feeling; she felt weirded out and numb all at the same time. She looked at Bree, wondering if the girl would ever recover from the shock.

"We'll be there in four and a half hours," Thaalu said quietly to Kate who nodded. She was squeezed in between Brianna and Thaalu, with one leg on either side of the gear shift, the cab definitely more suited to two people. Brianna had dozed off and neither Thaalu nor Kate wanted to disturb her.

"Do you know what to do?" Kate asked Thaalu quietly, "I mean when we get to the hospital?"

"Yes, I have a lot of doctor friends there. Many of the doctors in our country have a great respect for the traditional healers and they ask for our advice."

"Are you a traditional healer?" Kate asked.

Thaalu smiled. "Yes, I am a shaman or as you might call it, a *sangoma*. Like all things in this world, there are good *sangomas* and bad ones. I heal people."

"And you think she was poisoned?"

"I'm sure of it. But what I'm not sure of, is why she died."

"What do you mean? I thought you said she was poisoned and that's why she died?"

"She was poisoned yes, there is no doubt, but there had to be something about her that made her different, weaker than other people because she should only have had a terrible stomach ache. For her to have died from the poison, there would have to have been a big amount in the water, so big that she would have easily tasted it.

"And," he wiped a bead of sweat from his forehead, "why did she need to drink so *much* water? Jono told me that she drank all of her water and all of this other man's. A person in a healthy, normal state wouldn't need to drink that much water. That is why I don't understand it."

"How long will it take before we will know?" Kate's shoulder was getting sore with Bree's weight on it and there was a long way to go.

"I radioed ahead, they are expecting us and they will have everything ready to do an autopsy. It is important that we find out the reason as soon as possible — what if this was not poison, but some contagious disease and you are all in danger? And, if she died by poison, that means there is a murderer in the group with you and the police will have to get involved and the tour will have to stop."

"Disease." Kate had been so convinced Rydell had poisoned the water that she had not even thought of any other possibilities. She looked at Thaalu in shock.

"Disease is very unlikely. Let us change the topic. How are you enjoying your holiday?"

"I love Namibia," Kate said with great enthusiasm. "We could do with a bit less fighting in the group, though."

Thaalu glanced at the rearview window and at the body behind. "I think she would agree."

Back at Sossuvlei, Jono waited for the group to return from their walk. When they did, they were full of tales that Charles had told them, Bushman legends and fables. As they climbed down from the bakkie, happy and chattering, it was as if they had completely forgotten what had happened.

"I liked his stories about the tourists who suddenly think they are trackers." Jasmine said. "They see a bit of spoor and off they go, in hot pursuit. And Charles has to run after them and rescue them and they keep trying to go back to track the animal." She was flushed with happiness and covered in fine red dust.

"This is the most brilliant place ever." Richard wiped the sweat from his forehead with the bottom of his T-shirt. "I'm so glad the sun finally came out but I'm glad it was cloudy for as long as it was — we would have died in that heat."

The mention of death brought them back to reality.

"Any word on Charisse?" Eva asked Jono in the sudden quiet.

"I would imagine she's still dead," Richard tugged at the knotted bandanna around his neck, "unless Thaalu performed some kind of resurrection miracle."

"That's not what I meant," Eva said and her eyes filled with tears. "Honestly, Richard. I meant were they there yet and do they know why she died? Do we know anything new?"

"I'm sorry," Richard apologised. "That was a stupid thing for me to say, I wasn't thinking straight."

"They will probably be arriving at the hospital soon," Jono checked at his watch. "We will only know more late this afternoon. We must get on the road to Solitaire as quickly as possible and we will not be able to stop for lunch because we must get our camp set up before dark. We will eat on the bus if that is all right with everybody."

"That's fine," came the answer.

"I want to also say something else," Jono announced. "I have been thinking very hard and I do not think Thaalu was right about the poison. It would take a lot of poison to kill an adult and Charisse would have tasted that much poison and she did not.

"What I ask," he continued, "is that we stay calm and wait to hear what the doctors say. We will stop at the nearest shop and buy new fresh water supplies, new ice, new everything. Also, please do not worry, this has nothing to do with Treasure's cooking, she was very worried you would think she had poisoned you."

"Of course she didn't," Harrison replied hotly. "I've been by her side for every meal so if she's guilty, then I am too and I'm not guilty."

He marched over to Treasure's side and glared at the gathering, with Treasure smiling at him.

"Ease up, mate," Richard said, "no one would be so stupid as to think that. Besides the poison was in yours or Charisse's water and you're unlikely to try to kill yourself, at least not in that way, I would presume."

"The poison was in my water?" Harrison was astounded. "I thought it was in Charisse's water? What do you mean it could have been in my water? How do you know that? Who put it there?" His voice was filled with panic.

Jono shot a look at Richard who shrugged another apology.

"Harrison, please, calm down," Jono said, in what he hoped was a reassuring manner. "We have no idea if the poison was in your water or Charisse's or even if there was poison. Please calm down. Think about it, who here would like to kill you? We all like you."

"Of course we do, old chap." Richard said, "that was a stupid thing for me to say. Charisse was the one with the enemies, not you."

At that, Jasmine started crying noisily. "Oh, so now it's me who killed her? Don't you think I feel bad enough that she's dead, without being accused of murdering her? I feel terrible for how I treated her. I should never have interfered, her business is her business. I never would have killed her or anybody. That's just stupid."

"Best I keep my mouth shut from now," Richard muttered to Mia who gave him a look, nodded and went over to Jasmine.

"Jazzer, luv, Sweet Jesus and Mary, no one here would dream of finking that you offed her. Come on now, stop crying, and as for how you treated her, don't you worry, she was 'aving it off with someone else's husband and that made you angry, it's perfectly understandable."

The mention of Stepfan had all eyes turn to Lena.

"Yes," she said scornfully, "I killed her because she stole my husband." She gave a short laugh. "Don't be so ridiculous, all of you, look at him, do you really think he's worth killing for?"

The group turned towards Stepfan who was asleep on the bus, his head back, mouth agape.

"She would have been welcome to him," Lena said with finality.

"Everybody, no more talk of murders." Jono ended the discussion. "There is no proof of anything. Let us go."

Stepfan woke at the sound of their approach and watched his wife climb onto the bus. He suddenly felt a thousand years old. He told himself he would get his wife back, he knew he would. He was furious with Charisse for dying like that, the silly girl. He knew he needed to work on repairing relations with his wife but before anything, he desperately needed to sleep, he was exhausted.

Rydell climbed on the bus, relieved that Kate had gone to Walvis Bay. She was the only one who could tie him to Harrison and the poison. She had seen him on the bus, under Harrison's seat, and she was the only one who would know why he would want Harrison out the way. And although he had succeeded in distracting her by being as nasty as he could, he was sure she would not have forgotten he had been there.

He was irritated by how complicated this was becoming. It was not supposed to be like this. But he was not going to give up, Treasure would be his, she would. He was not going to lose what was rightfully his, not this time. He consoled himself by imagining Treasure as his bride, standing next to him with a lace veil framing her queenly face, her expression loving and tender and he strengthened his resolve.

He knew he still needed to find a way to get rid of Harrison. Perhaps if Harrison betrayed or frightened Treasure in some way, she would tell him to leave her alone and then she would be happy to have a real man at her side. He wracked his brains and he recalled coming across the so-called Jack the Ripper murders in his research on Namibia. They had occurred in July of the same year, and he knew the police had charged a

Windhoek doctor for killing four young prostitutes, decapitating and dismembering their bodies. Rydell figured that a copycat murder would not be too difficult to orchestrate. They had lots of time in Swakopmund and it was a big town; he would have all the resources he'd need. Yes, life as a copycat murderer was what Harrison's future held for him. He smiled broadly and his pouty lower lip curled down. He was unaware that he was watched by Marika who wondered why he was smiling if, in fact it could be called smiling. She knew now that Kate had been correct about him and she wished she had listened to her.

She turned to watch the scenery fly by, her expression worried, and she hoped Kate was okay out in the middle of nowhere.

In the van, with Brianna asleep on her shoulder, Kate concluded that she was Rydell's only weak link and that she would have to be careful. She wished Jono had listened to her and she also wished she had not encouraged Rydell to talk to her so much. She was only being polite. And yet, even while she knew how bizarre and even dangerous the situation was, her thoughts were distracted; Thaalu smelled wonderful. And his thigh, pressing up against hers, was unexpectedly arousing. She did not want to move — not that she could.

Kate was disconcerted by her reactions to the man next to her; she was powerfully attracted to him. She tried to tell herself that it was just the reaction to being "rescued" by a handsome stranger who rode in to take charge; a stranger with skin the colour of polished sandalwood and eyes the colour of amber gemstones.

But analyzing her feelings did not make them go away. She felt as if each cell in her body was on high alert, waiting to feel the subtlest movement from Thaalu; the shift of his leg, the in-out swell of his rib cage when he breathed.

She stared ahead at the long straight white road, white sand on either side, the cloudless blue sky above, hoping he had no idea what she was thinking.

"Thaalu," she said, before she could stop herself. "Do you have a wife?"

He smiled and glanced at her and she blushed under the gaze of his gold and brown eyes. "I have two," he replied.

"Oh." Kate suddenly felt deflated, reminded of the real life that awaited her once the holiday was over. She would have to find a job and a place to stay and she would be alone.

"Marriage is a good thing," Thaalu said.

"So good you had to do it twice," Kate teased him.

"Absolutely." Thaalu smiled at her again and she blushed.

The sun was blazing down on the small car and there was no air conditioning. The windows were wide open but that did nothing to help. Kate wiped the perspiration from her upper lip thinking that she was getting stuck to both Bree and Thaalu; they were melting into one person. Kate pushed the damp curls off Bree's forehead and gently wiped her face. A small trickle of sweat ran down Brianna's neck but she was breathing evenly, sound asleep.

"What pills did you give her?" Thaalu motioned to Brianna. "She is sleeping like a drunk person."

"Tranquillizers," Kate explained, "Which should last about four hours."

"Then she should be waking up just after we get there, so that is good," Thaalu calculated. "She was very upset. I would like her to preferably be in the hospital when she wakes up again."

"Yes, she's had a terrible shock, I wonder if she will ever recover." Kate voiced her earlier thoughts.

"She will, if she wants to," Thaalu said. "We can choose, every day, to be happy or sad. Or nothing. Some people choose nothing because it's easier for them."

"I like to be happy," Kate told him, "even though it can be tiring at times. How foolish is that, to say that happiness can be tiring."

"Not foolish. It means you make the effort. Making an effort is always tiring, even if you badly want the reward of what you are making an effort for."

"You know Thaalu," Kate burst out quietly, "I thought you would be short and wrinkled."

Thaalu snorted with amusement, then he looked over at Brianna and lowered his voice. "A common mistake," he said. "But, do you imagine every human to look like your ninety-year-old grannie? Most people have only seen pictures of older Bushman and that's why they think the way they do, that we are all ninety and shrunk. I always find it so funny."

"Sorry," Kate said.

"No need to apologize, as I said, it's a common mistake." He grinned at her and her heart quickened.

Brianna showed signs of restlessness and Kate and Thaalu both froze.

"We must be quiet," he whispered.

Kate nodded, "we must not wake her." She stroked Brianna's hair and she settled down. They were quiet after that. Brianna slept on, and behind them, Charisse lay wrapped in thick black plastic.

When they arrived at the hospital, Brianna was still asleep. "Wait here with her, in the car," Thaalu spoke quietly. "Try not to move or wake her up. I will get the doctors. It is better if she wakes up with them near to her and preferably with the dead girl's body removed."

Kate waited in the car which remained stifling and airless, although Thaalu's door and the windows were open. The parking lot was empty save for a handful of battered old Toyotas and Mazdas.

The hospital was white, single-storied, and governmental in appearance, sprawled across a large barren area of cleared red earth. A few geraniums bloomed in a flower bed near the main entrance that was flanked by young palm trees. "*Quality Care by People Who Care,*" Kate read the slogan under the hospital logo. The entire complex seemed brand new.

She was desperate to stretch her legs but she did not want to disturb Brianna. She was as stiff as a board, not having moved for close to five hours. She was beginng to think that she could not stand the heat any longer when Thaalu returned with two doctors, a security guard and a nurse.

"You go with Brianna and this man," Thaalu said to Kate, "and I will go with the body. I'll come and find you. Don't worry, I won't leave without you. Also, we need to find you a hotel for the night. We will sort it all out."

Brianna's doctor brought her a wheelchair and he and the nurse put her into it. She woke slightly but fell back into a doze. Kate collected their belongings and staggered slightly under the weight of the two backpacks and her camera bag.

Thaalu rushed up to her. "Don't be foolish," he chided her, "I was going to bring those. Give them to me."

Kate handed them over and followed Brianna.

They put Brianna to bed with a drip in her arm, and Kate began a long wait. She was concerned if she left Brianna's room that Thaalu would not know where to find her. She was hungry and tired. By 5:00 p.m., she was beyond exhausted. Kate drew her chair close to Bree and rested her head on her arms on the side of the bed and fell into an uneasy sleep. It was close to midnight when the doctor who had first seen to Brianna returned with Thaalu.

"We have checked their documentation," the doctor apologized for waking Kate. "They are covered for all sorts of travel insurance and their passports and visas are in order and we've got someone coming from the American embassy to help the girls get back home."

Kate thanked the doctor and asked him why Brianna had not woken up.

"We've given her a mild sedative and she's in shock and dealing with it by sleeping. Rest is the best thing for her now," the doctor told her. "Don't worry, she'll be fine, you know what they say about time healing all wounds." He shook Kate's hand and walked off.

"I found you a bed-and-breakfast for the night," Thaalu said, "and Jono will pick you up tomorrow morning." He picked up her camera bag and made to leave.

"Wait a moment, please," Kate said. "I must leave Brianna a note." She grabbed her journal and tore out a page telling Brianna how to get in touch with her if she wanted to.

"You have a good heart," Thaalu said, watching her.

Kate thanked him. She felt as if she'd been at the hospital forever and by the time they arrived at the bed-and-breakfast that was housed in a white, ranch-style bungalow, Kate barely felt capable of thought. Thaalu helped her to the front desk and got her signed in. They stood in the hallway of the house, with the outside security light throwing shadows of ghostly light through the burglar-bars and Thaalu prepared to leave.

"Wait, Thaalu," Kate said, "I'm so tired I nearly forgot to ask you. How did Charisse die? Did they find out?"

"Yes, they did. She had poison in her system from one of our local bushes but it was not enough to kill her. She had a very bad stomach ulcer and was dehydrated, which is why she drank all of her own and the other man's water. Because of the bad state of her ulcer, she very quickly got septicaemia and so they ruled it an accidental death and that is the end of the matter."

"How sad, poor girl." Kate was shocked.

"Yes," Thaalu agreed. He paused and looked around the living room. "But, you my dear," he said as he stepped closer to her, "must remember one thing." Her tired body was once more aware of his sensual beauty and she looked up at him, wondering if he had any idea what she was thinking. "Somebody did try to poison either this girl or somebody else. So you must take very good care of yourself and be careful like I said. I want to give you my cellphone number in case you need me."

"You have a cellphone?" Kate was surprised.

Thaalu laughed, a wonderful, deep sound. "I keep making

you astonished, don't I? First I am taller and less wrinkled and now I have a cellphone. Yes, drawing on caves to communicate takes too long these days especially if a person's life is in danger." He handed her a piece of paper with his number on it. He took her hand lightly and held it for a moment and Kate clutched him tightly and then with reluctance, let go. He walked out, closing the door carefully.

Kate wasn't quite sure what to do with herself. The owner, in dressing gown and pyjamas, had signed her in and vanished. It felt odd, being in this place, all alone. It was well after midnight and she grabbed her bag and headed for the washroom. As she stood under the steady stream of hot water, she felt immeasurably sad and she cried for a long time.

The Sixth Night

MEANWHILE, EARLIER THAT NIGHT, the gang had set up camp in Solitaire and Jono was preparing steaks on the braai. "Or, the barbecue, as you Americans call it." he said to a miserable Stepfan who was with him at the concrete open-air grill, the coals glowing red hot.

"We don't barbecue much in New York," Stepfan commented but there was hardly any energy behind his words.

Richard arrived with Mia and he handed Jono a beer.

"Thank you," Jono said. "Did anybody try the world-famous apple pie yet?"

"Not yet," Richard replied, "we don't want to spoil our appetites. This is a pretty deserted spot, wouldn't you say?"

Jono cracked open the beer, and took a long drink. "It was a refueling stop for vehicles and light aircraft, then they built some washrooms and the camping site. But the shop is a good one, lots of different things in it. Have you been in there yet?"

"Yes," Richard waved the beer at him. "That's where we got these and the girls immediately started shopping up a storm. Women."

Mia hit him on the shoulder and showed Jono a small, beaded copper lizard that she had bought.

"Very pretty," Jono said. He turned the steaks over and brushed them with sauce.

Sofie was doing yoga under a tree. Helen had gone for a run on the track around the airfield and Enrique was cleaning his camera. Rydell was nowhere to be seen and Lena and Gisela had gone for a walk. Marika was enjoying a shower and Eva was hunched over a poem, chewing on her pen.

Jono brushed the steaks again, thinking how normal and holidayish it all seemed, while under the thin skin of the surface, bad things were happening. And he knew in his gut that there was more to follow and that his biggest challenges still lay ahead. He looked over at Treasure and Harrison chattering away while they prepared the vegetables and he had to laugh, remembering how much Treasure had hated Harrison. He could not recall ever having seen her laugh so much or sound so happy.

He smiled to himself and poured a dash of beer onto the steaks. He wondered how Kate was doing and he wished she had not gone with the body for the simple reason that he missed her. He was determined to tell her how he felt as soon as she returned; he did not want to waste another moment. He thought about how she was supportive to those who needed it, and how she never failed to come up with a plan when one was needed. He decided that he would ask her out to dinner the following night when they were in Swakopmund.

"When do you want the vegetables to be ready?" Treasure called out.

"In about half an hour," Jono told her, "by which time Helen will be back from her run and we can eat. And I must make a phone call before we have supper."

Helen was flying down the track in fine style, relishing the heart-pounding familiarity of her faithful sanctuary. She rounded a corner and saw Gisela and Lena walking close together, deep in conversation and she thought how wonderful it was that Lena was no longer a slave to her husband's whims. Helen waved to them as she ran by and it seemed to her that they were startled to see her, but she figured it had been that kind of day and after everything that had happened, it was natural that they were all a bit on edge. She was curious if they had determined what had killed Charisse. Then she told herself to pick up the pace, there was steak for dinner and world-famous apple pie for dessert, and her heart swelled with contentment at a perfect moment.

"Good evening, everybody," Jono said, taking his usual position to the side of the group after they had finished eating dinner. He stood with his hands in his pockets, while the lights from the bus illuminated the group. "How is everybody tonight?"

"Why isn't there a bleedin' fire pit at this campsite?" Mia was truculent. "I feel like I'm sitting in an abandoned lot or something, smack bang in the middle of nowhere. I don't understand why there's no place for a fire."

"It's just the way this campsite is," Jono said, marvelling at Mia's self-absorption.

"How are we going to sit around the bleedin' campfire and drink, if there's no campfire?" she persisted.

"Light a candle, sit and drink around that," Sofie muttered but only Helen heard her.

Jono looked exhausted. "*Haw!* Mia, my dear," he said, "practice drinking in the dark, it cannot be too difficult. I am sure you will manage fine." He smiled at her but she was not happy.

"Not the same ambience," she grumbled, flicking a seed pod off her bare stomach; she was lounging on her camp stool in her bikini top and shorts.

Jono decided that he couldn't be bothered with Mia's need for ambience. "Today," he said, and he cleared his throat, "was, as you know, a most difficult day for all of us." He looked around at the circle. "It was very tragic what happened and I am certain we will miss Charisse a lot. I have just spoken to Thaalu on the telephone and he has given me an update and I am happy to say there was no murder involved whatsoever. So you can erase that from your minds entirely."

"How did she die then?" Sofie asked pointedly.

"She had a very bad bleeding stomach ulcer and then it got septic when she drank the water."

"There wasn't any poison?" Harrison enquired.

"Well, there was some poison," Jono admitted unwillingly, "but not enough to kill her, just enough to give her a stomach ache but because her stomach was so damaged, it killed her. They ruled it an 'accidental death.' "

Harrison cocked his head to one side. "Let me get this straight," he said, putting his tin plate on the ground and folding his arms. "There was poison in my or Charisse's water bottle. We will never know whose bottle it was in, but we know it was there? Am I correct?"

"That is correct, yes," Jono replied, again with obvious reluctance.

"Is there any way that the poison could have fallen into water by accident?" Harrison asked.

"No, somebody would have to had to put it there," Jono answered, with even more reluctance.

"Therefore," Harrison said, acknowledging Treasure who had come up to sit beside him, "somebody, on our bus, somebody amongst us here, tried to poison either me or Charisse. Does that not worry anybody except me? There is a murderer among us, does that not concern any of you? I suppose not since none of you were the intended victims."

"Harrison, there was no intent to kill anybody," Jono hoped he sounded convincing. "They only wanted to give you or Charisse a stomach ache."

"Oh, well, that's much better," Harrison said, sarcastically. "Forgive me, but the idea of somebody wanting to give me a stomach ache doesn't make me feel reassured either. Is it because I like to clean so much? I'm only trying to keep us in good health. I mean, some of you are strange too, we all have our own ways, but I'm patient with you, why would you try to poison me?"

"They could have been trying to poison Charisse," Richard

said. "Harrison, I know it's easy for me to say, since I'm not the one who was nearly poisoned, but the desert does strange things to people, loss of sanity and all that. We heard Charles tell us all kinds of stories."

"None of which has any bearing on me being poisoned." Harrison stuck to his guns.

"Why don't you have a beer?" Mia offered, "help you relax a bit, take the edge off."

"Alcohol is not the answer to my problems as it so obviously is to yours," Harrison said shortly, ignoring the offered beer.

"Don't you start attacking Mia now," Richard warned. "Let's keep our wits about us now. This is a time of stress, we need to pull together, not apart."

"I tell you what I need," Harrison announced, his arms still crossed. "I need the person who put the poison in my water to tell me why they did it. I'm going to sit here all night until they tell me. I want to know. I will not get angry, but I must know." He glared around at the circle, trying to determine who sat uneasily on their campstools, with no one making eye contact.

"But it may not have been aimed at you," Richard argued. "It may as easily been aimed at Charisse. Heaven knows people here had their issues with her. Here's the thing: we're not even halfway through our trip, well, maybe we're halfway, I don't know. But never mind, it's not important; what is important is that we don't let this ruin our holiday. Let's put it behind us and carry on."

Richard looked around intently. "I say we get it together, and stop attacking each other and carry on. This is a holiday of a lifetime for all of us, so, come on people, let's holiday for God's sake. I'm incredibly sorry for, and about, Charisse but you heard the man, she died because she had an ulcer that went septic and that's it. Let the consequence of this be that we unite, not that we crumble." He came to a close, his tone strongly persuasive. He had taken the time to shower after they arrived and he had shaved his facial hair into long thin sideburns that cut across his cheeks and met in a small goatee on his chin. This geometry, along with his hawk-like features and the pale untanned skin around his eyes, made him an odd, yet compelling figure as he gave his speech.

"I wonder if he's a politician in his spare time," Eva whispered to Marika.

"He's quite fascist with his horrible new shaved look," Marika agreed.

Sofie looked at Helen who was nodding in earnest agreement with Richard. Sofie shook her head, unable to see what Helen found so appealing in Richard; she found him arrogant and vain.

In the ensuing silence, Jono started to applaud. "I could not agree more, my friend," he said. "Let us move on and enjoy the rest of our holiday."

"Harrison, the decision lies with you, old chap," Richard continued, hoping the sheer force of his will would break Harrison down. "Either we go now and buy some world-famous apple pie and enjoy our holiday or we continue to interrogate and search for answers which, I can tell you now, we will not find. What's the call? It's up to you."

Harrison looked at him, and then at each member of the circle in turn. "Apple pie," he said, and he laughed. "My life comes down to apple pie. I'll tell you this," and he got up and dusted off his shorts, "you go and get your apple pie and continue on with your holiday, I won't stop you. As for me, I'm going to do the dishes now." He walked off, with Treasure and Enrique close behind him.

"Good man." Richard was relieved. "And now I am going to buy apple pie for the lot of you. My treat."

"I was going to do that." Helen sprang to her feet, "I'll come with you, we'll split it. And if they have ice-cream, we'll get that too."

"I'll get the plates ready," Mia got up and pulled a tank top over her raw sunburn. "And forks and spoons. I wish we had a bleedin' campfire," she muttered, "especially after today. I need to get blotto more than ever."

"I'm really sorry about Sofie insulting Mia earlier," Helen told Richard as they walked to the store through the thick coarse sand.

Richard glanced over at her. "Why are you sorry?" he asked.

"She said it, not you."

"Yes, but she's my tentmate, I would hate for you to think..."

"For me to think what?"

This was not going quite the way Helen had thought or hoped it would. "Richard, hang on a second, let me be frank," she said and stopped, catching him by the arm.

"You're a good looking man, a great looking man actually, incredibly sexy. And Mia, well, she's let herself go, not that she may ever have been different, I don't know. But I wonder, wouldn't you like to feel a taut, hard body underneath you rather than all that softness?" She took a step closer to him.

Richard went dead quiet. "Come again?" he asked softly.

Helen stepped still closer to him and looked up at him. "I was wondering," she said, "if you wouldn't like to have a body like mine underneath you — fit, tight, strong, lean. No strings attached, just you and me, work off some energy, have some fun together. I can bring you a lot of pleasure, trust me."

"Funny," Richard said, consideringly, "that's exactly what I thought you meant."

He turned off his flashlight. "Let me explain something to you, sunshine," he said softly, and he moved closer to her, his warm breath caressing her ear.

She leaned up against him, loving the feel of his chest through his thin T-shirt and enjoying the way he smelled clean and freshly shaven. She could see the wiry ginger hair on his neck below his Adam's apple and she felt a wave of arousal so strong she nearly clutched him.

"You repulse me," he whispered, "you're like a man to me,

no, you're something even worse. You're a finger-pointing, uptight, judgmental, know-it all bitch in trousers. No one will listen to you in the real world, so you seek out the vulnerable, the sick and the poor, and you form a little dictatorship, lying to yourself that you're bringing help and relief to the world, when all you're really doing is bossing people around who've got no choice but to listen."

He leaned in even closer. "You pretend to others that it's for the good of the cause but the truth is that you get off on it. And now, you want me to put my hand up your skirt and fuck you and tell you how sexy you are, tell you that I've been hot for you since the moment I saw you. I took one look at you and saw exactly who and what you are and I saw what you think of Mia, it's been written all over your unhappy, frigid face right from the start. Now," he added, running a finger up her arm, "here's how it's going to work. We're going to get this apple pie, which frankly I don't give a bastard's shit about, and then we're going to go back and you'll be all happy, like you were when we walked off. And if you ever come on to me again, or even so much as look in Mia's direction with any kind of holier-than-thou expression, I'll make sure you can't do your precious running for a very long time and believe me, I know how to do it. Do I make myself clear?" He held her chin for a moment and then he stepped away and waited for her reply.

"Crystal clear." Helen was quiet, with salty tears falling onto her cheeks.

"Excellent. Now, wipe your face and start smiling again. Imagine," he continued conversationally, "world-famous apple pie, right here, in the middle of nowhere."

Helen watched him walk off, then she ran to catch up with him.

To Swakopmund

Kate woke up early, disoriented. She could feel that her face was swollen from crying but she could not remember what she had been upset about. She raised herself up on one elbow and looked around the anonymous room. For a few moments she had no idea where she was or what she was doing there. She searched around for clues. She saw her camera bag next to the bed and then she remembered the hospital and all the events of the previous day came flooding back. Charisse was dead. Brianna was in a state of shock and sedated. Thaalu, with his spicy scent and beautiful tiger's eye gaze, was gone and she was alone.

She lay back down on the bed and pulled the thin sheet over her. She thought about her family, about her best friend Rachel, her ex, Cameron, and the job she had left. That life seemed like a distant movie from another universe. She rallied her thoughts back to the present, dismayed to feel a headache brewing in the back of her skull.

She wondered what the group was up to. Everything seemed so complicated and a part of her wished that she could phone Thaalu and tell him that she wanted to join him, that she wanted to live a life that was simpler, easier.

But then she tried to picture herself living in a hut, digging for tubers, collecting milk and honey, and washing her few items of clothing along the banks of a river. She tried to imagine herself skinning dead animals and drinking thick rich beer while sitting around a campfire with voices clicking in a tongue she could not understand. She told herself she was making assumptions and that Thaalu's life was in all likelihood far more modern than that but regardless, it would not work.

She sighed, rolled over onto her back and dug her fingers into the pressure points at the base of her skull. The pain was intense, the relief minimal. She pulled a pillow over her head and lay very still.

At Solitaire, the camp slowly came to life. Helen had gone out for an early morning run. She was still shaken by her encounter with Richard, and furious with him — he could as easily have said "no thanks," instead of being so vicious. She eased into her rhythm in the dusty fuzzy-peach light of the dawn and wished there was a way she could pay him back. There had to be a way. She felt sick with humiliation and incensed with the way both he and Robbie had treated her. Her face was grim, her body tight and focused. Toying with ideas of vengeance, she wondered if there was any credence to spells and curses. She had always scoffed at the idea but the locals at the mission had taken them seriously, even the educated women among them.

She pounded through the sand and the more she thought about it, the more she was convinced that it could work — she would find a person or a book in Swakopmund that would tell her how to do things. She smiled as she ran, thinking about her revenge.

It had taken Rydell a long time to fall asleep. He had been overwhelmingly relieved when he heard the results from the hospital but there had been a moment when he had been alarmed by Harrison's insistence to learn the truth. But who was there to point the finger at him? Kate was not there, which was a good thing, but what if she had already told someone about how he felt about Treasure? It would not take a genius to put two and two together: that Harrison was the target and Rydell the one with motive. And while Rydell had been grateful to Richard for turning the situation around, in the next breath, he hated him, hated him for his easy charm, his striking good looks, and his tall athletic body.

Rydell knew that there were women who found him attractive but he also knew that he was nothing compared to Richard. And, by taking control of the situation in the way that he had, Richard had unleashed a flood of distressing memories for Rydell, memories of his plump rejected youth, his troubled young adult life and the lonely stretch of his isolated later years. Sitting in the circle, waiting for Richard and Helen to return, Rydell had been filled with venom and hatred, so much so that he could taste the offending acid in his mouth; it was thick enough to choke on. Stung by the failure of his plan to get rid of Harrison and fearful of discovery, Rydell's anger and fear funneled into self-loathing.

"*Four and twenty blackbirds sitting in a pie, four and twenty blackbirds pecking out my eyes,*" he mumbled under his breath. "*The dormouse is a tea tray and the world is full of spies.*"

He felt as if the group had, with one united movement, banded together and forced him to the outside. Sure, when Richard and Helen returned, they had given him apple pie and ice cream, he could not argue that. They did all the right things outwardly, just as his mother had done but he knew that they despised him just as she had.

Later, he thrashed about in his sleeping bag, feeling boneless, fat and invisible, and hating himself for being such a nobody. He tossed and turned, feeling spiteful and restless. He wanted to hurt something, someone, but who, what? He shook off the sleeping bag, sat up in the darkness and listened to the thick silence, wondering what sounds of Africa Stepfan was always complaining about missing, because Rydell could not hear a thing; not a bird or a cricket or a frog.

Suddenly claustrophobic in his pajamas, he ripped them off and he felt a searing heat radiating off his tight, parched skin.

He felt his anger building up even further and he scratched at himself in the darkness, viciously scoring his arms and thighs. He realized he might have to take a couple of pills to take the edge off his anger; he could not afford to lose control now.

He turned on his flashlight and dug in his bag, quickly chewing two tranquilizers but they did not work fast enough. The need for release overwhelmed him. He clawed at his scalp, willing the anguish to lessen but the fury consumed him. He reached into his toiletry bag and found his nail scissors and began to stab at his thigh, deep enough to draw blood. "*Pop goes the weasel*," he said with each prick, and he slowly felt the pressure ease. "Pop, pop, pop."

His numb fury receded and in its place came calm. He could feel the pills beginning to work. He cleaned his wounds with antiseptic, set his alarm for 7:00 a.m, and finally fell asleep.

"Man, can that guy ever snore." Gisela lay in her sleeping bag, several tents away. "He's like a dying elephant in pain. Not that I've ever met a dying elephant but I'm sure that's what one would sound like."

Eva laughed. "I agree."

By silent mutual consent neither of them mentioned the events of the day.

"What's the time?"

"4:30 a.m." Gisela replied.

Eva groaned, "We're going to be so tired later."

"I'm going to try to get more sleep," Gisela turned over. "You know, the least he could have done was give us ear plugs when we started the trip."

"You're right. Jono said Rydell paid extra to get a tent all by himself and now we know why. He'd be impossible to share with. I'm going to listen to my music and try to drown him out."

In the next tent, Stepfan, in his sleeping bag, was watching Lena who was getting dressed despite the earliness of the hour.

"Lena, my love," Stepfan said pleadingly, raised up on one

elbow, "I know I did what I said I would not do. I said I'm sorry. Why will you not forgive me? I see that I've behaved badly, I do. It was wrong of me and I'm sorry for embarrassing you."

"The only person you embarrassed was yourself," Lena replied. "I'm going for a walk."

She climbed out of the tent and strolled around the airfield, enjoying the birdcalls and the cool air. She stopped to pick some of the long grasses, inhaling their raw woody scent. As the sun came up, she headed back to camp, and saw a sleepy Treasure at the back of the bus, with Harrison talking to her as he put the kettle on the burner. She thought they were becoming quite the couple.

She walked to the washroom and passed Richard and Mia's tent and she heard Mia shouting; "You should, just for fucking once, take me bleedin' seriously. I'm going off my rocker. If we don't get to do it soon, then fuck it, yeah, fuck it, Richard. I'm telling you, I can't take much more of this."

Lena heard the reassuring murmur of Richard's voice as she walked away and she wondered what Mia was so upset about.

"Good morning, Jasmine," Lena said, stepping up into the tiled washroom. Jasmine waved at her, her mouth full of toothpaste.

Ellie emerged from the shower. "Tonight, we go dancing," she announced.

"Dancing?" Lena exclaimed in surprise. "Where?"

"In Swakopmund," Ellie called out, toweling herself dry, quite unconcerned by her public nudity. "You must come."

"We'll see," Lena replied cautiously. "I haven't danced in years."

"I bet you're great at it," Gisela said, walking in. "I'm going, you should come."

"I'm too old," Lena protested.

"Nonsense," the others said. "You must come. It will be fun."

"I'll think about it."

Mia arrived, her eyes red and her face blotchy and swollen.

Ellie did not notice that she had been crying. "Mia," she said eagerly, "I can't wait for tonight."

Mia managed a pale smile and closed the shower door.

The others looked at each other and shrugged. To cover up the awkward silence, they fell into a fast chatter.

Later, standing around the foldout table at the bus, Jono pointed to the Wheetabix, Kate's favourite.

"The Wheetabix misses Kate," he said, holding a steaming mug of coffee close to his face.

"I don't know about the Wheetabix," Marika told him, "but I certainly do. I'll be glad when we have her back safe and sound." But all at once she remembered that it might not be safe for Kate to be back on the bus. She glanced around cautiously. Rydell was sitting at a picnic table, listlessly spooning cereal into his mouth.

"Isn't he a train-wreck this morning," Eva followed her gaze. "If I didn't know better, I would think he was totally stoned. He can hardly get his hand to his mouth."

It was true that Rydell was struggling. He had forgotten the power of his meds, how they knocked him flat. He had been foolish to take two. It had taken all of his resolve to get up, get dressed, take down his tent and get to breakfast. He hoped he would make it onto the bus where he would be able to sleep off the rest of the effects. He was gripped in chains of fog and he could not shake himself free. He watched his hand move from his cereal bowl to his mouth, and he commanded it to move faster but it failed to obey. He stared at the disobedient appendage with dislocated anger when he felt someone sit down beside him. It was Ellie.

Big brown moth girl, he thought as he spilled milk on his chin and struggled to wipe it off with his shirtsleeve. *No moths rhymes, they're too ugly.*

"Rydell," Ellie said brightly and he tried to focus and sit up straighter.

"We're going dancing tonight, will you come with us?"

"We missed you so much." Eva hugged her.

"Are you alright, *liefie*? It must have been terrible," Marika asked, also hugging her.

"We were very worried about you," Lena and Gisela said together and they joined the hug. "How are you?"

The unexpected affection brought tears to Kate's eyes. "I'm fine," she said. "I'm stupid for crying, but I'm so happy to see you."

"As are we, to see you," Helen gave her a big hug and Sofie did the same.

"I'm a man, I do not hug," Harrison declared, "but I'm delighted to see you, Kate. You are somewhat alright?"

"Yes, Harrison, exactly. Somewhat alright," Kate said. She was thinking how odd it felt, to be hugged by Helen, even when she meant well. "And how are all of you?" she asked.

"All the better for seeing you," Richard said heartily and Mia agreed.

"Now we will continue on to Swakopmund," Jono said. He had been quiet so far. "Kate, *haw* but we are very glad to see you. We missed you a lot." He cleared his throat. "I hope that everybody has remembered that we are all going out to dinner tonight?"

There was a collective nod.

Jono had been hoping to cancel the dinner as he had wanted to ask Kate out by himself, but Treasure had persuaded him that it was essential to stick to the plan for the sake of normalcy and he had agreed, albeit reluctantly.

"*Aikona*, my friend," Treasure had said when he had suggested cancelling, "it was on the itinerary, you can't start changing things however you feel like. These people need routine more than ever."

She was right but Jono was tired of the group and he wanted to be alone with Kate. Seeing her again after the short time apart had only increased his desire to be with her and he found it hard to concentrate on anything else.

"Then tomorrow is a free day for you," he continued, "and you can do adventure sports, which you can book this afternoon on our way. Or you can shop, or visit the Internet cafés in town. I am sure many of you would like to update your families and tell them what a great time you are having."

Great time? Kate was dumbfounded. A girl had died. No one had mentioned Charisse or Brianna; it was as if they'd never existed. She felt odd, despite the welcome she had received. Had they collectively decided to pretend none of it had happened? She looked for Rydell but he was nowhere to be seen.

When she climbed on the bus, she saw that he was slumped against the window, fast asleep. He was twitching and muttering and to her disgust, she noticed fine strands of saliva hanging from his chin. She looked questioningly at Eva who was behind her.

Eva shrugged. "He's been like that all morning," she whispered. "He could hardly eat his breakfast. None of us knows what's wrong with him. It's like he's drugged."

"Good," Kate said firmly. "Let's hope he stays that way."

"Here, I saved you a seat next to me," Marika said.

Kate sat down with a sigh of relief. "Marika," she asked in an undertone, "why isn't anybody talking about what happened? Do they know the results from the hospital? Tell me what happened after I left with Thaalu and I'll tell you about my trip."

"Hmmm," Marika said, "let's wait until it's just you and me this afternoon and I'll tell you. There's a big market in the centre of town that I really want to visit, if you're interested? We can chat properly then."

"Sounds like a plan," Kate said.

The bus pulled into the adventure sports centre at noon and the group tumbled off. They walked past three scornful camels lying in the sand and yawning widely with their noses in the air.

"Camels!" Kate slowed and reached for her camera.

"Come and check out the adventures with me first," Eva said, propelling her forwards.

The adventure centre was a cool hive of noiseless activity. Large TV screens had quad bikers flying through the air, while speedboats hurtled through foamy blue waters, and tandem skydivers shrieked silently with grins of panic and pleasure air-blasting their faces. A confident, flashy girl, shapely in extraordinarily tight jeans and a blue Adventure Group T-shirt clicked a remote control and the immediate sound was deafening.

Kate decided she was not interested in any of the activities and she went outside to photograph the camels, leaving Eva and Marika to debate the many choices, trying to balance their budgets with their wish-lists.

Kate was lying in the sand on her stomach, as close to the camels as she could get when she heard the bus door open. She sat up and turned around to see Rydell climbing down; he was unsteady and groggy. He stopped and scanned around him. He looked confused. He saw Kate staring at him. She stood up and brushed the dirt from her trousers. For a while, neither of them moved. Then he walked towards her.

"How are you?" he asked with his high-pitched boyish voice and a sideways glance.

"Considering the circumstances, I suppose you could say I'm fine," Kate said.

Rydell smiled and looked over at the camels. He seemed unsure what to say next. He scratched the back of his head and shifted from side to side, his mouth twisted in a small smile.

Kate waited.

"That whole poison thing," he said, eventually, tugging at his shirt, "I've got no idea how that happened or who would have done such a thing. Do you have any ideas?"

"I always have ideas," Kate replied, neutrally.

"You may be thinking that I did it, to harm Harrison because he hangs around Treasure all the time and you know I like her. Is that what you thought?"

"It certainly crossed my mind." She stared at him, knowing he hated direct eye contact.

Rydell shifted uneasily from side to side. "I would never do that," he stated. "Because I'm the better man for her and she'll see that by herself. But did you tell anybody about how I feel?" he demanded, and he scuffed his shoe in the dirt, glancing up and meeting her eye for the briefest of moments, and Kate was disconcerted by crazed malevolence conveyed in the brief look.

"No," Kate lied, concerned she would enrage him if she told him the truth. "I told you, I respect your confiding in me."

Rydell smiled his odd smile. "And," he said, "if you were to tell them now, no one would believe you, they'd say you were making up lies."

"You're quite right," Kate said. "I can't say anything now. No one would believe me. But what are you going to do, Rydell?"

"What do you mean?" Rydell was confused.

"Are you going to try to hurt Harrison again?"

"Hurt Harrison, hurt Harrison," Rydell mimicked. "No, Mother. I'm not going to hurt anyone."

Kate was unsettled by his sudden and obvious departure from rationality. "I'm not your mother, Rydell," she said. "How are you feeling, anyway? You don't look so good today."

"*Some like it hot, some like it cold, some like it in the pot, nine days old,*" Rydell muttered. "Don't ask me how I feel, Mother, you don't care, you never have."

"Rydell," Kate tried to keep her voice even and reassuring, "if you don't want to talk to me, fine. I don't want to talk anymore either. All I want to do is photograph the camels, okay?"

Eva, Marika, Richard and Mia came out at that moment and when Marika saw Rydell standing so close to Kate, she rushed up to her and grabbed her by the arm. "I must show you something," she said. "Excuse us, Rydell." She pulled Kate into the doorway of the adventure centre.

Rydell watched Marika drag Kate away and he yawned. He was grateful that the fog was beginning to clear from his mind, and that his body was returning to his possession. He could not wait to frame Harrison as the serial killer of prostitutes; he could imagine the group's horror and he chuckled in anticipation.

Rydell had not had time to plan it out as precisely as he would have wanted to, but he was not worried. There was still plenty of time.

"Yes, *dance to your daddy, my bonnie laddie, you shall have a fishy in a little dishy, you shall have a fishy when the boat comes in.*" He could not stop chuckling.

"What are you doing talking to Rydell?" Marika demanded. "You must be more careful — I'm convinced he poisoned the water."

"Sssh." Kate said. "I agree but he mustn't suspect what we think. That will make him go off the rails even more. I must talk to Treasure, where is she?"

"Over there," Marika pointed and Kate went over to her.

"Treasure, I must speak to you now," she said. "I'm going to the washroom, please come with me."

"Fine, my baby," Treasure said. She slid off the edge of a dark wooden table where she had been sitting and chatting to a blonde Adventure Centre girl. "*Ja, ja* Miss Kate," Treasure squeezed into the washroom behind her and tried not to knock over an arrangement of dried flowers. "What is this matter of such great urgency?"

"Treasure," Kate got to the point, "it's Rydell. He's in love with you. Or at least, he thinks he is."

"I know, my baby. Jono told me. That's why Rydell tried to poison Harrison but he poisoned Charisse instead. As if he has any chance with me, the stupid man."

Kate nodded. "I see you know everything. I didn't think

Jono would tell you."

"He told me the whole thing. But it's all over now, that nonsense. Rydell won't try anything again."

"How do you know?" Kate asked. "I doubt he's going to give up that easily."

Treasure's eyes filled with tears. "You really think Harrison's life's in danger?"

"Yes, I do." Kate bit her lip. "You must tell Jono to call the police."

"*Eish*, he will never do that. He will get into trouble with his bosses, the tour people. And the police are the corrupt ones too, and we have no proof of anything. Who would believe that a white man would try to kill another white man over a black woman such as me? *Aikona*, nobody. Nobody will take you seriously." Treasure pulled a wad of toilet paper from the roll and blew her nose. She inspected her face in the mirror and wiped her eyes. "*Haw!* My heart is beating so hard." She patted her chest as one would a colicky baby. "Later, when we get to the lodge, there is a briefing, come and talk to Jono and me afterwards."

"Good idea, let's both think about what to do and we'll talk about it later," Kate said and she slipped out to find Marika waiting.

"Marika, this is such a dangerous mess," Kate said. "How on earth did it get like this?"

"I've got no idea but yes, a mess it most certainly is. In fact if you ask me, that's an understatement."

When they climbed back on the bus, Rydell had straightened his clothing and returned to his semblance of normal.

The group excitedly compared activities. "Enrique and I are going tandem sky diving this afternoon," Eva announced.

"Together?" Sofie asked, "as in you are both jumping at the same time, strapped together?"

"No way!" Eva laughed, "I wouldn't trust him that much."

"And in this case, you're right not to," Enrique said. "No, Sofie, we each get our own professional guy to hold onto. I'm going to record my jump the whole way down so you can all see."

"I'm breathless with anticipation," Stepfan commented.

"I will leave the adrenalin junkie stuff to you young people," Harrison said. "I'm going to spend the afternoon at the Museum of Swakopmund. I hear it is full of wonderful things. If you like, Eva and Enrique, I can videotape it for you in exchange."

"Uh no, that's okay, Harrison, but thanks," Eva said, grinning.

"Everybody, this is the city," Jono shouted through the connecting window. "Here is the market. Lots of locals trading all kinds of souvenirs. And there is the sea but it is too cold to swim in."

"At least Harrison can't get hurt in a museum," Kate said to Marika. Then they looked at each other.

"Or can he?" Kate asked. "Should we follow him around?"

Marika groaned. "The last thing I want to do, is spend my afternoon in a museum," she said. "And don't you think it would be odd, us lurking around the corners?"

"Yes." Kate thought for a moment. "Unless we asked if we could join him?"

"Kate," Marika said, "don't get me wrong. I really do care what happens to him but honestly, an entire afternoon in a museum with Harrison, well, that just might kill *me*."

"Yes, I know what you mean," Kate said. "It's so strange, you know. If you'd told me at the beginning of this trip that I would end up caring for Harrison and worrying about him like I do, I'd have said you were crazy. But there's something endearing about him."

"*Ja nee*, well fine, as they say in South Africa," Marika said. "I wouldn't go so far as to call him endearing, but I don't want him dead or hurt either."

The bus pulled into a narrow driveway; they had arrived at

the lodge. The group investigated the lodge, dismayed to find that there were only two rooms, each sleeping ten people.

"The beds are so close we could hold hands while we sleep," Jasmine commented, inspecting the tiny low-ceilinged dormitory, with beds crammed in at every angle and stacked high.

"At least we are not in the same room as Rydell the Serial Snorer," Sofie said. "When he dies, he should donate his body to science. I think there is a whole crowd of people living inside his head."

Kate agreed and claimed a top bunk, climbing up the cheap wooden frame. She was distracted; there had not been a briefing as Treasure had said there would be and everyone had dispersed in a hurry. "You want to hold hands?" she asked Eva who was across from her. "Jasmine's right, we could."

"No thank you, you weirdo." Eva said, smoothing out a piece of paper. "But do you want to hear a poem I've been working on?"

"Love to," Kate said.

"Remember it's a work in progress," Eva warned.

"Just read it!" Kate said and the others in the room fell silent to listen.

"It's called *The Glass Circus Safari*, and it's about our trip, as you'll soon see," Eva said and the others shouted at her to stop talking and read.

The Glass Circus Safari

This travelling circus safari,
this glass house rolling
taking us further into
a party of madness

this hot dusty
topsy turvy
winter solstice

turned upside down
while
witchdoctors dance
on the morals
of madmen and
warriors

where will it take us
this gusting
lusty spell
of accidental madness
this mystic mayhem
spinning and weaving

we walk through
Eden twisted
and become
black against the sun,
silhouettes
cut from
dark cloth
waiting

"Well done," the others applauded and Eva blushed with pleasure.

"People in glass houses shouldn't throw stones?" Jasmine asked, thinking back to the night of Stepfan and Charisse at the pool.

"Or glass because something's going to break?" Sofie asked.

"You're certainly right about us being a travelling circus," Marika piped up.

"I don't know what I mean by any of it," Eva shrugged. "I write stuff down as it occurs to me and I'm happy to have my poems back again."

"Did you see that Mia and Richard got a private room all

to themselves?" Sofie asked. "They paid quite a bit but where obviously in the mood for romance."

"Good for them," Helen said heartily. "Now listen, everybody..."

"Yes, Jono." Ellie called out and Helen threw a pillow at her.

"You must be on your guard at the market. Be sure to watch out for..." and she listed a number of things to which the girls paid scant attention as they sauntered down the gravel driveway.

"We are in little Germany," Sofie said, pointing out the buildings that lined the street. "Only, with a colonial sort of feel. I am feeling positively Bavarian." She skipped, kicked up her knees, and swung Eva around.

Eva untangled her arm. "Better than negatively Bavarian," she said.

They walked down to the beach and turned towards the market, no sooner rounding the corner when they were accosted from all sides by a thick wave of aggressive sales vendors shouting with raucous cries. "Me madam, look at me, good prices madam, look at me," the vendors shouted, holding carved giraffes, hand-painted wall hangings, masks, jewelry, ostrich eggs, stone sculptures, wood artifacts, ivory, jade, feathers and ornaments of twisted metal.

"They could easily get violent," Helen warned. "There are too few buyers and too many hungry families, so be vigilant, I'm serious."

Even Marika, a seasoned African market shopper was taken aback by the vigour with which they were approached.

"These people are so desperate it's frightening," Kate whispered. "I'm sorry but I don't like this. Are you going to stay and shop?"

"Yes," Marika said, "but don't stay if it doesn't feel right. I'll be fine."

"Thank you." Kate felt relieved. "I'd rather try the souvenir shops in town than brave this. I'll either be at the Internet café we passed, or at the lodge. See you later."

Marika waved goodbye and dove into the fray.

Kate paused near a stall at the edge of the market and looked back. She saw Helen talking to a couple of shady characters and she was surprised — after all of Helen's dire warnings, she expected her to be with Sofie and rest of the gang. Kate half-heard a stall vendor shouting his prices in her ear as he thrust an ivory bowl at her. She turned and bumped into Rydell who smiled wetly. For a minute Kate stopped breathing and her heart pounded hard.

"Think you're so clever," he hissed at her and then he smiled again. "Little Miss Muffet sitting on your tuffet, so high and mighty. Be careful of spiders who sit down beside you." He snickered.

Kate turned and strode off, shaking her head. Despite her intentions to not be alarmed by Rydell, there were times when he truly frightened her.

The sky was cobalt blue, and powerful waves crashed onto the beach as Kate walked by but she barely noticed the scenery. She could not understand why no one had mentioned Charisse or Bree. None of them had asked her anything about the drive to Walvis Bay or what the doctors had said, or how Bree had been. It seemed disrespectful to her, as if the most important things in life had been put aside; civilized human responses had been stopped by the press of a pause button, with "play" to be resumed after an intermission of superficial pleasures — or perhaps never to be resumed by some at all.

She found an Internet café and logged onto her email, quickly scrolling through the messages. Rachel wanted to know how she was. Her father was also keen for an update — apparently her parents were having a great time with their new life in Florida. Mum was playing a lot of tennis, Dad was reading the classics and they were taking salsa lessons at night with another couple they had befriended. He hoped Kate was safe and being careful. There were also close to ten emails from Cam. Kate stared at his name, feeling utterly dislocated from the man she had once loved; she could hardly summon up a picture of what he looked like. Cam was deeply sorry for what he had done. He would make it up to her, he said. Bethany had used him to make her ex-boyfriend jealous and now she was back with him and not even talking to Cam. He said he felt very bad for having upset Kate.

He was sorry he had *upset* her? Kate laughed as she read his increasingly panicked emails but she also felt angry. He had done a lot more than *upset* her. Then again, if he had not done what he had, she would never have taken this trip.

She wrote long replies to Rachel and her father, omitting the parts about Charisse and Brianna. She ignored the messages from Cam. She logged off and walked around the town, sticking to the politely-staffed and brightly-lit stores, secretly ashamed for being frightened by the chaos of Africa.

She arrived back at the lodge to find the room buzzing with happy chatter; gifts and purchases spread out on every available surface. Marika had two large bags stuffed with tribal masks, ornamental carved gifts, hand-painted blue-and-orange batiks and all kinds of trinkets, and even the usually-contained Helen was bubbling with excitement as she held out a necklace she had bought: silver ovals linked with elephant hair.

"It is lovely," Sofie said, "I also want one. I didn't see any like that at the market."

"I got it in the town," Helen explained. "I'll take you tomorrow, if you like."

"Please." Sofie said. "Is there time for a quick shower?"

"Probably not," Ellie told her, "because only one of the two showers is working and there's a big lineup."

"Good grief," Marika said. "Where's Harrison? He'd tell management what's what."

"He's probably inspecting the kitchen to see if breakfast will pass muster," Jasmine said.

"Pass muster?" Ellie enquired. "Since when did you use words like 'muster'?"

"Since I met Harrison," Jasmine retorted. "Observing him and his obsessions has brought out the muster in me."

Kate lay on her stomach and watched all the activity, hoping that Harrison was safe.

The Seventh Night

LATER, THEY GATHERED ON THE LAWN, waiting to go to dinner. "Where are Mia and Richard?" Jono asked.

"Doing the naughty, I would think," Rydell stuttered.

"The naughty?" mocked Stepfan. "You bad man, to even mention the naughty."

Rydell blushed a furious purple.

"Yes, Stepfan, the naughty," Sofie said, "or has it been so long since you did it that you have forgotten what it's called?"

The others laughed and Rydell looked relieved.

"Don't you worry about me..." Stepfan said, catching a look from Lena and falling silent.

"I bumped into Mia and Richard at the market," Ellie said. "He bought an evil-looking mask that he put the whole way over his head. It was one of the expensive ones, with cowrie shells and beads and cloth, and it had things drawn onto it, like black and white zig zags and triangles and patterns. He looked like a monster with it on."

"It sounds like a dance mask that Richard was trying on." Jono was thoughtful. "From Zaire. If I am right, then the mask is of a beautiful female spirit, named Ngady aMwaash, who was the incestuous sister wife of Woot. Woot was the first human on earth and creator of the world. It is said that the skin of the people at this time was white but Woot dyed them black so they could hunt better, because their white skins were too visible to animals. When Woot became king, he said that only kings should have the privilege of living with their own sisters; that ordinary people had to mix with other clans."

"I thought woot meant 'we own the other team' on a video game," Enrique said, "Or if you think something's cool, you say woot. Kind of like wow."

Jono laughed at this. "But you know," he added, "Richard should be careful because it is said that when you put on a mask, its spirit takes over."

"I get the impression that's exactly what he wants," Gisela commented.

"They were buying so much stuff," Ellie said, "other masks, and carvings, and a really huge box covered in cowrie shells. I even asked them how they were going to fit it all on the bus but they said they were going to post it all home tomorrow."

"Clearly they're not coming to dinner," Jono decided, "so let's depart."

On the way to the restaurant, Helen sidled over to Rydell who regarded her with suspicion and disinterest. He was concentrating on the ground to avoid watching Treasure smiling at another man. Treasure, with her hair newly braided in cornrows; his Treasure, beautiful in a bright yellow sundress.

The group walked up the wide, empty street. The sun had set, and the evening was filled with a dusky light. Festive German beer taverns and turreted European hotels lined the way but Helen was single-mindedly focused on her task. "I hear you're our resident expert on all things African," Helen tried to ease into the conversation with flattery.

"I'm not an expert," he said shortly, refusing to look at her. "Jono's the expert, you heard him. He knows about everything, whatever you want, ask him."

"I have asked him," Helen lied, "and he doesn't know, so I thought I'd ask you. I know you've read a lot of stuff."

He did not respond, so she abandoned her efforts to charm him and got to the point. "Rydell, how would I go about putting a spell or a curse on someone?"

He snorted. "Oh, I see," he chortled, his plump cheeks babyish. "No wonder you didn't ask Jono, you want to do something bad."

Helen flushed red. "Whatever," she said shortly, "do you know or don't you?"

"You'd have to become a sorcerer first," he said, thinking she was already halfway there. He did not care for Helen and her brittle anger.

"That's not very practical advice," Helen commented. "Come on, Rydell, there has to be a way."

"You're so desperate," he remarked, as they walked up the hill. "She who is desperate has given away her power."

Helen clenched her jaw. "I was wrong to ask you," she said, through gritted teeth. "You haven't been helpful at all."

"Here's something that might be more up your alley," he said. "There once was a woman who wanted to put a spell on her husband, so he'd love no one else but her. The witchdoctor told her he needed three hairs from a lion's eyebrow for that. The woman came back with the hairs. The witchdoctor told her if she could put a spell on a lion so that he didn't wake up while she was snipping off his eyebrows, she could put a spell on her husband just as easily."

He snorted again and glanced at her to see if she had gotten the point but Helen scowled.

"I don't want them, him, whatever, to fall in love with me, I just want them to suffer a bit," she elaborated. "He deserves it, they both do."

Rydell lost patience with her. "I don't know," he stuttered, "and I don't care either. Please, leave me alone, Helen, I need to think. Go and do your own research."

Helen was not happy. She had not wanted to resort to asking Rydell, but she had felt certain that he would know what she could do. She did not want to hear stupid things about sorcerers. She had enquired about spells at the market but they had only laughed at her, offering her impotent love potions instead.

She thought about Robbie's letters. She had reread them a number of times during the trip. She had bought a yellow highlighter and a red ballpoint pen from one of the spazas along the way and she had gone through each line and highlighted all the promises or references to their future, or how he had felt about her, or the time they had spent together. Then, in tiny capital letters, above the yellow, she neatly wrote: YOU LIED. YOU LIAR. Soon the letters were painted with yellow, the tiny red words biting into the page like stinging ants.

Helen had thought about posting Robbie's letters back to him, marked with his lies but she did not want him to scorn her or be relieved he was free of her. She wanted him to be inexplicably, shockingly filled with pain just as she had been; devastated by a blind-siding blow that came out of nowhere, and she was growing increasingly frustrated.

"Everybody, we are here." Jono announced.

Helen shook her thoughts aside. She would be resourceful in the morning.

The restaurant was enormous and filled to capacity. The crowded wooden tables were covered with red and white checked tablecloths and there was a bar area in the back and it too was packed, filled with noisy patrons swigging beer. It took a while to get settled; tables had to be rearranged to accommodate the size of the party.

"This restaurant is incredibly busy," Kate said to Jono who was seated to her left.

"What is that?" He leaned into her, "I did not hear you. It is quite noisy in here."

"I said the restaurant is very busy." Kate yelled back.

"Yes it is. They make good ribs and steak so it is a popular place."

Kate studied the menu. "I'll have pizza," she said loudly to Jono.

"What?" he asked.

She decided to try the reverse tactic and she lowered her voice and said quietly, "I'm going to have pizza."

"Good choice," he said, "I am going to have the ribs and steak combo."

Kate looked around at the group, thinking that apart from the trip, she really did not have much in common with anyone except for maybe Marika and Eva. She smiled across the table at Eva who smiled and waved back. Although they were directly across from each other, it was so noisy they could not hear each other speak.

"What are you having to eat?" Eva mouthed slowly with accompanying hand movements to further demonstrate her message.

"Pizza," Kate replied, also using her hands. "Do you want to share one?"

"Yes," Eva nodded and gave Kate a thumbs up. "No meat or anchovies."

Kate nodded, picked up the menu and pointed to a selection. Eva nodded.

"Where's the man to take our drinks?" Kate asked Jono in the same low tone that had succeeded before.

"He is busy. He will get to us," Jono said, wondering why his lot were always in such a hurry except when he was trying to get them back on the bus.

Kate had been circumspect about drinking since her wild hangover on the first day of the trip but she decided she needed a very large glass of wine.

Jono turned to her. "Tell me," he said, badly wanting to talk to her on a real level but feeling overwhelmed and unsure how to begin. "Are you enjoying your trip?"

"Yes, I am, Jono, I am — but I have to say there have been some extremely concerning elements which haven't been resolved and…"

"Kate," Jono put his hand over hers, "I know what you are going to say and please, do not think that I disagree but for tonight, let us have a good time. It has been tough for everybody, really it has. Let us relax tonight and discuss happy things, please?"

"Okay, fine," Kate said, resigned and she pulled her hand away, "but let's also try to get a waiter."

She looked around the table. At the far end, Treasure and Harrison were arguing good-naturedly about something and it seemed each had their supporters; Gisela and Lena were rooting for Treasure, while Jasmine, Enrique and Ellie supported Harrison.

Kate noticed that Ellie had given up her fascination with Rydell and had turned her attentions to Enrique, The only problem was that Enrique seemed equally as smitten by Eva as Ellie was by him.

"You are in another world," Jono shouted to Kate.

"Not really," she said. "It's so noisy in here that I find it hard to talk. Jono, I'm going to find a waiter."

"No, no," he got up, "I will." He fought his way among the crowd and returned with a waiter.

"We must order our food now too," Eva insisted loudly to the resistant waiter who scowled. He took all their orders slowly and vanished.

Eva leaned across the table. "I hope he comes back," she yelled to Kate, "he didn't seem very with it."

Kate nodded in agreement.

"Kate," Jono asked abruptly, "if you did not have a boyfriend, would you ever consider dating a black man?"

"Of course I would," Kate said, immediately remembering Thaalu's long limbs, his dark gold eyes, strong jaw and high cheekbones.

"This boyfriend of yours, why have you not married him yet? Perhaps you do not want to marry him?"

"That's a very personal question," Kate felt uncomfortable, even irritated. "Why does it matter to you?"

Jono was taken aback. "You are right, it is none of my business. I am just curious. If I was your boyfriend, I would have wanted to marry you a long time ago."

Kate was silent.

Jono sighed. "Kate," he said and he scooted closer to her, "I must tell you something. Forgive me and do not be angry with me for being so forward with you, but I have strong romantic feelings for you." He blurted out the last bit and stared at his place-mat, waiting to hear what she would say. Every inch of him hoped that her response would be a positive one.

And, despite the din, Kate heard him clearly. She sat motionless, unable to say a word or form a thought. She finally gathered her wits about her. "Um, Jono," she said, carefully, "oh dear, what can I say? Because I am sorry, I don't have any romantic feelings for you, I can't tell a lie." She clutched at the tablecloth, certain there was nothing she could say to ease the situation.

"But perhaps," Jono was desperate, "that is because you are a loyal person to your boyfriend and you have never given another man a thought? And perhaps if you gave it a thought, those feelings might grow?"

"No, I'm sorry, Jono. For me, those kinds of feelings are either there immediately, or they'll never be there. And I don't have those feelings for you."

She knew she had to be blunt. She could not package her rejection of his love with any kind of comfort because she had no doubt he would mistake it for hope.

Jono was quiet for a while. "I see," he said. A certain numbness had overtaken him and the din of the restaurant had fallen away; it was as he was standing in the middle of the silent desert, alone. "You do not have feelings for me," he repeated. "Maybe it is because I am black man, no matter what you say."

"No, Jono, don't say that. That's calling me a racist and I'm not."

"Have you ever had feelings for a black man in your life?"

"Yes, I have and who it was or when it happened is none of

your business." She was amazed it had only been yesterday when it felt like a lifetime ago.

"And why did this so-called relationship not develop?" Jono asked. "I will tell you why. It is because he is black. Like me."

The drinks arrived and Kate quickly ordered a second glass before the waiter disappeared. She took a deep gulp of her wine, grateful for the generous glass. "This is good," she said, not answering Jono because she could not think what else to say. Across the table, Eva raised a glass and Kate smiled at her and toasted her in return.

"Listen, Jono," Kate said quietly, "I'm very sorry."

He toyed with his knife and fork, his face inscrutable. "Sorry for what?" he asked. "All the injustices, all the pain I have suffered, all the death I have witnessed?"

"Yes," she said. "I'm sorry for all of that."

"It is easy for you to be sorry," he was bitter. "What do you know? It is easy to be sorry when you have it good, when life is a big fat cushion for you to sit on, since the day you were born."

"I'm not going to argue with you, Jono," Kate wished she had not been forced to hurt him, "But that's too broad a statement, that it's easy for me. Every person has their own burdens to carry. I'm not going to argue that mine are as heavy as yours, of course they're not, they could never be. And I'm deeply sorry for each injustice. I'm sorry for every pain, for your losses of which I'm sure there were many. I can't even imagine the hardships of your life and I'm sorry for all the bad things that have happened to you. And I'm sorry I'm not in love with you, because you're a good man, a decent man."

"Sorry does not make anything better," Jono said. "It does not bring back my dead wife, my two dead babies, my burnt house, my lost life. Sorry does not fix my bad health, or give me the money that I need to survive or help me do my job day after day. If you truly cared and were not only *sorry*, you would love me back and that would make a difference. So you do not care, and really all you want to do is say 'oh I am sorry you've had a tough life, good luck with that' and walk away. If you honestly cared, you would love me because that would help me. Saying sorry does not help me."

"I realize that." Kate drank more of her wine. She did not know what else to say.

"Is it your parents?" he asked. "I can talk to them, talk to your father, prove to him I am a good man, a trustworthy man." He sounded excited, as though he had found the solution.

"No, Jono, it's not my parents, it's me. I'm not in love with you for no other reason except that that magical thing didn't happen. That's why."

"Magical thing. Now you are speaking like a child, not a grown woman." He was angry now. "If that is the way you think then perhaps it is better that you do not love me as your love does not mean a lot. I feel sorry for your boyfriend. He is a foolish man or perhaps he does not care deeply for you either. Perhaps he is waiting for magic to happen to him too, with somebody else, have you ever thought of that? Any real man would have insisted you marry him by now and particularly if he was a man in love, he would demand it. You should be worried about him."

Without any warning, all the pain of Cam's betrayals rose up in Kate's heart as strongly as the day he had told her about Bethany. Her chest slammed tight and she felt as if she could not breathe. The restaurant was closing in on her and she had to get out. "Excuse me, please," she said thickly, and she climbed out of the bench and ran to the washroom.

The washroom doubled as a messy storage area for chairs and bicycles and toys and Kate sat down in a yellow rocking chair, crying and vaguely registering a hand-written sign on the mirror offering psychic readings. She had no idea why she felt as hurt as she did. She had felt bitterness and anger when she read Cam's emails but not hurt. She had thought she had moved beyond the pain. She was still crying when the door opened and Eva and Marika came in.

"Kate," Marika asked, "what was going on with you and Jono? We were watching and it didn't look good. What happened?"

"It was so horrible," Kate said and she got up and fetched some toilet paper to blow her nose. She told them what Jono had said.

"Whether he was heartbroken or not," Eva declared, "that's no reason to attack you, none whatsoever. Men. I tell you."

"I'm sorry Kate," Marika said. "Honestly, what did Jono expect?"

Back at the table, the subject of their discussion had put his head in his hands and felt terrible. He could not believe he had been so cruel to Kate and he asked himself what he had become — what had he let his life do to him? While it was true he had suffered many tragedies, so had countless others. He had never thought of himself as a bitter and angry man but that was how he had behaved.

The bench was shaking and he turned to see Rydell giggling a hyena chortle.

Jono stared at him

"Good one," Rydell laughed. "You got her good. Kissed the girl and made her cry."

Jono was disgusted by Rydell's freakish enjoyment. "Yes, Rydell," he said and he turned to face him squarely. "And I can also make you cry. Would you like to see me try?"

"No. No." Rydell stopped laughing and sat up straight. "No. Don't make me cry. That's not nice. Boys mustn't do that to other boys. Boys must be friends."

"I am your friend, Rydell, but you must promise me something, something very important, or I will make you cry."

"I promise." Rydell licked his lips, furtive and trapped.

"You have not even listened yet. You must never, ever hurt

Kate. If you promise me that, I will be your friend and you can be mine. What do you say?"

"I won't hurt Kate," Rydell agreed. "Not me, I won't touch her," and he laughed again.

"Good man," Jono said. "Shake on that," and he held out his hand.

"I'm not touching you," Rydell recoiled. "You must never touch me. If you touch me, I'll die. Men in Africa are full of AIDS disease. They think if they sleep with a virgin it will go away but it never goes away."

"Fine, whatever." Jono did not care. He wondered if there was any end to Harrison and Rydell's crazy obsessions. "I will not touch you but for your information, I do not have any disease."

The food arrived and Jono looked at Kate's pizza, her empty seat. "Helen," he leaned across the table, "Kate went to the washroom, would you please go and tell her the food is here?"

"Ask Eva or Marika to go," Helen said, looking around. "They're there too? Fine, I'll go and get them, but I don't want my food to get cold, I waited long enough to get it."

She got up, went to the washroom and returned almost immediately with Kate, Eva and Marika.

Kate slid back into her seat.

"Kate," Jono was quiet, sincere. "I am very sorry. It is not your duty to love me back. I am sorry I attacked you. Your boyfriend is a good man I am sure, and a lucky man I know. Please, forget what I said, please accept my apology."

"You have got nothing to apologize for," Kate assured him and Jono smiled.

"Thank you. Now I am going to enjoy my nice big supper," and he attacked his stacked platter of steak, ribs, onion rings and fries.

Rydell had lost interest in Kate and Jono, and was avidly watching Treasure and Harrison. "Enjoy your last night with her, little pixie man," he hissed under his breath. "Because from tomorrow night, she will be mine." He cut his steak precisely into the same tiny, bite-sized pieces.

Shortly after dinner, Kate had had enough. Jono's pile of gnawed rib bones were making her nauseous; she had finished both glasses of wine and she was tipsy and exhausted.

"*Haw!* but I am so full." Jono leaned back and patted his rounded stomach, his jeans and T-shirt straining.

Kate agreed. She leaned across the table. "Are you going dancing later?" she yelled at Eva and Marika who nodded.

Kate got up and went around to them. "I can't be bothered to yell anymore," she said, her mouth close to Eva's ear. "Can I get the key to our room? I'm going to go back to the lodge to have a shower and go to bed."

"Oy! You're tickling my ear. Here's the key. Are you okay to walk back by yourself?"

"Fine. Have fun, party girls."

She waved goodbye to Jono and the others and made her way outside, enjoying the fresh, cool air and the quiet of being alone.

Back at the restaurant, Jono ordered an Irish coffee. "Double whiskey and only a small amount of cream," he told the waiter.

"What are you drinking there?" a flirtatious voice giggled in his ear. He jumped, and turned to see Ellie.

"Ellie, I am drinking an Irish coffee. Would you like to try it?"

"Yes," she slurred.

"I see you have been enjoying yourself," he said, thinking he might end up having to carry her back to the lodge.

"A wonderful time! We're going dancing soon, will you come with us?" She wrapped her arms around his neck, dangling her body against his and against his better judgment, he was instantly aroused. He told himself that it was that accumulation of his desire for Kate and he untangled himself.

"Here," he offered her the glass. "Try some but be careful, it is very hot and it is strong."

"There is nothing I can't handle," Ellie declared drunkenly.

"Hmmm," Jono kept his hand on the glass in case she dropped it.

"Ow. It's hot. Why didn't you tell me it was hot?" Ellie giggled. "It's like a hot toddy when you have a bad fever. Do you feel sick? Can I make you feel better?" She put her hand on his forehead and stroked his face in a clumsy childish way.

Jono looked around in desperation. He had been so wrapped up in his own thoughts that he had not noticed the group getting increasingly drunk. Enrique and Eva were howling with laughter, their heads close together while Jasmine and Gisela were lining up another round of shots. Stepfan, with a sour expression, was watching Lena giggle and take sips of Gisela's drink. Treasure had her arm around Harrison's neck and she was whispering in his ear with Harrison loving every moment.

Jono turned around to see what Rydell was up to but Rydell had vanished leaving a small pile of money on the table. Jono's first thought was for Kate's safety but he remembered Rydell's promise never to hurt her and he believed him.

He decided to leave the party to its madness and visit some friends; stay with them for the night. He needed a respite from all the goings-on and he would tell his friends everything that happened. Maybe they could help him figure out what to do if anything else popped up, which he was certain it would.

He pulled Ellie off him and made his way over to Treasure. "Treasure," he caught her attention with difficulty, "listen to me for a moment. Are you listening?"

"*Yebo*, Jono, I'm listening carefully. What do you want? Talk fast. I'm busy."

"Yes, I can see that. I am happy to see you having fun. I am going to stay with Betty for the night. You can have the room all to yourself and perhaps a friend if you like."

"*Haw* Jono!" Treasure got up and flung her arms around him. "You're a good man, Jono. A great man."

"Why do you hug my woman?" Harrison demanded.

"She is hugging me," Jono said, "but here, you may have her back."

He sat Treasure back down next to Harrison and she whispered in his ear and a look of delight crossed his face.

"Let's go," he shot to his feet and tossed a bunch of cash on the table.

"Goodnight people," he said and he and Treasure pushed their way through the crowd, laughing so hard they could hardly walk.

Jono turned to find Ellie once again attached to him and he thought she was like seaweed in a dam. Once it got its grip, it did not let go until it drowned you. He slipped out of her embrace and rushed away before she could follow.

"Aw, you're no fun," she yelled after him.

"Ellie," Stepfan called her, "come and sit here, next to me, I'll take very good care of you."

Lena gave an unladylike snort. "Said the wolf to Red Riding Hood," she remarked, drawing patterns in the spilt salt on the rumpled tablecloth.

"You're talking to me now?" Stepfan said. "Too late. I don't care. I'm going to have some fun. Come here, Ellie," he repeated as she wove her way over to his side of the table.

"What you deserve..." Gisela began but Lena put her hand on Gisela's arm and shook her head.

"I don't care, Gili," she said.

"If you don't care Leni, then I don't either." Gisela said, "although..."

Lena patted her arm "No althoughs tonight, we're having too much fun."

"More shots, more shots," Jasmine shouted.

"Yes, more shots." Enrique and Eva cried.

"Marry me," Enrique handed Eva a ring he had fashioned by dismantling the bread basket. "Be my wife and have ten babies."

Eva collapsed in merriment. "Ten babies? When will I have time to be a poet?"

Enrique gave her a beautiful smile and shrugged. "Babies are better than poems. Babies *are* poems," he declared, throwing his arms out wide and narrowly missing the waiter.

The manager appeared at the table. "It's high time you guys took the party somewhere else."

"Now you arrive!" Sofie shouted. "All night long we wait for service, we wait for drinks, we wait for food, we wait for the bill, and only when we finally start to have a good time, does anybody come and then it is to tell us to move on."

Helen tried to quieten Sofie down but Sofie was having none of it. "Just like everything in life," she shouted. "You have to make noise to get your way. I want to tell them what I think. I am tired of being quiet." She continued to rant at the top of her lungs.

"Okay, enough already, please pay up immediately and leave," the manager said, his accent thick with Afrikaans, his bearded face unamused, "or I will have you escorted out."

"I'm paying for her and me," Helen quickly put the money down. "We'll meet the rest of you outside."

The others paid up and followed, trying to contain themselves. When they finally got outside, they doubled over with laughter.

"My stomach hurts from laughing," Lena said. "Are we going dancing or what?"

"Yes, but where?" Gisela lit a cigarette. "We don't want to end up on the wrong side of town."

"I don't think Swakopmund's big enough to have a wrong side," Lena commented.

"There's always a wrong side," Jasmine said, peering down the main street where the streetlights did little to illuminate the dark alleys. She missed Mia and felt a little stung at being so unceremoniously ditched by her friend, even although the evening was turning out to be a great one.

"I'm going to ask the security man at the restaurant where we should go," Helen said and she darted back into the restaurant, returning a few minutes later.

"There's a club down the road, to the right. He said once we get Sofie in, no one will notice the noise she's making, but he wishes us luck in actually getting her in."

"What noise?" Sofie grumbled. "I am merely conversing with my good friends." She lurched off.

"Hang on there," Helen grabbed her arm, "no walking in the middle of the street."

Behind them, Stepfan was trying to convince Ellie to go to a hotel with him.

"But I want to go dancing," she objected, pulling away from him. "Mia said we were going dancing. Where is she? She promised."

"One drink at this hotel right here," Stepfan pointed, "and after that we will go dancing."

Ellie glanced up. "I don't like that hotel," she said sulkily. "All that horrible gold and red, it looks like a whorehouse. I'm not going in there, I'm going dancing with the others." She tugged her arm free of his vise-like grasp and ran up to Sofie and Helen.

"Stepfan wants me to go to that horrible hotel with him," she said, "but I want to go dancing with you, is that alright?"

"Absolutely," Helen told her. "In fact that's an order, young Ellie."

"Aye aye, Captain," Ellie saluted Helen. "Yes ma'am. That's an order." She skipped ahead and Helen turned to Stepfan, her expression one of sheer disgust.

He shrugged, then turned and headed toward the hotel that he had pointed out to Ellie.

Stepfan walked quickly through the red and gold carpeted reception area and was struck dumb to see Rydell at the bar, in deep conversation with a tall dusky woman with an exotic hairstyle.

Stepfan approached them and saw a dozen reflections of himself in the mirrored baroque walls. "Hello Rydell," he said, smiling, "and who is your lovely lady friend?"

"None of your business," Rydell said, "and she's *my* friend. Go and get your own."

Rydell clutched the woman's hand and led her to a private booth. "Allow me to buy you another drink," he stuttered and he blushed, "and I apologize for my rudeness back there." His lips twisted with his odd, wet smile. "I don't like to share."

The woman laughed. "I don't mind sharing but if you want me all to yourself, that's also fine by me." She adjusted a drape of sheer bronze fabric across her shoulder and downed the glass of the cheap champagne that Rydell had bought her.

"I don't like sharing," Rydell repeated, and put his nose close to the large amber crystal buried between the woman's plump breasts, "but I do like other things." He reached for the necklace, twisted it tight and pulled her towards him. "Tell me, are you strong enough to make a bad boy feel good? Because I've been a naughty little boy, and I need to be punished. Can you do that or are you too pretty?"

She took his chin in her hand in a way that left him in no doubt and he sighed with relief.

Back at the bar, Stepfan had a hard time making up his mind who to choose and he silently thanked his wife for being a bitch and for giving him his freedom, and he settled back to enjoy the party of the century.

"Hey there, gorgeous lady," he said to a leggy bronze-skinned, blonde-wigged Lolita, "let's have some fun, what do you say?"

There was a moment, shortly after she left the restaurant, that Kate was delighted to be alone. The cool night was refreshing and she savoured the ocean-scented air, glad to be on her way back to the lodge and it was only after she had turned off the main street that she began to feel uneasy. She quickly dismissed her fears as a reaction to the silence around her after the noise of the restaurant. Nevertheless, she walked faster, pulling her sweater tightly around her. She strained to hear if there were any other footsteps and while she could not hear anything, she could not shake the feeling that something was very wrong. Her heart began to pound and she told herself not to panic, not to run.

The wide street leading down to the lodge was devoid of movement except for the flitting shadows of the tall palm trees that swayed in the breeze. The only sounds were the rustle of the leaves and the clacking of a tin can as the wind kicked it down the hill. The amber pub windows glowed but gave no comfort and the locked-up houses were dark and tucked far away behind bougainvillea-covered wrought iron fences.

Kate tasted fear, bit her lip and stared straight ahead. She told herself to stop scaring herself with foolish thoughts, told herself she was frightening herself for no good reason.

But just as she was convinced there was nothing lurking in the shadows, that it was all in her imagination, a boy of about eighteen stepped directly in front of her.

Kate gave a quick harsh grunt of fear and the sound held in her throat. She knew from what Helen and Marika had told her that these boys had nothing to lose; he could kill her for twenty rand and feel nothing for it.

"Madam must not be afraid," the boy said, talking softly, with his hands in the pockets of his cheap tan jacket. "I am Dumi, from the market, do you remember me? You did not buy anything but you said you would come back later and I waited and waited but you did not return. That is not polite, Madam." He looked at her, his eyes small in a narrow face, his lips thin, his chin sharp and pointed.

She did remember him. When she stopped to look back at Helen, Dumi had thrust a carved wooden bowl at her, shouting. She did not recall saying anything to him, she only remembered her fear and that she had wanted to be as far away from the market as possible.

"I'm sorry, Dumi," she said, stepping around him and walking fast. "I didn't buy anything from anyone today, but I'm going to come back and buy from you tomorrow. Remind me," she said, conversationally, "what did you have at your stall?"

The boy was lanky and his trousers were too short; a length of gray sock was showed and his shoes were that of a businessman, only cracked and old. "Madam, I have bowls and big spoons. You liked the bowl with the lions drinking at the edge, do you remember?" He kept his hands in his pockets and matched her stride for stride.

"I do," she said, "but do you have any other kind of bowls?"

"Yes, Madam, I have ivory bowls and the green soapstone ones."

"Hmm," Kate said. "I would worry that the soapstone one would be too heavy for me to carry all the way back home." She wanted to keep him talking. "How much was the ivory bowl?"

"It was three hundred rand, Madam."

"Ah." Kate saw the lodge come into view, "Well, Dumi, that's a lot of money. Tell me, what's the best price you can give me? Because I can't pay three hundred."

"What is Madam's best price?" he asked. "You tell me and we will negotiate."

"Let me think." She picked up her pace. "How about two hundred?"

"Oh no, Madam, that is too low. Two hundred and seventy."

"Two hundred and thirty?"

"Two hundred and fifty, Madam, is as low as I can go."

"What is that in U.S. dollars?" Kate fervently wished the lodge would miraculously rush up towards her.

"Divide it by seven, so just over thirty dollars."

"That is a good price," Kate agreed and she quickened her pace even more.

The side door to the lodge pub was open and a wonderful warm light spilled out and with it, the noise of people laughing and talking. Kate had made sure she was on Dumi's right and, ready for this moment, she dove through the door and quickly ran into the milling crowd who were drinking tequila shots from a wall-mounted springbok's rear end, and licking salt off its balls. Kate, leaning against the bar counter, was never been more delighted to watch inane drunken activities in her life.

Outside, Dumi was furious. "Madam," he called repeatedly into the crowd until one of the local white men shouted at him to stop.

"Hey, you, boy, *voetsak*! How many times must we tell you not to hassle the tourists? Do you want to go to jail, is that what you are want? I recognize you, boy, now get lost or I'll come out there and help you."

Dumi shot off into the night and the man turned to Kate but she had left. Her heart still racing, she practically ran to the room, scrambling to find the key and locking herself inside. She made sure the windows were locked and she closed the curtains. She checked the washrooms, the one with the broken shower and the one with the broken toilet.

"Area secured," she said aloud, sinking down against the frame of the bunk bed. Sitting among the comforting holiday mess, she began to feel better.

"That was so stupid." She took deep breaths. "I could have ended up a statistic. I'll never be careless like that again. The first thing I'm going to do tomorrow is buy something to protect myself. I won't be caught off guard like that again."

She saw Marika's bottle of Old Brown Sherry sticking out of a bag and she helped herself to a few generous swigs to help calm her nerves.

Then she had a long hot shower. Her heart was still beating fast.

Kate's sleep was disturbed by the drunken arrival of the rest of the gang. She could hear them fumbling for their key and she jumped down off her bed and let them in. "You do look worse for wear," she said, "that must have been some party. Eva, you're pale as a ghost."

Eva groaned and crawled facedown onto her bed.

"I see," Kate was amused. "Marika and Helen, you're the only sober ones. I guess it would be safe to say that a good time was had?"

Helen laughed. "Yes, it was fun. Now listen up all of you, there's only one toilet, so if you are going to get sick, do not do it in the toilet that doesn't work. Eva, do you hear me?"

Eva gave a muffled moan.

"Good," Helen said. "Ladies, if you need me to get trash cans ready for you to throw up in, let me know now."

"Eugh. This is so gross." Kate climbed back into bed. "Too much information. I'm going to back to sleep."

A series of groaned apologies rose up to her.

In Swakopmund

THE NEXT MORNING KATE SLEPT IN and woke to find that the others had as well. She rolled over and squinted at her watch. It was nearly 9:00 a.m., but the bed felt wonderful and she snuggled back down. After her fright with Dumi the previous night, she was glad to be safely surrounded by the familiar gang. She decided once again that she needed to arm herself with some kind of protection. She dozed for a while but the sunshine outside was too tempting and she slid down off her bed.

Marika sat up slowly, looking like a startled sparrow, her hair sticking up in all directions. "I should get up too," she said, lying back down, "but my bed feels too good."

Kate grinned at her. "Then you should enjoy it," she whispered. She dressed quickly, grabbed her camera bag and left, closing the door quietly behind her. She contemplated grabbing breakfast on her way out but could not be bothered. She made for the beach and enjoyed a long walk, with the blue-green waves curving high and crashing down hard beside her. The sea seemed so energized and powerful compared to the deep still lakes of Ontario. Kate studied the strength of the frenzied water and tested the frothy white foam of the Atlantic Ocean with her fingertips, but Jono was right, the water was freezing.

And while she was happy to be by herself, with only the swooping seagulls for company and a tiny crab scuttling across the sand, she nervously kept one eye over her shoulder and was careful not to walk too far from the main street. She was more shaken from her encounter with Dumi than she liked to admit. She sat down for a while in the soft white sand, enjoying the hiss and pull of the water as it reached for the shore and then sank back into the sea. She dug in her camera bag for an energy bar but came up empty and decided it was time to head back into town.

Kate scoured the stores and found what she wanted: *André's Guns and Ammo*. The sign hung above a bright yellow door; the store front was sandblasted red brick and barred windows were set high up near the roof. Kate looked up and noticed a security camera. She pressed the small white buzzer.

"Yes?" the voice did not sound particularly welcoming.

"I ... uh," Kate cleared her throat and spoke into the intercom. "I'd like to come in" A buzzing noise sounded and Kate pushed at the heavy reinforced steel door. She walked up to a glass counter filled with knives and gun accessories. The walls displayed all kinds of weaponry; antique rifles and spears, and ornamental antique jerry cans were stashed neatly in the corner.

A large muscular man was leaning on the counter filling in a crossword puzzle. His shaggy dark blonde hair was in need of a comb and his yellow Che Guevara T-shirt was wrinkled. He glanced up briefly and did a double-take. Kate assumed she was not his usual clientele.

She cleared her throat. "Um, hello. I'm traveling through Africa by myself and I need something to protect me, can you help me?"

"I'm sure I can be of assistance." The man stood up and groaned as his back made a cracking noise. "What did you have in mind?"

He leaned forward, so close to her that she could see the blonde, brown and gray of his facial stubble. She looked into his deep-set blue eyes and thought that he smelled good, a combination of aftershave and gun oil.

"I'm not sure really," she said, "having never been in this situation before."

"And what situation would that be? I'm André by the way, owner of this fine establishment and purveyor of all manner of protective devices."

"I'm Kate. I'm with a tour group and it's just that there's been some weird stuff going on and last night I walked home from the restaurant by myself..."

André scowled at her. "You walked home by yourself at night? I'm sorry but are you looking for trouble or what? I don't get you tourists, always going on about the crime and then you do a stupid thing like that."

Kate was defensive. "I wasn't thinking. I was exhausted and I just wanted to be by myself. And then this young guy from the market suddenly appeared, Dumi, and he seemed to be friendly but I've got to admit I got a fright and it just made me think."

"Ja, well *jong*, best you don't do stupid things like that again, hey? Dumi? I'll keep an eye out for him. Odds are, I hate to tell you, that he would have hurt you if he could have. How did you get away from him?"

"I talked like crazy until we got to the lodge which wasn't too far, thank heavens. Then I ran into the pub. But now I really want something to help me feel safer, and I won't ever go strolling around at night by myself."

She sat down on a tall stool next to the counter. "I don't know what I want," she said. "What about a switchblade?"

André laughed, deep from his belly. "What do you think this is, the *Gangs of New York*? But, as a matter of fact, I do have one." He ducked down and pulled open a drawer, brandishing a traditional switchblade, leaning towards her and pressing the switch. Kate shot backwards off her chair, her heart pounding in fright and her face turned bright red when she saw that all it released was a man's hair comb.

"Very funny," she said, feeling stung.

"Caught a *skrik* did you?" André replied, laughing. "It's

a 1980 classic I got off ebay. But in all seriousness *bokkie*, I don't have any switchblades. What's next on your shopping list? A gun? I can't sell you that either because you need a license that you register with the police — it's a whole song and dance, believe me."

"I don't want a gun," Kate was horrified. "What about pepper spray?"

"Now you're talking. I've got the perfect thing. It's a very dynamic combo of pepper spray, tear gas and UV dye. Plus it comes in a nice little pouch so that you can keep it with you all the time. Here, I'll show you."

Kate examined it. "Yes," she said, "this is more me." She gave a sigh of relief. "Just looking at it makes me feel safer."

She found she was in no hurry to leave the sanctuary of André's store. Sunlight streamed in through the small barred windows and dust motes floated on stripes of warmth while township jazz played a pennywhistle jive. "This is nice," she said dreamily and André grinned and his dimples cut deep into his cheeks.

"That will be a hundred and fifty dollars," he said, leaning forward. "Namibian dollars, not U.S."

"I can manage that," she said, "it's only about twenty dollars back home." She dug in her wallet and handed him the money.

"So, *jong*," he said, "are you free for lunch now, even if it's a bit early?"

"Yes," Kate said, astonishing herself with the speediness of her reply. She wondered what was going on with her; her attraction to Thaalu and now André but she pushed her analyzing thoughts aside.

"Good. I'll take you somewhere nice." He grabbed a knapsack from behind the counter and threw a few things into it. He locked his laptop away, turned off the radio, and set the security alarm for the store.

"Come on." André put his hand on the small of her back and led her down the street. Kate felt a thrill of heat at his touch and she noticed that André appeared to be in no hurry to remove his hand either.

"Up these stairs," he said, guiding her into a small courtyard. The whitewashed walls were covered in scarlet bougainvillea and the sounds of the busy town faded away.

"*Le Bistro Afrique.*" Kate read the restaurant's name that was scrolled in gold script. "This looks very five-star. I'm not exactly dressed for it." She looked down at her white shorts and yellow T-shirt and wished she'd known that her day was going to entail meeting a gorgeous man who'd take her out for some fine dining.

"You look fantastic," André said with enthusiasm. Enthusiasm that was matched when the owner came over to greet them, giving André a complicated hand-shake and Kate an admiring glance.

He led them to a table out on the open balcony overlooking the ocean and Kate sank into her chair and smiled. She spread her linen napkin over her lap and admired the view. "Very nice," she said, the breeze lifting her hair. "Very, very nice."

André was studying the wine menu. "Like I said, it's a bit early in the day but what the hell. Chardonnay, Sauvignon Blanc or Pinot Grigio? I recommend a lovely South African Sauvignon Blanc, if you're game?"

"André, I know as much about wine as I do about switchblades, so you go ahead and order for me."

She realized she was ravenous. "I feel as if I haven't eaten properly in days," she said. "although we did go to dinner last night but I just had pizza." She opened the menu and read the quote embossed on the first page. "*All glory comes from daring to begin.* Kind of weird, to have a quote on a menu. It's by Eugene F. Ware and I like it."

"Well *bokkie*, let's you and I begin," André said, having ordered the wine. He leaned close to her and she immediately lost interest in food and wished they were lying on a blanket behind a dune on the beach and letting things develop as they may.

Lost in her daydream, she lost track of what he was saying and she blushed when she had to ask him to repeat his question.

"Where are you from?" he repeated. "Thought I'd start with the easy questions first although even that one seemed to baffle you."

Kate, not used to being teased, turned plum. "I'm from Canada," she said. "A town near Toronto. And you?"

"I was born here. Then my parents separated and I moved to Boston to live with my mom from when I was eight until I was sixteen. I got myself into a bit of trouble there, substance over-enthusiasm and all that. So my mom shipped me back to my Afrikaans dad who knocked some sense into me and I liked it better here, so I stayed. I still visit my mom, pretty much every year. If you think about it, Toronto and Boston aren't that far away from each other."

"Practically neighbours," she said, smiling, wishing she could grab him and wondering how she was going to get through lunch without doing just that. She could feel his knee touching hers and just that slight touch had her feeling like a schoolgirl on a date with the quarterback hero. She gulped back some wine and reminded herself that alcohol was not going to help her curb her inhibitions. She reached for a crisp breadroll and broke it in half, scattering crumbs across the table and quickly brushing them off the pristine cloth.

André laughed and pushed the dish of butter towards her. "We're going to make much more of a mess than that, trust me."

She grinned at him and then a thought occurred to her and her face fell. "André, do you have a girlfriend, or a wife?"

He raised an eyebrow. "Do you think I'd be here if I did? I'm a one-woman man, when I have a woman that is, which I currently do not. You're single too, I presume?"

"Yes, single. But from what I gather, lots of men these days like to have a few women to choose from."

"Not me, sweetheart. Now, as for food, unless you object, we're having prawns." He poured more wine into their glasses that were the size of jam jars. "And lobsters and langoustines and more prawns. With lemon butter and garlic butter and peri peri sauce. Is that okay? You do eat seafood?"

Kate nodded enthusiastically and took another generous sip of her wine. She giggled and then frowned. "I never giggle," she said, "look what you're doing to me."

He laughed. "You're on holiday. That means you're even allowed to partake of a giggle or two."

"André," she said, serious for a moment, "you would not believe some of the things that have happened on my trip and I'm not going to go into them because it's too perfect a day. But let's just say that this is exactly what I needed."

He pulled his chair even closer to her and brushed her hair away from her neck. "And you, sunshine, were a very nice surprise in my day too, believe me."

Several hours later, they were still at the restaurant. The food had long since been cleared and they had nearly finished a second bottle of wine.

Kate looked at her watch with regret. "I have to get going soon," she said. "We get back on the bus tomorrow and I've got a whole bunch of stuff I must get done at the lodge. Everything's a mess, I need to pack."

"Really?" André leaned in and cupped the back of her neck with his hand. "Or we could take this back to my place and..."

Kate burst out laughing. "A nice thought," she said, "a very nice thought but hardly likely."

André grinned. "I had to ask," he said. "Where does your trip end?"

"Windhoek."

"Then, I'll come and see you there. I simply cannot not see you again, it's as simple as that."

"I think there might have been an easier way to say that," Kate said, wishing she had agreed to go back to his place but knowing that she could not.

"At the very least, let me walk you back to your lodge," André said. He bounded up out of his chair, looking way more sober than she felt.

Outside on the sidewalk, in the hot sun, André took hold of her hand and before she knew it, Kate grabbed him and pulled him towards her. Kate, whose sex life with Cam had been predicable at best, and whose sexual history before him had been pale and disinteresting, was kissing a man she hardly knew with passion she had no idea she possessed.

"You see, that's why you should come home with me," André said, when they finally pulled apart. He sounded out of breath.

"That's exactly why I shouldn't," Kate countered. She grabbed his hand and started walking in the direction of the lodge, her thoughts spinning with desire and every nerve ending in her body aflame.

André pulled her to a stop for a moment and dug in his knapsack. He tore a piece of paper out of a notebook and fished for a pen.

"Here's my home phone number, my cell number, my work number and my email address." He smiled at her and handed her the list which she folded and tucked carefully into her money belt.

"Kate, wait, do you have a cellphone with you?" he asked.

"No, I don't," she said.

"*Jirre*, so how were you going to phone me? Trying to pull a fast one, were you?"

"I thought there must be payphones," Kate said. She had no intention of seeing him again; he made her feel reckless and crazy, it was safer to avoid him entirely.

"We're going to get you a pay-as-you-go phone," he said, guiding her into a store. "My treat, okay?"

He bought her a phone and showed her how to use it, storing his numbers in the memory.

"One more thing," he said. "A souvenir for you." He

handed her the fake switchblade comb and Kate pocketed it with delight.

They reached the lodge entrance and André walked her to her room. "*Jirre*," he said, peering inside the doorway, "not exactly the lap of luxury, *né*?"

The tiny room looked as if a frat house had exploded and Kate nodded. "Close quarters," she said, "and I need to tidy up my part."

"Can I see you tonight?" He stepped inside the room with her, tempting her.

She looked up at him. "Not tonight," she said, caressing his forearm, unable to resist touching him.

"I thought that's what you'd say. Okay, Miss goody-two-shoes that's fine by me. But I'll tell you this much, this could be the start of a very nice friendship and it would be a pity to let it go to waste. It's not every day that a gorgeous little *meisie* walks into my shop and gives me CPR. Because that's how it felt, hey, like you gave me the kiss of life by showing up like that. Listen to me, talking too much, and saying stupid things but I'm scared you're going to disappear and I'll never see you again, so I'm saying anything I can think of." He grinned at her. "But I'm going to shut up now for sure." He kissed her lightly on the forehead.

"Come on, Kate," he said, "please, tell me you won't just disappear."

"André, I promise I won't just disappear," she said, "I promise."

She pulled his head down and kissed him. She took his hand and slid it up inside her T-shirt, inside her bra. She cupped his thick, strong fingers around her breast and she felt the breath catch in his throat and his body tense. He caressed her; her nipple was so taut it was nearly painful and his hand felt hot against her skin. She could feel his erection digging at her through his trousers and before she knew it, her hand was rubbing him and he was groaning with pleasure.

"What on earth's going on?" A dislocated voice spoke from the depths of a bunk bed.

Kate and André shot apart, and Kate could not help smiling at the tent pole projection of his trousers.

It was Ellie waking up. She rubbed her face and looked around. "Oh, it's you, Kate." She hardly seemed to notice André. "I must have a shower." She climbed down off the bed and ambled past André. "Hello," she said vaguely and went into the washroom.

Kate and André looked at each other and doubled over laughing.

"A couple more seconds and we'd have been naked on the floor," he whispered and Kate nodded.

André ran a hand through his hair and let out a whistle. "Okay *bokkie*, I'll respect your wishes and be on my way before we ignite our flame again. Not that it's going to be easy to walk, if you get my meaning. But listen, I want to hear from you often, okay?"

"Constant updates," she said and he grinned.

He walked away, down the driveway, stopping to look back. She waved and he smiled. Then he turned the corner and was gone.

Kate sank down on her bed and touched her lips with her fingertips. "What on *earth* was that about?" she asked herself. "Oh, my."

While Kate was out having a fine adventure, the same could not be said for other members of the group. Helen, in particular, was not having a good day. She was sitting at the top of the stairs that led down to the market, feeling angry and resentful. She had had no idea it would be this hard to get what she wanted.

Helen's revenge had fast become Helen's frustration. No one was willing, or able, to help her. The only spells she could find were tourist potions for love which were useless to her, while all the really virulent stuff was apparently locked up in the vault of some secret society that would not let her in.

She had thought that Peter's Antiques, self-proclaimed stockist of a wide range of fetishes, would be able to help her and she had marched in the minute the store opened. But all she found was a wide array of German antiquities, jewelry, statues, masks and calabashes; an amazing plethora of artistic African treasures as well as a few fearsome objects, but nothing of any use to her.

She was also facing the problem of postage. She could not send Robbie a godawful ugly fetish telling him he was cursed, because it would lead straight back to her. Besides, her goal was not to momentarily alarm him but to infect a virus of hurt into his life that would leave a permanent scar just as he had done to her. But she was coming up short and she was running out of time.

As for Richard, she had been luckier there. She had stopped in at a pharmacy and found a shelf stocked with herbal African *mutis* and cures. She picked up a large plastic bottle of *Ingwe Izifozonke, The Strong One, Amazing Mixture for All Diseases*. She examined the label; an orange cheetah roared with teeth bared and the logo was a fearsome yellow and black, and it looked, she thought, like pretty authentic stuff.

"Whatever you do, don't drop that or open it," one of the shop assistants walked up and warned her. "*Ag, liewe hemel*, that stuff stinks to high heaven. I can't imagine why they'd ever drink it. We opened a bottle one time out of curiosity and the smell was enough to kill seven cats."

Helen laughed. "That bad?"

The girl held her nose with two dainty fingers, her little finger stuck up in the air. "We couldn't get it closed fast enough, I tell you. Let me know if I can help you with anything." She wandered off to straighten the fragrance bottles.

Helen wondered how Richard would feel, climbing into his sleeping bag at the end of the day and sticking his feet into this gunk. Or maybe she would pour it into his backpack and ruin his things ... yes, she would find a way to make his life as unpleasant as possible.

But Robbie was proving to be tough. She was beginning to wonder if she should fly back to Cape Town from Windhoek, and confront him. Perhaps seeing him face to face would give her the closure she needed. Or she could scratch the beloved convertible he had talked about so often, gouge the paintwork and rip the upholstery into shreds. He would never know it was her; he would think she had long since left the country.

She sat on the stairs in the hot sun, staring down at her mannish, capable toes and feeling miserable. Below, the market vendors outnumbered the buyers thirty to one, with old men selling postcards for a rand a piece, while the young boys fought with each other and squabbled like chickens scratching in a yard.

Helen wondered idly what to do with the rest of her day. She had longed for this time to be alone but oddly enough, all she wanted now was to be back on the bus with the group, reading while they talked and argued and slept around her. There was something reassuring about being carried along on a wave of communal activity; it offered a sanctuary from loneliness and the bigger questions in life.

She sat up straighter, and rested her elbows on her knees and realized that the last thing in the world she wanted to do, once the trip was over, was return to Canada. There was nothing there for her, apart from her drunken mother shrieking to pass the time while she waited for her next welfare cheque, or a visit from her crackhead brother. Helen was friendless and without a job or a home to return to, and the bleakness of her future settled in her chest like a large stone. She pulled at the strap of her shoe, thinking that she had somehow had it in her head that she would find a way to stay in Africa and when Robbie had fallen in love with her, it had seemed like everything had fallen into place and all the hurts and battles she had suffered were part of a terrible past, a past soon to be banished and replaced by her happy-ever-after life. She had worked so hard, she deserved things to be good at long last, but now what did she have? Nothing. For the first time in her life, Helen was without a clear sense of purpose, and it was not, as she discovered, a pleasant place to be.

She stared at her feet again, not wanting to think about her mother but unable to push back the unwelcome memories. When she was growing up, she had thought that everyone had a mother like hers, that the way her mother behaved was normal. It was only when she went to a friend's house after school one day, that she realized the chasm of differences that existed.

Standing in her friend's kitchen, Helen had dropped a glass of milk. Her hand shot to her mouth in horror as she watched the glass falling in terrible slow motion, while the milk fanned out in a graceful arch and white drops sprayed the room. The glass had finally hit the floor and shattered.

Wide-eyed with terror, Helen held her breath, waiting for the shrieking and the yelling. Her hand was still pressed to her mouth. She was seven years old.

But her friend's mother had laughed kindly, "I'm sorry, love," she said, "my fault for giving you a glass straight out the dishwasher; they're always wet and slippery. Did you get any on your dress? I hope the glass didn't cut you."

She wiped Helen's dress and to her everlasting shame, Helen began to cry, silently, endlessly. To the startled mother, it seemed as if she had opened an endless reservoir of pain, her kindness only making it worse. In the end, she had taken tear-stained, weeping Helen home. She had waited with Helen on the doorstep, holding her hand, until Helen's mother, Carol, answering with screeches from deep inside the house, had come to the door in a cheap pink satin negligee that barely covered the top of her thighs, with all manner of stains encrusting the fabric.

"Ya, can I help ya? What the fuck ya want?" she had asked

the woman, provocatively posed against the peeling doorframe, smoothing her flyaway wiry bleached blonde hair, her fingernails filthy and ragged.

"I brought Helen home," the woman tried to explain, "something upset her, she dropped a glass of milk but it wasn't her fault..."

"Ah, it's always her fault, eh, stupid kid." Helen's mother's smile was gapped with missing teeth. She cuffed Helen on the head. "She's clumsy, I tell ya, you should have kids like mine, you got kids? Tell me? You got kids? Ha? Well my kids are a fuckin' nightmare, I tell ya. You didn't need to bring her home, she woulda found her own way, she's got ways, that one."

The woman, horrified, did not know what to say. "I'll leave you now," she said, and she rubbed Helen's back, a departing gesture of kindness Helen would never forget. Then she turned and walked down the narrow muddy pathway that was lined with dead weeds and junk and made her way out through the chickenwire gate.

Helen's mother watched her go and she flipped the finger at the woman's parting back. She looked down at Helen, her mouth twisted around her cigarette, one hand on the torn screen door, the other holding a beer. "Ya gonna get ya skinny ass in here or what?" she barked at Helen who slid inside underneath her mother's arm.

Her mother sneered at her and slammed the door shut. "You think ya fancy, coming home with ya friends, who do you think ya are, missy? You think ya better than me? You're not better, I'm your ma, you never forget that." She pointed at Helen as she spoke and her hand shook, her eyes rheumy in her sallow, haggard face.

She was twenty-eight, she looked fifty.

Helen tried to escape to the relative sanctuary of her tiny attic room. She slipped past her mother and ran up the steep wooden stairs of the dark, narrow house.

"Oh no, you don't," her mother screeched, and her furious

scream pierced every cell in Helen's body. Her mother rushed up after her, stamping loudly on the old wooden stairs that echoed and reverberated as if an army were marching through.

Helen dove onto her bed and lay face down, her hands over her ears. Her mother rushed into the room after her and slammed the door with a loud bang. It seemed to Helen that there were three parts to her mother; the cigarettes, the beer and the endless slamming. Cupboards, closets, doors, drawers, shelves, stairs; she slammed and stamped, shrieking all the while like a banshee.

Her mother stood, quiet for a second, inside the closed door of Helen's room while Helen waited for the onslaught of deranged agony to spew forth. But then her mother paused, her ear cocked, listening for a sound.

"Jimmy's back," she exclaimed, "ya lucky kid. But I'll be back."

She flung the door open and rushed down the stairs, pounding with the force of a three-hundred-pound woman, although she was no more than a hundred, soaking wet.

"Jimmy!" she yelled, "ya got the beer, eh? Ya lousy fuckin' loser, turn the fuckin' music down, what's the matter with ya, ya come in and the first thing ya do is turn on the fuckin' radio station to ya stupid rock music, you know the neighbours call the fuckin' police when ya does that, for fuck's sake..."

And on it went.

Helen, never wanting to be vulnerable again, had refused to visit any of the other children from school ever again. She also refused to have them come to her home. She rarely spoke to anyone outside of class and walked to and from school by herself, with her head down. She studied hard and would not participate in extracurricular activities, mainly because she lacked the necessary gear. She learned to fend for herself at home; she padlocked the door to her room from the time she was ten, even when she went to the bathroom.

Helen's father was a high-school teacher, he'd had the two

kids, Helen and Tommy, and then he'd left in a hurry when it was clear that Carol had lost her marbles. Helen's little brother, Tommy, was a loser from the start, born to be a druggie. He had learned to swig beer when he was four; Carol thought it was cute. "Thanks dad, for taking us with you," Helen told him, the one time she met him. She had tracked him down, though he had been slippery to find, and not keen to reunite.

He shrugged. "Sheila said no contact was better," he said. Sheila was the second wife, a churchgoing teetotaler he had met at an A.A. meeting.

"Your mother was a real looker once," Helen's father had said, smiling at the memory. "Before she started hitting the booze big time. And she had to take those meds, they said she was bipolar, manic depressive, borderline personality, you name it. Course, she never stayed on them like she was supposed to, only stayed on them long enough to feel better, then she'd go off them and wham, the maniac was back. But my theory is that getting pregnant screwed her up, all those hormones out of whack, or maybe the hard work of being a mother. She was pretty good fun when I met her. I mean she'd party hard but she wasn't crazy, not like she is now."

Helen, sitting across from him at a McDonald's, looked him in the eye. "Help me get through teacher's college," she'd said, "and I'll never ask you for anything again. And I'll never contact you again, either."

She was fourteen at the time. "You've got a deal," he said. She never saw him again but he put money into a bank account for her, while he went off and had two more kids with Sheila. Helen never met them, never wanted to.

Helen distanced herself from all her family. She came and went like a quiet ghost, learned to earn her money, and she found ways to shave what she could from what her mother and Jimmy carelessly left lying around. She guarded her belongings, studied at the library, and took up running. She had a clear goal for her life and with that, came hope.

She took to sex with the same passion she had taken to running; it was a way of working off her pent-up energies, it was a release. She joined an online dating site making sure that her prospective lovers knew the emotional boundaries were set at point zero; encounters were physical only and that had worked fine–until Robbie.

And as much as her mother was an untidy, out of control slagheap of a woman, Helen was precise, neat, practical, contained. These traits were woven into the fabric of the life-raft that saved her, but now she had nothing, no plan, and no recourse to rescue from any quarter. Without warning she began to cry and the market vanished in a blur. She brushed the tears away with her capable fingers and hugged her knees to her chest. She had no idea what to do next.

Kate looked down the driveway that André had just left. She could still taste him and smell his skin, feel the coarseness of his unshaven cheek, and her breast still tingled where his hand had been. She lay down on her bed, thinking she would just rest for a moment when the next thing she knew, she was waking from a deep sleep, disorientated and confused.

"You were fast asleep," Eva laughed. She was sitting on her bed across from Kate, scribbling in a notebook.

Kate sat up. "Look at the time, and I still want to go shopping."

"Let's go then." Eva hopped down off her bed and Kate followed.

"How was last night?" Kate asked, not really interested but hoping to distract herself from thoughts of André.

Eva laughed. "We had great fun. Enrique and I are now married and we're going to have lots of babies. We were so drunk, I felt really sick. Still, it was fun. Wait, we must go into this store." It was a small boutique with an unusual window display; three wooden giraffes of varying sizes had purses and scarves slung around their necks, with brightly-coloured cushions at their feet.

Kate was quickly enthralled by the one-of-a-kind couture garments she found on the racks. "I love this skirt, it's so vibrant."

"And I want to try this on," Eva held up a short dress with zebra patterns and splashes of vibrant green.

Kate bought the brightly-coloured skirt, while Eva bought the dress.

"Let's go into the thrift store," Kate said as they stepped out into the bright sunlight. She pointed to a dimly-lit shop next to the boutique. The store had stacks of brown ceramic glazed pottery in the window, and a dusty spider plant hung from a macamé basket.

"Really?" Eva was disbelieving.

"I'll find a treasure," Kate assured her.

She quickly scored a gem that had Eva shuddering; an unusual handmade doll with long skinny witch-like fingers and a little hat fashioned like cattle horns. Her long, pale blue, thickly-padded Victorian dress was patterned with cornflowers.

"Fourteen dollars," Kate calculated the price from Namibian dollars and paid while Eva shook her head.

"Totally creepy," she said. "I need to go and email but first gossip: Ellie hit on Stepfan last night but only after she hit on Jono and she was aiming for Enrique first but he wasn't interested."

"Not Stepfan," Kate said. "No way."

"Yes, way. Stepfan wanted her to go to a hotel with him."

"That's too gross for words. I hope she didn't go?"

"No, but he did. Into a totally trashy place. Ellie ended up coming with us and carried on drinking and some local guy tried to chat her up but she threw up on him."

"What was he like, this local guy?" Kate thought that perhaps André had been out on the town, chatting up tourists.

Eva gave her an odd look. "Average height, dark hair, kinda skinny, about twenty. He was disgusted and he left but we stayed. Sofie was so drunk, she was talking at the top of her lungs but the music was so loud no one could hear."

"And Harrison?" Kate asked. "Was he okay?"

"Last I saw of him, he had Treasure hanging all over him and they left the restaurant in a big hurry — they didn't come dancing. Harrison looked like he was having the time of his life. Don't ask me about Rydell-the-psycho because I've got no idea where he was and I couldn't care less. I'm going to email, see you later!"

Eva hugged Kate and rushed off up the street.

The Eighth Night

KATE SAT DOWN ON A LOW BRICK WALL and dug out the cellphone that André had bought for her. As she'd hoped, there was a text message.

Hving fun bokkie? Hope so. Dinner?

She grinned and texted back: *fell asleep aftr u left. Shopping now. Raincheck dinner for now*

Still smiling, she headed to Peter's Antiques but was startled by a sudden reflection in the window behind her; a man was a hair's breath away from her back. She leapt to the side, swung around and came face-to-face with Rydell who smiled his wet smile. "Why are you following me?" she demanded.

He chortled. "I was just crossing the street the same as you. I'm allowed to, you know."

She ignored him and went into Peter's. Rydell followed her. She was soon distracted, marvelling at the store's variety, and she soon forget about Rydell. After she paid for her souvenirs, she left and went into to the local grocery store to pick up supplies for the following day. Once again felt someone standing too close for comfort. She turned and for the second time, it was Rydell too-close and personal. She was about to say something to him when he laughed eerily and she realized there was no point. She paid and walked hurriedly away, checking behind her to see if he was still following her. She got to the lodge and rushed into the room.

"Are you okay?" Eva was lying on her bed reading.

"That darn Rydell, I swear he's been following me. I confronted him but he just laughed at me." She sat down on her bed and looked into the distance, chewing on her lip.

"What are you doing tonight?" she asked Eva. "I feel really unsettled." She was thinking about André and wondering whether she should change her mind about dinner.

"Anyone would be upset by Rydell-the-psycho. I went to the Internet café but it was too full, so I'll have to go back later. We're all going to the Cape to Cairo restaurant tonight. Nobody's heard from Mia and Richard; it's like they've disappeared. Speaking of disappeared, Harrison and Treasure have been outta sight all day, too. And Rydell's been following you. So that's where the group is, or isn't."

"Yep, that's the whole crazy deck of cards. Maybe I should have another nap or something."

"Are you okay?" Eva sat up on one elbow, "you seem... I don't know..."

"Discombobulated? Yes, I am." Kate pushed her purchases to one side and lay down on her bed with her hands behind her head. She was dying to see André but she was too afraid to.

"I'm going to have a shower." Eva got up. "Come to dinner with us, you'll enjoy yourself."

"Maybe," Kate said. "But I should pack."

"Pack in the morning like the rest of us," Eva advised, grabbing her towel.

Kate lay there, thinking about André, wishing she had taken a picture of him. She decided not to join the others for dinner but stayed in the room, reading instead, unable to really concentrate. She suddenly could not wait to be back on the bus, travelling along the lonely roads with the vast blue sky above and miles of dust on either side. She turned out the lights and quickly fell asleep, tired out from all the excitement of the day.

Outside, Jono watched her room grow dark and he wondered how she was going to take the news. He sighed and decided to go the bar and drink the night away.

To Uis and Aba Huab

KATE WOKE EARLY THE FOLLOWING MORNING and slipped out for a walk. She stopped at the end of the road and aimed her camera back at the lodge, surprised to see a couple rushing through her shot. She focused her viewfinder and was startled to see Richard and Mia, carrying all their luggage and a number of other bags.

Kate was confused but she shrugged and walked along the jetty, her thoughts focused on André. She felt angry with herself but she could not figure out why.

A runner pushed towards her at a steady pace; it was Helen. "We missed you last night," she yelled at Kate as she pounded by. "See you soon."

The wind picked up and the sky turned gray, whipping with blustery clouds. Kate was cold and she walked back with brisk steps. She was close to the lodge when a man stepped out in front of her and she stiffened with fright but it was only Jono. Jono, battling a spectacular hangover and the weight of terrible news.

"Ah, Kate, back from her early morning walk," he said, jovially but his face looked strained and he could not quite manage a smile. "I am waiting for my eggs, so I thought I would see what the weather is doing. Nearly everybody is at breakfast, come and join us."

The group was gathered at the wooden tables to the side of the bar and it was deliciously warm inside.

Kate saw the wall-mounted springbok tequila dispenser and

remembered her relief the night she had escaped from Dumi and she felt that same comfort now. She would sit next to Marika on the bus and they would share music and laugh and nothing would be complicated.

She helped herself to a bowl of cornflakes and reached for the milk, stopping abruptly.

"Mia, what in God's name happened to you?"

Mia was badly bruised and beaten. She had a swollen blood-caked black eye and the right side of her face was a mess of deep cuts and scratches.

"What happened?" Kate asked again, the milk jug still poised.

"Hello Kate," Mia said, nonchalantly shovelling cereal into her mouth, "good fing you arrived now, I was just about to tell everyone the boring bleedin' story and God forbid, I'd have to repeat myself. I was pissed as a coot, three sheets to the wind and I fell flat on my face on the corner of a chair on my way to the lav. And no, before any of you start finking stupid rubbish, Richard didn't do this to me, I'm not covering up for him. I can get a bit wild when I drink, isn't that so, luv?"

Richard nodded and spooned sugar into his coffee.

Mia continued. "I'm bleedin' lucky I didn't take me eye out. I fell into a fire once and I never even realized I was getting burnt."

She and Richard chuckled at this.

"And Richard, what happened to you?" Helen asked from the doorway where she'd been standing unnoticed.

Diagonally, across the right side of Richard's face, were the clear track marks of fingernails; fingernails that had raked deeply and drawn blood.

Richard ran his fingers lightly over the deep grooves. "Like she said, my sweet lassie here can get a bit carried away when she's in her cups. No real harm done, we had a riot." He shrugged.

"Good morning everybody," Jono interrupted, spreading his hands in a gesture of supplication. "Everybody, I have some very bad news. Please prepare yourselves."

The small assembly immediately fell quiet and waited.

"Yesterday afternoon," Jono's bulging eyes pleaded with them for understanding, "I got a phone call from Treasure. She and Harrison were shopping in town when Harrison was stabbed in the back and in the ribs, just under his heart. Please, do not worry, he will be fine; he will live, but he is in the hospital and he is lucky to be alive."

"Do they know who did it?" Richard asked into the shocked silence.

"Yes. They arrested a local boy. He dropped his knife, which led them to him."

"Is Harrison going to be able to come on the rest of the trip?" Ellie asked, a piece of toast stopped halfway to her mouth.

"What kind of stupid idiot are you?" Stepfan barked. "The man was stabbed. He's lucky he didn't die! He'll have to stay in hospital for weeks probably. He should sue you." He shouted the last at Jono. To the group's surprise, Stepfan burst into tears. He put his head in his hands and sobbed.

No one seemed to know what to do. No one moved to comfort him, not even Lena.

"How is Treasure?" Sofie asked. "It must have been a terrible shock for her. She and Harrison where getting really close."

"Yes, well, that is the thing," Jono was hesitant. "Treasure will not be coming with us for the rest of the way. She is going to stay here with Harrison, to help him get better. We have a new cook, Betty. She's an excellent cook and she will be joining our tour."

Kate, ice cold at the news about Harrison, turned to glare at Rydell. She watched him turn puce, and then immediately go equally as pale. He laid down his spoon, and as she watched, he picked up his bread knife and dug it forcefully into the palm of his hand.

"Can we visit him?" Eva asked.

"He is in critical condition but he can talk and I am very sorry to say that he does not want to see or hear from any of us. He said first he was nearly poisoned and no one wanted to talk about it in case it ruined their holiday and now he nearly died. He is very upset. And so is Treasure. It would be better if we leave them alone like they want."

"No!" Enrique slammed his hand on the table. "I want to buy him a card and deliver it myself. I don't care if he throws it away but I'm not leaving Swakopmund until I see him. He's my friend."

Like Stepfan, Enrique's face was wet with tears and Eva went and sat down next to him and patted his shoulder. Stepfan was still crying noisily. One of the women brought in plates of fried eggs but no one noticed.

"We want to take things to him too," some of the others echoed.

"Fine." Jono said. "We will stop at Pick 'n Pay, you can buy whatever you like. They have cards and flowers and then we will drop them off."

Enrique suddenly turned to Eva. "You know what we were talking about?" he asked and she nodded. "We should do it for real."

Eva shot a guilty glance over at Kate and then she nodded her head in agreement.

"Do what?" Jasmine demanded.

"We're going to hire our own car and leave the group," Enrique said. "Eva and I first had the idea when we went skydiving and I figured it all out: hiring a car, the route, hostels, campgrounds and equipment we'll need. Last night we thought all the nonsense was behind us but now, hearing this today, we were right to come up with alternative plan and we're going to do this our way. There's room for two more, and we can all split the costs."

"You've got a point," Marika said. "Isn't it time we all admitted that this holiday is well and truly cursed? Death, poison, strange bedfellows," she shot a glance as Rydell who went from ice white back to puce, "and no one in charge," she glanced over at Jono. "And now stabbings too. I'm sorry but this is not what I signed up for. I want my money back and yes, Enrique, if you and Eva will have me, I'll come along too. And if it doesn't work out, I'll find a ride to Windhoek and fly to Durban and meet my parents there. I've had enough too. Kate, I hope you'll come with us."

"Very quick to jump ship, aren't you?" Helen sneered. "Not that you're wrong. There are some serious head-cases on this bus."

"Anyone in particular you'd care to name?" Richard asked, evenly.

"No," she answered coldly, "I'd hate to lose a leg, or shall we say, a ligament. But one thing's for sure, for a holiday, this sure hasn't been much of one." She sat down and methodically untied her running shoes.

Kate eyed her cereal as if it held the world's greatest secret. She was amazed by how hurt she felt by Eva's news and she could not believe that Eva hadn't told her that she and Enrique were even considering leaving the group. And when Marika agreed to leave too, she felt doubly betrayed.

As if reading her thoughts, Marika spoke from across the table. "I'm so sorry, Kate," she said. She looked guilty and unhappy. "But I'm really scared. Please come with us, please."

Kate knew she was being childish but she refused to look at her.

"Jono," Marika said, "I know you did your best, but this trip has become dangerous. Who's next? You should cancel the rest of the journey."

Eva agreed loudly. "And I'm going to say it right here, if anything happens to Kate, if she so much as gets a scratch, it's this man here," pointing directly at Rydell, "this psycho bastard, who did it."

She turned purposely toward Jono and added, "You should kick him off the bus, Jono, I'm telling you now. And Rydell, you listen to me, don't you touch Kate, you sick bastard."

Rydell gave a cry and lunged across the table at her but she saw him coming and jumped out of the way. Rydell landed next to Stepfan who grabbed a fistful of Rydell's hair in a harsh grip and then punched him hard.

"Ow!" Rydell yelped as blood poured from his nose, "what did you do that for? What have I ever done to you?"

"You destroyed my holiday," Stepfan roared and he punched Rydell again. Rydell's lip was cut and bleeding and his nose, flattened in the centre and misshapen, appeared to be broken.

"You snored every single night, like a train or a whale or some kind of terrible machine. Who comes on a group holiday with a bunch of strangers when you have a problem like that? You inconsiderate idiot. I have not slept one single night because of you, and then when I'm trying to watch the scenery and enjoy my holiday, I fall asleep on the bus, all because of you!" Stepfan seemed set to punch Rydell one more time but Jono grabbed him.

"*Eish*, enough." he said. "I keep telling you, buy some earplugs. Now, Rydell, what Eva said is true. If anything, and I do mean *anything* happens to Kate, I will cut off your ears and I will take out your stomach while you watch. Do you understand me?"

"That's disgusting," Marika got up. "Forget breakfast, I've had enough of this. Kate, I'm really so very sorry and I wish you'd change your mind and come with us."

She looked pleadingly at Kate who shook her head, still refusing to meet her eye. Eva walked out, followed by Enrique and Marika.

"Dear God in heaven," Richard exclaimed. "I've simply no idea what to say, or where to start untangling this mess." He stared down at his hands that were bruised and cut from whatever he and Mia had been up to the last few days.

"This is the way I see it," Jono said loudly, from the head of the table. "*Yebo*, terrible things have happened but none of them have been my fault or the fault of the tour. I am very sorry about Harrison but he was stabbed by a local boy..."

"Who could easily have been paid to do it," Helen stated. "I've seen it more than once. They'll never find whoever paid him to do it."

"...The police *will* find the perpetrator behind it," Jono continued as if there had been no interruption. "I am going to start up the bus at 8:30 am and then I am going to go to Pick 'n Pay and after that I will stop at the hospital. Any of you wishing to drop off a card or gift to Harrison may do so.

"Rydell, you will get your nose and lip taken care of at the hospital and Mia, you should get looked at too. Then I am continuing with this tour and those of you who choose to continue will behave yourselves, from this moment onwards or I will drop you off in the desert and say oh, I am sorry, I did not realize what happened, when they find your dead bodies. Do I make myself clear? You will do your dishes according to the roster, put up your tents, and then take them down nicely. You will keep the bus nice and tidy, look out the window at wild animals and enjoy your holiday. You will welcome Betty the new cook, and you will eat her food without complaining, and we will not talk about any of this again.

"And," he added, "you are free to tell my company your versions in as much detail as you would like. Also, any and all of you are welcome to leave right now, if you would like to do so. What do you say?"

"I need time to think about it," Sofie said, sounding shell-shocked. "It is not easy to know what to do."

"Like I said, the bus leaves at 8:30 am and you have until that time to think about it. Either you are on the bus or you are not," Jono said, shortly. "At this point I really don't care. *Aikona wena*, you people act like I should have done things differently, well, let me tell you I have never met a more strange bunch of crazies in my life and believe me, I have seen some things. You attacked each other right from the start. Did you think I did not notice what was going on? All of you, with the exception of a few, need your heads read. You come from so-called civilized countries and you behave like this? Come or do not come, I really do not care. *Eish.*" He walked out, throwing his hands up in frustration and disgust.

There was a long silence.

Mia let loose a high pitched giggle and they all turned to her. "I'm so sorry," she said, clapping her hand to her mouth. "It's a nervous reaction of mine, to laugh when I get upset." She must have been very upset because she started giggling again and this time she couldn't stop.

Richard sighed. "Come on then, come outside with me," he said, "and we'll figure it out." Mia was close to hysteria, tears streaming down her cheeks, and her whole body shaking, as he led her outside.

Kate got up and made a cup of coffee. She returned to the table and sat down. "I'm going ahead with my holiday," she said, "and this nonsense will stop." She turned to Rydell, adding harshly. "And you leave me alone from now on! No more following me around, do you understand?"

"Yes," Rydell got up, his face was broken. He could hardly talk through the mess of blood and mucus. "Don't worry, I'll leave you alone. I'm sick and tired of this abuse from all of you. I haven't done anything wrong. And I might lay charges against you," he said to Stepfan. "You hit me because I snore. You're not allowed to hit a person because they snore." He was indignant and agitated.

You're not allowed to poison a person because you have a crush on their girlfriend, Kate thought but she did not say it, looking at her untouched coffee instead, and thinking about Harrison in hospital.

"I'm continuing on," Lena said calmly. "You do whatever you want to," she said to Stepfan.

"I'm continuing too," Gisela said.

"And so am I," Helen spoke up. "This is my vacation. I

worked hard for it and I'm going to have a good time, dammit."

"We'll carry on too," Jasmine and Ellie said after a quiet conference.

"What about you, Sofie?" Helen asked. "Come on. Please come."

"I don't know," Sofie said, sounding fragile and unsure. "Well, okay then, okay." She got up. "I am going to get my things."

The rest of the group got up too. Bowls and plates with untouched breakfasts lay on the table, and some servings lay shattered on the floor, a scramble of broken china and fried eggs.

The only person left seated was Stepfan. He buried his face in his hands and realized he had no choice but to carry on.

"*Haw!* What happened here?" one of the cooks walked in and demanded to know. "All this good food gone to waste. And broken plates. Did you have a fight or what? *Haw!* You people, really, what a mess." She shook her head and grumbled under her breath.

Stepfan ignored her and walked back to his room. He grabbed his bag off his bed and headed to the bus. He climbed onboard, sat down and stared out the window. He felt intensely sorry for himself and filled with misery. His trip of a lifetime had turned into the nightmare from hell and he had no idea how to fix it. And he still had to go the entire way to Nairobi.

He wondered if he might meet a new woman at one of the new campsites they would be stopping at and the thought cheered him up. He decided to have a nap on the bus while he waited for the others.

Kate was still reeling from hurt by Marika and Eva's departure. She felt crushed as if by a blow. She got to her tidy bed and found a note on her pillow.

Dear Kate, I'm so sorry, I certainly didn't plan this but it seems like the best and safest thing for me to do. You've been a very good friend and travelling companion to me. Please forgive me. And please email me when you're not angry with me anymore and please don't stay angry forever. I wish you wouldn't carry on with the trip, there's something very bad about that bus. With lots of love, your friend, Marika.*

Kate picked up her bags and lugged them to the bus where Helen and Sofie were helping each other up the ladder.

"All this shopping." Sofie was subdued. "I am so stupid. I should have posted stuff home. Mia and Richard where at the post office when I mailed a postcard to my sister and they where sending dozens of packages, wich was much more sensible."

Rydell arrived. He had not changed his shirt or cleaned his face. "Will you take a photograph of me so I can press charges?" he asked Kate and he held out his camera.

"No," she said, shortly. "Ask someone else."

Jono climbed into the back of the bus. "Everybody here yet?" he asked. "They have got ten minutes more. How is everybody?"

"Fine, Jono," Sofie, Helen and Kate answered, none of them sounding too cheerful.

"Good," he said absently, "very good."

He stepped aside to let Gisela and Lena climb up, followed by Mia and Richard.

"Oy, sorry you all," Mia apologized and patted her fairy-floss hair, "about going pear-shaped in there. I lost it, gobsmacked by the shite going down."

"Not your fault," they reassured her.

"It was hard to believe what we were hearing," Jasmine said.

"Yeah, crazy," Ellie agreed, secretly thinking it was exciting.

"Are we are all here?" Jono called through the cab window.

"Yes," they shouted back at him and he started the bus.

And then there were twelve little Indians, Kate observed in silence. *Like the Agatha Christie story, we are all being picked off.* She sighed. The bus felt oddly empty: *Charisse, Brianna, Harrison, Marika, Eva, Enrique and Treasure — gone.*

As promised, Jono pulled over in front of the Pick 'n Pay. Kate got Harrison a selection of gifts and she picked up the daily newspapers for herself as well as two magazines for Treasure.

They got to the hospital and trooped in while Jono waited outside. The receptionist pointed them down the hall and they peered inside Harrison's room. Treasure was asleep in a chair pulled up close to Harrison, her head resting on his bed.

Helen opened the door gently and they crept inside and left the gifts near Treasure.

"They were both sleeping so we placed our gifts on a chair near Treasure and left as quietly as we could," Helen reported back to Jono. "Harrison looked in really bad shape."

Jono nodded. "We must wait for Rydell." He leaned against the bus with his arms folded. "Mia, are you sure you do not want to get your faced checked out?"

"Nah, it's fine, looks much worse than it is," Mia said.

"Two stitches in my lip and my nose is broken," Rydell said, returning half an hour later. He had difficulty talking. "I'm going to press charges, the nurse took pictures."

The others ignored him except for Stepfan who commented that a broken nose might be the best thing to help cure his snoring.

"And now we will pick up our new cook and then we will be on our way," Jono interrupted any retort Rydell might have made.

Jono drove to a suburb on the edge of town and stopped at a small bungalow with lace-curtained windows and a neatly trimmed lawn. He sounded the horn and a couple in their late forties emerged. The man was tall and thin, dressed in a black suit and a black fedora, while the woman was small and round in a colourful dress.

Jono got out of the bus and took a bag from the man, shook his hand and said something in Xhosa. The man hugged the woman and kissed her.

Jono said something to the woman and she laughed and he led her to the bus and opened the door. "Everybody, this is Mrs. Betty Nwosu, please make her feel very welcome."

"Hello, Betty," came the chorus, "Welcome. Thank you for joining us."

Jono put the bus into gear and they drove off.

Despite the drama of the morning and her concern for Harrison, Kate felt a glimmer of happiness stir in her chest. There was something wonderful about being back on the open road, having a day without plans and a clear blue sky above.

She checked to see if André had sent her a text but there was nothing. She desperately wanted to send him a message but could not think of anything so say so she settled down to read a small volume of African poetry she had found the day before in Peter's Antiques.

Two seats ahead of Kate, Rydell explored his injuries. He felt clearheaded and peaceful. The pain felt good and he repeatedly tested his lip to taste the blood of his wounds. His nose was too excruciatingly raw to bear touching, so he patted his brusied black eyes instead and revelled in his war wounds. He felt as though he had triumphed in some way; indeed, he felt vindicated.

He had been devastated yes, and filled with fury, when he first heard that Treasure was not going to rejoin the bus. But oddly enough his violent anger soon subsided, and he realized that he did not care much at all.

He fingered the vial of painkillers in his pocket. The nurse had not understood why he had refused to take any. He'd thought about explaining how pain made him feel alive, but he thought better of it, and asked for Harrison's room instead. He had not been sure of his intentions, but when he saw Treasure asleep and Harrison so frail, his rage and envy left him. In fact, he felt nothing much at all except a modicum of surprise at how ordinary Treasure was. He looked at the gifts and cards that the others had left and he was amazed by their actions, unsure why he had never felt that kind of kinship.

He thought about Treasure, asleep at Harrison's bedside and

how, at that moment, she had seemed too real for his liking; a woman of flesh and blood, not the goddess he'd imagined. He realized that he'd been so eager to find The One that he had fallen for the first woman he met. Sure, she was beautiful but she had turned out to be very ordinary — only a very ordinary woman would have fallen in love with Harrison. No, things hadn't gone according to plan but in fact they had turned out just fine. And, he reassured himself, there was no way they would ever be able to trace that boy to him. And he was glad, now, that the boy had not managed to get to Kate. With his desire for Treasure gone, there was no need for collateral damage. Not that he really cared one way or the other. He glanced over at Kate, hugging the secret that she would never know how close she had come to being hurt too.

Rydell's head was filled with a beautiful silence, there were no jabbering voices and no chattering rhymes and he was perfectly happy.

The bus drove smoothly along the coastline and turned east, stopping at Uis to get gas. Kate finished photographing the toilet; a masterpiece of disparate dirty pieces, and she saw Jasmine, Ellie, Sofie and Helen running up to her, all of them out breath.

"What wrong?" she asked with trepidation.

"We saw your doll! Alive. In the same dress! Hurry up, she's in the Spar, you must see her!"

Kate had received many comments about her doll's unusual appearance; her uncommon hat and her strangely long and witchlike fingers.

Not understanding what they meant, Kate followed them to the general grocery store and saw a regal woman who was indeed dressed exactly like her doll.

"What on earth?" Kate exclaimed, startled, and she craned to get a better look inside the dark store crowded with locals lining up at the cashiers.

"You see," Sofie said, "isn't that the most amazing thing?"

Kate got close behind the woman and peered at her horn-shaped hat, her tightly-waisted buttoned bodice, and her long floor-length Victorian skirt. The woman turned and glared at Kate.

"Pardon me," Kate apologized and stepped back. "Would you mind if I took your photograph?"

"She wants to know for how much?" the cashier translated the woman's reply.

In answer, Kate held out a handful of coins. The woman looked at them scornfully, but nodded and took the money. Kate followed the woman outside to a brightly painted wall lined with post-office boxes and photographed her.

"She is from the Herero tribe," Betty explained, joining them. "They have dressed like that from the days of the German settlers. Their clothes are very beautiful. The Herero became successful cattle farmers in the central grasslands of Namibia but then they came into conflict with the Nama people, and then later with the German colonial armies."

"Can the conversation please continue on the bus?" Jono asked. "We have a long way to go and we had a late start."

"I will sit in the back," Betty said and they got back on the bus.

"The Herero tried to make peace with the Germans," she said, "but the Germans continued to exterminate them in the most horrific of ways. It took the Germans just three years to reduce the Herero population from 80,000 to 15,000."

"Yes, Jono told us about the concentration camps," Sofie said. "Unbelievable."

"And then," Betty explained, nodding at Sofie, "in 1915, after South Africa got control of Namibia, the Herero were pushed into South African style 'homelands'. But today the story is a happier one, and the Herero population is up to 100,000."

"Why do they dress like that?" Helen asked.

"In the early days, the Herero dressed much like the Himba do today — and the Himba do not wear many clothes.

During the nineteenth-century, the German missionaries took exception to Herero's nakedness and clothed the women in ankle-length dresses with long sleeves and bodices that button right up to the neck. Today many women wear shawls, and six to eight petticoats under the dress to make the skirts so nice and full. Their horn-shaped hats pay homage to the horns of their cattle. You may also wonder how the Herero women don't get too hot in those clothes, but they do not appear to suffer."

"And how do the Herero men dress?" Sofie asked.

"For every day, they dress like ordinary men but for special occasions, they have a suit that is like the military uniform of the Germans, from the nineteenth century."

"Why would they want to dress like them, when the Germans killed them and treated them so badly?" Sofie said. "Seems weird to me."

Betty had no answer to this.

"How do you know so much about the Herero?" Helen was curious.

Betty blushed. "I'm a schoolteacher," she said, "so you mustn't let me talk too much about these things or I'll bore you."

"But you are here to cook?" Sofie enquired.

"Jono's a friend and he needs my help. I'm a good cook, don't worry."

"I am not worried," Sofie assured her.

"I am," Mia said, under her breath to Richard, "because I hate bleedin' history and teachers."

"Relax," Richard said, "sleep or think about our adventure. It went better than I ever could have imagined."

"Yeah, it did, didn't it?" Mia brightened. "I didn't really fink we could pull it off but we did."

"We can't talk about it," Richard snuck a look around, "but think about it. I know I am. You never let me down, Nurse Teller, you do know that, don't you?" He kissed the top of her head.

She smiled and leaned against him. "Right you are, luv."

The bus entered a new Africa; the earth was claylike and parched and the carcasses of black trees lay strewn at random angles under the empty blue sky.

"Look at that woman!" Kate cried out, pointing out the window to a near-naked woman who was standing with military precision and staring fiercely at the bus. She was camouflaged in pasted mud and would have been easy to miss, were it not for her fury that glowed like a beacon.

"She is a Himba," Betty explained, "as I was mentioning a moment ago. And you must not take a photograph of her without her permission or she will get terribly angry. They are a very violent people. If you murder somebody in the Himba tribe, there is no punishment except that you must buy fifteen cows for the murdered person's family. The Himba wear very few clothes and they smear a mixture of red ochre and fat over their bodies to protect them from the sun, and that is what gives them that beautiful colour. The red also symbolizes the rich earth as well as blood which symbolizes life. The women work much harder than the men; they milk the cows, take care of the children, carry water and build homes."

Kate was poised for Stepfan to make a sexist comment of approval but to her surprise he remained quiet.

"They have managed to keep their traditional lifestyles because of where they live," Betty added as the bus drove past the angry woman and drew closer to a group of Himba and Herero women. "The harsh desert climate and their seclusion from outside influences help them keep their heritage. The Himba also struggled badly at the hands of the Germans, but they have made a comeback and they now live on nature conservancies where they have control of their wildlife and of tourism."

Mia yawned widely and sighed.

Jono stopped the bus. "You have fifteen minutes at this stall of the Herero and the Himba," he called out. "Remember to ask permission for photographs, do not just take them."

Kate rushed off the bus and hurried toward a Himba woman who glared at her. The woman was naked except for an extremely short skirt of leather strips. The woman's skin, hair, clothes and jewelry were all coloured with the same polished red paste, and white cowrie shells were sewn onto leather straps that were fastened under her knees. Her neck was decorated with copper and leather necklaces, and a beaded shell pendant hung between her long flat breasts.

Kate purchased a tiny doll that was fashioned in the woman's likeness; a doll she was sure customs departments the world over would reject as it was covered in red paste and felt sticky to touch.

None of the others approached the women, apart from Jasmine who cautiously bought a doll and quickly rejoined the others.

The bus continued down the deserted road with no signs of life as far as the eye could see. Kate studied her doll. Sofie and Helen were reading; Jasmine, Stepfan and Ellie slept while Gisela and Lena chatted quietly. Richard and Mia were looking out the window and Betty had returned to the front of the bus with Jono.

Kate was about to pick up a newspaper when the bus stopped in what seemed like the middle of nowhere.

"We are now at the petrified forest," Jono announced, his tone flat. "There is a short guided walk here that will take you three quarters of an hour."

Jono's recalcitrant mood was largely due to his disenchantment with the current situation. He missed Treasure and the easy rhythm of their familiarity. He felt like he had to entertain Betty. He had also hoped that Kate might have had a change of heart, but it was clear this was not the case and he was disgruntled by how things had turned out. He rubbed his suffering eyes and yawned, thinking he must ask Betty if she had a headache tablet. He watched the group raggedly following the guide;

they did not seem too interested and were dragging their heels.

"This is like a school tour," Stepfan said, scratching a bite on his arm.

"I am surprised you can remember that far back," Sofie commented, pushing past him. "Stay on the bus and sleep."

"He'd rather come with us and complain all the way," Ellie pulled on a sunhat.

"That's right, pick on me." Stepfan whined but they ignored him.

The guide on the walk appeared as disinterested in his subject matter as his tour were hearing about it. "Dead tree," he pointed. "It turned to stone. They are about 250 million years old. Please do not touch anything and please do not take pieces of the stones."

"What made this happen, mate?" Richard asked idly, the scratches on his face vivid.

The guide went on to describe the geological forces behind the petrified wonders while Kate wandered off to investigate the welwitschia plants. "Stay on the path please," the guide called out to her. "I will explain the welwitschia to you later."

Kate knelt down to photograph the strange, multi-leafed plant that lay in thick tangled ribbons on the ground. She marveled at the shape of the curved leaves and waited for the guide who strolled over at his leisure.

"That ancient plant in front of you is actually a tree," he recited, his gaze at the sky. "It has the appearance of having many leaves but in fact there are only two leaves. There is a male plant and a female plant. This plant is a living fossil."

"Look, Stepfan, you have a relative," Sofie pointed.

"Very funny," Stepfan said.

"The plants are many hundreds and even thousands of years old," the guide continued, "and they live on the dew they collect on their leaves. That is the end of the tour. Let me show you our market stall where you can buy souvenirs and cold drinks."

"Cold drinks!" The untidy and thirsty gang shouted their

appreciation as they rushed down the steep, rocky path, glad to escape the blistering heat.

Kate wished Enrique was there, so she could chat to him about welwitschias and flowers and oddly-coloured tree bark. She missed him, and Marika and Eva.

"I would prefer," Jono announced loudly through the connecting window, when the group was seated on the bus, "that we do not stop for lunch but continue straight on to Aba Huab, would that be fine with you? We are late running behind today."

Everyone agreed and Jono set off down the bumpy road.

Kate dug out an apple and opened up a newspaper, stopping short, her heart leaping in fright at a headline: "SERIAL KILLER STRIKES AGAIN?" She put her apple down and concentrated on the article, her eyes wide.

> Just when the police thought they had the correct suspect in custody in Windhoek, "Jack the Ripper" strikes again, this time in *Swakopmund*. The naked, headless body of a woman identified as Rosalee Khumalo, 23, was found dumped in the industrial area, just off Mandume Ya Ndemufayo Road sometime yesterday. Rosalee Khumalo was a sex worker, working out of the Old Colonial Hotel, distinctive for its gaudy red velvet and ornate gold-leafed ornamentation, where, despite efforts on the part of the police, the hotel operates a lively sex trade.
>
> In July of this year, the bodies of Melanie Janse, 22, Juanita Mabula, 21, and Violoa Swartbooi, 18, were identified, all three murders attributed to the work of a serial killer. The police dubbed the killer "Jack the Ripper", suspecting the killer might be a doctor, as the bodies had been precisely dismembered, indicating a knowledge of human anatomy.
>
> The police are also still seeking the identification of a fourth woman, whose body had been discovered in a rubbish bin at a lay-bye along the busy road between Windhoek and Okahandja in May. The body of the woman, believed to be in her 20s, was found with the head, arms and legs cut off and the torso slashed into two pieces.
>
> Despite calling in help from the South African Police Service, no

progress had been made. The police continue to hold a doctor in custody who confessed to the murders when he was stopped for drunken driving, but the police were uncertain as to whether he is actually the killer, despite his startling confession.

"The SAPS Investigative Psychology Unit will be helping us catch this killer," the inspector general of the Namibian police, Lieutenant General Sebastian Ndeitunga is quoted as saying. "Because this monster is living among us whether being on a farm, settlement, a church member, a restaurant frequenter, a doctor, a street vendor, you mention it, the monster will continue to attack of his own accord and stir fear and panic until someone comes up with information about his whereabouts."

An official with the Namibian government forensic unit said "The perpetrator is a professional who knows what he is doing. The legs and arms were cut off was done in a way that you would think it was done in a butchery or a science lab."

Namibian president Hifikepunye Pohamba has made an impassioned appeal to law enforcement agencies to trace the murderer and ensure that he faces the wrath of the law.

And now the discovery of Rosalee Khumalo leads police to suspect that the killer has struck again or a copycat has emerged. Sources have revealed that there are differences in this killing to the others; while the body was neatly dismembered, as in the cases of the other victims, and the head was also missing, there appeared to be evidence of a muti murder: the woman's genitals had been cut off which had not been done to any of the other victims. Also, the breasts had been removed and fat sucked from the abdomen which is considered to bring good luck in muti.

Rosalee Khumalo is survived by her elderly mother, 83, and her two children, a girl, 8, and a boy, 5. The investigation will continue.

Kate folded the paper, appalled. Despite the heat of the day, she cold and covered in goosebumps.

She was convinced that Rydell had killed Rosalee Khumalo. She glanced over at him; he was fast asleep, still wearing his bloodied clothes, with his head leaning against the window.

While she was certain it was him, what could she do? She could not tell Jono; he would not believe her.

She decided to put the newspaper away so none of the others would see it. She was rearranging her bag when she spotted André's phone and she grabbed it with relief.

There was a message: *mornin sunshine! Where r u? did u forget me yet?*

She smiled and replied; *near Uis. I remember evrything! Can I phone u 2nite? Smthing wryng me.*

She sent it and did not have long to wait.

Problms? With? U ok? Tell more

u know jack serial killer? I think he's on bus

no! 4real?

yes, 4sure. Cant talk now, call l8r?

yes. going 2 ask frnds 4 intel 2day. I know pep in know. r u safe?

yes I'm fine, don't wrry

where r u 2night?

aba huab

thats not far. I can b there in 3hrs if u need me. Try2 need me.

I'll be fine. But good to know

will fone u 6pm. b safe

I will, talk later

She signed off and put the phone back in her bag, exhaling a huge sigh of relief. At least she had André for an ally.

The road had become a series of supersized bumps and she hung on to her seat, glancing furtively around the bus. Her companions were lost in their own worlds and Rydell woke up and was rubbing his eyes.

Kate could not shake the sick feeling in her stomach that the worst was yet to come.

They arrived at Aba Huab mid-afternoon. The campsite, set under immense acacia trees, was picture-postcard Africa with a traditional low pebble-stone wall and a thatched rondavel bar. The veldt and bush were quiet in the afternoon heat, with only a few birds and crickets calling out lazily.

Kate thought about telling Jono about Rydell and the death of Rosalee Khumalo but before she could open her mouth, Lena distracted them all with an announcement.

"I'm sharing with Gisela now," she called out to Stepfan. "Put up your own tent."

"I had better help him, *eish*," Jono said in an undertone to Kate and trotted over to Stepfan who was standing helplessly, looking around.

The tents assembled, Jono called everyone over. "Tonight the locals will dance for us," he announced. "There is no fee, but contributions are welcome as this is a poor area and it is very tough for people to make a living."

"Dancing!" Mia gave a loud whistle. "That's bleedin' brilliant! The Marula, here I come." She whooped, shook her shoulders and stamped her feet. Mia's antics threw aside the heavy cloak of gloom that had shrouded the group since breakfast.

"My girl always wants to party," Richard said theatrically with a sigh.

"She certainly parties enough for two," Lena whispered to Kate.

Kate was startled. "What do you mean?" she asked.

"She's pregnant," Lena said. "I heard her telling Jasmine like it was something funny."

Kate stared at Mia who was still practicing her dance, her bruised face horrifying. A thought occurred to Kate and she looked at Richard whose face still bore the deep tracks of fingernails.

Kate sidled closer to Mia who had stopped dancing and was standing with her hands on her hips. Mia's nails were bitten to the quick and Kate frowned, thinking that the story of Richard and Mia's night of drunken debauchery did not ring true and she wondered what had really happened.

And now there was the news that Mia was pregnant.

"I wish I had a mask for the dance," Ellie said. "Richard, are you going to wear yours?"

"Depends," he said, "I was saving that for our trance dance, when it's just us. We'll see, Ellie, we'll see."

Later, Kate was not sure why she was not in a better mood. She felt tired and grumpy and out of sorts. She had lots of reasons to feel ill-tempered but still, it was not like her and she wished she could shake the mood off.

"It's fifty degrees in the shade," Richard reported, studying his portable barometer. "That's 122 Farenheit."

"I'm going to have a shower," Kate said to the others. "It's too hot for me."

She stood under the cold water and felt her good spirits start to return. She pulled on the new African skirt she had bought with Eva and went up to the cool verandah. She settled into a lounge chair and closed her eyes, enjoying the fragrance of hot veldt grass and spicy thatch. Others from the group drifted up to join her and they were soon all dozing or writing in their journals.

Kate fell asleep and woke disorientated.

"What time is it?" Sofie asked in a similarly confused waking state, with deep sleep creases on her face.

Kate looked at her watch. "5:45," she said and her heart skipped a beat. "I must get my phone," she said and she dashed off.

"What phone?" Sofie called after her. "Wait for me."

But Kate ran like the wind, her long African skirt whipping in the breeze. The air was hot and dry and filled with a rich mix of evening African smells: campfires, the cooling earth, a hint of the mysterious night to come. Kate rushed into her tent and grabbed her phone. Her heart was beating fast but there were no missed calls. She climbed out of her tent and zipped it up, thinking there was nothing she could do now but wait.

What if he didn't call? Should she call him? It occurred to her suddenly that she was more concerned about the possibility of André not calling than she was about Rydell being the copycat killer of the murdered Rosalee Khumalo.

She sat, uneasy in the shade on the stone wall. She was wondering whether she should go for a walk when she heard the unmistakeable sound of a car engine. She looked up in disbelief, and yes, there was André, spinning into Aba Huab in a bright green Porsche, whipping up a cloud of dust.

She ran up to the boma where he had parked and called his name.

"Don't you look very *lekker* in your nice new skirt," he said and she blushed. He was much better-looking than she remembered, and bigger too.

They stood awkwardly and then Kate advanced a step. "I, um, I'm glad you came," she said.

He flipped his car keys around his fingers and looked around. "Sounded serious, thought I'd better check out what's going on."

"André," she said suddenly, "I must tell you something..."

"Let me guess," a scornful voice said, close to them, "your boyfriend has arrived all the way from Canada." It was Stepfan. "It seems," he continued, "that our good girl is not quite as good as she made herself out to be. Miss holier-than-thou turns out to be quite risqué after all." He smiled smugly and walked off.

André cocked an enquiring eye at Kate.

"I can explain, let's go for a walk," she said, and he nodded, his expression not particularly forgiving. They walked in silence until they had rounded a corner of the sandy road.

"When were you going to tell me?" he asked her.

Kate sighed. "There's no boyfriend. There was — he's the reason I'm on this trip. I thought he was going to propose marriage and next thing, I'm listening to him tell me all the advantages of an open relationship."

"Ah, I see. He had someone in mind then?"

"Yes, he did. I left him and came on this trip and then, on the first night, Jono seemed interested in me and I didn't want to hurt his feelings by not liking him and I told him I had a boyfriend. It seemed like the nicer thing to do. And I was right, Jono did, or rather does, have a crush on me, he told me so at dinner, the night before you and I met."

"Goodness gracious," André said, and the expression sounded quaint coming from him. "You have been having an interesting go of it. Okay, well, fine then. But now, listen, tell me about this serial killer."

"It's quite a long story if I start right at the beginning in Cape Town when our trip began."

"We've got all the time in the world."

"Not really, because it's nearly suppertime and then some local dancers are doing a show for us — will you stay for that?"

"That and more." He looked around Aba Huab. "I hate to see this. The campsite's not nearly as busy as it should be, for this time of year. There should be three or four camps set up, meanwhile there's only you guys. That's not good, the locals will suffer badly."

Kate was dying to grab André's hand but she resisted, wondering if he thought he'd made a mistake in coming to see her.

"Mevrou Nwosu," André exclaimed in surprise, when they got back to the bus, "*Wat doen jy hier?* What on earth are you doing here?" He ran over to Betty who was stirring a pot on the gas burner and he swept her up in his arms.

Betty responded like a giddy schoolgirl. "André Markus Bartaiah, I might ask you the same question, what are *you* doing here? And put me down, you naughty boy."

"I'm here to visit my excellent new friend, Miss Kate," André explained. "And you?"

"I'm here to help out my excellent and very *old* friend, Jono, who is the guide on the tour. I think you know him? He lost his cook who lost her heart to a man who got off the bus and she stayed with him."

"You're cooking?" André had a gleam in his eye. "You will not know this," he said to Kate, "but this esteemed lady is not only a wonderful teacher, but also a great cook. Her skills are in high demand in Swakopmund. I'm very glad I'm staying for dinner."

"You're staying?" Betty laughed. "Thank you for giving me good warning, because now I must double my ingredients — I know how much you can eat."

"André, my man, what are you doing here?" Jono walked up and offered a traditional African handshake.

André swung around. "Hey, Jono," he smiled broadly, "*howzit my bru?*" He grasped Jono's hand and pumped vigorously.

"You know everyone," Kate commented.

"Just in my corner of the desert," André replied, "which in reality, is only a very small piece of the world. Jono, I'm here to visit this gorgeous woman who I had the pleasure of meeting yesterday, the lovely Kate."

"Yes, she is lovely, I could not agree more." Jono sounded slightly strained. "You are going to stay for supper? Did you fly up in your green Porsche?"

"*Ja*, man, of course I did. The super green flying machine."

"Supper's ready," Betty announced and as if by radar, people had already gravitated to the side of the bus where the food was laid out. "Vegetable curry, mielie pap and curried meat in that dish there. Enjoy."

"The famous mielie pap," Kate said. "Marika told me about it. It's a pity she didn't get to enjoy it." She prodded the stiff white mound on her plate. "It looks like Cream of Wheat made without enough water or milk." She sniffed it. "It doesn't have much smell."

"It's ground maize," Betty explained, "made from white corn kernels. It is a staple of my people, good for breakfast or supper. Foreigners sometimes find it a bit dry, so add more sauce if you need to."

The group fell on the food as if they had not eaten for a week.

"Hey, Jono, my china, have you been starving your crew?" André laughed. "I've never seen such a hungry lot in my life."

"We need energy to dance later," Sofie said.

"Are you going to stay for the dancing tonight?" Helen asked flirtatiously.

"I wouldn't miss it." André tucked into his plate of food and waved his fork at Betty in appreciation.

"We are going to do the Marula," Mia declared. "I've only been waiting the whole bleedin' trip to learn it."

"You've even got me interested in it." Gisela had decided to put her misgivings about Mia aside for the evening.

"I'll try too." Lena announced.

"That I must see," Stepfan said.

"And you shall, tonight." Lena said, smoothing down her long skirt. She had managed to remain polished and fashionable throughout the entire trip; it was as if she had access to a hidden ironing board and a secret washing machine.

"I'm on dish duty tonight," Sofie said. "Don't start without me."

All the men and women were flirting with André and Kate was amused to watch them succumb to his charm and she thought that he was the kind of man who, with little effort, could cause a woman to throw caution to the wind. She reminded herself that she had already had that opportunity; she could have had dinner with him that last night in Swakopmund but she had resisted. But he was here now and she was dying to touch him, kiss him again.

She finished her supper and took her plate to the bucket.

"Where did you find him?" Sofie and Helen joined her and asked in an undertone. "he's totally awesome."

"My God, girl," Sofie added, "you are a quiet one but when you come out with it, you don't just do half the job."

"I met him in the town," Kate said, unable to hide the delight in her eyes. "He dazzled me."

"I'm sure he did." Sofie said, "and from the look of it, you dazzled him too!"

Kate helped Sofie and Helen wash the dishes, and then they trooped off to the boma to watch the local dancers.

The Ninth Night

KATE THOUGHT THE DANCING WAS WONDERFUL but she also knew she'd she would remember nothing none of it later because all she could think about was André. She was acutely aware of him: his touch when his skin brushed against hers, the feel of his hand caressing her back, the warmth of him as he leaned into her, and the heat of his breath on her ear.

"Will you teach us the Marula now?" Mia leapt to her feet as soon as the dancing ended and the dish on the ground was filled with money.

The women found her request funny and they giggled and chatted in Xhosa.

"Please," Mia pleaded, "give us lessons. We really want to learn."

The dancers soon had the whole group on their feet to learn the Marula, including Rydell and Stepfan.

"Come walk with me," André whispered to Kate and they slipped away.

"Let's go to the camp," he said, "I'll light a fire and we'll be able to see if anyone's coming and you can tell me everything."

He built a fire in one of the small pits that faced the boma and Kate pulled up two camp chairs.

"*Ag nooit bokkie*," André said, "No way, my angel. I want to fill my arms with you. Come sit here with me, against the tree, *ja*, like so. That's better, *né*? So now, Katie, tell me about this serial killer idea you have and everything that goes with it."

Kate told him the story from the beginning, starting with Rydell's oddities, his theories about African women, his search for a Bushman wife and his desire for Treasure. How Richard seemed so obsessed with witchcraft, drugs and muti. How Stepfan and Charisse had carried on an affair right in front of Lena, Stepfan's wife. She told him about Sofie and Stepfan's constant political arguing; all the in-fighting, flirting and aggression that had been rife since the start of the trip. She described how Harrison's cleaning fetishes had led him to hang around Treasure, which incited Rydell to poison Harrison's water which and had then mistakenly killed Charisse. She told him about her trip to Walvis Bay with Brianna and everything that happened right up to the loss of Enrique, Eva and Marika. She told him about Stepfan breaking Rydell's nose because of his snoring and she explained why both Richard and Mia looked as if they'd they had gone several rounds in a heavyweight fight, and finally, she wrapped up with Treasure staying to take care Harrison in Swakopmund, hence Betty being their new cook.

The only part Kate judiciously left out was her attraction to Thaalu.

"My goodness gracious me," André said, stroking her hair, "with all that poison and intrigue, no wonder you wanted to buy a switchblade. I'm surprised you didn't rush to my shop and demand an AK47. Why didn't you bail and stay with me in Swakopmund? You could have, you know. You still can. I could give you a real holiday. You know, the kind, with fun, laughter, good times, things like that. Tough concept I know, but you never know, you might like it."

"I have to do this," Kate explained. "I started this tour and I'm going to finish it. I finish things and not only that, I try to do them right. I don't leave off halfway because the going gets tough, although in this case, given that lives have been lost and threatened, perhaps not finishing would be the more sensible thing to do. But this is my adventure, my holiday, and I won't give up on it."

"Hmmm, *ja*, I get that much," André said, "but if you ask me, it's not a good idea for you to stay. Let's think this through."

He massaged her shoulders while he thought out loud. "In terms of evidence, you have none and that makes it tough. It also explains why Jono let the wheels of this particular bus keep turning; he had no real reason to stop it and ditch the suspect player or players. He too had no facts. I mean, for sure, Rydell is one strange goofball, you can see that right off the bat, but what can you do? Arrest him for weird body twitches and a crazy look in his eye or the fact that he's covered in clothes like an Arab?"

"True," Kate sighed.

"What can you tell me about the others?" he asked.

"Jasmine and Ellie are fine, Helen's a moody man-eater, she'll try to steal you out from under me and Sofie's lovely, all she'll do is talk your ear off."

"*Ay yai yai,* so I'm going to be under you, am I?" André clearly relished the idea.

Kate smacked him lightly on the arm. "Isn't there anything we can do?" she asked, "about the serial killer? Can't we tell the police our suspicions?" She leaned back against him.

"Kate, they'll laugh at us," he said thoughtfully, "They want DNA, a weapon, a missing body part in someone's luggage, that kind of thing and that's not going to happen. This Rydell guy may be one crazy oke but you can tell he's clever, he'd never do something stupid. Everything you've told me points to how he does a neat job, tidy from start to finish. No sunshine, we cannot do anything, but what we can do is keep you safe, and that, for me is priority number one."

They could hear the yells and whoops of the Marula dancers.

"Come back with me to Swakopmund," he said again. "Just come back with me, we'll leave in the morning. You deserve a real holiday and I can't bear to think of you in danger."

She turned around to face him, hiked her skirt up her hips,

and straddled him. She put her arms around his neck and leaned in close. "There's only one thing I want right now," she said. "And that's you."

They kissed and he cupped her buttocks with his hands and held her tightly.

André pulled away for a moment. "Let's get ourselves inside your tent," he said, his voice hoarse. "Before they all come back and find us naked in front of the campfire."

They unzipped her tent and climbed in hand in hand. André's huge bulk proved a tight squeeze in the tiny tent.

Kate pulled his T-shirt off him and she reached to unzip his trousers while he hurried to get pull her clothes off.

"Murder and mayhem aside," he whispered, "you have no idea how glad I am that I met you."

To Okaukuejo
and the Etosha Pan

KATE WOKE WITH HER ARM AROUND ANDRÉ'S NECK and her leg draped over his hip. She tucked herself closer into him and he wrapped his arm around her waist and held her tight.

"Good thing it's still early, *né?*" he whispered in her ear. "Time for a quickie, if you're in the mood."

"I believe I'm in the mood," Kate smiled, "but let's not rush."

Later André groaned. "I don't want to leave but I must to get my shop open on time. But I'll see you when you get to Windhoek."

He looked at her, his hair sticking up in several directions. "You okay, *bokkie?*"

"Fantastic."

They climbed out the tent and she waited for him at his car while he was in the washroom. She was filled with a sudden fear and she knelt down and was peering at the underbelly of the Porsche when she heard André laughing.

"Are you going to give her a quick service before I go?" he joked.

Kate got up and brushed the sand off her knees. "André," she asked, "is there anyway you can check the brake line, stuff like that? You may think I'm paranoid but a lot of weird stuff's gone on, and better safe than sorry."

"But why would someone harm me?" He was puzzled.

"Who knows," she said, "these people haven't needed rational reasons to do anything, that's for sure."

André considered what she'd said. "From what we saw and heard last night, they would have had difficulty finding their own tents, never mind a piece of my car in the dark. But I hear what you're saying and it makes me ask you this: please, come away with me now, just come. You're right, there's danger here."

"I can't, André, I must finish this. I know what you're saying but I'll be fine. Trust me, I'll be careful. Please don't worry and I'll be in touch all the time."

"You'd better," he said and he kissed her. "Well, I must away. See you soon, sunshine, but not soon enough." He smiled at her, and spun down the road in a cloud of dust.

Kate watched him leave and then she went back to pack up her tent and have a shower.

"Happy, are we?" Stepfan's tone was bitter, as he stepped into her path near the breakfast table. "You think it's so easy, find a good-looking man and get him in your grip. You women are all the same, faithless, fickle, no morals."

"Whatever, Stepfan," Kate said and she stepped around him and filled her bowl with cereal and milk.

"A good night was had?" Jono enquired, trying to be casual. Seeing Kate so happy with André had hurt him deeply. He felt betrayed. She had dumped her boyfriend back home without a second thought; of course she had, for a white rugby player in his fancy Porsche, whereas he, Jono, had nothing to offer. He thought that she'd lied to him, lied to herself and a part of him hoped that André would break her heart, just as she had broken Jono's.

"Yes, very nice," Kate replied, "did you stay and dance the Marula?" She was well aware of Jono's thoughts and she felt bad for him but there was nothing she could say.

"I watched for a little bit," he said, "but then I came to bed. We have another long drive today and I wanted to be fresh and alert."

"Fresh and alart are very good characteristics, particularly in a driver," Betty commented, "Are you trying to tell me there are times when you are not so fresh and alert? Franz, dear husband of mine, he has given me a bad scare more than once. He falls fast asleep behind the wheel and I have to hit him hard on the head and shout at him."

"So we're in safe hands, thanks to you," Richard said, taking a plate of fried eggs and bacon from her.

"I am always fresh and alert," protested Jono, "really, I am."

"Which is more than I can say for myself," Helen walked up and groaned. "Oh, my head. I never drink like that. That Mia. I hope she's suffering as much as I am."

"She is," Richard assured her.

"I couldn't even wake Sofie up," Helen said, "I'm sure she's in an alcoholic coma. I shouted at her and she moaned a bit so at least I know she's not dead. I can't eat a thing this morning. I'm just going to have some coffee with a lots of sugar. Kate, where's your gorgeous man, you sly thing? So, it's a quick sayonara to the boyfriend back home, I take it?"

Kate shrugged. "I'm going to hang out with André when we get to Windhoek," she said, "and we'll take it from there. Who knows."

Sofie staggered up at that moment, groaning. "Please somebody, get me a chair."

"Here," Richard helped her sit.

She put her head in her hands and gave a heartfelt groan.

"You're in your pajamas," Helen pointed out to her.

"I don't care," Sofie said. "I might stay in them all day. Jono, if the road's a bad one, I might cry all the way too. Is it very bumpy?"

"The usual," Jono said.

Sofie made a noise of pure agony.

"Everybody, are we ready to hit the road? Where's Rydell?" Jono asked but no one had seen him.

Just then Rydell's tent opened and one of the dancers from the night before clambered out, in none too graceful a fashion.

"Knock me down with a feather," Kate said, the others

equally open-mouthed and all eyes fixed on the tent.

Rydell emerged swathed in his usual copious layers of clothing. His bruises had deepened in colour and his entire face was a mottled patchwork of purple, red and blue.

"I thought I didn't hear him snoring last night," Stepfan said. "How nice. Everyone was making whoopee except for me. This certainly is not how I imagined my holiday would be."

"A consequence of severe mismanagement by your own hand, I'm afraid," Richard told him shortly. "I am going to see what my buttercup is doing. She went to the washroom a while back. I'm afraid she might have drowned in a toilet bowl." He walked off and the rest of the group started packing up.

Half an hour later, they were back on board, ready to bump and jolt their way to the Etosha pan.

Sofie made a bed in the racks, double-mattressing. She curled up and quickly fell fast asleep, still in her pajamas and wrapped in her sleeping bag despite the heat.

"I gave her a couple of strong painkillers," Jasmine said, "I thought she needed to sleep off her hangover. Hola! Kate! I like the look of your new man. You lucky girl, where did you find him?"

"In Swakopmund, in one of the stores," Kate was evasive. She surreptitiously checked her phone and was delighted to find a message from André: *hey sunshine, am back in Swkp, hope ur ok? Last nite was gr8t*

Kate smiled. *It was fantastic! I am fine! Don't worry!*
u be safe now. xoxo
I promise. Will be in touch.

In the front of the bus, Jono was still thinking about Kate and André and he was driving at breakneck speed.

Betty glanced over at him. "What are you thinking?" she asked. "Are you sad because André arrived to court your girl?"

"I am not sad," Jono said through gritted teeth, "And she is not my girl. Whatever gave you that idea?"

"Maybe the fact that you told Franz and me for hours when you came over after the big dinner? After many beers and a half a bottle of brandy you couldn't stop talking. Don't you remember?"

He did, once she reminded him. "Ah," he grimaced. "Well, look at her, she likes a flashy no-good gun dealer, what chance do I have?"

"Oh, Jono," Betty said softly, "I am so sorry your heart is sore."

"My heart will be fine," Jono growled. "Enough of that conversation, if she wants a no-good loser man, then to hell with her."

At the back of the bus, Helen was deep in thought. She bit her lip and stared out the window, her face severe. She was furious with Mia for catching her off guard and getting her drunk like that. She had taken a couple of aspirins and was steadily drinking water to rehydrate her body.

She was thinking about Kate and André and how life was so unfair; she should have been the one to meet him in Swakopmund. She reasoned that Kate would go back to her life in Canada and pick up where she had left off — she was hardly likely to stay in Swakopmund and Helen could not see André living away from Africa. Which meant that once Kate left, there would be a nice juicy romance left for her, ripe for the picking. She decided she would ask Betty and Jono about André and gather as much information about him as she could, and then, once the trip was over, she would go back to Swakopmund and find a way to hook up with him.

She clenched her jaw tight, ignored her queasy stomach and throbbing head and pulled her hair into a tight ponytail. No way was she going back to her family; she would be happy to never see any of them again and all she had waiting for her in Canada were dismal gray days and an endless array of salt-covered winter boots. It was high time life served her up something good. Encouraged by the prospect of a romantic future with André, Helen fell asleep, with dreams of Porsches and flashing smiles playing in her mind while the hot African sun beat down on her head.

Rydell was thinking about his African dancer and he smiled his twisted smile, licked his bruised lips and cocked his head to one side. He massaged the bites he'd had the dancer inflict into the tender soft skin of his inner upper arm. He thought how stupid he had been about Treasure; sure, she was beautiful but last night's woman was much more to his liking — she had done exactly what he had wanted. He rubbed the bite marks even harder and chortled, causing Kate, sitting across from him, to glower at him suspiciously.

She was badly in need of the washroom and the way Jono was flying along, like a bat out of hell, her discomfort was even more pronounced. As if reading her mind, Gisela got up. "I'm going to ask him to stop," she said, as she stumbled toward the cab window. "Jono! We need to stop the bus for a toilet emergency."

Jono grunted and pulled over abruptly. Lena, Gisela, Kate and Helen piled off and squatted in a line behind the bus.

"How far we've come in losing our manners," Lena commented. "When we first started out, we would all disappear behind a bush, very self-conscious. Now we go right next to each other, in the middle of the road."

The others laughed. "Yes, one does adjust," Helen agreed. "When in Namibia…"

"Are we ready to go now?" Jono called out shortly.

"A bear with a sore head today, are we?" Helen asked, climbing back on the bus.

"I want to get us to Etosha, that's all," Jono said brusquely.

"To see giraffes." Gisela shouted.

"Lion kill!" said Lena.

"Elephants for me," Ellie cried out.

"Zebras," Jasmine added.

"What is all this yelling and screaming?" Sofie demanded,

sticking her head out, high above the seats.

"What animal do you want to see the most?" asked Jasmine.

"I just want the blood to stop pounding behind my eyeballs," Sofie said, vanishing back inside her sleeping bag.

"Don't drink if you can't handle the day after," Stepfan called out.

"That's a bit sanctimonious old chap," Richard said. "At the rate you knocked it back yourself."

"Ah yes, but unlike others, I can handle my alcohol," Stepfan was smug. "I'm always in full control of my physical, mental and emotional capacities."

"What emotional capacities?" Lena enquired.

"It is due to my martial arts training," Stepfan ignored Lena. "I'm a black belt in many kinds of martial arts, jiujutsu, wing chun, tai chi, karate, judo."

"You can't be a black belt in tai chi," Jasmine laughed at him. "Because if there's one thing I'm an expert in, apart from yoga, it's tai chi."

"I'm highly trained, that's all I'm saying," Stepfan continued, giving Jasmine a dismissive glance. "My body is a weapon, a finely-tuned machine. That is why I can handle my alcohol. I'm always in full control. Feel this arm," he said to Ellie, offering her his flexed upper arm.

"No thanks," she said.

"I'll show you some moves," Stepfan said. "A young girl like you needs to protect herself...."

"...From men like you," Lena interjected.

"...in today's world," Stepfan continued.

"We should do a yoga class tonight," Helen interrupted him, "It will be good for us, detox."

"Yoga would be wonderful," Jasmine agreed. "Stretch out our aching muscles."

"Jasmine, you could do with some high intensity fat-burning training," Stepfan started. "I could show you..."

"Stepfan, sit down and shut the fuck up," Richard said. "You don't want to get me started on you, so drop it. Sit down and look at the window. Lovely scenery, lots of rocks and sand, go on, admire it."

Stepfan sat down, his face black with anger. "I was only…"

"I told you," Richard said, evenly, "to shut it, and I mean it."

"What's going on down there?" Sofie stuck her head out. "I'm coming down, you are all making too much noise for me to sleep. Are we there yet? Where are we going and why is it taking so long? Oh, my head. Why didn't anybody tell me I was in my pajamas. How embarrassing."

"I wish I'd stayed in my pajamas," Mia said. "My whole body hurts today." She had been silent all morning and was pale with dark shadows under her eyes. Her face was healing slowly but she still looked a mess.

"We are stopping for lunch now," Jono announced loudly and flatly through the cab window. "As you can see, we are at the gates of the Etosha National Park. Betty has gone to pay, then we will pull over and have lunch and go to our camp from there. Etosha is known as 'the great white place of dry water,' and it offers a large variety of wildlife. The waMbo name, eTosha, means 'white place of mirages'."

He leaned closer to the cab window. "We will be staying at Okaukuejo which means 'place of the fertile women.' Okaukuejo started as a veterinary post in 1897, then later a small fort was built here as the military stronghold. There is a very high limestone tower which gives you excellent views of the camp and there is also the floodlit watering hole that is very nice at night."

He brought his emotionless recital to an end. "Ah, here is Betty, we are ready to go."

They drove inside the park.

"I'm so excited." Jasmine exclaimed as they got off the bus. "I've always wanted to come to Etosha. This is so cool."

"Actually, it's mind-blowing hot," Richard admitted, red-faced from the heat. "I don't want to be naff or anything, but I've got to dunk my head under a tap and sit down in the shade. I don't even know if I can eat anything."

"Come on, you naff old geezer, you," Mia pulled out a chair for him. "I'll pour some water on you if you like. You poor sod."

"Cheers, love," he said as she emptied a bucket of tap water on him.

The others doused themselves with water and crawled to their camping chairs in similar fashion.

"Lunch is ready, everybody," Betty said.

"Richard," Mia said, "would you mind getting my burger for me? I feel a bit pale."

"Of course, my love," Richard stood up.

Lena went over to Mia while the others formed a line for their burgers. "Are you okay?" Lena asked, "you don't seem well."

"I lost the baby this morning," Mia said in an undertone. "It probably didn't like doing the Marula last night, poor bugger. Oh, well. It's not like it was planned or anyfing, so it's probably for the best. I do feel pooped though and I've got a headache the size of a brick shithouse but that could just be a hangover. This bleedin' road doesn't help much. Don't worry, I'll be right as rain soon, ta for asking though."

Lena was about to say something but Richard returned and Mia shut her down with a look and Lena went to get her burger, piling it high with every relish and condiment on the table.

"And how do you plan to eat your leaning Tower of Burger?" Gisela asked her affectionately.

"With a lot of mess." Lena laughed, balancing her plate carefully on her knees.

"After lunch," Jono announced abruptly, apparently still in a bad mood, "we will go on a game drive, which will take us right to Okaukuejo where we will arrive this afternoon. We might get a lot of rain tonight and if not tonight, then tomorrow night for sure."

"Are our tents waterproof?" Kate looked up the sky which

was amassing heavy dark purple clouds that made the colours of the day seem even more intense.

"For the most part, yes," Jono frowned at the question.

"For the most part!" Ellie and Jasmine cried out. "That's not very reassuring."

"Come on girls, don't be afraid of a little African rain." Stepfan puffed out his chest, "we're tough here."

"I am reminded of short poem," Jono said, leaning against the tree. "It is called *The Big-Game Hunter* and it goes like this:
*A big-game hunter opens fire once more,
Raconteur, roué, sportsman, millionaire and bore—
But he only shoots his mouth off, knowing how
He's safer on a sofa than on far safari now.*
Everyone found this hilarious.

"What are you trying to say?" Stepfan demanded and he looked accusingly around.

"I've got no idea," Lena was doubled over in laughter, "since you're certainly no millionaire."

Stepfan scowled and marched off to put his plate in the bucket.

"You are very poetic, Jono," Helen said, "If you don't mind my asking, how come?"

"Before I studied International Politics and Philosophy, I wanted to write poems that would change the world and free the black man from apartheid and slavery." Jono said. "But my kind benefactor, a farmer in Zimbabwe, persuaded me to get a degree first. 'Study first,' he said, 'you can write poems later,' but then I got caught up fighting in the wars and poetry did not seem so important and my own poetic voice died. I still read a lot of poetry. But enough of that," he said, washing his hands. "I'm sure you are eager to see the animals."

"Yes, yes, yes," they chorused, each shouting out the name of the animal they wished to see: "zebra, lion, kudu, giraffe, elephant, hyena, meerkat, baboon, oryx, springbok, warthog, wildebeest, rhino, hippo, cheetah, leopard!"

"They may be a little disappointed by the animals," Jono said to Betty in the front cab.

"They always are." Betty told him, "you know that. No matter what they see, they want more, or different. You can't win here, Jono. Don't even try. You're not responsible for their expectations."

"I always feel bad if they do not see some good things, even now when I am so cross with them."

Kate got her camera ready for the game to come and she thought about Jono's poetic leanings and felt guilty for having fallen for André instead.

But André was a doer, and independent by nature, and that attracted her. Jono, she felt, would wait for her to guide the relationship, hoping that her enthusiasm for life would enter his heart and soul by osmosis and that he would suddenly wake up a happier man. Jono was simply not for her. She tried not to think about it, craning her neck, and wanting to be the first to see wild game.

"Giraffe!" Gisela screamed at the top of her lungs. "Stop the bus! Jono, giraffe!"

Jono dragged the bus to a halt.

"Here we go," he said to Betty, "they will be yelling at me to stop for every springbok, dassie and tortoise from now until Windhoek."

They admired the giraffe for a while and then drove on, pulling up next to a watering hole.

"Over there," Jono shouted, pointing, "elephants, zebra, giraffe, springbok, warthog and wildebeest. That should keep them happy for a while," he said aside to Betty.

"Where are the lions?" Lena asked.

"Hey, I have found a new function on my camera," Sofie marvelled.

"Can't we get any closer?" Jasmine asked.

"None of this is what I expected," Ellie commented, "I thought it would be much more jungle-like."

"Oh, cute," Mia sprawled back in her seat and flicked something off her thigh.

"The elephants don't seem all that big," Richard craned to get a better look.

"No rhino, no leopard?" Rydell asked nasally. "I'm disappointed."

"Disappointed?" Kate said, "I'm in heaven! Never mind the animals, they're fantastic, but the whole scene: the colouring's like nothing I've ever seen before. Black and white with shades of tan, gray and caramel. It's spectacular and so different to what we've seen so far. Even the sky seems a deeper blue and those purple clouds are incredibly majestic."

"It's very beautiful," Gisela agreed, "you're right."

They stayed at the water hole for half an hour and then the group began to get restless. Jono moved forward slowly, hoping to find a fresh lion kill in the middle of the road but nature did not oblige. He turned into Okaukuejo Etosha National Park and waved at familiar faces at the gate.

Jono swung the bus into the camp site, climbed down and stretched his back. He felt as if he was covered in a dozen layers of sweat and caked in dust. All he wanted was a cool shower and a nice cold beer under the shade of a tree.

The group fell into their usual routine of setting up for the night and Kate asked Jono to help her with her tent. "I'm getting better at this," she said, "but it definitely takes two to put up these tents."

Jono nodded. He paused, then helped Kate with her tent in silence. He felt guilty about his earlier hateful thoughts but did not know how to make amends. "I better go now and help Mr. Tough Guy over there," he said instead, gesturing at Stepfan who was standing waiting, not making any effort on his own.

Kate thanked him and looked around; it was as if they were camping in the middle of an open sandy road. The bush was off in the distance, not like the Fish River Canyon where they had been in the thick of it. It also seemed liked they were the only people there and it seemed eerie, she thought, how deserted it all was.

She turned around and noticed that her tent was lifting off the ground in the gusty wind and she ran to the bus to get her big water bottle to weigh it down. Strong surface winds whipped back and forth, and the dust swirled wildly, blowing the contents of the overturned trash cans across the ground. Kate darted to pick up the debris, her hair catching in her eyes and mouth and she felt stung by the sun, wind and heat.

She decided to head toward the tourist shop and bumped into Sofie and the girls near the swimming pool.

"We're going to check out the top of the tower," Helen said, "and we're thinking of doing yoga up there at sunset, it's too hot now. Do you want to join our reconnaissance?"

"Love to, thanks," Kate said.

They walked slowly in the thick afternoon heat to the tower. The stairs were narrow inside the dark passage and Kate went first, climbing quickly.

"Wow," she called out, "the view's incredible." Tiny insect-sized giraffes grazed at trees while the various colours of the desert earth and the tight acacia trees formed a patchwork blanket that spread out for miles.

"You can see our camp," Sofie leaned over. "There is our bus! It's a tiny, dinky thing, and there's the swimming pool, it looks really small too; this tower is very high."

"What a perfect place to do yoga," Jasmine said. "We'll fit fine."

"There might be some overlapping," Helen said, and she frowned. "How many of us will there be?"

Jasmine did a count. "Six, without Mia or Kate. Kate, are you sure you don't want to do it?"

"Absolutely sure," Kate said vigorously. "We've been eating up the miles like nothing else, and I'd love to do a bit of nothing."

She did not want to admit that she had never done yoga. She realized then that her entire life had been about pleasing Cam, keeping her dead-end job, making her parents happy, and phoning Rachel. Without knowing what her future held, she knew for one thing for certain: that meagre existence was over.

She waved goodbye to the yoga girls and headed back to the camp which was still eerily quiet. She could see Betty's form moving in the kitchen area, a shadow behind the fly screens.

Kate did some laundry, and lay down for a nap. It was stiflingly hot, and the scorching dry wind was still gusting hard. Jackals lurked everywhere and Kate could hear them nosing through the garbage cans. She found it hard to believe that she had initially thought they were cute; they were like horrible big rodent scavengers, dog-sized rats.

Kate thought that her attempt at a nap might be futile when the next thing she knew it was 6:00 p.m and her alarm was beeping. She got up, groggy and disorientated and stepped outside. The sky was crayon slashes of orange and red, vivid, nearly violent. The hot wind continued to blow forcefully and the jackals were still searching through the garbage cans.

Betty came out of the kitchen. "Dinner will be ready in two hours, everybody," she called.

"We'll be here," the yoga girls yelled back. They were on their way to the tower and Kate noticed an ignored Stepfan tagging along behing them.

Kate walked down to the waterhole and was dismayed to find hordes of chattering tourists.

"This camp is such a dive," one woman proclaimed loudly. "I'm very happy we are not staying *here* overnight."

Kate felt suddenly restless and she decided to phone André. She dialled his number, her heart fluttering in her throat.

"Sunshine," he said, picking up on the first ring, "are you in one unbruised piece? How goes life on the bus of travelling horrors?"

Kate laughed. "It's all very zen as we speak," she said, describing the yoga girls' plan. "But why do people come to water holes and talk at the tops of their voices?" she asked, straining to hear him and André chuckled.

"That's because you are with the flotsam and jetsam of the game-viewing world. Now, if you were with me, I'd have you at an exclusive lodge, with only you and me in a lookout with a nice cold gin and tonic keeping us company. We'd watch the wonders of nature far from the madding crowd."

"What do you know about the madding crowd?" Kate was surprised.

André gave a theatrical sigh. "Ah. She thinks I'm all brawn, no brain. I can think every now and then and you know, I can even read. Yes, not only can I, but I love to. Some days I lie on the couch and do nothing but read."

They continued to chat, and Kate was soon laughing and making as much noise as the others around her.

Up in the tower, the girls had spread out their mats and had started with warm up stretches.

"Let's each do our own routine for a bit," Helen suggested, "and after that, we'll each take turns to lead. Even if we end up doing a position twice or more, that's okay. Let's take this slowly. We've been sitting for days, our muscles are tight and sore."

The others followed her advice; bending and stretching slowly, absorbed in the quiet, high above the camp. The wild crimson and orange sky turned gold and purple and diamond rays of white light fanned out from behind the thick, dark clouds. Deep in concentration, none of them took notice when Stepfan started vying for attention.

He started to make small noises: grunts and moans. Then he lay down on Ellie's mat.

"Stepfan," she asked, "what are you doing? Get your own mat. Get off mine."

"With the mats all together, there's room," Stepfan protested. "I hardly take up any space."

Ellie was not happy but she moved over.

Lena threw a glance in Stepfan's direction but he ignored her. Some minutes later, he broke the peaceful silence. "Try this," he said to Sofie. He was on his side, doing a pushup on one arm.

"No thanks," Sofie replied, refusing to even look at him.

"You're angling your body wrongly," he told Gisela.

"She knows much more about this than you do!" Lena spoke up, despite her best intentions to not be baited by him. "Why do you always have to ruin everything? You're such a know-it-all. And to think that for years, I really thought you did know it all. I listened to you, I believed you, I trusted you, your lies, your promises, your empty charm. Why are you here now, ruining our lovely time? You're not welcome here! Why don't you leave?"

"This is my holiday too," Stepfan retorted. "I'll do as I please. Where I please and with whom I please."

"You already proved that." Lena got up and went to him, her hand on her hip, one leg jutting forward. "How dare you behave like you did with Charisse? Who do you think you are to do that to me? How dare you?"

Jasmine got up and joined Lena. The light was liquid gold in the sky, the clouds burst of violet, but no one noticed the beauty.

"And," Jasmine said quietly, "what gives you the right to judge me? You hateful, arrogant man, how dare you? You've judged me for my weight this entire trip, and you've said the most disgustingly, unforgivable things that no one in their right mind would think, never mind say." She glared at him.

"I have something to say too," Ellie unfolded her bony limbs. "How dare you try to take me to that gross hotel to have sex when I was drunk? What kind of disgusting man are you? You sat at dinner across from your wife and hit on me." Ellie, in a yellow tank top and purple shorts, looked like a tall, thin angry bumblebee.

"You were asking for it," Stepfan retorted. "If it wasn't me you were going to have sex with that night, it would have been somebody else. You seem to have forgotten that you hit on Jono first, but he ran off like you had burnt him with a hot poker, and next thing you were on my lap. I just thought you would be more comfortable lying down on a nice hotel bed."

"You see!" Lena cried out, "even now you lie. Even now, the thoughts you have are beyond me. What kind of man even thinks the things you do?"

"A sick, arrogant, deluded man," Gisela came up closer, her eyes wide with anger and her nostrils flaring. "A man who needs to be taught a lesson."

"Here comes your butch lover to rescue you, Lena," Stepfan sneered. "Poor little Lena, always needing to be rescued by a man of some kind. You're welcome to her," he said to Gisela. "She's an old burden to me, of no use any more. Besides she has no respect."

"What did you say?" Helen joined the circle around Stepfan. He did not seem to realize he was alone, surrounded by a band of hostile and angry women.

Stepfan turned his back to them and placed his hands on the top of the tower ledge. "While all of you whine and complain," he said, "I'm going to prove my prowess to you. Not that it needs proving. And I invite you to join me, if any of you have the courage." He hoisted himself up onto the top of the tower's ledge and straightened up slowly, a tightrope walker finding his balance.

"Don't be stupid," Lena said. "Get down, now. Only an idiot would do that. But do you think I care what you do? I don't."

"Come down, Stepfan," Sofie was insistent. "It is much too dangerous up there. And the rest of you," she turned to the women, shaking her head in disapproval, "leave him alone. Yes, he says unspeakable tings, yes, and he treats vomen very badly, there is no doubt about dat, but this is crazy. Come on," she pleaded, "get down, Stepfan. It is beginning to get dark, this is madness, please."

Stepfan ignored her and worked on steadying himself.

Lena stared up at him. "As far as I'm concerned, do whatever you like, we're going back to doing our yoga," she said.

The women returned to their mats and sat down, watching Stepfan wordlessly.

"I have had enough of this," Sofie said, and she gathered her mat. "You are all playing with fire. I am leaving." And with that, she scurried away, her head down, the thumping of her mat sounding upwards as it bounced on each step on the way down.

Stepfan stretched out his arms and began to walk along the top of the turret. The evening light deepened to darkness, the kodachrome sunset gone, replaced by a bruised sky that would soon turn to black.

"Look at him," Lena said quietly. "He always does what he wants to, regardless of what I say, or what anyone else says."

Stepfan walked across three blocks with his arms stretched out wide and his concentration fierce. "You see," he called out, "once again I can do whatever I say. I am at one with my body, I am the master. Watch and learn."

"You are nothing," Lena called out and she stood up. "You are nothing!" Then shouting, she added. "Do you think I don't know about all your affairs? I do. Every last one of them." She had her hands on her hips, her face red with fury.

"You have no idea," Stepfan retorted. "You think you know, but you don't."

"What? What now? Tell me, since we are finally having a real conversation."

But Stepfan did not reply, focusing instead on crossing another three blocks. He frowned, his jaw set, his arms outstretched, the muscles in his body tensed and his abs showing clearly through his black mesh T-shirt. He crossed another two blocks.

"Tell me," Lena screamed. "Tell me what it is you think I don't know."

She advanced on Stepfan who was studying his next step. He sensed her approach and he looked up, startled. He seemed surprised at how dark it had become and he glanced to the west in alarm.

"What are you doing?" he shouted, "I'm trying to concentrate here. You stupid bitch…"

"Tell me!"

"Your sister," he yelled back. "Yes, even your sister! You didn't know that, did you? Did you?"

Lena gave a savage growl and she lunged at him in fury. Instinctively, he backed away from her but he had nowhere to go. He windmilled his arms desperately, but his body weight was leaning out too far and he fell backward from the tower ledge, screaming wildly.

Lena gave a high-pitched cry and grabbed the edge of the tower wall, as if hoping she could pull him back up.

The women turned to look at one another in horror. Lena let go of the wall and sank to her knees and buried her face in her hands. Gisela rushed over to her, her face white with shock.

"Do you think he's dead?" Jasmine asked. "Did he die?" She peered over the wall ledge. "I can't see anything," she said, and turned back to the others, pressing her hand against her mouth, her strange green eyes enormous and threatening tears. She started running towards the stairs, with Ellie close behind her when Helen blocked the doorway to the stairwell.

"We need to think for a moment," Helen said. "Maybe he just broke a few bones, but what if he *is* dead?"

"It wasn't Lena's fault," Gisela said, her voice shaking. She knelt down next to Lena and put her arms around her. "You all heard her. She told him not to go up there."

Lena looked up, obviously terrified and shaking uncontrollably.

"Listen to me, all of you," Helen said brusquely, "listen to me carefully." And such was the force of her tone that they all turned to her, numb and silent.

"He went up there all by himself," Helen said. "Lena told him not to and we all heard her. Nod if you are keeping up with me," she barked at them and the women nodded.

"And then she got up to try to talk him down but he lost his balance and fell. It wasn't anybody's fault, least of all Lena's. Are we all together on this?"

Gisela had her arm around Lena who stood up unsteadily. Gisela nodded. "Of course we're together," she said.

"Who else?" Helen glared around the group.

"Don't worry about us," Jasmine reassured her, "Ellie and I are together with you."

Helen looked at Ellie. "Are you?" she asked. "Can you be relied on?"

Ellie nodded. "I don't really care," she said, "whatever."

Helen slapped her face, hard. "You have to care. That's exactly what I'm trying to tell you. You need to care because if we don't care, if we don't pay attention, then Lena will end up in big trouble and she doesn't deserve that. He went up there alone while she told him not to. Ellie, you start caring now, do you hear me?"

Ellie nodded, rubbing her cheek that had turned a bright red. "You didn't have to hit me," she complained.

"Wrong," Helen said, "I did. Time to go downstairs." Her voice softened. "You all good, ladies?" she asked.

"All good," they chorused quietly.

Jasmine swallowed hard. "I admit it. I'm afraid of what we'll see. Don't worry, Lena, you really didn't do anything wrong."

They all nodded in agreement and then, as one, they turned and filed down the stairs in silence.

By the time they reached the bottom of the tower, the women were sobbing and the security guards from the gate had gathered around Stepfan's body.

"*Haw!* But are you ladies okay?" a shocked security guard asked them. "We watched this crazy man, what was he thinking, *eish*? Stupid tourists, they come here and think they are Bushmen or Rambo and they do such stupid things."

"We told him not to do it," Helen cried, "but he wouldn't listen."

"He would not be stopped," Gisela said, gulping. "We tried."

"Come now ladies, let us take you away from this terrible thing. Who is travelling with this man? Any of you? All of you?"

"We are all traveling together," Jasmine said.

"I am his wife," Lena managed to say, and Gisela held her tight.

"Come this way," one of the guards said. "Let us go into the main lodge while the other guards will take care of the body. Who is your tour guide?"

"Jono Odili," Helen said, wiping tears from her face.

"Not that it matters," Jasmine's voice shook, "but our mats are up there. We were doing yoga in the sunset and our mats are there and it's dark now."

"I will send somebody up to get them and I will get them delivered to your campsite," the guard said, leading them through the lodge lounge and into a conference room of some kind. He closed the blinds. "I will have the cook make you some tea, you need a hot drink with sugar, wait here. I will go and find Jono."

He disappeared. Helen shot the others a warning look, no talking. The tea arrived but the women ignored it. After what seemed like an eternity, the guard returned with Jono.

"I hear we have had an accident," Jono said, dryly. "So let us hear how this one happened. Who wants to tell me?"

"I will," Helen said firmly, "It was Stepfan's idea, to walk on the top of the wall, you know what he is like, he wouldn't listen to us…"

Jono nodded. He poured himself a cup of tea, added three sugars and stirred, listening to Helen without saying a word.

The security guards had radioed the police and they had logged in the incident. The security guards who had witnessed Stepfan walking around the top of the tower confirmed that he lost his balance and fell; there was no suspicion of foul play.

The security guards had taken Jono to Stepfan's body and Jono stood looking down at the broken wreck of the man before covering him with a sheet.

"He will have to wait here until the hearse arrives," the security guard had said to Jono. "Don't worry, we have already phoned for the undertaker to come, and he will drive him to Windhoek."

Jono nodded and then he went to meet the women in the lodge and he wondered how much of what Helen was saying was true. He felt numb with exhaustion, thinking that he was beyond caring about any of them, except for Kate and Betty.

"It must have been very upsetting for you," he said wearily, when Helen finally finished her tale.

The Tenth Night

BACK AT THE CAMP, Kate was looking for Betty, to see if she could help out with dinner. She found her in the kitchen, washing dishes.

"It was wonderful down at the waterhole," Kate said. "There were lots of noisy tourists but then they left and the sunset was just incredible. And elephants, giraffes and even a rhino showed up to drink. Now, can I help you with anything?"

"Yes, I want to make a kind of Tiramisu for dessert, with finger biscuits and Kahlua. You can help me layer the ingredients. It's good if the biscuits can soak for a bit and I even have ice cream for the top which we will put on later."

Rydell walked in. "Is it time for supper?" he said nasally, through his gruesome face. "I'm very hungry."

"Yes," Betty said. "Yes, everything is nearly ready. I wonder when the others will get back from their yoga. It was a very nice sunset for it."

Mia and Richard wandered up. "Not to rush you but is supper ready yet?" Richard asked. "I'm starving."

"Me too," Mia was less pale than she had been earlier. "We had a good old sleep this afternoon. I was feeling like death warmed up but I'm all nice and refreshed, tada!" She leapt into a wobbly pirouette of sorts and staggered slightly. "We're going to head off to the waterhole after supper, if anyone wants to join us."

"I came from there and I already planned to go again," Rydell gave his lopsided, wet smile "You never know, a leopard might come out of the bush and sink his claws into a huge elephant and the lions might attack a rhino."

"And the moon will turn to green cheese," Betty commented. "Speaking of cheese, Kate, would you grate some for me please? To go on the top of our vegetable lasagna."

The others gave groans of delight. "You're spoiling us rotten, dear Betty and I love it," Richard said. "I'll carry things outside."

They found Sofie sitting outside on one of the camping chairs. Her face was pale and she looked miserable and lost. Bits of her braided hair had come undone and she had dark shadows under her eyes.

"Oy, you okey-dokey, luv?" Mia went over to her. "You look like you've seen a bleedin' ghost or something. Spot any witches did you, riding their hyenas with fire coming out their bums?" She snickered.

"No, I just don't feel too good," Sofie said quietly. "I didn't even stay for yoga. Are the others back yet?"

"No, and we'll start without them," Betty said. "I wonder where Jono is though. He wouldn't want to miss my famous lasagna!"

They heaped the lasagna onto their plates, and sat down their camping chairs that they had arranged in a circle on the dusty ground, next to the bus. They had nearly finished eating when the others began to arrive: first Jasmine and Ellie, then Helen, then Gisela, and Lena and Jono.

Betty took one look at them. "What happened?" she demanded. "Are you alright? What happened?"

Helen sat down heavily on a campstool. Her eyes were red and swollen and her face was blotchy.

Kate paused, her fork halfway to her mouth. The women looked as if they had been crying for hours. "What happened?" she echoed Betty.

"We were up in the tower," Helen said, crying quietly, "doing our yoga and Stepfan was there too and he started to get really irritating as you know he can. Could. Anyway, he kept telling us what to do and how to do it, but we weren't paying him any attention so he told us he could walk around the top of the tower, the whole way around. We didn't take him seriously, or think for a moment he would do it, so we ignored him and next thing, there he was, walking around the top. We carried on with our yoga thinking he'd lose interest and come down but he didn't. The light was fading and we got worried and Lena tried to persuade him to come down and I don't think he realized how dark it was getting and next thing he lost his balance and fell."

"He's dead?" Kate gasped and lowered her plate to the ground, feeling instantly sick. "What do you mean? What happened?" She was horrified. A thousand thoughts crowded into her mind and she fought to sort them all out.

"Of course he is dead," Jono said, bluntly. "You cannot fall from that tower and live."

"Good God," Richard exclaimed, "that's ... well, that's just..." He seemed at a loss for words.

"Incredible?" Jono said. "*Yebo*, I would have to agree. I have never heard of anybody, in all my years of coming here, who wanted to walk the perimeter of the top of the tower. But I suppose you could say that is the joy of my job, never knowing what to expect next. I tell you though, you lot certainly have taught me a few things."

Jasmine looked at Jono. Her face was so swollen her eyes had all but disappeared. "What exactly do you mean by that?" she asked.

"Do not pretend you do not know," Jono stated, his arms folded. The hot wind lashed dust across the darkness of the campsite. "But I am not going to discuss any of it with you, *eish*. Let us try to get through the rest of the trip without anybody else dying, okay? Betty, I am sorry, I cannot eat anything right now, I have no appetite."

"What are you going to do now?" Betty asked Lena who blew her nose loudly.

Gisela answered for her. "The security guards helped us and let us use the lodge phone. Lena's already contacted Stepfan's brother and told him the bad news He is going to make arrangements for Stepfan to be flown back home and he will meet the body. Lena has decided to stay on though. She still wants to go to Nairobi and I've decided to take Stepfan's place; I was only booked up to Livingstone."

"All neat and tidy," Richard commented dryly.

"How dare you?" Lena turned on him, startling them with venom of her anger. "What do you think? That I'm happy he's dead? Of course, I'm not happy he's dead, but I've lived under his thumb all my life and this is *my* holiday and I'm not going to lose it just like I lost everything else to him. Do you *mind*? Is that all right with you? Do I have your *permission*?" She began to choke with sobs and Gisela grabbed her and hugged her and glared at Richard.

"Sorry, sorry," Richard leaned back on his campstool, raised one hand in the air and picked at his teeth with the other. "Peace out, it's none of my business anyway."

"Stepfan deserved to die," Rydell announced. "And the way he died says it all. Macho showoff. He hurt me and now he's dead, so I'm not sorry." His shoulders shook with contained laughter.

Jono rounded on him. "*Eish!* You people are crazy. No one deserves to die! I am going to my tent. I do not want to be around any of you. I cannot wait to drop you off at Windhoek! I wish I could leave you all here, right now."

He turned swiftly and marched off.

"I thought you were taking some of us to Livingstone?" Ellie called after him.

"Not any more," he shouted over his shoulder. "I get off the bus at Windhoek. Those of you continuing will get a new driver."

"What's his problem?" Rydell was genuinely bewildered. "I am going to the waterhole. I want to be there a nice long time in case there is a kill."

Later, Jono was inside his tent, his head in his hands, crying. He looked up at Betty as she climbed in. "Betty, did I do something wrong? Did I let it get out of control? Is this my fault? What happened?"

"*Aikona*, Jono, of course it wasn't your fault." Despite his protestations that he could not eat, she had brought him his dinner, and laid the plate carefully down, then wrapped her arms around him. "It's simple. Too many bad apples in one place. One bad apple goes unnoticed; it has no allies, but if they are all rotten, there is no hope, they all go bad."

"Kate is not like them," Jono blew his nose. "But the others … well maybe Sofie is not so terrible either."

"You see," Betty said, "that's not so bad then."

"Betty," he exclaimed, "we started off with twenty of us, now we are are eleven. And three of the ones left look like they have been in the ring with Muhammad Ali: broken noses, stitches, black eyes. I mean think about it, nearly half the people on this trip have left, by choice or death or misadventure."

"Don't you think this was an accident?" Betty asked. "Stepfan dying?"

Jono considered the question before he answered. "No," he said shortly. "I do not. If he had been the only one to have come in harm's way, or if he was a stupid, drunk youngster acting out a dare, then perhaps. But *aikona*, Betty, not even a stupid, drunk youngster would do that unless he was trying to kill himself. Stepfan said a lot of ignorant things to try to impress women and he was very proud of his body and his martial arts and things, but no, I do not think he would have done this stupid thing."

"But he did," Betty said, "you heard Helen, they tried to stop him…"

"They LIE!" Jono shouted, frightening Betty with his vehemence. "They hated him, they wanted him dead, I know they did. Who is next? Rydell, because they do not like him either? Or me, because I suspect them?"

"Jono, you need to calm down," Betty got up. "I am going to get you some brandy from my tent. A little bit at bedtime always helps me sleep. You need something." She slipped out.

"I just need this terrible nightmare to end," Jono muttered to himself as he lay back on his sleeping bag, exhausted.

By the time Betty got back, Jono was fast asleep, snoring lightly, his hand over his face. She picked up his untouched plate, zipped his tent closed, and walked back to camp.

Jasmine and Ellie were finishing their supper. They were the only two in a ring of empty camp chairs.

"Where's everybody?" Betty asked.

"Most of them went to shower," they replied with their mouths full. "Rydell's at the waterhole with Mia and Richard. This was excellent lasagna, Betty."

"Good," Betty muttered. She was disgusted by them and by the night's events. She hurried by them and went to clean up the kitchen area.

She could not wait to be back home in Swakopmund again. Only one night left to go, in Fort Namutoni, then on to Windhoek and straight back home. She hastily washed the dishes and packed them away into their plastic buckets. Then, she crossed the campsite and spotted Kate climbing out of her tent. Kate looked ill at ease. She quickly zipped up the tent flap and shoved something into the pocket of her baggy camouflage pants. "How's Jono?"

"Not good," Betty sighed.

"I'm sure he isn't," Kate said. "Does he think Stepfan was responsible for what happened?"

"He doesn't know what to think," Betty answered carefully.

"Neither to do I," Kate said. "Good night, Betty, I'm going to my tent now, I don't want to bump into any of the others, I don't want to talk to them right now." Kate smiled and walked over to a different tent.

Was that her tent? Betty was flummoxed. *So, whose tent did she climb out of?*

She was determined to find out and made her way over to the tent she had seen Kate emerge from. She unzipped a tiny part of the tent door and shone her torch inside, immediately perplexed as to what Kate would want in Rydell's tent. She closed the tent and stood for a moment, thinking. Then she walked off to her tent and climbed in, still confused, and a little afraid, too.

Back in her own tent, Kate put her hand into her pocket and withdrew the item she had found in Rydell's sock. It was her underwear. What was Rydell doing with her underwear? She felt nauseous and violated. She looked at her bikini panties with tiny yellow daisies patterned along the waistband. She had thought the design so cheerful and happy, now the flowers seemed abused, sullied. But shocking as it was to find these in Rydell's tent, she came up empty with any evidence linking him to Rosalee's murder.

His tent was not as neat inside as she had expected and it was easier than she had thought it would be to rifle through his belongings and then to put things back exactly where she found them. She stumbled across her underwear in a rolled-up pair of socks near the end of her search; she potted a tiny part of a flower peeking out and she had grabbed the socks, and then pulled out her panties, in disbelief.

"Sick *bastard*." She looked at her watch. She was not ready to go to bed and she decided to go for a walk and phone André. She made her way over to the swimming pool, thinking that it would be deserted but to her surprise she found Richard and Mia reclining on the deck chairs, casually drinking beer, and commenting on the night sky.

"Come and join us," Mia called out.

Kate went over and sat down. "I don't know if you'd want me," she said, "if you knew the sort of mood I'm in." She tried to laugh.

"Understandable. Vile, absolutely vile what happened," Richard said languidly. "We saw Sofie earlier, she was on the phone in the security guards area. We've got no idea who she was calling but she was crying."

"Where's she now?" Kate asked.

"Don't know. We haven't seen her walk by since, and we've been keeping an eye out for her. What do you think really happened?" Richard asked.

"Not a clue," Kate replied, and she shook her head at the beer Mia was waving at her. "No thanks, Mia."

Sofie appeared out of the darkness, a glassy-eyed wraith with a flashlight in her hand. She seemed to be heading back to the camp. "Sofie," they called out to her, "We're here, come over."

She looked over at them, not sure who it was.

"It's Kate, Richard and Mia," Kate told her.

Sofie gave a slight start and wound her way through the deckchairs. "Why is this place so deserted?" she demanded. "Where's everybody? I mean the other tourists? Why are we the only ones here? Where are all the other people?"

She began to cry. Kate leapt up and helped her sit down. Sofie put her head on Kate's shoulder and sobbed. "This is all so sick," she sobbed. "I want to go home. I never want to come to Africa again in my entire life. If I get out alive, that is."

"Ah, it's not Africa's fault," Kate soothed her and stroked her hair, "It's true that things have gone terribly wrong but why do you think anybody would want to hurt you? We all love you, you're probably the safest person on the entire trip."

"Because ... because ... I saw, I heard ... oh nothing, nothing at all. I'm going to bed. But I *really* don't want to share with Helen any more, I don't." She started to cry again.

"Come and stay with me," Kate said firmly. "There's only me in my tent now, what do you say?"

Sofie nodded and wiped her face. "Will you come with me to get my stuff?" she asked.

"Of course I will," Kate said. "Come on, let's do it now. Have you had a shower?"

"No," Sofie was crying again. "Somebody was in there, so I was frightened."

"We'll go and shower together and get you nice and clean, but first we'll get your stuff and set up your bed. Hey, you guys," she said aside, to Richard and Mia, "I thought you were going to the waterhole?"

"Didn't feel like it," Mia said. "We thought we'd have a nice cool swim and go to bed. It doesn't get cold here at night like the other places so a swim would be nice."

"Did Rydell go to the waterhole?" Kate asked.

"I imagine he did," Richard said. "To be honest, I didn't notice."

"Me neither," Mia wriggled her toes. "Barking mad, he is anyway."

"Well, it doesn't matter. Come on, Sofie, let's get you settled."

She helped Sofie to her feet, said goodnight to Mia and Richard and they walked off, Kate's arm protectively around Sofie's shoulders.

Helen was lying on her stomach on her sleeping bag and reading with her camper's light on. She looked up when Sofie stepped through the tent door. Sofie wordlessly gathered her gear and quickly handed her things to Kate who waited for her outside. Helen watched silently, then she rolled over onto her back and carried on reading. Kate found it awkward and uncomfortable. Sofie was even more subdued after seeing Helen and sank into silence.

Kate led Sofie over to her tent and helped her settle in and find her toiletry bag. Then she guided Sofie over to the washroom. "Sofie, let's have a nice, long hot shower," she said. "Don't go back to the tent without me, okay?"

Sofie nodded. Kate propelled her towards a shower cubicle, trying to get her started. Sofie was becoming increasingly withdrawn.

"Sofie," Kate's tone was sharp but kind, trying to jolt Sofie back to reality, "get undressed and shower, dear. Now." Sofie started to undress in slow motion with Kate helping. "I'm not going to wash you in the shower too," she said, "in you go, turn on the water." She finally managed to get Sofie under a steady stream of hot water with a bar of soap in her hand.

Kate had a quick shower and washed her hair. She got out and dried herself quickly. She peered into see how Sofie was doing and saw her in the same spot, the soap unused, the water running cold.

"Oh, Sofie, I'm so sorry," Kate said and she led Sofie out of the shower and gently dried her off.

Betty came in. "Hello ladies." She did not seem to notice anything unusual in a blank-eyed Sofie being dried off by a naked Kate.

"I'm so glad to see you, Betty," Kate exclaimed with relief. "I think Sofie's gone into shock." She quickly explained about meeting Sofie at the pool, getting her things from Helen's tent, and how she had stood in the shower, not moving.

"*Eish*, poor girl," Betty said, "here, let me help you."

Sofie was docile and unresisting as they dressed her.

Kate quickly got dressed and brushed her teeth. "Betty, is there a doctor here? I think Sofie needs one."

"I agree, she's in a bad way. I don't think there is a doctor here but we can ask Jono to radio ahead to Fort Namutoni."

"I guess I could ask Mia for advice..." Kate took a quick look around and spoke in an undertone, "she's a psychiatric nurse, but don't tell her I told you, she asked me not to say anything to anyone. Besides from what I've seen, I wouldn't have much faith in her nursing abilities and by this time of night, she's most likely drunk."

"Let's not even ask her. Did you know," Betty whispered,

her mouth close to Kate's ear, "that Richard is a surgeon? It said so on the forms he filled out to come on the tour, Jono told me. But he told me that Richard has told everybody he does life insurance or something, so I don't think he would help either — for some reason he wants to hide the fact that he is a doctor."

"A doctor? A surgeon? Knock me down with a feather." Kate was shocked into immobility. "And yet he did nothing to help Charisse. Not too big on the old Hippocratic oath is he?"

"*Eish*, I shouldn't have said anything, please never tell anyone I told you," Betty looked anxious. "I wasn't supposed to know except that Jono told me that night in Swakopmund, the night you all had the big dinner together, and he came to see us afterwards and he was really quite drunk. I'm sure he doesn't even remember that he told me, and he also said, like you, that he couldn't understand why Richard hadn't tried to help Charisse when she was so sick." She spoke in an anxious rush.

"Don't worry, Betty," Kate reassured her, "I won't breathe a word of it, we'll keep each other's secrets. Let's have a doctor at the ready at Fort Namutoni and we'll try to get Sofie there as soon as we can. Will you let Jono know?"

"Yes, I will let him know. Let me help you get her to bed."

"That's okay," Kate said, "I can manage. It's late. You have your shower, you must be exhausted. By the way, I'm doing all the dishes from now, I see that we've lost our roster, so count on me for that."

"*Yebo*, thank you, Kate. I'm very tired."

Kate gathered her and Sofie's things and led Sofie to their tent. On the way, she saw Rydell on his way back from the waterhole and she was relieved that he must have been there the entire time. She had been worried he might have seen her go inside his tent.

She helped Sofie climb into her sleeping bag and then she checked her phone.

Sunshine, so quiet, no goodnite? U ok? Miss you. Luv talkng 2u

Kate sighed with relief and punched in her reply.

miss u2. BAD nite, Stepfan 'fell' off twr. Cldnt call cos Sofie in shock. Will fone 1st thing

She lay back in bed and switched off her flashlight. She was certain she would lie awake all night but before she knew it, she was fast asleep.

Two tents away, Rydell was on his hands and knees inside his tent, sniffing his bedding. "Someone's been snooping around *my* tent," he chanted quietly, again and again. "Someone's been going through *my* clothes, someone's been eating *my* porridge, someone's going to be *very sorry*."

The Etosha Pan
and on to Fort Namutoni

THE NEXT MORNING KATE WOKE to find Sofie sitting upright, and staring straight ahead. "Sofie?" Kate asked gently, "How are you?"

There was no reply.

"Let's get you dressed, will you help me?" She struggled to get Sofie out of her pajamas and into a pair of shorts and a T-shirt.

"We're going to the washroom, here's your toothbrush."

Kate climbed out backwards, leaned into the tent and held out her hand to Sofie.

Sofie stepped out of the tent and let out a bloodcurdling scream that turned Kate's blood to ice. She swung around to follow Sofie's gaze. Directly in front of the tent was a dead jackal, hanging upside down over a garbage can with its tongue lolling out to one side and its eyes wide open.

Kate was unable to move. She stood stockstill. Sofie carried on screaming and her high-pitched siren call brought the others running towards them in various states of dress.

"What's going on now?" Jono demanded.

Speechless, Kate pointed to the jackal.

Jono put his arm around Sofie and led her away.

"Betty," he yelled, "I need you *now*."

Betty rushed up to him and they conferred while Sofie stopped screaming and stared unblinkingly ahead. Jono took out a phone and began dialing. He talked to someone in Xhosa, his voice agitated, his hands waving. The others milled around, some with toothbrushes in hand and tousled hair.

Rydell looked over at Kate when no one was watching and made the sign of a slit throat and she marched up to him. "Got something to say to me?" she said, her hands on her hips, her eyes boring into his.

He giggled. "Someone's been eating my porridge, someone's been touching my socks, someone is going to be very *sorry*."

"Jono," Kate called out loudly, "I want security to arrest this weirdo, I'm not getting back on the bus with him. He was in my tent, he stole my underwear, it was hidden in his socks. Let me ask you this, who killed the jackal? Huh? It was him. We're leaving him behind, Jono, I'm telling you now. I hope he dies here."

Jono looked uncomfortable. "*Ei*, Kate, we cannot do that. He has committed no crime that we can be sure of, I cannot leave him behind. Maybe your underwear got caught up in his laundry. We have no proof that he killed the jackal, it could have been a local person. Only yesterday security was saying they were having real problems with things such as these."

"Ah. There you go again, Jono. The quintessential man of inaction. Wonderful. I see." She turned back to Rydell, her mind whirling for a solution. "Rydell, you've been a bad, naughty, worthless boy, no wonder your mother hated you and had to punish you like she did. If you don't behave, I'm going to hate you just like your mommy did, do you understand me, because you're such a bad boy."

It was a desperate move on Kate's part but to her surprise, it worked and the scales of love and hate that Rydell felt for Kate tipped and broke. She had reminded him of his mother from the start; the similarity in their appearance, as well as the memories of that erratic maternal affection followed by her inexplicable and bullying cruelty all swirled and mixed in Rydell's psyche and his fragile hold on reality snapped like a twig. He fell to his knees like a child and began to cry, clasping his arms tightly around Kate's legs.

"I'm sorry. Don't hurt me, mommy, love me, don't hurt me. I'll be a good boy, mommy, I promise I'll be a very good boy."

Kate pushed his face back and stared at him. "Go and tidy your tent," she said, sternly. "Then go and sit on the bus and stay there, do you understand?"

"Yes, I do, mommy, I'm sorry," Rydell sniveled, untangling himself, and got up. "I'll be a good boy and you'll love me, I'll be a good boy, you'll see." He walked back to his tent, still crying, his head down; for all the world a dejected, five-year-old boy.

"That's the most disgusting thing I've ever seen," Helen was revolted.

Kate glanced over at her. "I'm sure you've seen and done worse," she said pointedly.

"I didn't mean you," Helen was quick to reply. "I meant his reaction. Do you think he killed the jackal?"

"I have no idea," Kate said, acidly.

"We're going to wait for a helicopter," Jono announced. "They're sending one from Windhoek and they'll take Sofie to a hospital. It should be here within the hour and we'll leave directly after that. Kate, please let me talk to you," he called after her, but she marched off and he watched her go. "*Ei*, I do not blame her," he said to Betty, "but honestly, what else could I do?" He and Betty looked helplessly at one another.

At that moment the security guards arrived to investigate the dead jackal.

"Excuse me, don't touch that," Kate reappeared with her camera. Anger radiated off her. "Step back for a moment, please."

"What are you doing?" Jono asked.

"Collecting evidence." Kate photographed the animal's corpse from every angle: close up, footprints in the sand, pieces of garbage. When she got closer she saw that a piece of twine had been used to strangle the jackal and she peered at it more closely, thinking that it looked familiar.

"Jasmine," she called. "Get me a pair of tweezers."

"I don't use tweezers," Jasmine objected.

"Well, go and get some from somebody else then," Kate shouted.

Ellie rushed off and returned with tweezers.

Kate dug inside the jackal's torn neck and pulled out the piece of rope. She knelt down and fished a ziploc bag from her camera bag, emptied it of flash cards, and put the rope inside. She closed her camera bag, swung it over her shoulder and walked off.

"*Wag 'n bietjie,*" one of the security guards called out. "Wait a moment, that rope belongs to us, it's evidence."

"And I'm simply making sure it doesn't disappear, do you have any problems with that?" Kate swung around and confronted the guard angrily.

"Uh no, *mevrou*," he stammered. "That's fine, but don't lose it, *asseblief*."

Kate went over to Betty. "Betty, we need to make sure Sofie's papers are in order so they know who she is, who to contact, who her embassy is, that kind of thing. I learned this well from Charisse's death, the first death of many shall we say." She tried to be less sarcastic; none of this was Betty's fault. "Can you accompany her?"

"*Ei*, Kate, believe me, I would love nothing more but there's no room on the helicopter, they are very small."

They turned to Sofie who was singing to herself and pulling at strands of her hair.

Betty and Kate both looked over at Richard and Mia who were helping themselves to breakfast, pouring milk onto cereal, unconcerned by the bedlam around them.

Kate and Betty exchanged a look. "You can't explain some people," Betty said, shocked nevertheless.

"Yes," Kate agreed. "A nurse and a doctor too. Well, let's get Sofie's things ready. Jono should try to have someone at the hospital to be with Sofie. She shouldn't be alone like this.

I'm sorry I snapped at you Betty, it was rude of me."

"Don't be silly. Terrible things have happened. I agree, I will tell Jono now. I know he always has a list of emergency contacts and such on these trips." Betty went to talk to Jono while Kate sat with Sofie. She longed to phone André but it would be impossible to talk to him, given the situation. She grabbed her phone; she had not had the chance to look at it since she had texted André about Stepfan's death. There were three messages from him, all saying a different version of the same thing: *That is* BAD NEWS. *I must come+get you? I will. Plse tlk 2me, am v worried*

She thought about it. There was only one more night left and besides she calculated, it would take André too long to get to Fort Namutoni.

Don't worry, but I will need u asap in Wndhk, cant wait 2cu.

He replied almost instantly:

Kate, am NOT *happy bout this. Call me 2day soon as u can I will I prmse, at namutoni, don't worry tho. But is v ugly b safe. Talk soon, be safe xo*

Betty arrived with Jono. "Where are Sofie's bags and documents?" he asked.

"In my tent, I'll show you," Kate said shortly. She had not forgiven him for not standing up for her. She marched off to the tent and placed Sofie's things outside the door. "There you are," she said to Jono.

"Kate ..." he pleaded, but she ignored him and climbed back inside her tent.

Kate packed her things and took down her tent. She carried her bags to the bus but did not go in, wanting to avoid Rydell as much as possible. Then she remembered something, how drugged he had been the day she had rejoined the group in Walvis Bay; how he had drooled and slept and she realized that he must have meds with him. She climbed inside the bus. Rydell was sitting in his usual spot and he looked frightened to see her.

"Rydell," she said sternly, "mommy wants to know where your medicine is? Show mommy your medicine now."

Rydell obediently reached into his bag and brought out a three large amber prescription bottles. Kate read the labels and had no idea what any of them were. *Take as prescribed.*

"Rydell, mommy wants to know, which of these must you take to make you sleepy?"

Rydell pointed to the Alprazolam. "Rydell must take two if he feels bad," he said. "Then he will sleep for a long time and he will feel much better."

Kate shook out two of the pills and pocketed the bottle. "Rydell, mommy wants you to take two, right now."

"But why," he whined, "I don't feel bad mommy, I don't feel bad."

"You've been a very BAD boy," Kate said and he flinched. "Even if you don't feel bad, you must take two, now, while mommy watches. Then you will be a good boy."

"Good boy, good boy," he sighed.

"Here's your juice," she handed him his water.

She watched him carefully and he swallowed the pills.

"Open your mouth so I can see they are gone," she said.

He opened his mouth wide.

"Good boy," she said, "and now, Rydell must sleep."

"Hungry," he said, "very hungry."

"Okay," she said, "you stay here, mommy will bring you breakfast. Be a good boy now, Rydell, and stay here."

She climbed off the bus and went to get him a bowl of cereal. By the time she got back, the drugs had started to work.

"Mommy?" he slurred, and the milk dripped down his chin.

"Yes, Rydell, what is it?"

"I didn't kill the jackal, mommy, I was only trying to make you scared and pretend I did, but I didn't. I'm sorry I made you scared. I'm going to be a good boy now, you'll see and then you won't have to be dead anymore." And with that he fell asleep.

Kate took the bowl from him, puzzled. She wouldn't have to be dead anymore? What was that supposed to mean? That he wouldn't have to kill her anymore? He must mean that. Or was he talking about Rosalee Khumalo? Or his real, dead mother? She resolved to keep him drugged at all times.

Kate took his bowl to the bucket, remembering that she had told Betty that she would the dishes. She stopped in front of Helen. "How about you clean up breakfast, Jasmine and Ellie do lunch, and I'll do supper?"

"Sounds good." Helen leapt to her feet.

A long black hearse pulled up slowly. The driver got out and looked around, at a loss.

Jono waved a greeting and approached him. They spoke and Jono pointed to Lena. They walked over to her; she had been warned by Gisela of their approach.

"We need you to sign a release," Jono said gently.

"Is he in there?" Lena's mouth was pressed tight and she nodded in the direction of the hearse.

"*Yebo*," Jono said. "They are taking him to Windhoek and he will fly home from there and his brother has confirmed that he will meet him."

"He is in a coffin now?" Lena asked.

The driver did not seem surprised by her questions.

"Yes, Madam, he is."

"I want to see him," Lena said.

"That is not advisable, Madam, the bruises, the head wounds…"

"He's my husband, I want to see him," Lena insisted.

"Sign these papers, Madam and I'll show him to you," the driver acquiesced.

Gisela took the papers and read them carefully. She nodded approval and passed them over to Lena who signed them, and gave them back to the driver. They walked over the hearse, and the driver opened the back. He went around to the front and activated the mechanism that slid the coffin out.

Just as he was doing that, a small bubble helicopter approached, hovered and looked for a place to land. It descended and showered the onlookers with sand and they all ran for cover, except for Lena, who remained motionless beside the coffin. The driver of the hearse looked perplexed and once the helicopter had landed, he brushed the dust off his black suit, clearly unimpressed.

The helicopter blades spun slowly and finally came to a stop. The pilot emerged, and scanned the group. A second man got out of the helicopter with a doctor's bag. Jono ran up to him, explained at length with many hand movements and pointed to Sofie. The pilot went back to the helicopter to get a stretcher while the doctor approached Sofie.

"Madam," the driver of the hearse said to Lena, "I would like to leave soon, Madam, forgive me."

Lena lifted the lid slowly with the help of the driver.

"Hold it up for me, please," she said, "I need both hands."

The driver held the lid up while Lena tugged off her wedding ring. She looked at it for a moment and she peered in at Stepfan. Then she threw the ring into the coffin and walked away.

The driver shut the coffin without comment, got into the hearse and drove off.

Meanwhile, the doctor gently questioned Sofie but he did not receive any answers. Sofie continued to sing quietly and gaze into the distance.

"Is she going to be alright?" Kate asked. She could not help but think what a rough lot they must present to the dapper little doctor. They all looked worse for wear one way or another with only Lena her usual elegant self.

"She's suffering from severe emotional trauma due to shock," the doctor said. "Will there be anybody who can fly out to be with her in Windhoek?"

"She listed her boyfriend as her emergency contact," Jono said, "and I called him. He said both him and Sofie's sister would get on a plane today."

"That's good," the doctor said. "Time, medication, the love of her family and a lot of support and she may recover. But it won't be easy and won't be quick."

He moved out of Sofie's sight and filled a syringe then he patted Sofie's arm, gave her the shot and applied a Band-Aid.

"She will soon sleep," he said and even as he spoke, Sofie slumped against him. He and Jono laid her on the stretcher and strapped her in. Two of the security guards from the camp picked her up and carried her to the helicopter. "There's a good chance she'll never remember what happened," the doctor said "but it would of course, be helpful for me to know, so that I can help her. Can anybody tell me anything?"

"She saw something she shouldn't have…" Kate said slowly.

Helen rounded on her. "How do you know that?" she demanded.

"Because she told Mia, Richard and me last night. She didn't say what, but she said she was worried she might be killed because of what she had seen."

"But do you know what she saw?" the doctor asked and Kate shook her head.

"Doctor, a man fell from the tower yesterday," Jono admitted uncomfortably. "There is perhaps a chance she witnessed that."

"Good God," the doctor was shocked. "That could have done it for sure."

"It was his hearse that drove off," Jono pointed.

The doctor stared at the ground, thinking. "It would not have been good for her to have seen that," he said, "but it's too late for that now." He looked around. "Can anybody add anything else that might be helpful?"

The group shook their heads.

"I've got all your contact information," the doctor said to Jono "in case I have any other questions."

He walked off neatly holding his black bag at his side and climbed into the helicopter. The blades slowly started turning and the bubble took off in a whirlwind of hot stinging sand.

Too late, Kate wondered if the doctor had seen the jackal and she realized that she should have told him about it. She decided she would visit the hospital when they arrived in Windhoek.

"Everybody, are we ready to leave?" Jono asked.

"Are we bloody ever," Richard exclaimed. "Never been more ready in my life."

They packed the bus and climbed on board. Rydell was fast asleep with saliva gathering on his chin.

"The delights of self-medication," Richard commented. "Delights for us, that is."

Kate looked through the window for the jackal's corpse but it was gone. She dug into her bag for the plastic bag with the bloodied rope and studied it surreptitiously, wondering who it belonged to. She thought about what Rydell had said about not killing the jackal and she wondered if someone else had done it to send Sofie over the edge. Sofie had hinted that she had seen something up at top of the tower, before Stepfan fell, and Kate wondered if this latest atrocity was designed to send Sofie further into shock and deeper into silence. Kate came up with a list of possible suspects: Gisela, Lena, Jasmine, Ellie and Helen, but she could not figure out anything further. She stared at the stark burnt earth flying by and she moved to the front of the bus to ask Jono a question. "We're still going to stop at the Etosha Pan, aren't we?"

"*Ei*, do you really want to?" Jono sounded doubtful.

"Yes, of course."

Jono sighed and turned down a road. "Good timing," he said. "We nearly drove past."

The early morning sunrise had been ruby red but the sky quickly turned dark, with large storm clouds forming on the horizon. The Etosha Pan itself was vast white salt lake with a domed ceiling of roiling purple anger.

"You have fifteen minutes," Jono announced loudly and pulled to a halt.

The group rushed off the bus.

"No wonder they used this a backdrop for *2001: A Space Odyssey*," Richard said, for once awed by something. "It's prehistoric ... it's like the bleached bones of a thousand disintegrated dinosaurs..."

"Listen to you, waxing bleedin' lyrical and all that," Mia mocked him. "When you stop talking poetic, run out into the middle and Jazzer, you take a picture, so it looks like he's standing on the palm of my hand."

"Eight million years and all she sees is a practical joke," Kate said to Betty who was standing next to her. "But you know, I mustn't get bitter, each of us has our own ways of doing things."

Betty grimaced in reply.

"Time to go, everybody," Jono shouted out the window, and he started the bus.

"A bit speedy, there, eh?" Mia puffed in her haste to get to the bus. "Oy, that was a good bit of fun."

They turned down the road and drove directly towards the threatening clouds. Lightning flashed in the distance and dust devils whirled towards the bus.

Kate thought they had been lucky to escape wet tents thus far, but she feared their good fortune in that regard was coming to an end.

"No lunch. We are driving straight through, I am worried about the storm," Jono yelled through the cab hatch.

"No lunch?" Ellie complained. "But I'm hungry."

"Here," Richard got up and opened a bag of supplies. "Chips, chocolate, all the junk food you could possibly want and more."

Ellie's eyes lit up. "Ooh, lovely," she said and she, Jasmine, Richard and Mia tucked in.

Lena was fast asleep on Gisela's shoulder and Rydell was out cold.

Helen stared out the window, her chin on her hand.

Jono stopped briefly to point out a watchful large male lion under a tree, guarding a dead zebra, but for the most part the ride was focused on getting to Fort Namutoni and they arrived in the early afternoon.

"The last campsite," Jono said in an undertone to Betty. "And thank God for that, or I might have killed them all myself. Only one night left." He smiled at Betty who patted his knee.

"Only one night left, Jono," she repeated.

The group quietly and efficiently set up camp on the patchy lawn. The tents were scattered haphazardly, and the only tree, a thin, scrawny acacia, was next to the bus, with the fire pit and concrete picnic tables nearby on the bare soil. The usual jackal-raided bins lay on their sides, with the garbage spread around.

As soon as her tent was up, Kate called André and told him what had happened.

"I can't wait to see you," he said, after he had listened to the whole story. "Take it easy tonight. I guarantee there'll be some good old white mischief because you know they've got nothing to lose. Be careful and stay out of their way."

"I couldn't agree more," Kate said and they said goodbye.

Her phone call made, Kate considered how to while away the time. She strolled down the blood-red road towards the old castle-like fort and watched a large warthog snuffle on the bright green grass while the threatening purple sky hung low and heavy. Like the other campsites, Fort Namutoni was deserted; the poolside was spotless and silent and the only sound came from the subdued rustle of the palm leaves.

Kate slipped into the fort's courtyard and found a large, closed restaurant and a souvenir shop that was open for business. The tourist shop offered some unusual and eye-catching wares but she was disinclined to shop. She was anxious. There was a long way to go before she would be safe in Windhoek with André.

She thought about Rydell, fast asleep back at the campsite.

Kate and Jono had put up his tent and arranged him inside with his belongings. Kate had made him take another pill and she planned to keep him drugged and harmless the entire way to Windhoek. Once they were there, as far as she was concerned, he was Jono's problem.

Kate examined a basket fashioned out of twisted wire and decorated with Coke and Sprite bottle tops but when Helen, Jasmine and Ellie came in, she quietly slipped out. She climbed the stairs to the deck overlooking the waterhole which was little more than a muddy man-made pond surrounded by a swampland.

"Hardly a waterhole, is it?" Helen piped up, suddenly next to her.

"More like a mini golf course gone wrong," Kate agreed. "The only wildlife I can see it attracting is mosquitoes."

Helen laughed. Jasmine and Ellie bounded up the stairs, followed by Richard and Mia. Mia's arms were full of beers and vodka.

"Aha, the gang's here. Come on, y'all," Richard said in an imitation Western drawl, "we've come to the arse-end of our weird and certainly less-than-wonderful magic carpet ride through Namibia and if you ask me, it's time to get wasted off our faces."

"As if a dozen beers and a bottle of vodka will do it," Ellie laughed.

"Never fear young lassie, there's a lot more where that came from." Richard said. "Ladies, I propose we get absolutely hammered from now until sunrise. What the hell, let's party like it's the end of time."

"Woohoo! We can finally have our trance dance." Mia raised her arms to the sky and skipped a few dance steps. "Tonight's the night. No one's allowed to be a soggy old blanket. I've got brill music, the place is deserted, the setting's bleedin' perfect, let's do it. All in favour, raise your beer."

"I'm in." Jasmine gave Mia a high five. "But does anyone

have the mind-altering chemicals?"

"I am, shall we say, an expert shopper in all things local," Richard smiled. "Anyone for a little wacky tobaccy, the old evil weed?"

"You are good," Ellie said. "I'm impressed. When did you get it?"

"Acquired it along the way," Richard waved a hand.

Helen turned around to see what Kate would say but she was gone.

"Forget about her," Mia said, reading Helen's thoughts. "She's a damp squib if ever I saw one. Come on, HellsBells, let's get this party started."

She threw a beer at Helen who cracked it open and took a quick, reluctant sip. She was on her guard though. Mia would not get her drunk again, she would keep up social appearances, no more. She hated beer, hated the taste, the smell, the associations. She hated the way people spoke about drinking beer as if they were actually *doing* something, watching a movie, reading a book, having a beer.

Having a beer isn't doing anything, she thought, and there was no way she was smoking pot either.

She sat down primly on the bench and put her sandaled feet up on the white railing, dourly surveying the scene in front of her and trying to ignore the enthusiastic party erupting beside her.

Jono arrived at the top of the stairs. "Supper will be early tonight," he announced shortly. "Please check your tents are tightly closed because we are going to get some heavy rain tonight."

He left as abruptly as he had arrived and Helen rushed after him, leaving her beer behind.

"Old Jono's got his knickers in a right knot, hasn't he?" Mia observed.

"I'm going to get some chasers," Richard said. "I'll be back."

"You'd better." Mia wiggled her bare toes on the railing, leaned back and sighed with contentment.

The courtyard was a lonely queen with no courtiers. Beautiful wooden tables sat on brickwork paving, tall palm trees waved in the hot wind and rich red geraniums bloomed in large earthenware pots. But Helen noticed none of this as she ran through the courtyard and out of the fort, trying to catch up with Jono who had carried on walking despite her calls. "Jono," she caught up with him, slightly breathless, "you know Kate's André?"

He stopped, taken aback by this entirely new curve ball thrown his way. "What about him?" He was guarded.

"It's just that I like Kate a lot," Helen was earnest, "and I don't want her to get hurt, so I want to find out if you think he's a good man, you know, good enough for her. What does he do anyway?"

Jono looked at her, thinking he knew exactly what she was after. "I do not know much about him," he shrugged and walked off.

She bounded up beside him. "But you and Betty seemed to know him well," she objected, "I saw you both talking to him. Kate said she met him in town, do you know where?"

"How would I know?" Jono replied. "I was not following her around." He shrugged again.

"But you do know," she insisted, "I know you do. Why won't you tell me?"

"Because it is not for me to tell you," he said shortly, "if you want to steal Kate's man, do it by yourself."

"You've got it wrong, it's not that. I just want to know about him. Maybe he's married and she doesn't even know. I don't want her to get hurt, I keep telling you."

They had reached the edge of the campsite and Jono stood still for a moment and then he turned to face her. "Enough," he said and he held his hand up like a traffic officer. "I am not going to talk to you any more. And by the way, don't ask Betty any of this nonsense either, because I am going to her now to tell her not to say a word to you. Go back and get drunk with the others and pray tomorrow comes quickly so we can leave each other and go our own ways. I have no idea what job I am going to do once I offload this terrible tour, but it is never, ever going to be this again. In all my years, and they have been many, I have never met such a bunch of crazies like you people. Now please, do not follow me anymore, I do not want anything to do with you."

Helen watched him walk away and she sat down, pulling at strands of grass and nibbling on them, thinking. She was suddenly concerned that Kate would change her mind and decide she liked André enough to stay in Namibia and where would that leave Helen?

She looked up and saw Kate photographing the warthog and she jumped up and went over to her.

"I like your latest supermodel," she said casually and Kate mumbled a response, her face squashed up against her camera. "I really don't feel like drinking with the others tonight," Helen continued, conversationally. "It's really not my style at all. Look, there's Richard, going back to camp to get more beer. They're chugging it down like there's no tomorrow."

Kate did not say anything. She put her camera down, rubbed her face and sighed. "I couldn't get a good shot of him," she said, "such a great opportunity and nothing." She stared at the warthog who snuffled on, oblivious.

Helen made no move to leave and she kicked at the grass with her toe. "What are you going to do while they're all trance dancing tonight?"

Kate snorted. "They're still going to do that, are they? What I'm going to do is stay as far away from them as I can."

"And phone your hunky man."

Kate looked at her and did not reply.

"Kate," Helen said, "you're very lucky to have found him. I thought I had found my knight in shining armour but now I don't have anything or anyone."

Kate continued to ignore her and waved at Lena and Gisela

who were on their way back to the fort with Richard. Gisela called out, inviting her to come drinking and dancing and Kate thanked her and shook her head. "I'm admitting defeat on the warthog front," she said to no-one in particular, and she started to walk back to camp. "I'm going to see if I can help Betty."

"She's fine," Helen lied, having no idea one way or the other. "You want to go for a walk?"

"I'm okay, thanks. Aren't you going running?"

"Not in the mood," Helen said. "I feel restless. I'm not sure what I'm going to do when I get back to Canada, if I even go back."

Kate looked at Helen, at her strong profile and high cheekbones and she thought she could be lovely were it not for her hard expression and scraped-back hair. Give her a dose of happiness, a bit of a makeover and she'd be a real knockout.

"Kate, have I done something to offend you?" Helen grabbed her by the arm and Kate pulled away, not enjoying Helen's energy.

"It's not you, Helen," she lied. "I'm tired of this trip, too much bad stuff's gone on, enough already. I want this to all end."

"I don't know what to do with my life," Helen blurted out. "I've got less idea than ever and I hate being like that. I always known what I'm supposed to do next and now I don't have a clue."

Kate felt sorry for her despite their differences. "Why not go back to Canada for a bit?" she asked. "You could try to get another volunteer job from there; you could get a new visa — how bad could that be?"

"Worse than you could ever imagine," Helen's face fell. "You've got everything in life, Kate. You have no idea what it's like to have nothing, to have worked so hard since the day you were born, fight the odds and end up with nothing."

"Don't I?" Kate asked drily. "I do have the best parents ever, that much is true; I'm very lucky there. But from the time I was twenty-three until two months ago, all I did was wait for this loser guy to marry me and I spent the same eight years working in a dead-end job because my father thought it offered good security, and I didn't do any of the things I really wanted to in life. I thought I wanted to marry Cam and have a house in the suburbs and a bunch of babies and that's all I was waiting for."

"Why did you break up with him?" Helen asked.

"What makes you think I broke up with him? He told me he wanted an open relationship and off he went. I fell apart, spent a week in my best friend's apartment, crying day and night. When I finally got myself out of bed, I went to the mall and I saw a travel store and booked this trip, mainly to try to escape my life. When my boss wouldn't give me the vacation time I was owed, I resigned. I don't have anything to go back to either."

Kate sat down on the grass and Helen joined her.

"Yeah, but now you've got André," Helen argued and Kate burst out laughing.

"Get real, Helen. What do you think, that after seeing him twice, that he's going to rescue me from my life? That's the biggest loser fairytale ever."

"Aren't you going to see him in Windhoek?" Helen sounded hopeful.

"Of course I'm going to see him. He's going to take me to a proper game lodge for a bit of rest after all this. But as for what happens after that, who knows? I'll probably end up going back to Canada too, in which case, I'll stay with my best friend until I find my feet. Don't you have anybody you can stay with?"

Helen thought for a moment. "I stayed in my teacher's basement before I left for Africa and she said she'd keep it free for me, in case."

"There you go then," Kate said. "Life's not a holiday, Helen, not that this has been much of a holiday either, but you know what I mean. We can't be on a bus forever, or in a nice mission, or whatever. I'll tell you what this trip has taught me: that I can live my life my way, meet interesting people, do fun stuff and see the world." She laughed. "Thank God my boyfriend didn't marry me and buy us a house in the suburbs. I'd still love kids some day but my life's going to be very different to the way it was before."

"I wish I had your optimism and confidence," Helen said, bitterly. "I'm out of both."

Kate got up. "Can't help you there, Helen. If you ask me, you've got a lot going for you and you're the one who gets to make the choice. You can choose to live a happy life or you can be a bitter woman because the rewards didn't drop into your lap when you thought they should. You still get to choose whether your glass is half full or half empty."

"I hate that kind of clichéd fortune cookie moralizing." Helen stood up and brushed the dirt off the seat of her shorts. "A load of crap if you ask me."

She walked off quickly, turning away from the fort and striding briskly down the road that led out of the camp. Kate watched her, thinking that Helen was playing with fire heading out of the camp. This was not a zoo with caged animals but a real jungle. Kate decided not to worry. When it came to Helen, self-preservation ran stronger in her blood than hemoglobin.

She headed toward Betty to see if she needed her help and as she passed Richard and Mia's tent, she suddenly stopped dead in her tracks. A thought suddenly flashed through her mind.

Richard was a surgeon, and Mia a nurse. What if they had been the ones to murder Rosalee Khumalo in Swakopmund? Both Richard and Mia would be battered and bruised if the girl had put up a fight. Heart pounding, Kate suddenly thought it all made sense. Richard had been preoccupied with *muti* and witchdoctors from the very beginning. And Kate had seen them scurrying back to the lodge before anyone else was awake, so they had lied about staying there in a private room.

Convinced she had stumbled on the truth, she wished she

could duck into their tent and search their belongings, but she had no way of knowing if Richard would return for more alcohol. She decided to wait until they were drunk and deeply into their dance and then she would sneak into their tent.

She walked into the kitchen and found Betty mashing potatoes.

"Burger patties of the meat and vegetarian kind and mashed potato, that is as good as supper is getting tonight, and I don't want to hear any complaints." Betty smiled, her traditional blue and white patterned apron fastened tightly around her.

"And you won't either," Kate assured her. "That sounds delicious. Can I help you?"

"You can put the plates out under the awning. Supper will be ready soon."

"I must warn you, Betty," Kate said, "they might be more than a little drunk when they arrive back from the waterhole."

"They've started already?" Betty commented.

"Yes, and they're intent on it being a big one. They want to try a trance dance."

"I might as well have given them day-old bread and cheese," Betty grumbled. "They won't even notice my famous mashed potatoes."

"Do not worry, Betty," Jono walked in, "my appreciation will make up for everybody's."

"As will mine," Kate agreed. "Let me go and set these out. And I must check in on Rydell."

"What pills are you feeding him?" Jono leaned an elbow on one of the concrete ledges. "Do not give him too many."

"Don't worry," Kate said, "it's his prescribed medicine, I just want him to stay safe and sound, and us too."

"What is the name of the tablets?" Jono asked and Kate pulled them out of her camera bag.

"It's a standard tranquilliser of some kind," Jono said, studying the label and handing the bottle back to her. "Be careful."

"I promise. But we can't have any more dead jackals you know."

"I do not believe Rydell did that," Jono put his hands in his pockets and looked calmly at Kate. "You know that piece of rope you pulled out? I recognized it from Jasmine's sleeping bag. She had it outside at the Gariep River, out on the grass there, under the tree and I thought then that it was a nice rope."

"Why would she be so stupid as to use something from her sleeping bag?" Kate asked.

Jono shrugged. "Maybe she could not find anything else. People do strange things when they panic. I doubt she would have done it alone anyway. But even so, Kate, so what if she killed a jackal? I do not mean 'so what' really, but I mean what can we do, what does it prove?"

Kate spoke in a rush of pent up fury. "It proves, Jono, that she's a sick and disgusting person who killed and dismembered an innocent animal in order to destroy the healthy functioning of a another person's mind, when that person had already been subjected to untold trauma and was on the brink of going either way. That's what it proves. It proves, beyond any doubt, she had something to hide. That Sofie must have seen something. That Stepfan's death was not an accident. It proves all of that, Jono, can't you see that?" She glared at him, stiff with anger.

Betty rolled meat patties and watched them both out of the corner of her eye.

Jono shrugged again. "Then, tomorrow, when we are in Windhoek, take the rope to the police and tell them your story. I will tell it my way. A dead animal was found, and yes, the rope looked to be the same kind that was on Jasmine's sleeping bag. And then what? You have allegations about a man dying mysteriously when an entire crowd tells the exact same story with no evidence to prove anything the contrary?"

"Why are you sticking up for Jasmine?" Kate cried. "Or any of them? They are killers."

"You do not know that," Jono stated. "Even if you think you know it, you do not, because you have no proof. And I am not *sticking* up for them. That is a childish way to look at it,

Kate. They have either been brilliant or lucky or both because there is *nothing* I can do and it is eating me up inside. There's nothing I can do, can you not see that?"

He looked at her, his arms folded, his face impassive. "For you — a rich white girl — there is always a solution; do this, do that. We blacks, we know how to keep quiet and suffer the weight of the burdens we have to carry. You whites, you stand around, asking who can take this load from me? It cuts into my back, it hurts my shoulders, I do not like it, you say, it is not comfortable you complain, so we step in and carry it, not a word said."

"It comes down to black and white, does it, Jono?" Kate was hurt and angry. "I don't want to solve this because it's an uncomfortable load on my white back. I want to solve this because its murder and it's wrong."

"All murder is wrong," Jono said, softly, "and most of it goes unchallenged. Truly, only you privileged whites think everything must be solved, that the 'bad' man will be brought to justice. Justice, what is justice? Here is a Xhosa proverb for you, Kate, on how we think your famous justice works:

The ox is skinned on one side only.
Ponder well this saw, and do not go to the law,
For, like an ox with half a hide, justice has oft one side."

They stared at each other, an impasse.
"Let me help you with the plates," Jono said, ending the discussion.
Kate picked up the sauces and walked out.
Betty looked at Jono, and said nothing.
He shrugged, and loaded up a tray.
"At least," he said to Betty, "I have your mashed potatoes to look forward to, tonight. That is the only reason I will even go near these people this evening."
"Oh, Jono," she turned to scold him but he had already left.

The Eleventh Night

WITH CRIES OF DRUNKEN HILARITY, the others made their way back to camp. "I'm so hungry." Ellie cried.

"Starving." Mia agreed.

"I could eat a horse," Richard said. "One can't help wondering why it's a horse they always suggest you eat? I mean who would eat horse really? Not me or anyone I know, that's for sure."

"The saying," Jasmine was already slurring, "has two possible origins of meaning. The one is that you are so hungry you could eat all of a horse, which is a huge amount of food. The other is that you are so hungry that you are willing to eat a horse, which is considered to be the most disgusting of meals, the last resort."

"I don't know about that," Richard considered. "Surely gnawing one's arm off would be the real last resort? As opposed to horse I mean?"

"It would be the only resort if you were chained up *and* you were hungry?" offered Ellie.

"Why not get on the horse and go and find more food?" Lena asked, "that would be the most sensible thing to do, as far as I can see. After all, don't eat your transport, use it to find more food, simple."

"But," argued Jasmine, "even if you were on your horse, there might be no food to be found. That's the whole point, you could ride for days and find nothing and you'd be so hungry, you'd consider eating your horse, your last resort."

"The poor horse would be so hungry," Ellie said sadly.

"If the horse 'ad any brains, he'd eat you," Mia kicked at a pebble.

"He can't," Ellie told her earnestly, her long skinny legs sticking out of her short, bright red sundress, "he's a hervibore."

"You mean herbivore, old Ellie, and we've just about flogged this horse to death." Richard aimed an empty beer bottle at nearby trashcan and missed.

"He'd be easier to eat if he were dead," Gisela stopped to light a cigarette. "I mean then you wouldn't be responsible for actually killing him, and you could light a fire, roast some horse meat and thank him for dying and therefore saving your life."

"How did he die?" Ellie asked, upset.

"He starved," Jasmine told her. "No wait, he was flogged."

"Ladies. Please, leave the road kill alone, can we please move on from the horse?" Richard begged.

They walked on in silence.

"Gisi, luv, can I bum a fag off you?" Mia asked, and Gisela handed over her pack of cigarettes. Richard looked questioningly at Mia who shrugged. "Just for tonight luv." She inhaled deeply. "Fuck a duck, talk about a head rush."

"Was it a grey horse or a bay?" Ellie asked.

"Ellie! Stop with the horse!" the others yelled.

"I'm trying to imagine what I'm leaving behind," she said sulkily.

They reached the camp and lined up under the awning to get their food.

"Mashed potatoes, burgers, meat and vegetarian, enjoy." Betty pointed.

"Kate," she said aside, "would you mind clearing it away and doing the dishes? I'm so tired, I am going to sleep now."

"With pleasure. Take some food with you," Kate said, "I'll come and get your plate later. I must take some to Rydell anyway."

"*Aikona*, that's fine, I have eaten enough today. I want to take a nice long shower and go to sleep. Kate, don't listen too much to Jono, he likes you very much, he doesn't mean to attack you."

"He didn't attack me. Don't worry, Betty, you go and rest now and thank you for a delicious supper."

Kate put a plate of food together for Rydell and she noticed Helen arrive.

"Where did you go?" Ellie cried noisily. "We missed you. Have some schnapps."

"I went for a run," Helen said. "I'm going to have a shower then I'll join you."

"Why the sour puss?" Gisela called out.

The others found that hilarious.

"No reason," Helen said. "I'll get cleaned up and party with you in a minute."

She headed for the shower and Kate went to give Rydell his supper.

Rydell was sitting up groggily and rubbing his face, scratching his unshaven jaw.

"Must go to the toilet," he said to Kate as she climbed in and his voice was thick and gritty.

Kate looked at him sitting on his sleeping bag in his hot, airless tent, his clothes sweaty and disheveled. His hair was pasted to his skull and the bruises on his face had turned yellow. She suddenly felt sorry for him. She wondered if his perspective had returned to present-day adult or whether he still believed she was his mother and him a naughty, scolded boy.

"Come on," she said, "I'll help you. Where's your toiletry bag?"

"You should know," he yawned. "You went through my things, remember?"

Clearly his psyche had bounced back to normalcy and she thought he might be waking up a bit too much.

"Don't worry," he said, as if reading her mind. "I'm only

joking. I don't care what you did. I don't care about any of this anymore. All I want is to get to Windhoek, go to the airport and go straight home. I just want my nice clean life back. Why's the wind blowing so hard?"

Kate had not noticed. "It must be getting ready to storm," she said. "It's been threatening all day. I must go and close my windows. I'll close yours too. Take some new clothes to change into. The washroom's over there, you see it?" She pointed, and held the tent door open.

"Yes," Rydell said, still yawning. "*It's raining, it's pouring, the old man is snoring.* Please don't make me take any more pills tonight. I hate them, they make me feel terrible. I promise you I'll take more in the morning and I'll stay in my tent and sleep but please, no more tonight."

"Let's see," Kate said cautiously. "The others plan on partying hard, the noise might keep you awake. It will be easier for you to sleep if you take a pill."

"I'll sleep, I promise. Who's partying?"

"Whoever's left," Kate said and she tidied his belongings to make space for his plate of food. "Not me though, I'm going to do the dishes and go to bed. You go and shower. I'll fix the tents and I'll leave your supper for you here, okay?"

"Okay," Rydell sounded sleepy. "Have you had supper yet?"

"Not yet, but I will."

She watched him walk to the washroom and marvelled at how normal he could be at times. She zipped the tents closed and walked back to the awning where she saw that the party had already accelerated beyond the point of no return. She wondered if she could risk going into Richard and Mia's tent but decided to wait a little longer and then she went to gather up the plates. Hardly any of Betty's food had been touched.

"Come and have a drink." Jasmine shouted at her. "Stop working so hard."

Kate shook her head.

The sun had set and the sky was dark violet with a yellowish tinge to the fading light. A strong gale slapped the sides of the tents with noisy force.

"Perfect for a trance dance." Mia yelled. "Richard, make a fire, here under the awning. We're going to 'ave to dance in here and then if it gets really muddy, we can roll around in it out there."

Richard spotted a steel garbage can. He turned it upside down, and tossed the rubbish to the ground.

Nice, Kate thought, stepping over a disgusting compost of rotting food and waste.

Richard dragged the can under the awning. "We need wood," he announced.

"We'll get it." Ellie and Jasmine yelled and they ran to the back of the bus, returning with their arms full.

"I'm in charge of the music," Mia said, a cigarette hanging from her mouth as she worked on the ghetto blaster.

Richard passed a joint around. "Share the love, loves." he said.

Mia fired up the music. "Righty-ho," she said and started to move in time to the music, waving her cigarette around. "'Ere's how it works. Us girls sit around in a circle and Richard dances around us. We clap and yell at him right? Then I get up and dance around wif him until he's too shattered to dance or he needs a drink or somefink and then he sits down. You got it?"

She peered around and continued. "As soon as he sits down, the person who was sitting next to me, gets up and she dances wif me until I need a toke or a drink or whatever, and then I sit down and the next person in line gets up. You see how it works? Whoever is sitting must be clapping and yelling, okay? And this is the perfect music, yeah, it's drumming stuff from Ethiopia, this DJ gave it to me back in England, And remember the idea is to have visions and fings, and get into the zone, connect wif spirits and get out there."

"Sounds good," Jasmine said and her pale green eyes gleamed in the light of flickering fire.

"Okay, one more shot each, pass the joint, hit the music and we're bleedin' ready!"

The wind blew harder than ever, mixing sand, dust, twigs, small stones in a frenzy. The dancers arranged themselves in a circle under the awning and the fire in the bin sputtered and smoked and the music was deafening.

"Ah, bollocks," Richard yelled. "I want to get my mask, shite, sorry girls, I forgot. Hang on a mo', you carry on drinking."

He ran back to the tent, grabbed his mask and dashed back. A smattering of rain had begun to fall in small, fast, stinging drops. Richard ran for cover under the awning and flipped the mask up over his head, screaming in shock and horror as a waterfall of black muck poured down his face, filled his mouth and his nose, and stung his eyes. He cried out in terror and disgust while the girls shrieked and screamed in fear with Lena and Gisela jumping to their feet, their hands pressed to their mouths in panic and disgust. Richard howled and yanked the mask off as fast as he could, ripping the delicate ancient fabric of the cowried hood.

"Ah! Fuck!" He clutched his face, unable to open his eyes. "An animal shat in my mask, ah fuck, that's disgusting, I'm going to be sick." He doubled over and vomited, hanging onto the awning pole for support.

"What happened?" Ellie was still shocked. She leaned over him and patted his back. Mia had recovered quickly from her initial fright and was shrieking with laughter, lying on the ground and kicking her heels in the dirt.

"Fuck me gently with a bargepole," she finally managed to say and sat up, tears streaming down her face. "Didn't that take the cake? Are you alright, luv? What the fuck happened there?"

"I've got no fucking idea," Richard said grimly. He remained bent over, his face black with stinking sewerage, "unless a jackal with the runs and fucking bad body odour got into our tent and pissed and crapped in my mask which is highly unlikely, if you ask me." He gagged and coughed, the smell of the black gunge rancid on his skin.

"Och, come on now, luv," Mia got up and went over to him with a dishtowel. "Go and wash your face, take a big swig of Jack's, take a hit off the old weed and get wif the program. I'm sorry your mask's right fucked yeah, but here, look, we'll hang him up, on this pole thing, so he can watch us all nice, like this, he's still with us, yeah?" She patted Richard on the arm, and started to laugh again, the others joining her and their giggles soon escalated to a crescendo of howls.

Kate, in the kitchen, heard the bloodcurdling screams and rushed out, her heart racing. She rounded the corner to see Richard doubled over, his face blackened and Ellie patting his back.

"What happened?" Kate asked. At first she thought something was seriously wrong and it was hard to get a reply from the stoned and drunken group who were giggling uncontrollably again.

"A jackal pooped in his mask," Jasmine finally managed to say, gasping and pointing at the mask.

Kate looked at the sullied mask. Its hood was filthy and torn and mud and dirt streaked the ornately-decorated, carved face. She turned back to Richard who was wiping his face with one of the kitchen tea-towels. He went over to the camp tap, stuck his head under the cold water and scrubbed vigorously. He walked back in the rain, beginning to see the humour in what had happened, the shock wearing off.

"I need a moment," he said, sitting down and gargling with Jack Daniels. "Don't worry, girls, I'll get back into my party spirit, but fuck me, that was disgusting. I smell like shite and the taste was terrible."

"Ah, but we love you even if you smell like rotten meat," Gisela giggled and passed him a joint. "This is very good stuff, have some more and you'll feel better in no time."

Richard took it, and inhaled deeply. His face was streaked

and dirty, his hair a Mohican spike. Mia, still cackling uncontrollably, got up, and pulled Jasmine to her feet.

"Well, luv, "she said to Richard, "you sit there and get yourself together all nice, me and Jazzer are going to begin. Right you all, start clapping, go on, get it on, yeah."

The rain had begun to fall in earnest, big drops, flat and hot, the beginning of a torrent.

Kate picked up the last of the dishes and escaped to the privacy of the kitchen where she could still hear the raucous insensible shouts and the high-decibel industrial-techno music layered with heavy tribal drums.

She did not see Helen leaning on the other side of the bus, out of sight, a smug smile on her face.

Kate, wishing more than ever that night was over, filled the two sinks with water. She arranged the stacks of dishes, wondering how Eva, Marika and Enrique were doing. She thought about Charisse, Stepfan, Harrison, Treasure and Sofie, and how things had turned out. Her face was creased in a frown of concentration. She hoped Rydell had gone back to his tent like he had said he would. She also hoped that her tent was not going to leak in the downpour. She picked up a frying pan and eased it into the soapy water.

She felt rather than heard a presence and she swung around. It was Helen, sidling in. She was wearing her raincoat, a thin floppy dark green jacket, and she had the hood pulled forward to protect her face.

Kate looked pointedly at the second pair of gloves but Helen made no move towards them and she leaned against the counter instead with her arms folded and her expression fierce. "I thought about our conversation," she said, and the ghostly black shadows under her eyes coupled with her cowled head covering gave her an almost ludicrous grim reaper look and Kate turned away, unnerved.

"I can tell you categorically," Helen continued, "that my

frickin' glass is half empty, no matter which way you look at it. I have to say, Kate, you've driven me nuts on this trip. I've hated your stupid optimism, how you get so excited by such ridiculous things. How you manage to have fun all the time, be so happy, and entertain yourself with things that bring me no pleasure. I watched you from the start, taking photographs of crap everywhere. And what about your irritating enthusiasm for Kleine Skok? For God's sake, you even held that disgusting rabbit's blood."

Kate scrubbed a pot wishing that Jono or Betty would come in but she remembered that they had gone to bed. Monstrous hairy brown and gray moths crowded their way inside the small room and their scattered fluttering wings, along with Helen's unchecked fury, made Kate anxious but she told herself that her fear was simply a reaction to everything that had gone wrong. She reassured herself that Helen was not dangerous but she recalled Stepfan's death and the mutilated jackal and her dread thickened.

"And how come you took control when Charisse died? I'm always the one in charge. And you got to drive off with the good-looking Bushman and I bet you charmed the pants off him too, didn't you? Even that weirdo Rydell likes you when he's not busy losing his mind. Jono missed you when you went, of course he did, he fell in love with you, just like the rest. And when we fetched you from Walvis Bay there you were, pale and fragile but still happy. I could tell.

"And you know what else?" she said, and she moved closer to Kate. "You know what bugged me about you the most? That all of us on this trip have behaved badly at one time or another except for you. You're the only one who hasn't done something bad."

"That's not true." Kate said and her voice sounded trapped in her throat. She was cursing herself for having left her pepper spray in her tent; she had been so sure that nothing else could go wrong.

She fished around in the soapy water, trying to find a bread knife or anything she could use for her own protection. "Sofie didn't do anything wrong. Or Eva or Marika or Enrique, or Harrison or Treasure."

"No. *You're wrong.*" Helen's breath was hot against her ear. "They all left before it counted and Sofie went crazy, so she doesn't count either. But I came here to do good and look at what I did. I didn't stick up for Harrison and I could have stopped Stepfan from walking around that wall but I didn't. I hoped he would fall, that's the truth, I did. He was such a showoff and I thought it would serve him right if he fell and then he did. And then I was beyond cruel. I was all the things I've hated my whole life. I watched Sofie that night in my tent, getting her things and I could see that she was in so much pain but I didn't help her."

"Since we're being so brutally honest here," Kate said, her fingers finding a knife among all the cutlery, "let me ask you something." She was afraid to confront Helen but she could not stop herself. "Did you and Jasmine kill the jackal to drive Sofie beyond the limits of what she could handle? So she wouldn't be able to tell anybody what really happened up in tower?"

Helen clenched her jaw in anger. "I've told you what happened up in the tower and Stepfan was responsible for his own death. And I didn't help Jasmine kill the jackal, if in fact she even did. I think it was that weirdo Rydell or some locals, not that I care either way. But back to the things that irritated me about you. Next thing, you scored André, and who knows where you found him but you did and, like Prince Charming, he rushed to see you, in a Porsche for God's sake. You never lost your frickin' happiness, not even in the darkest moments of chaos, and that really pisses me off in a very *big* way. I thought that I'd tell you how I feel, given that the trip's coming to an end." She gave Kate a strange smile.

Kate pulled the knife out of the water and shot backwards towards the screen door.

"Stay away from me, Helen," she said, brandishing the knife, her heart pounding. "I'm not going to be another casualty of this trip, I won't. You think I'm stupid? I know you think you've got a chance with André, with me out of the picture. Well, whatever you're planning, you can forget about it."

To her surprise, Helen burst out laughing. " Look at you, all Angelina Jolie with a knife! You think I came in here to kill you? Is that what you think? I guess this trip has been filled with all kinds of violence but you've got me wrong. I came here to thank you. Granted I had to tear a strip off you first but I want to thank you."

"Thank me?" Kate was perplexed but she did not lower the knife.

"Yes. Because you helped me get my power back. I've got my focus back. You're right, my life's up to me, not anyone else and waiting for someone to rush in and sort it all out for me is stupid. I fell so hard for Robbie that I lost my way, lost my sense of who I am. I guess what I'm really trying to say is that even although you've bugged the crap out of me, thanks. Seriously, you can put the knife away now."

Kate looked doubtful and Helen laughed again. "And if I'm honest, André wouldn't look twice at me," she said, "not even if he was single. I know that. I'm too bossy for him. I just daydreamed that's all. There you see, I've got no reason to kill you."

Kate glanced back over her shoulder. The rain was a torrent. "How about finishing the dishes then?" she said. "For a save-the-world-do-gooder you've reneged more than once on your washing up duties."

Helen obligingly snapped on the gloves.

"And take your hood off. You look like something out of a Wes Craven horror movie."

Helen brushed the hood back with her elbow and started scrubbing.

"And if in fact you really were trying to thank me, it's not the most gracious speech I've ever heard but then again, it was bona fide Helen." Kate thought for a moment. "Helen," she said, "what's your take on Richard? Do you still find him as attractive as you did at the beginning of the trip?"

"No way. I'll tell you this for nothing, he's a really nasty piece of work," Helen's face was grim. "And since I'm spilling my guts to you, I may as well tell you this. He threatened me big time once, in Solitaire. Granted I was coming onto him and I shouldn't have but still, he threatened to cut my ligaments so I'd never run again. And all he had to say was 'not interested.'"

Kate took a chance. "This might sound crazy but hear me out. I think Richard and Mia might have killed Rosalee Khumalo."

"That sex worker who was murdered in Swakopmund when we were there? I read about it in the papers, I figured it was some local did it. Richard likes to be cruel all right but don't you think you're making big assumptions?"

"Did you know that he's a surgeon?"

"No! No way! Really? Wow. Then he could have done it like they said. And remember, he was totally obsessed with all that *muti* stuff."

They looked at each other.

"And that would also explain their disapearance in Swakopmund and the fact that they looked so beaten up. But still ... murder? And Mia? Come on, she's nothing but an airhead and a stupid drunk."

"She's a psychiatric nurse."

Helen was shocked into silence and Kate nodded. "You see? And they never wanted to really do any of the tourist stuff unless it involved witchdoctors and magic. And then, we got to Swakopmund, they disappeared, a woman was murdered in true *muti* style and they get all banged up?" Kate shrugged. "Who knows, there's a good chance I'm wrong since it would really be crazy if it was true, but I'd love to find out."

"We can search their tent," Helen said confidently, pulling the gloves off. "They're all so out of it, we wouldn't have to worry about them finding us. And I've already been in there, to put that stuff in Richard's mask – I gotta tell you, watching that disgusting stinking stuff pour down his face was one of the best moments of my life. Who says revenge isn't fantastic? Come on let's go and search their tent."

By now the ceiling was covered with fist-size moths and the kitchen light had begun to flicker on and off, and little could be heard above the sound of the rain pounding on the tin roof, with torrents of gushing water pouring down the eaves.

Helen stopped. "Fuck," she said, "fuck, fuck, fuck."

"What?" Kate froze, her heart was already beating hard with fright at the possibility of them being discovered in Richard and Mia's tent.

"I wasted my entire holiday on Robbie. How stupid was that? I can't believe how stupid I was."

"You were heartbroken, Helen," Kate said, "there's a difference between heartbroken and stupid. And now you're not heartbroken. Be happy about that, okay, instead of mourning the loss of a holiday that really wasn't a holiday anyway."

Helen laughed. "You see, there you go again, looking on the bright side. Okay, you ready? I've got a flashlight. Don't worry, they're so out of it, they won't know we're there."

Kate and Helen stepped out into the deep mud. The flashlight illuminated a small area in front of them in the dense wet darkness. They headed for Richard and Mia's tent, passing the wild party along the way. By now the group was buck-naked, singing and shouting as they danced around the trashcan fire under the awning. Entwined and entangled, they caressed one another, their bodies smeared with thick red mud, their faces war-painted masks with howling mouths. Kate stopped, mesmerized. The pounding music along with the primeval storm ignited the certain pull of animal lust in her and for a moment she too wanted to tear off her wet clothes and join the insensible party and dance with abandon. She too wanted to lose herself in the glory of Africa; Africa, a goddess of rage and fury. She turned to Helen, wondering if she felt the same crazy madness but Helen just laughed.

"They look like such idiots, don't they?"

Kate turned back to look at the crazed group but Helen grabbed her hand and dragged her forward.

They found Richard's tent and Helen unzipped the sodden fabric and crawled inside, with Kate following.

"Don't worry about making a mess," Helen said. "The place is a pig-sty anyway."

She was right and Kate looked at the chaos of jumbled items and wondered where to start.

"You grab Mia's bag over there," Helen told her and Kate took the items out, one at a time while Helen grabbed Richard's bag.

They searched in silence. Kate was halfway through the bag when Helen suddenly snapped off the flashlight.

"Ssh," she said, "can you hear something?"

Kate strained to listen. "It's raining too hard to hear anything," she whispered. She broke out in a cold sweat and crouched deadstill over Mia's bag.

"I can hear something," Helen insisted. "Someone's coming."

They waited in the darkness when suddenly the tent door was unzipped and Kate and Helen grabbed at each other. A body tumbled inside and fell top of them and they all screamed. Kate and Helen both realized that it was neither Richard nor Mia and Helen clicked on the flashlight.

It was Ellie, drunk, stoned and muddy, deciding she'd had enough for the night.

"Why are you in my tent?" she asked, looking confused.

"This is *my* tent," Helen asserted, "and Kate's sharing with me because you guys are making too much of a ruckus out there. Go and find your own tent, you're getting crap all over us."

Ellie sat up and burped. "I feel sick," she announced.

"Take it outside," Helen said brusquely. "Now!"

Ellie clambered over them and crawled out into the night.

Helen stuck her head out and watched as Ellie took two paces and then fell down in the mud, retching.

"Eugh," Helen said. "Listen, we'd better hurry up." She balanced the flashlight on a pile of dirty clothes and they resumed their search, working in silence.

"I've got nothing," Kate said, coming to the end of Mia's possessions, disappointment in her voice. "And I was so sure."

But Helen had gone oddly silent. "Uh, no, actually, you were right. Funny, I feel sick. I mean I didn't really think that it could be true."

"What did you find?" Kate felt a headache starting and she realized that she had been clenching her jaw. She crawled over to where Helen was kneeling.

Helen wordlessly held up a ziploc bag that held a necklace with the name 'Rosalee' written in gold cursive script.

"Oh my God," Kate said, shaken by the discovery. It was one thing to harbour suspicions and another to discover the truth.

"But wait, I found more..." Helen held up a torn piece of newsprint with an advert for an escort agency that had a picture of Rosalee.

"Why would they be so stupid as to keep this stuff?" Kate whispered.

"Because they're that arrogant," Helen said, digging deeper among Richard's things and pulling out a pair of high-heeled silver platform shoes with glittery sequinned straps. The shoes were worse for wear and a large rust-coloured stain covered the one heel. Kate grabbed a plastic bag that had held liquor and Helen dropped their findings inside.

"Let's go," Helen hissed, "we've got enough stuff. The police will do the rest. Come on."

They ran back to the kitchen where the light continued to flicker on and off.

"Should we tell Jono?" Helen asked and Kate shook her head.

"He won't do anything." She dug out her cellphone. "There's no signal." She shook the phone as if that might help.

"It's the storm," Helen said. "We'll have to wait until the morning. In the meantime, let's go and wait inside the bus, our tents will be soaked."

Carrying their precious cargo carefully, they ran back out into the rain and towards the bus.

Under the awning, the dancers had lost their manic energy. Gisela and Lena had passed out and were lying in each other's arms. Jasmine was out cold, her head in Mia's lap. Mia was smoking a joint, her eyes closed and Richard was leaning up against a tent pole, cradling his ruined mask and finishing off a bottle of bourbon. The music had stopped and even the storm's fury was beginning to abate. No one noticed Kate and Helen climb into the bus.

"Here," Helen threw a T-shirt at Kate. "The advantages of me drying my stuff everywhere."

Kate tried to summon a grateful laugh but she was wrung out by the events of the night and she pulled the T-shirt on in silence, appreciating its dry warmth.

"Drink this," Helen said, handing her a can of Coke. "Lots of sugar, good for shock."

Kate cracked it open and even managed a smile. "You are good in a crisis," she said. "If anyone can save the world, it's you."

"Gotta save my own world first," Helen said dryly, spreading mats out on the floor. "Come on, lie down, get some rest."

"I'll never manage to sleep," Kate said but before she knew it, it was morning.

She sat up, groggy, while the events of the previous night sorted themselves out in her waking mind. Helen was still asleep and Kate grabbed her phone and quietly made her way outside.

The sky was clear and cry of the ring-necked dove sounded its haunting melody. The air was washed with a spicy clean fragrance and Kate took a deep breath, drawing the purity deep into her lungs. Around her, the others slept on, oblivious.

She got André on the second ring and she explained the situation to him.

"I'll get my cop friends," he said. "We'll be there in two hours max. Are you safe till then?"

"Yes, fine, the rest of the gang are all out of it. They'll most likely still be drunk when you get here."

She closed the phone and looked up to see Jono climbing out of his tent. She called out and walked towards him.

The Aftermath

TRUE TO HIS WORD, ANDRÉ ARRIVED with the police, two hours after having spoken to Kate. Helen and Kate explained the situation and handed over the evidence and the police made a thorough search of Richard and Mia's tent while snapping handcuffs onto the sullen pair.

"Helen and I remembered Sofie saying that they posted stuff back to England from Swakopmund," Kate added. "There may be more evidence on its way to the UK."

The constable in charge nodded and made a note. "The good news is that you guys found enough to put these two away until we come up with more — and we will."

Kate turned to say something to Helen and saw her chatting happily to one of the helicopter pilots, a small man with dark hair and a sizable nose.

André followed her gaze and he laughed. "Got her sights on Kevin, does she? She could do a lot worse. But he's got two kids. I don't know how she'll feel about that when she finds out. His wife left him a couple of years back, left him with a baby and a toddler. He's a good guy."

"I think she'd make a good mother," Kate said. "If you ask me, all she's looking for is a family to love."

"And you and me, *bokkie*, are you still going to let me treat you to the lap of luxury before you head off back home?"

"André," Kate said, "I'd love nothing more than a real holiday, I can't tell you…" She was interrupted by the arrival of another helicopter that landed in a cloud of dust and she turned enquiringly at André who shook his head. As they watched, the pilot climbed down and unlatched the back door, holding it open for a police officer who helped a thin black lad in handcuffs climb down.

"My goodness," Kate said, "that's Dumi. What's he doing here?"

"That's the boy you mentioned to me, the one who followed you that night?"

Kate nodded.

Dumi pointed to Kate and the police officer led him over. "This is the guy who stabbed the fellow from your tour," the police officer explained. "And he's here to identify the man who paid him."

Dumi started to cry when he saw Kate. "Madam, I am very sorry," he snuffled. "He said he would give me a hundred dollars if I hurt you. He said I mustn't kill you but I must hurt you, I am very sorry."

Kate felt the coffee rise in her throat and before she could help herself, she threw up into the mud, with André patting her back. She straightened up and wiped her mouth. She looked at the police officer. "I'm not going to jeopardize anything but I'm quite sure I know who's responsible."

"It is that man over there," Dumi said, pointing at Rydell who was yawning and stretching, having just climbed out of his tent. Dumi continued. "He said he would pay me one hundred and fifty dollars for stabbing the man and one hundred for you. He said I must not hurt you as badly as the man. That is why I was following you that night, Madam, I am very sorry, Madam."

Rydell saw Dumi and his face paled. To the everyone's amazement, Rydell started to run, heading towards the bush with his strange jerky stride.

André watched him for a moment. "I think it's time I practised my rugby tackle," he said and he took off after Rydell, catching hold of him easily and leading him back by the scruff of his neck.

"I don't even want to look at him," Kate said, staring at the ground as the policeman snapped handcuffs onto Rydell who looked amazed, as if he could not believe what was happening.

The officer led Rydell back to the helicopter along with Dumi and the small aircraft took off.

Kate watched it become a tiny dot in the sky and she started to shake. "For the first time," she said, "I truly understand what it means to have one's life threatened. I was so full of myself. I never thought Rydell would harm me. I even thought he liked me."

André hugged her close. "He's deranged, *bokkie*. I bet he'll get off on an insanity defense and go to a mental home. But Kate, I promise you, I'll help you get over this, okay?"

She nodded, her head buried in his chest.

"The police are packing up," he said, stroking her back. "We should be able to leave soon."

Three weeks later, Kate was waiting to have lunch with André in *Le Bistro Afrique* in Swakopmund.

They had just returned from a long safari to the Okavanga Delta and had gone on to the Chobe National Park and then Victoria Falls. From there they had flown down to Cape Town and stayed at the Mount Nelson hotel for a few days before heading back via Sossusvlei so Kate could get to see the heart of the Namibian desert that she had missed out on. Following that, they had flown back along the coastline with spectacular views of the Skeleton coast. Kate enjoyed every magical moment of her second, real holiday. She and André quickly fell into an easy rhythm and the horror of her overland journey had, for the most part, faded.

She opened a newspaper to see a familiar story:

> A London couple was yesterday indicted on several charges: first

degree murder, trafficking human body parts, violating international and national postal customs, and smuggling.

Dr. Richard David Conlon, 34, and Mia Amanda Teller, 31, both of Kensington Gardens, have been in custody in Namibia for several weeks and have now been formally charged. Evidence has shown that the couple went to Namibia on an overland holiday to select and kill a victim for body parts that they sent back to London.

When asked why she had engaged in the 'muti' killing, Teller said she'd "done it for kicks", that it was "something different to do."

Dr. Conlon said that he had been studying traditional African healing techniques for some years and he'd been curious as to whether there was any truth to the muti legends.

"We felt compelled to investigate further, to see for ourselves. I know it seems shocking in London, but in Africa, it's perfectly normal," he's reported as saying. "As a doctor and a surgeon, I was interested from a research and development point of view. It's unfortunate that the woman had to die, we obviously do understand that, but research is research; I'm a scientist, and I stick by my decision to have killed in the name of science; that's how we've evolved as a species and made some of the most important discoveries of our time."

The body of Rosalee Khumalo, 23, a sex worker, was found in December, with her limbs severed, her genitals and breasts cut off, her head missing, and fat removed from her abdomen.

The British police, working with the Namibian task force, alerted the British postal service after evidence of the murder was found by two women on the trip, and an interception by British Post and the police led to the discovery of packages containing a human eye, a severed human head, human genitals and breasts, and a bag of what appeared to be human fat, all packaged inside tourist souvenirs and addressed to Dr. Richard Conlon.

Access to the couple's computer revealed that they intended to sell some of the body parts, hoping to extort exorbitant sums of money. Parties who expressed interest in purchasing the body parts are also being investigated and will face charges.

The case continues.

Kate showed André the newspaper when he arrived at the restaurant and his face darkened. "*Ja,* that poor woman lost her life and Jono and Betty had a very bad time because of them. If those two hadn't been obsessed with bad *muti,* a lot of the bad stuff wouldn't have happened. I mean Rydell was one crazy dude regardless, that's true, and Stepfan was such an arsehole, so with him, it was simply a matter of time."

He rubbed his jaw. "*Ja,* and the fact that Charisse died and Harrison got hurt had nothing to do with them, so *nee* man, I guess bad things would have happened anyway."

Kate leaned over and tousled his hair. "I'm glad Sofie's going to be okay. She's lucky she had such a good doctor. And I got emails from Jasmine, Ellie, Enrique, Eva and Marika," she said. "They're all back home and fine, and they had a great time on their roadtrip. Oh, and Lena went back to Sweden with Gisela. I got a lovely message from them too, they sound very happy."

"And Jono will bounce back," André said. "I meant to tell you, his bosses were sorry he had to go through that hell, and they gave him a month off with full salary paid, the works, and they're going to give him a new tour route. And, like I thought, Rydell the weirdo ended up back in Kansas, in a mental home. His mother and family doctor flew out and saved him. You wouldn't believe it, but Rydell comes from big money, he's been crazy all his life. He used to kill the family pets willy-nilly but they never thought he'd actually murder anyone or hire someone to do it."

Kate shuddered. "I still can't bear to think about me walking down that street all alone that night, with Dumi sent to hurt me. I hope they lock Rydell away forever. How do you know all this stuff anyway?"

"Friends in lowly places, what can I say?" André grinned at her. "And Harrison's fine. He made a full recovery, and Treasure's moved to Seattle with him and her kid and her mother, and she's going to have a baby, did you know that?"

Kate nodded her head and laughed. "Actually yes, I did

know she was pregnant," she said. "Jono told me at the start of the trip but what with all the mayhem, I forgot. Treasure and Harrison, what an unlikely pair to find love. What other news do you have?"

"Only that Helen's pretty much moved in with Kevin and the kids," he said. "The murder helped her get a visa to stay in Africa because she's got to give evidence, just as you will too, *bokkie*. I chatted to the guy at the consulate and he said you can stay as long as you like, if you want to stay that is. And you know how much I'd love you stay with me, not that I want to pressure you or anything, but I just want you to know where I stand."

"I've been thinking André. Yes, I'd love to stay, thank you. I can try to find a job teaching English as a second language or even find a job in a camera store. Then at the same time, I can study photography and work at getting better doing that … so, yes, André, I am definitely staying."

His face brightened and he sat up straighter in his chair. "That's great news. Listen, what's that quote on the menu again, the one you liked before?"

Kate flipped the menu open: "*All glory comes from daring to begin*. Well, I dare us to begin a whole new adventure together." She fell silent for a moment as her mind flashed back to everything she had been through and she wondered if now was a good time to let him in on her thoughts.

"Actually André," she said, leaning in to kiss him, "I do have something in mind…"

Acknowledgements

I thank Luciana Ricciutelli, my extraordinary publisher and editor. Thank you, Luciana, for polishing my prose and for always encouraging and supporting me. I really cannot describe how much you mean to me, nor can I thank you enough for having enriched my life in the many ways that you have, and for making all my writing dreams come true. That my words reach the world is all thanks to Luciana and the wonderful team at my Inanna family.

To Bradford Dunlop, thank you for having the patience of a saint and for reading (and rereading) draft after draft after draft, and for bearing with me through title options and opening lines — the words "Sixteen strangers..." will live with us forever!

I thank Doug O'Neill, Dorothy McIntosh, Liz Bugg, Brenda Missen, Joan O'Callaghan, Alexander Galant, Terri Favro, Rob Brunet, Brenda Hammond and Bianca Marais for their wonderful blurbs and endorsements, and for all their words of encouragement and support along the way.

Thanks to the always-inspiring Liz Worth for supporting this book, as well as Rosemary McCracken, Mandy Eve Barnett and Mayank Bhatt.

I thank my family who have believed in this book wholeheartedly, right from the fledgling idea. Dad, like I say, this one's for you. Thank you to my generous and kind extended family, my Dunlop/ Abrams/ Looney/Bradley/Johnson family, thank you for all your support too, you are simply wonderful.

I thank all my friends at the Crime Writers of Canada, the Sisters in Crime and the Mesdames of Mayhem, as well as all the talented authors and readers I meet online and in person at the various launches, readings and publishing events; writers who make up the incredibly rich fabric of the Canadian Literary world. The breadth of talent is inspiring and the camraderie and support such a joy. Thank you to the hosts of reading series such a Plasticine Poetry, ChiZine Reading Series, Makin' a Racket At the Red Rocket and all the other avenues where we get to showcase our work.

The Toronto Public Library is fantastic in helping authors and we owe them all a heartfelt thanks. In particular, Pam Mountain of the Annette Street Branch is such a great supporter, and I value our friendship that has grown over the years.

A big thanks to a lovely writer with a keen eye for art, without whom we would not have the beautiful cover art for this book: Dawn Promislow. Dawn found a rare book with artwork by Wopko Jensma which in turn led me to this artwork. A huge thanks to Dawn for this.

I'd like to thank GAP Adventure Tours for the journey I took with them in December 2007, from Cape Town across Namibia. I wrote the first draft of the book in 2008, and while I used carefully documented travel details in the novel, it is important to note that none of the characters on the trip served as inspiration for the characters in *The Witchdoctor's Bones,* except for Jonna Nummela who knows that she was a muse (and friend!) to me. The GAP Adventure holiday was an excellent vacation, offering none of the madness and drama in the book and my fellow travellers were all delightful.

It is always sad to acknowledge friends who have left us and there is one in particular who is very sorely missed: Anne Redpath. Anne, you are dearly missed but your wonderful spirit shines strongly and I hope you will be proud of this book.

Thanks to Cathy Douwes for an accurate and respectful simulation of witchdoctor's bones.

And finally, the most important thank you goes to the readers. Without readers, all this effort and passion would be in vain, so thank you, for reading.

Glossary

ag – Afrikaans for "oh"
bakkie – Afrikaans word for small van with an open back
bokkie – Afrikaans word for small buck or affectionate term for a female
bomvu – red in Xhosa
chana – my mate (from Zulu, "my nephew"); umshana
eish! – cross-cultural, an interjection expressing resignation
haw! – cross-cultural expression of disbelief
howzit – cross-cultural hello, how are you
inyanga – Zulu word for traditional herbalist and healer (compare with *sangoma*)
ingcibi – Zulu word for circumcision expert
ja – yes in Afrikaans
jirre – expression of surprise in Afrikaans
jong – informal Afrikaans address for friend
lekker – Afrikaans word for alluring, enticing and tempting, very nice
liewe hemel – good heavens in Afrikaans
mense – people in Afrikaans
muti – medicine (from Zulu *umuthi*) – typically traditional African
mnyama – white in Xhosa
mnyama – black/darkness in Xhosa
my china – English/Afrikaans slang, a friend; as in the greeting *howzit my china*
nee man – no, man! Afrikaans

"n//au" spot – typically traditional word for hole in the neck of a *sangoma*, where sickness escapes

sangoma – Zulu word for witchdoctor or traditional healer or diviner

skrik – Afrikaans word for fright

tolokoshes – Zulu word for a water-sprite, supposed to haunt certain rivers, to be very fond of women, to be mischievous to people, and to be used by witches for nefarious purposes, and said to resemble a tiny, hairy dwarf. Can have alternate spelling: *Tikoloshe, Tokolo* or *Tokolosh*

wena – Zulu meaning "you." Commonly used in a sentence "*Haw wena!*"

yebo – Zulu meaning yes

Bibliography

"Albino Blacks Sought by African Witchdoctors for Ritual Murder 'Medicine.'" *The New Observer* 30 May 2013. Web.

Berglund, Axel-Ivar. *Zulu Thought: Patterns and Symbolism*. Bloomington: Indiana University Press, 1989.

Braid, Mary. "Africa: Witchcraft returns to haunt new South Africa." *The Independent* 21 January 1998. Web.

Chapman, Michael and Tony Voss. *Accents: An Anthology of Poetry from the English-speaking World*. Cape Town: Paper Books, 1986.

Clark, Michael. *The Saga of the Sani Pass and Mokhotlong*. Himeville: Author, 2001.

Corbin, George A. *Native Arts of North America, Africa and the South Pacific: An Introduction*. Boulder, CO: Westview Press, 1988.

de Waal, Mandy. "Witch-hunts: The darkness that won't go away." *Daily Maverick* 30 May 2012. Web.

Early Man: Time Life Books. New York: Time-Life Books Inc., 1979.

Finck, Henry T. *Primitive Love and Love Stories*. New York: Charles Scribner's Sons, 1899.

Gordon, Robert J. and Stuart Sholto Douglas. *The Bushman Myth: The Making of a Namibian Underclass*. Boulder, CO: Westview Press, 2000.

Heale, Jay and Dianne Stewart, eds. *African Myths and Legends*. Capetown, SA: Struik Publishers, 1995.

Illustrated Guide to Southern Africa: Second Edition. Cape Town: The Reader's Digest Association of South Africa (Pty.) Limited, 1980.

Knappert, Jan. *An Encyclopedia of Myth and Legend: African Mythology*. London: Diamond Books Inc., 1990.

"My Lioness." *South African Love Poems*. Web.

Off The Beaten Track. Cape Town: AA The Motorist Publications Ltd., 1987.

Olivier, Willie and Sandra Olivier. *Namibia: Travel Guide.* Chatswood, Australia: New Holland Publishers, 2006.

Pelton, Robert Young. *The World's Most Dangerous Places.* New York: Harper Collins, 2003.

Phythian, B. A., ed. *Considering Poetry.* London, UK: Hodder & Stoughton, 1981.

Poland, Marguerite, ed. *The Mantis and the Moon: Stories for the Children of Africa.* Johannesburg: Ravan Press Ltd., 1979.

Roberts, Jani Farrell. "Modern Witches: Saudi Arabia and Africa." Excerpt. *Seven Days: Tales of Magic, Sex and Gender.* 2000. Web.

Salopek, Paul. "Children in Angola tortured as witches." *The Chicago Tribune* 28 March 2004. Web.

Shaw, Serena. *Pucketty Farm.* Durban: Author, 1999.

Thepa, Madala. "The devil in our midst." *Sunday World* 25 March 2012. Web.

Photo: Bradford Dunlop

Originally from South Africa, Lisa de Nikolits has been a Canadian citizen since 2003. She has a Bachelor of Arts in English Literature and Philosophy and has lived and worked in the United States, Australia and Britain. As an art director, she has worked on *marie claire, Vogue Australia, Vogue Living, Cosmopolitan* and SHE magazines. Her first novel, *The Hungry Mirror,* was published by Inanna Publications in 2010 and was awarded the IPPY Gold Medal for literature on women's issues in 2011, as well as long-listed for the 2011 ReLit Awards. Her second novel, *West of Wawa,* was published by Inanna in 2011, was one of four *Chatelaine* Bookclub Editor's Picks, and was awarded the IPPY Silver Medal for Popular Fiction in 2012. Her third novel, *A Glittering Chaos*, was released in spring 2013 to literary and reader acclaim. Lisa lives and works in Toronto.